D0121465

EVERY SECRET CRIME

EVERY SECRET CRIME

DOUG M. CUMMINGS

FIVE STAR

A part of Gale, Cengage Learning

GALE
CENGAGE Learning™

Detroit • New York • San Francisco • New Haven, Conn • Waterville, Maine • London

GALE
CENGAGE Learning

Set in 11 pt. Plantin.

Printed on permanent paper.

LIBRARY OF CONGRESS CATALOGING-IN-PUBLICATION DATA

Cummings, Doug M.
    Every secret crime / Doug M. Cummings. — 1st ed.
      p. cm.
    ISBN-13: 978-1-59414-665-7 (hardcover : alk. paper)
    ISBN-10: 1-59414-665-9 (hardcover : alk. paper)
      1. Television journalists—Fiction. 2. Chicago (Ill.)—Fiction. 3. Political corruption—Fiction. 4. Psychopaths—Fiction. I. Title.
    PS3603.U65555E94 2008
    813'.6—dc22
                                                                2008001700

First Edition. First Printing: June 2008.

Published in 2008 in conjunction with Tekno Books and Ed Gorman.

Printed in the United States o
1 2 3 4 5 6 7 12 11 10 09 08

In loving memory of JohnElla Perrin

ACKNOWLEDGMENTS

Evan Lipkis, M.D.; Capt. Pete Negro, Illinois State Police; Lt. Mike Sliozis, Illinois State Police (ret.); Tim McGrath, PhD, Chief, Gurnee (IL.) Fire Department (ret.); Jim Wipper, former/future Coroner, Lake County (IL.); Pat Camden, Chicago Police Department; Rusty McClain, Firearms Examiner, Illinois State Police Crime Lab (Rockford); David "Eagle Eye" Lasker; Ken Herzlich; Tom Keevers, J.D.; Joe Zima, J.D. Every librarian, book store owner/manager, and book club sponsor kind enough to invite me to speak and sign books; Tess Schmieg; Lydia Steck; Linda Mickey; Tom Gancarz; Susan Driscoll, Mike Altman, and Pam Anderson; Randy, Laura, Kathy, Mark, Jan, Jeannette, Cheryl, Laurie, Kelly, and Gail, for providing wisdom, energy, and humor; the staff of "News Blues" for daily alerts, editing help, and hilarity; and last, but not least, William, Henry, Zac, Sam, Ellie, and Alex, six of the nicest young people I know.

Whenever a man commits a crime
God finds a witness.
Every secret crime has its reporter.
—Ralph Waldo Emerson

Earlier . . .

Older Brother shivered as he descended the basement steps.

It wasn't the cold that raised the gooseflesh on his arms, or the fact the concrete basement floor would be wet under his bare feet and the air would smell of damp earth and rotting leaves. Nature's own sweet decay. None of that bothered him.

Fear wasn't the culprit, either. The darkness held no demons. In fact, he felt there was a texture to the dark and that, if he practiced often enough and concentrated, opening his mind to the concept, he would someday find he could reach out and manipulate the inky void like so much black clay.

He curled his toes around the edge of each stair, enjoying the sensation and delaying completion of his errand as long as he could, given the fact Mama was in the kitchen awaiting his return. Her rules never changed. Do it quietly and quickly and don't turn on any lights. Your brother is not down there playing. He's being punished. If you stop to visit, I'll lock the door and you'll stay there with him.

Older Brother couldn't allow that, of course. So, as he stepped from smooth wood to chilly concrete, he called out very softly to the person he could not see.

"Hey. I got a ham and cheese sandwich and some chips."

He wasn't surprised when the response came from off to his right near the opening that led to the crawlspace. It was a grunt, no more of a sound than an animal might make at being awakened in surprise, but he recognized it. His brother had learned the hard way to keep talk to a minimum. Mama liked a quiet house. Older Brother imagined him crawling silently out of the hole cut halfway up the wall, his oversized shoulders squeezing past the edges.

"C'mon, little bro," Older Brother said. "Take this. I don't want to just lay it down." *That wasn't a lie. The smells he'd expected were joined with another, more acidic, odor. He knew it emanated from the floor drain off to his left. With no bathroom in the basement, his little brother occasionally urinated there.*

Older Brother shifted his feet, squirming at the thought that the drain might be closer to the stairs than he remembered.

"C'mon, man," *he spoke into the darkness again.* "Mama—"

"She had no right!" *The urgent, whispered words seemed to come out of the air itself. He had not felt his brother's approach and now, even though they stood barely a foot apart, he could summon no sense of his brother's exceptional bulk. The hair along the back of his neck tingled and he felt a nudge of jealousy. Little Brother embraced the darkness, too.*

"I made my bed. I cleaned my room. I done it right after I cleaned yours, just like you told me. When I came home from school, she said I didn't make my bed. But I did!"

Older Brother leaned away from his sibling's feral breath.

"She probably messed it up herself just so she could fuck with you. I'll fix it, though. Like I always do. I'll get you out of here." *Actually, while she was a bitch-goddess in her own right, this time hadn't been their mother's doing. He had pulled his younger brother's bed apart.*

"Here, take the food," *he whispered.* "She doesn't know I'm down here so I gotta get back."

Thick fingers gripped his shoulder. "Why's she always doing this to me? I haven't been bad or nothing. She's always picking on me . . ."

Older Brother reached up and took his sibling's hand, pressing the foil wrapped sandwich and then the bag of chips into it. They made a crackling sound. "I'll tell her you said you're sorry and that you won't let it happen again, okay? You just have to promise to do everything I say, always. You got that?"

"Yeah, but—"

"Promise!" Older Brother insisted.

Silence. Then, "Yeah. Okay."

Older Brother mounted the steps two at a time, eager to get to a shower and cleanse himself. As he closed the door to the basement and locked it, his mother looked up at him. A thick-bodied and large-breasted woman in a too-tight house dress, she sat at the kitchen table holding a half-smoked cigarette in one hand and a half-empty bottle of Tab in the other. A newspaper was spread out in front of her. Despite her size, she looked insubstantial. Had her dress and the wallpaper been the same color, he might not even have noticed her sitting there.

"Been down three hours. Another fifteen minutes, I guess you can let him out." Her voice pushed through thin lips was hoarse from the yelling she'd done earlier and from the three-quarters of the pack of Marlboros she had smoked.

"He pissed in the drain again," Older Brother said.

His mother stared at him for a moment, almost as though she hadn't heard. Then, very precisely, she licked the fingers of her right hand and ducked her head, turning the page of the newspaper.

"Leave him," she said.

CHAPTER ONE

The house was a three-story, red brick Colonial with white columns adding an extra touch of elegance to the small portico at the front door. Set back from the road on a three-acre lot heavy with trees, it featured a thick, professionally maintained lawn and lush gardens. Most important for the man who was about to break into the house, the backyard was full of shadows and as dark as the woods it abutted.

He stepped into the yard from a trail that snaked through those woods. He wore dark designer jogging clothes and a White Sox cap pulled low over his face. While he was as fit as a serious runner, he had no patience for the mindless routine. He'd developed the muscles in his legs and upper body from daily work with weights. The expensive outfit merely helped him blend in.

He liked the feel of the backyard and the patio so he stopped for a few moments to sit in one of the cushioned chairs arranged around a glass-topped table. He smiled at the two chaise lounges drawn up next to each other with a small table between. There was an ashtray on the table and he leaned over and sniffed it.

Bingo. Just as he'd thought. The fading fragrance of fine quality weed.

He wondered if the mother or the stepdaughter ever laid out in the buff, smoking dope. Probably. Maybe they did it together. He would have liked to watch that. Both of them had excellent bodies. Looked obnoxious, especially the teenager, but hot.

He examined the house. Reconnoitering earlier, he'd noted no alarm company sign on the lawn or stickers on the doors or windows. That, of course, wasn't information you wanted to depend on to keep your ass out of jail so he'd checked the Wihega county clerk's office for the plat of survey, hoping to find blueprints. Even better, the file contained a recent building permit application for what the owners called a "media room." Plans for the room had obviously been copied from a master drawing that included the handwritten notation in one corner: "No sec sys, no pets, client will leave back door open for contractor entry."

He spent several minutes enjoying the humid fall evening, then stood and stretched. He felt the weight of the Maglite in his left jacket pocket, a Glock automatic in the right. The old man had said a gun wouldn't be necessary but carrying it had become second nature to him. Screw the old man.

He withdrew a pair of thin and supple plastic gloves. Slipping them on, he reviewed what he knew about the whereabouts of the homeowners and their children.

The parents? Out of town. Their reservations included tonight, Sunday. They'd still been registered as of an hour ago when he called to check.

The nineteen-year-old son, Trey? Party hound. Friends had picked him up. Drove him to a house filled with teenagers just a few minutes away, where loud rap music rolled out the front door. That had been an hour and a half ago. The boy was no doubt drunk and getting his knob well honed by some babe.

The busty seventeen-year-old daughter, Emily, a senior in high school? She'd be screwing her math teacher boyfriend about now. He'd seen her leave with the guy in his brand new Ford Thunderbird convertible. Followed them too, just to be sure.

16

The Hayden home was empty. He glanced at the Timex strapped to his wrist.

Time to make the donuts.

He approached the back door and almost laughed. He had expected this. Wood below, glass panels above, and a cheap spring lock with no secondary deadbolt. A buck-ninety-eight worth of security for a home that would easily go for two mil in this fancy neighborhood. He shook his head, took one long deep breath, and tried the knob. What the hell. If they left it open for the contractors, maybe they left it open all the time.

Sure enough. It turned silently in his hand. He paused.

He listened. He listened a little longer. Longer. Concentrated on nothing else. He stood in the doorway not daring to move or to let loose of the knob. Maintained the same pressure he'd used to make it turn while his heart bumped along in sudden overdrive.

Perfect silence greeted him, although he knew there really was no such thing. Houses always emit little noises of some kind. Central air-conditioning systems cycle. Wood creaks. Tree limbs scrape against glass.

Finally, he drew a deep breath, released the knob, and pushed the door wide enough that he could enter. He found himself in a hallway and knew from the drawings he'd studied that the kitchen was to his left. He closed the back door and winced at the small click the latch made as it engaged. He listened again.

He heard only the low-level hum of a refrigerator. He counted off five minutes in his head. With a tiny shudder, the refrigerator shut down. He detected no other sounds in the house.

He took one deep breath and let it out in a sigh. Felt sweat on his forehead and blotted it with a jacket arm. This, he thought, was going quite well.

Since he was already inside, he missed seeing the brief flash of light from a bedroom window on the second floor.

Trey Hayden lay with his back on four pillows pushed up against the headboard of his bed and listened to Korn thumping through his expensive headphones, all the while feeling the pain of his bruises and his broken heart. The tiniest butt of a roach had burned out in the clip he held, forgotten, between the thumb and forefinger of his right hand.

Even dim light hurt his eyes. For that reason, he'd left the house completely dark, not even stopping in the kitchen to check the refrigerator after stumbling home from the party. He knew he would have a brilliant shiner in the morning and from the way his mouth hurt probably a hell of a fat lip, too. The fight had only lasted a few minutes, but Lucas was a boxer and had nailed him good.

Trey wanted to get up from his bed and go puke but he didn't have the energy. The grass hadn't done anything for him except leave him feeling drained and remote and able to identify the pain radiating from each of his injuries.

The whore! The slut bitch. He couldn't help thinking about her and the party at Jeremy's folks' place. He'd walked in not suspicious at all. Looked around for his girlfriend, Lindsey, and his best friend, Lucas, and when he didn't see them asked others where they were. No one seemed to know. He wandered some more. Smoking one joint and then another. Drinking some rum. Kickin' it. Caught her on the floor in an upstairs bedroom, sucking away.

Lucas, that son of a bitch. Grinning when Trey walked in. Their eyes met just as Lindsey pulled back in surprise from the act she was performing. Jesus!

Some fuckin' party. Hadn't even been there a half-hour before he stormed out.

Trey lifted the .38 revolver off his chest and, for the fifth time since he'd been home, pointed it at a collage of pictures mounted on the wall of his room and let his finger curl around the trigger. The piece was loaded, too; 195 grain jacketed hollow points from the box good 'ol Lucas had bought for him. Wouldn't it be just fuckin' awesome, not to mention ironic, to put one of those slugs right through his ex-friend's nose?

He let the pistol drop to his side and felt it bounce on the covers. Became aware of the roach clip in his fingers and tipped it off the side of the bed. Still burning? Who gave a fuck?

Damn Lindsey anyway. What had she gone and done that for? Had she been playing him all along? She'd probably been doing Lucas the whole time.

Trey fumbled with the small flashlight that hung from the side of his bed and snapped it on, then quickly off again when pain flared behind his eyes. Her picture. The image burned itself into his retina. The one she had taken and sent to him on the computer. Standing there topless.

Damn her. Damn Lucas, the cocky shit.

Trey began to cry and touched the gun beside him. He wanted to shoot Lucas. After that, he wanted to point it at his stepmother. Maybe goad the bitch into a nice loud argument, and when she started taking on that condescending I've-been-to-law-school-and-you-don't-have-the-smarts-or-balls-I-do tone, then lift the .38 and push it into her face and tell her to Shut the Fuck Up. Argue with *this*, you cunt.

Or, maybe . . .

Trey had to think about this for a minute. Not an entirely radical concept but . . . what if he put the .38 into his own mouth and pulled the trigger?

Would it hurt, he wondered? No. Just a flash, probably, and then nothing . . .

He slid the gun out of his mouth, a taste of oil and metal left on his tongue. Gross. He placed the .38 on the bed beside him and squirmed around to reach into the headboard. As he did, the headphones pulled away from his ears. Disgusted, he yanked them off and let them fall to the mattress. He withdrew a small baggie of weed and a packet of rolling papers. He needed another hit something fierce. No way would the 'rents be home until at least early afternoon, and by then, the air cleaner would have done its thing and they'd never know.

He was disappointed by the small amount left in his stash. Especially since Lucas was his dealer. Trey knew others, but none of them had the quality of product that Lucas could provide. Shit.

Trey rolled a joint and sank back into his pillows as he lit it with a lighter from the bottom of the bag. It failed to fire the first time and he had to snick it twice more to get flame.

A "clunk!" from out in the hall lifted his head off the pillows and had him fumbling around, trying to mash his joint into the ashtray he'd laid down beside him. The sudden movement sent a spasm of pain flashing behind his eyes.

Whatthefuck? His parents? No fucking way. He picked up the .38.

"Lucas? I'm going to kill your ass if that's you, motherfucker," he shouted into the darkness. He pulled back the revolver's hammer.

"Police!" A man's voice called out. "If you have a weapon, put it down and step out of the room with your hands in the air."

Terror immobilized him. His thoughts zigzagged. That isn't . . . can't be . . .

Wait.

Something was weird. The idea that cops would just sneak into the house. Unless . . . a raid? But on *Cops* they always made a lot of noise during raids.

He was stoned. Concentration was difficult.

20

A raid. Now that was weird, too. He wasn't a dealer. Never bought anything more than half an ounce. What was going on?

He didn't believe the guy. Had to be Lucas. Playing one of his stupid-ass games. Yeah.

The checkered wooden grip of the .38 felt small in his hand. The gun wavered. So did his voice.

"How do I know you're a cop?"

"C'mon, kid. You want to see my badge, come on out into the hall and I'll show it to you. Just do you and me both a favor and put the gun away. We don't have a problem yet. No need to cause one, you know? Just put the gun down and step out here."

Trey glanced out his window into the backyard and saw nothing. Something's not right here, he thought. If they were cops, why hadn't they just stormed his room? They always came in bunches during a raid, didn't they? Why hadn't he heard them bursting in and clomping up the stairs?

Trey got up off the bed and held the gun out in front of him, turning it sideways like he'd seen gangbangers do in the movies. The voice had come from right outside his room. The guy in the hall called to him again. He didn't answer. This was too weird. It had to be Lucas or one of his creepy friends. Probably making a joke, trying to get Trey to look stupid. Then Lucas would come in and apologize and try to make it all okay. But it wasn't okay.

Trey said, "Lucas, you're so fucking lame," and walked out into the hall . . .

. . . And saw a man standing in the shadows of the hallway. *Not Lucas.* Fear hit him like a static charge.

"What the fuck?"

The guy jumped toward him. Trey fell back. Felt his finger spasm on the .38's trigger. *Shit,* he thought, as his gun went off.

Followed by . . . two more explosions. Two blinding flashes.

Trey felt like he'd been punched in the center of his chest.

21

Fucking Lucas, he thought. He tried to raise his gun. Couldn't.

Felt something tear loose inside.

"Fuck," he said. At least his brain formed the word. But then he was on the floor and something white-hot was sizzling through him, cutting off his air. Like when he was about nine and fell off a swing set and landed flat on his back. Couldn't get air then, couldn't get any now.

Felt his eyes bulge as he tried to force oxygen into his collapsed lungs. It didn't work.

His last thought was that dying hurt a lot more than he figured it would.

No! This isn't happening. There wasn't supposed to be anyone here!

The intruder let the Glock fall to his side, smoke still trailing from the barrel, and sank to his knees next to the kid. For all of a minute, Trey Hayden looked like a fish out of water, back arching, his mouth open wide as he tried to suck in life. It did him no good. After a couple of minutes, he flattened out on the floor. Fists opened. Bladder and sphincter released.

The intruder's ears rang from the three gunshots. The pressure in his head was building, too, the way it did when he was about to get a migraine.

Jesus. Jesus! What have I done?

He was holding his breath. He let it out. Then he had to think. Breathe. Slow and easy. Don't hyperventilate. Don't panic. Ignore the headache. Ignore the smell of death.

That little fucker.

A shudder started in his shoulders and traveled throughout his body. He slipped the Glock into his pocket. Touched his face. His gloved finger came away sticky.

Get out *now!*

Gun first, though. Gotta get what he came for.

He leaned across the kid's body and tugged the revolver from his lifeless hand, glad it wasn't stuck. Exactly what he'd been directed to retrieve. It was a Smith & Wesson, one of the old K-frames, with a four-inch barrel. *"An easy way to make five hundred bucks. It's probably rusted junk by now,"* the old man had said. Yeah. Right. Junk my ass.

He stuck the Smith into the back of his pants. The ringing in his ears and the pain in his head rocked him back on his heels, and he had to put a hand out flat on the wall to keep from falling. He couldn't hear a damn thing except that damn high-pitched whine and, in the background, a muted replay of the gunshots' roar. He had to go. Had to *go*.

Wait. Could anyone outside have heard? No way. Humid evening, big house, AC on. Everyone else in the neighborhood used AC, too. These were all big houses, well spread out. He got to his feet. Looked at the body. The boy was shirtless in jeans. His mouth was open, arms flung out to his sides.

The killer touched his face again. Looked around. Stepped into the bathroom at the top of the stairs and risked the light for a moment. Blood spatter speckled his face and neck. He found a washcloth and scrubbed face, hands, and jacket. Once finished, he squeezed the cloth tightly over the sink then put it into his pocket. He ran water in the bowl for a long time.

Back on the first floor, he strode quickly to the front door, snapped open the dead-bolt lock, and tried the knob. It turned easily. Wait. Leave the door ajar and go out the back? Yes. Misdirection. Good. Breathing hard, feeling suddenly giddy, he stuck his head outside and inspected the front yard and the street. Bright light from the carriage lamps on either side of the entrance hurt his eyes and he drew back. No cops. No threat. He was going to make it.

★ ★ ★ ★ ★

The black Jeep Sahara sat shadowed and hidden by the leafy overhang of a sugar maple in a turnout midway up the Hayden's driveway. Behind the wheel, Lucas Bremmer had been staring at the front door of the Hayden's house for several moments, aware of nothing but the buzz from the weed he was smoking and the sensation of Lindsey Sears's excellent mouth working in his lap. Then, whoa, the door opened and somebody stuck his head out.

One thought fired across the weakened synapses of Bremmer's brain.

"What the hell is *he* doing here?"

CHAPTER TWO

The kid in that movie saw dead people. I dream about them.

More often, though, I dream about their murderers. Faceless wielders of guns and knives and blunt objects spattered with blood haunt my sleep. I see them stalking their victims, feel their presence. I often awake with the covers tossed aside and sweat turning to ice on my skin.

It's been worse lately. In the past few months, one of those killers from my nightmares has had a face: my own.

Mostly, my dreams wake me. This time it was the phone. My bedroom was dark, a little of the night's chill breathing in through my open window. I felt Socks, my black and white cat, jump off the bed as I answered.

"Reno McCarthy?" A female voice, flat, hard-edged. Used to making middle-of-the-night calls.

"Who's this?" The ID display read "Private." Had to be a cop.

"Gorz, Eighteenth District watch commander. We just put Vinnie Seamans in an ambulance. He's going to Roosevelt Lakeshore."

"What happened?"

"We were having coffee when this 'shots fired' call came in. Vinnie said he'd run over there with me. It was just a dumbass domestic, couple of drunks popped each other. Vinnie thought he knew one of the mopes so he says he's going take a look. Next thing I know, he's down on the sidewalk. I thought somebody shot him, but it's his heart. Medics were bagging him in the ambulance, Reno. I'm not gonna lie to you. Full cardiac arrest. He went down hard."

Jesus. Vinnie. Jesus.

If you've visited enough hospital rooms, you've noticed that most of them look the same. An unthreatening color of paint, the smells a blend of life and death and cleaning agent, not in equal measure. Hi-tech equipment jammed into all the available space.

How much of that expensive gear you rate, of course, is dependent on how close to the edge you are.

Vinnie Seamans was teetering.

There was a lot of stuff, and it blipped and beeped and whirred, charting each bump of his heart and every liter of oxygen flowing through his breathing tube. I guessed as much for billing purposes as for the medical folks trying to keep him alive.

"Are you OK?"

The question posed by the attractive twenty-something nurse in faded blue scrubs was directed at me, not my father's best friend. She came into the room at Roosevelt Lakeshore Hospital not sixty seconds after I arrived and found me standing at the foot of Vinnie's bed.

"I'm . . ." I began. Thought about it. Then shook my head. Nope, I couldn't answer. Strange. Wasn't as though the paramedics had scooped *me* off the street outside a crime scene and carted me here. I'd come in under my own power, fully rational and alert. But I was as incapable of forming a sentence as Vinnie was, lying over there on the bed, looking not at all like the man I'd grown up knowing as "Uncle."

The blue-eyed nurse said to me, "Why don't you sit down?"

She was pretty, with her blond hair clipped back and a smiley face button displayed just above her hospital ID. Normally I'd have something snappy to offer up in response. I couldn't manage that this time.

I groped behind me for the stiff visitor's chair and sank down on it. Nurse Janney poured water from one of those cheap carafes made from the same plastic as the bedpans and handed it to me. I knocked it back.

She watched me. "How you doing? Better?"

Other than a headache that started below my shoulder blades and traveled up the back of my neck, squeezing all the way, I guessed I was.

"Yeah," I said. "Don't worry. I'm just a little out of it. Bad night."

She started a little smile, "This is cardiac intensive care. How did you get past the nurses' station without us seeing you?"

"If you look like you belong, you can get in anywhere."

"If these rooms didn't have so much glass, I wouldn't have known you were here. Even so, you just . . . appeared. Gave me a shock."

"I guess I haven't mastered total invisibility yet."

"Well, sneaky or not, it's six in the morning. Even family isn't supposed to be here now." She glanced pointedly at Vinnie and then looked back at me. I'm not black.

"Adopted."

Her eyes registered equal parts concern and surprise. My lie didn't matter, really. As much as I hated being there, I wasn't leaving unless she called security. And, even if what a colleague nicknamed "the small brains with big radios" showed up, they would have to use force to move me out. I didn't think Nurse Janney wanted that. I'm a big-shouldered white guy with a thrice-broken nose, but I wasn't exhibiting any aberrant behavior. And, given the suit I wore and my recent expensive visit to the barber, I could also be a fellow who kept a very high-priced attorney on retainer.

"Tell you what," I said, trying to make it easier for her not to dime me out. "I talked to Dr. Fong on my way here. He's coming in to meet me. If he doesn't show in the next few minutes, I'll leave."

I saw it then. The brief flicker in her expression that I'd been anticipating. I waited for her to say something.

"Wait. You're that TV guy, right? You did the story about the Russians who killed all those people."

"Yes," I waited again. It's a two-step process for most people. Her brow furrowed.

"You're not here . . . reporting . . . are you? The hospital doesn't allow . . ."

I held up a hand. "Dr. Fong will explain."

I watched her decide.

"I have to call my supervisor. It's . . . the rules." She started for the door, stopped, looked over her shoulder. "I'm sorry."

She went back to the nurses' station and spoke to a black guy in scrubs who was typing on a computer keyboard. He glanced at me and picked up a phone.

There was just enough water in the carafe on the cart next to Vinnie's bed to refill my cup. I willed myself to look again at my father's best friend. Up to a couple of months ago, I'd thought of him as one of mine, too.

He was unconscious, head and shoulders propped up, breathing through a ventilator tube and wired neck and arm to a cardiac monitor about six feet off the floor. Normally he's a robust guy, roughly shaped like a couple of boulders piled atop one another. Lying under the threadbare white blanket, he appeared to have dwindled in size. I could have been looking at sandbags instead of rocks. The only way I could tell he was still alive was from watching the slow rise and fall of his chest and the marching graph of green lines across the heart monitor screen.

My Uncle Vinnie. My dad's partner for nearly all of the time he spent as a detective. Burglary. Organized Crime. About ten minutes on the mayor's protection detail. Finally to Homicide. My dad swilling Jack Daniels as he slogged his way through the Job, Vinnie watching his back, carrying him on days he could barely function because of the booze he consumed the night before.

After my dad killed himself, after my mother died, Vinnie retired and took a job with the Cook County state's attorney. Working for F. T. "Jim" Quinn he was unofficially official. He carried police credentials and acted as a combination investigator and political fixer. The job allowed him to roam the night streets amongst the only family he'd really ever known. Cops. Mopes. The in-betweeners. What he referred to as his "night crew."

For a goodly amount of time after my dad's suicide, I'd taken to riding along with Vinnie on his nightly rounds. He was still a detective then, but with a pretty open job description. I was in high school, a big kid for my age, but still a kid. He never treated me as anything less than an equal. I think it pleased him, especially on those occasions when he could introduce me by saying, "Reno is Frank McCarthy's boy. I'm breaking him in."

An equal. A partner of sorts. A friend. Until it all crashed down.

We hadn't spoken since June. Three months. During which time I'd managed to explode the major story of the year in Chicago and, as a result, reestablish myself at Channel 14 after a two-year hiatus.

I took a breath. At the same moment, the pager clipped to my belt began to vibrate. Its alphanumeric display told me to call the newsroom, ASAP. I felt like grinding it under my heel.

I shut the pager off. Focused on Vinnie's hands. They were rough, thick-knuckled. I remembered them wrapped around the steering wheel of his county car, a cigar that was often unlit jammed between the fingers of his left. Always the left. The right he kept free to work the radios stuck into the console between the seats. Or, if the need arose, to grab the .45 Colt he wore cross-draw on his left hip. Now both hands lay at his sides, palms down, an IV needle stuck into the back of one and a pulse-oxygen clip on one finger of the other.

Annoyed with myself, I rose from the chair. Forget childhood memories. He'd betrayed me. End of fucking story.

I felt myself compacting inside, closing doors to all the rooms that mattered. Shutting out the wintry cold that blew through them. There was nothing I could say to him now that would make a difference, either to me or to him.

I needed to call the station and I couldn't use my cell in the hospital.

I took a last look at him. I wasn't sure if he was at peace or not. There was no benign smile on his face, no softening to his features. He was an old man asleep on a hospital bed.

"Sir?" Nurse Janney was back. No cheer this time. "My supervisor says . . ."

I knew what was coming and raised a hand. "That's okay. I need to leave anyway. Tell me this. What's his status right now?"

"He's resting comfortably."

"Beyond that."

Through the glass I saw the black guy step from the nurse's station and lean on the front of the counter, arms folded, watching us. Backup. Nurse Janney glanced at her patient and then at me.

"Beyond that, sir, I really can't say. I'm sorry, those are hospital regulations. You'll have to talk to Dr. Fong. If you give me your number I can ask him to call you."

A late September weekday morning was in full swing when I reached the street. Light sport coat weather, if that. I was okay in a worsted wool suit. We were enjoying a nice transition from the humidity of the summer. Just a hint of October and beyond rode in on the lake breeze. No rain in the forecast. A couple of early morning sailors in what boaters call the "playpen" next to Navy Pier and the water treatment plant provided a lazy counterpoint to the traffic already building on Lake Shore Drive.

And Vinnie Seamans was dying. I punched Ray Fong's number into my cell. Voice mail. Annoyed, I redialed. Same thing.

"Where the hell are you?" I snapped the phone closed.

I put Vinnie into a quiet room at the back of my brain for the moment and called the guy who had thought something was so urgent that he paged me at 6:30 in the morning and stuck a 9-1-1 at the end of his message.

"Yogi, it's Reno. What's up?"

"Hold on." I heard two-way radio traffic blatting in the background and shut up to let him listen to whatever it was that had caught his ear. A motorist sneezing at just the wrong moment can clog Chicago expressways for hours and traffic news is a Big Deal for both TV and radio. Yogi is a traffic producer whose job is to listen to the police and fire scanners during Channel 14's morning drive programs and keep both the traffic reporter and the assignment desk up to date on any breaking news or significant tie-ups.

"Okay," he came back to the phone. "Car under a semi on the southbound Ryan so I only got a second. About fifteen minutes ago, I picked up some traffic on the channel the state police evidence technicians use. There's a crew going to Wihega County for something."

31

It piqued my interest and quickened my step. I was six blocks from the station. "No address, no explanation?"

"They asked for something called a 'laser trajectory kit?' You know what that is?"

I knew. "Anything else?"

"No, man, but I'll keep listening."

I needed a distraction from the dark thoughts dogging me ever since the cop's phone call woke me. A good story with a lot of weird angles was just the ticket to keeping my brain occupied. This might be just that kind of story.

While Illinois State Police evidence technicians are on-call to any police agency that needs them, I doubted a team would routinely be sent on such a mission to Wihega County. Having recently become the first in the state to consolidate its city and county law enforcement operations, it had its own crime-scene processing unit. Yogi was right. Odd call. If something was up that required added help from the state police, it was worth my attention.

Channel 14's studios and offices are in the old Cartage Building that used to be known as North Pier. I took the stairs up to the newsroom two at a time. One thing you learn early in this business: the good stories don't wait. Someone at another station could have heard the same radio traffic and be checking it out.

A former transmitter engineer, Yogi created a closet-sized and soundproofed radio-monitoring shack behind a window overlooking the newsroom. He sits there throughout the morning surrounded by counters filled with scanners, two-way radios, and television monitors that display traffic activity at key intersections and on expressways throughout the city. A sign Scotch-taped to the window reads: "Don't tap on the glass." As if he could hear it if anyone did: the sound level inside roughly approximates that of feeding time at the primate house at

Brookfield Zoo. He saw me and waved, phone to his ear. As I opened the door, he smacked a couple of keys on his computer. A map of Wihega County appeared. Address-finder software took over, zooming in on the county seat of Falcon Ridge and targeting a street in a section called The Heights. Yogi thanked whomever he was conversing with and hung up.

"They keep using the street name, Warwick, but haven't said the house number. Hey. I saw a story in the Sunday *Trib* about Falcon Ridge Heights, didn't I?" He has a large head and squarish face that appears out of proportion to the rest of his body. Blond hair, looking like he combed it with WD-40, hung in his eyes. "Huge bucks in that neighborhood."

He was right. Even when the dot-commers in other ritzy communities were selling multimillion dollar mansions for bus fare out of town, the *Tribune* reported life in the Heights went on as usual. A murder there would play into the universal fascination with celebrity crime. Maybe *Entertainment Tonight* would send a crew. Maybe Dominick Dunne would come.

"No other radio traffic?" I asked.

"They said something about trying to find the victim's parents. Oh and the state's contact is a guy called Sergeant Esperanza."

I knew Master Sergeant Rudy Esperanza. He was the senior evidence technician on the squad. In my office on the other side of the newsroom I punched his name into my Outlook contacts file. Cell and pager numbers appeared. I tried the cell first. No answer. As I punched in my number on his pager, an incoming call beeped. Yogi.

I switched over. He read off an address.

"I got that off the coroner's channel. The coroner's investigators aren't being allowed into the scene, and there's some bigtime drama. It sounds like they're reporting to their head Fred. Some woman. She sounds supreme-o pissed off, too."

"Got a name on the victim?"

"Negative. And the address ain't in the cross-reference or up on Google or Intellius. Here's something to think about, though. You know how radio traffic has a feel to it? Slow, kinda relaxed or really tight when it's a heater case they're working? This is the tight kind."

Heater case. Major players. Political and media interest.

That nailed it for me: we were talking homicide. My heart rhythm ratcheted up a notch.

The adrenaline rush. No doubt it's akin to the sensation a skier gets at the top of a run or a swimmer waiting for the starter's gun. It's one of the reasons I love the news business.

On the downside, waiting for my friend, Master Sergeant Esperanza, to call me back wasn't cutting it. My patience level, never very high, kept dropping as the minutes ticked past.

I called the Wihega County Public Safety Center, identified myself, and asked what was happening in Falcon Ridge Heights. The dispatcher hung up on me. I noted that, along with the time and the guy's name. Tried the coroner's office. Another hang up. I wrote it down. I take a lot of notes when I'm working. Sometimes they turn out to be relevant. Sometimes I think I'm just tempting carpal tunnel syndrome.

My notebook had the names and phone numbers of the few residents Yogi found listed on Warwick. I started dialing. The first and second went to voice mail. Third was answered.

"I'm hoping you can help me," I told the righteous-sounding female voice. "I'm from Channel 14. We're getting information about some police activity in your neighborhood." Nice and bland. Don't want to cause a panic.

"Well, yes. There are police cars all over the street. Obviously, someone's been killed."

"Why do you say that, ma'am?"

"I've just counted ten police cars and a large white truck

with 'Command Center' painted on the side. No simple burglary requires the deployment of so many resources and I seriously doubt Croix and Margo Hayden are hiding Al-Qaeda terrorists in their home."

"Say that again? Who owns the house?"

"Why, the Haydens of course. They live two doors down from us. Croix and Margo Hayden?" Like everyone should know them.

In this case, everyone did.

CHAPTER THREE

Three minutes later, I stuck my head into the news director's office and rapped on the doorframe.

"Hey, Reno. What's up, man?"

Charles Chezwitz, known as "Chucky Cheese-Whiz," leaned against the corner of his desk like an executive action figure: shirtsleeves rolled halfway up his forearms, English regimental tie knotted and centered below his Adam's apple. Rowena Florbus occupied his visitor's chair. She's the day-side assignment editor. A gloomy dumpling of a woman at thirty with hair the consistency of broom bristles. She scowled at me.

I said, "Someone's been killed at Croix and Margo Hayden's house out in Falcon Ridge."

He frowned. Chucky's about schedules and image and butt-kissing. Breaking news stomps on the structure of his day.

"No shit. Where's that come from?"

"Neighbors. I'm waiting for a callback from a cop at the scene."

He glanced at Florbus, who leaned back in her chair and let out an exaggerated sigh, showing off ample cleavage. What annoys him annoys her. "Who's the victim?"

"From radio traffic, it could be a kid or a teenager. My cop buddy may be able to shed some light when he calls."

"Who's the cop?" Florbus asked. In the job for less than three months, she's too curious about other people's sources. Newsroom gossip has her sleeping with Chucky. Yogi says they

36

do threesomes with her autographed photo of Connie Chung.

"Buddy from the old days. He's solid. When he can talk to me, he will."

"So we have no confirmation except from a neighbor who may or may not know what she's seeing."

"She says the street's full of cops. Cops going in and out of the Hayden house. And the cops have called for help from evidence techs from the state police with a laser trajectory kit . . ."

"Whatever. Who's your original source?"

"Yogi."

"Great." Rowena once called Yogi "an unnecessary little goon." He refers to her as "the sawed-off bitch."

"What's a laser whatever?" Chucky asked, tearing his eyes from Florbus's chest.

"Device the cops use to figure out either where a bullet came from or where it went."

"So you're saying someone's been shot."

"That's a reasonable assumption."

Florbus counted on her fingers. "State's attorney's news conference at nine on the nightclub fire deaths. The governor's announcing the closure of the Burke Campus. Cops say they're holding a 'person of interest' in the Lincoln Park rapes. And this crash on the Ryan. We're stretched a little thin this morning, Reno. It would be helpful to confirm that this is something more than a suicide before we send a crew all the way out to Falcon Ridge."

"What's enough confirmation for you? When you see it on Channel 7 at noon?"

"Reno . . ." Chucky appeared to think better of continuing. He turned to Florbus.

"Rowena? Why don't you check with Yogi and see if there's anything new and then put a crew together to start toward

Falcon Ridge? Let us guys have a little room here."

Her mouth turned down at the edges at the "us guys," and she seemed to pause for him to tell her he was kidding. When he didn't, she hustled past me without another word. I got a whiff of cigarette smoke and a lemony fragrance as sweet as furniture polish. Chucky told me to close his door.

Oh boy, I thought. Here it comes. He got up and walked to the other side of his desk, putting something solid between us.

"I have no problem assigning you to this story," he began. "I know it's right up your alley. But we need to have an understanding."

"Meaning?"

He picked up a yellow tennis ball and squeezed it with his right hand. Among the plaques on the wall were several touting his prowess at the game. Where his predecessor, Frank Hanratty, loaded the walls with photos of politicians and news media luminaries, there were now shots of Chucky with Billie Jean, with Sampras, with the Williams sisters. There was even one of him smashing down a lob while Andre Agassi looked on.

He placed the tennis ball in the middle of his desk blotter, a hand flat on either side. "Elise and I are concerned about your . . ." He hesitated. "Emotional status." Elise was Elise Bascomb Hanratty, owner and general manager of Channel 14.

I've been startled enough over the years that keeping my features blank is no problem.

"Why is that?"

"You blew up at a producer in the edit bay last week. He's considering filing a grievance with the union. You have a generally defiant attitude toward Rowena. And calling Alderman Mundt an asshole was a bit intemperate, don't you think?"

"Mundt has an IQ two points below plant life and he's been sexually harassing our Northwestern intern for a month. You want to get sued because we didn't step up for her?"

"Be that as it may. We all just want to be sure you're in an okay frame of mind, Reno. I know the last few months have been difficult. I like to think of the newsroom as a family. We're concerned about you."

"I'm fine." Why were we having this discussion now? I was like a kid who wants to pitch his homework and follow the fire engines down the street. "So why don't I . . ."

"Whoa, my friend. I sure don't know all of the particulars of the Russian mob piece you did this summer but it was primo. I told you that when I first took the job and I mean it. You deserve all the awards you're nominated for."

My hands squeezed into fists and released. It was good he'd put the desk between us.

"If I let you have the Hayden story, I need your word it's not going to get out of hand. No . . ." He paused while his eyes seemed to search the wall behind me for some kind of guidance. Maybe he found it on one of his tennis plaques. Very Zen.

"No off-court moves. No . . . hissy fits."

You have to admire a guy who has such a command of the language.

"We work together," he continued. "You check in with Rowena or me as the coverage progresses. No going off on your own. Exclusives of any kind we talk about first. You're free to use your usual enterprise but not at the cost of prudence. I need to know all of your confidential sources for anything you put on the air. I'm willing to give you leeway for keeping them confidential, if necessary, to get their information but you don't get to hide them from me. We straight so far?"

"Sure." His conditions weren't unreasonable. They just didn't fit my approach to handling a story. Mr. Autonomous, that's me.

"I mean it, Reno. No surprises. And absolutely no rough stuff." His attempt at a stern look came off more Elmer Fudd.

"I ordinarily don't shoot people if that's what you mean."

He colored a bit and yanked his hands from the desktop. In doing so, he knocked the tennis ball to the floor. Even in our first conversation after he came aboard as news director, he'd avoided discussing the fact that I had killed someone earlier in the summer.

The topic frightened him. I frightened him. Understandable as hell. The state's attorney ruled I shot the guy, a Russian mob flunky, in self-defense, but that frightened and confounded a lot of people. For me to have killed a man, not as a soldier and not in war, and still be working in television news was the subject of ongoing ethics discussions. Professional journals called for my firing or resignation. Bloggers and talk show hosts debated it. Leno joked. Letterman came up with a Top 10 list. The both of them, along with Anderson Cooper, Meredith Viera, and a half dozen news organizations, issued me invitations to explain what happened and elaborate on it.

I refused.

Oh yeah. And three women proposed. By e-mail, no less.

Now Chucky waved the subject away again.

"What I'm trying to say is that you're a fine reporter. We recognize that. But you need to rein in that temper of yours. And that rebellious streak. Solo acts close the show, Reno. Clear?"

Before I could answer or even nod, there was a knock at the door. Florbus poked her head in. Face flushed.

"The Haydens' producer is in meltdown. Apparently Croix and Margo are in Lake Geneva. They have two teenagers at home. They can't reach them. They've been calling her every five minutes to get briefings and she doesn't know any more than we do." The couple hosted a hardnosed law and commentary show called *Hayden v. Hayden* that was produced in one of Channel 14's studios.

40

"What's our status?" Chucky asked.

"Peter had truck three on the Kennedy for Traffic's live shot so I sent him. Al Greco's coming from home. Reno'll have to drive himself. And Gervais, one of the stringers, called. The Haydens' neighborhood is crawling with cops. They're keeping everyone a couple of blocks away. Even residents who were out jogging aren't being allowed to go home. Gervais says she'll sit on the story for now, as long as we guarantee we'll use her stuff at premium rate, but she says there are all kinds of looky-loos with cell phones."

"Fine," Chucky said. "Reno, get out there."

A greyhound at the starting gate had nothing on me.

"Wait a minute," he said. "Take that new producer. Jody. Take her with you."

"I don't think that's a good idea," Florbus said. "It's her first week . . ."

"Her last boss told me she's a pit viper. Take her along."

"Your wheels or mine?" Jody Taggart asked on our way out of the building.

"Yours," I said.

She was parked in the open lot across from the station on Illinois Street. She was a couple of inches past five feet tall with short blond hair and a narrow face and bright inquisitive eyes. Her bio tacked up in the newsroom said she'd worked three years at a St. Louis TV station. The durable slacks, sweater, and low-cut hiking boots told me she knew something about working in the field. Fashionable enough, but comfy when spending a few hours in the back of a live-truck making calls, setting up interviews. From her practicality of dress, I expected she'd have practical wheels, too. She pointed us toward a late-model Ford Explorer with tinted windows. She walked briskly to keep up with me.

"I reviewed some clips off the Internet about Wihega County. This guy, Theo Zak? What's up with him?"

I smiled. "Otherwise known as Uncle Theo." It had been barely fifteen minutes since she'd been assigned the story. I was curious what research she'd done. "What did you find?"

"Wihega County state's attorney about thirty years ago. Ended up serving the most terms of any county board president in the state, merged city and county law enforcement. Controversial now because he's trying to get a casino for Falcon Ridge. Has ties to organized crime."

"With Uncle Theo, you better throw in the word 'alleged.' He's sued more than a few reporters who claimed he was mobbed up. Has good enough connections to get a federal judge to order the FBI to back off him a few years ago."

"So everybody knows he's a crook but nobody can prove it."

"Give the poor guy a break. Here he is, probably just left public service to have a little time with his grandkids before he dies and the big bad media is trying to make him into some kind of dirty politician."

She unlocked the passenger-side door of her Explorer and grinned up at me. "Are you always this sarcastic?"

"Frequently."

But I got into the Explorer thinking about Zak.

Though he was ostensibly retired, the Feds believed "Uncle Theo" was still calling the shots in Wihega County, albeit through cut-outs and a cooperative county board. In fact, an FBI agent I'd interviewed once called Uncle Theo a "collector." Instead of stamps, paintings, or expensive figurines, however, Theo Zak had reportedly spent the last thirty years amassing J. Edgar Hoover–style files on anyone who might further his ambitions or help him turn a buck.

Jody took us down Ontario Street and up on the ramp to the Westbound Kennedy, then slid the Explorer smoothly into the mid-morning flow of outbound traffic. Her vehicle was spotless. Even the cup holders in the console were retracted. I bet if I opened the glove compartment in front of me, I'd find it neatly stacked with everything a driver might routinely need. The only anomaly was the white plastic tip of an asthma inhaler peeking out over the rim of the ashtray built into the center console. I glanced at the notepad affixed to the windshield. A printed top sheet showed a list of what looked like errands, numbered one through five. There was a hand-drawn line through each one with a small smiley face at the end. Affixed to the top of the pad was a picture of a little blond girl wearing a broad smile.

"Your daughter?"

"Yep. That's my gorgeous child. Second grade and her daddy is a great Mr. Mom, God bless him."

Her phone rang, putting further small talk on hold. She listened for a moment, nodded, and said in a no-nonsense voice, "Dig for more but send the bios to my email. I'll pick them up when I get to the scene. Could you find anything about the neighborhood? Who else lives there, crime stats, anything like that?" Another moment of listening and then she thanked the caller and slipped her phone into a power converter mounted between the seats.

"I had an intern pull the network's bio on the Haydens. The kids are his, not hers. I didn't know she was his second wife. He's in his mid-fifties and she's barely thirty-five. Looks older. Must be those big plastic lips of hers. A federal judge and the head of some big electronics firm live in that same neighborhood. Falcon Ridge Heights. Not near the scene, though."

Her phone rang again. Good producers are seldom off the phone. While she talked, I reviewed my mental files on Croix Hayden and Margo Malveaux-Hayden.

They were the James Carville and Mary Matalin of the Juris Doctor set. He'd been a high-priced criminal defense lawyer.

She was a former prosecutor turned court-TV analyst turned wife. Their nationally syndicated show was just going into its second season. I'd watched it a few times. Their guests often left the studio looking like they'd gone three or four rounds with a team of boxing kangaroos. The type of show it was, and the irony of a murder in their own household, guaranteed the story would go network. I just hoped we'd get it on the air first.

Jody hung up her phone. "Al Greco just pulled up. He says the cops have a two-block perimeter but he's upstairs in a house nearby and has good line of sight."

"Competition there?"

"Just two stringers. One's in the weeds out back if the cops haven't found him already."

I smiled. If we hustled, we could break the story.

CHAPTER FOUR

Robert "Pike" Wescott burst from the Forge Global Technologies boardroom and loped down the long corridor leading to his private elevator. His administrative assistant and his secretary flanked him, nearly jogging to keep up so they could hear his orders for the day. It didn't help that he spoke in the low tones of someone accustomed to discussing sensitive and sometimes highly classified projects.

The brief elevator ride offered a couple of moments to clarify their boss's directives but, once the car arrived on the fifth floor, Wescott didn't pause for further questions. As the women glanced at each other in surprise, he stepped off ahead of them with uncharacteristic rudeness and walked directly to the door that led to his office and private electronics lab.

"No interruptions," he said. If either woman responded, he didn't hear. He closed and locked the heavy oak door and bolted for his rest room, shedding his suit jacket as he flung himself to the floor in front of the toilet.

He threw up with such force it would leave his throat raw for days.

His cellular ringing in the midst of a board meeting had startled him as much as if someone had crashed into the room.

The voice told him, "We have a serious problem."

"What do you mean?" He heard himself as a slight echo in the transmission, a function of the phone's high-security digital encryption. It was a feature he'd designed into the software to remind both parties that their conversation was protected from eavesdroppers.

"A fatal problem," the caller had said. "The boy is dead."

Only rigid self-control allowed him to hear his caller's message and still finish the meeting without any outward display of emotion.

He pushed away from the commode and stood up. His legs trembled. Washing his hands and face, gargling with a strong mouthwash, he stared at the mirror. Saw his father's heavy features and his mother's dark eyes. A face where emotions found it easy to hide. "A face made for deception," a woman once told him.

Now was not the time for self-assessment. Wescott found a fresh shirt and put it on, then straightened his tie and squared his shoulders. He needed to move, to act. Always more comfortable when walking the plant floor or investigating the work being done in the numerous development areas and labs throughout the Forge Global campus, he would apply that oversight to the problem at hand.

He stepped to his desk. A photograph on the wall behind it caught his eye. At twenty-five, his first board of directors meeting as president of Forge Technologies. Shaking hands with his mentor, Eldon Forge. A worn-out Eldon Forge, body overwhelmed by cancer and grief, barely strong enough to summon the requisite smile for the camera. Wescott remembered the pride in Eldon's eyes that day and felt ashamed.

He turned away from the photo and used the phone to summon his driver.

He would see firsthand what his fear had wrought.

CHAPTER FIVE

The cops had yellow barrier tape wrapped around two trees and stretched so it blocked sidewalks and the street for twenty-five yards in both directions from the Hayden's house. There were several cars that looked like antenna farms parked along the remainder of Warwick Avenue. A fat Hispanic guy with the logo of a local radio station on his tape recorder stood in a group of about half a dozen still-photographers right next to the police line. Occasionally one of the photogs would lift a camera and click away at something the cops were doing. The radio guy barked into a cell phone.

It was the sort of neighborhood I expected. This was Old Falcon Ridge. Like east Lake Forest or Winnetka, well-established homes surrounded by impossibly green lawns and thick stands of mature trees. Prices probably started at two million and climbed to the stratosphere. A couple of acres per house. As we drove in I saw some hiding from the street behind dense undergrowth and even a couple of them ringed with iron fencing and security gates. The Hayden house was well back on its lot but visible through the trees.

I was glad to see our microwave truck parked at the bottom of somebody's non-gated circular drive, well out of ticketing range if the cops turned nasty. The remote camera on the truck's mast pointed toward the action.

Whoever came up with the idea of sticking a camera on the microwave transmitter mast was a genius. It often gives us a shot unobtainable from any other vantage point, especially in cases where the cops throw up an unreasonable, wide perimeter and scurry from view any time they see a lens pointed at them. The beauty of the remote cam is that it's unobtrusive. The nifty thing about ours is that they're rigged with zoom lenses controlled in the truck.

Jody parked around the corner and we walked up to the truck together. She was on the phone again, trying to round up the stringers who claimed to have video. I looked around, half-expecting to see one jumping out of a tree. They take risks to get to a scene fast and sneak in close to the action. It's the only way they can sell what they shoot. All I saw, though, was a clutch of onlookers across the street, including one guy with wraparound dark glasses and a shaved head beside whom a Mac truck would have seemed like a Tonka. He looked to be in his mid-twenties but his outfit was pure high school: painter's paints hanging low on his hips and a T-shirt that looked ready to split at the shoulders. He squatted on the parkway grass munching jelly beans from a white paper sack and staring at us as we approached the truck.

Peter Prasad sat in the front passenger seat eating an apple and reading the *Sun-Times*. He's a camera guy, a "shooter" like Al, but he's also responsible for running the truck's electronics and feeding live shots back to the station. He keeps his shoulder-length hair neatly tied in a ponytail, but has the rumpled appearance of someone who got dressed in a marijuana fog. I introduced him to Jody and she hopped into the swivel chair in the back of the truck and began setting up her computer and wi-fi connection.

"Al schmoozed the woman who lives here and he's got a clear shot from up on her third floor. One of the stringers, Dave Philke, got the best stuff of the morning, though." Peter gestured to one of the video screens. Jody reached over and clicked the mouse.

The camera was zoomed in on what appeared to be a back door. A plainclothes guy was getting in the face of a patrol officer in a white shirt with a commander's insignia on his lapel. Plainclothes shouted that *he* was in charge of the scene. The white-shirt suddenly shoved him backward and snarled something the audio didn't pick up. Two other uniforms appeared from inside the house and got between the two men.

"Hope we can use that. The cops nearly busted Philke when he came out of the bushes."

Hearing that, I felt a jolt of irritation. I grew up in a cop's household and I'm probably more pro-police than a reporter is supposed to be, but law-enforcement agencies that go out of their way to play games with the media annoy me in a very dark way. I'd had some personal experiences with that over the summer, nearly being arrested by a federal task force when I got a little too close to the Russian mob.

I was still pissed when I noticed the white stretch limo in my peripheral vision. By the time I turned my full attention toward it, the Lincoln was parked at the corner near Jody's Explorer. A slender man in a sharp suit and sixty-buck haircut stepped out, glanced at the media throng, and walked briskly toward the police line on the opposite side of the street. Odd, I thought. Dropped off by the limo because he lived in the area and the car couldn't get any closer? Back from a business trip? If he was headed home, he carried no luggage or briefcase and cops don't arrive at crime scenes in stretch limos.

From across the street, the guy appeared middle-aged and moved with a stride that suggested he was on home turf. He looked halfway familiar but I couldn't come up with his name. The quick glance he gave us wasn't hostile or even curious. It was the sort of reaction we sometimes get from celebrities, politicians, and other public figures who aren't surprised to see a gaggle of reporters, cameras, and microphones tracking them. I wondered who he was.

"Heads up," I said to Peter. "Let's get a shot of this guy."

Yellow tape stretched from tree to tree, blocking the street. It flapped in the breeze. Two Wihega County squad cars sat idling just inside the perimeter, facing our way. As the guy approached them, with us trailing behind, an officer stepped from one of the squads and lifted the barrier so the guy could pass underneath it. No hesitation. They shook hands and the cop got between us and the guy. Regardless, Peter stayed with the shot and the still photographers in the gaggle of media a couple feet away kept their cameras clicking.

I nodded toward the man just as the cops led him inside a large RV with county markings parked across the street from the Hayden house.

"Anybody know who that was?"

A dark-haired guy in a rumpled Harris tweed sport coat, media ID clipped to his pocket, stared at me as though wondering if I was serious.

"Most of the money in Wihega County," he deadpanned. That brought a laugh from the group. I shook my head and shrugged.

"Pike Wescott. Forge Global Technologies? He's sort of like our own Bill Gates."

FGT I knew. I'd probably seen Wescott being interviewed somewhere. "He lives nearby, right?"

"Four, five blocks. He has Eldon Forge's old place." Harris Tweed gave me a thin smile. "You big-time TV guys outta the city, you're kinda lost here in the sticks aren't ya?"

"Yeah, yeah." I went back to the live truck, leaned in to Jody.

"Throw Pike Wescott into your notes. When you have a minute, see if you can find a connection between him and the

Haydens." I kicked myself for being slow off the mark. Should have been up there with a microphone and stuck it in his face as he passed by.

Still eyeing the RV where Wescott had disappeared, I asked Peter, "What do we know?"

"Couple people came by while I was setting up. They say Hayden's got two kids. They didn't know which one is supposedly dead. I asked 'em for, you know, reaction. Typical rich folks. Wouldn't go on camera."

"I take it the cops haven't talked?"

"Not yet. They're being hard-ass, like I said. Said they don't care who we are, if we sneak past the tape, they'd send us to jail. Scared me so bad I ate an extra donut."

"Reno?" Jody still held the phone to her ear. "Yogi says seven and two have their helicopters headed this way. Leaving from Schaumburg so they'll probably be here any minute."

Our helicopter, naturally, was grounded for maintenance. I looked at my watch. It was closing in on nine o'clock, the hour when Channel 14 flips away from local news to a network talk show. "Can we get a minute or so for an update?"

"Chucky says we're clear until we go to network. After that, he'll only take us if we confirm somebody named Hayden's been whacked."

"What if one of the Haydens was the whack-er?"

"Whatever!" She waved a hand in dismissal, grinning.

I considered the possibilities. The victim could have been a Hayden kid. Could also have been one of their friends. A Hayden employee. A home invader shot by one of the kids in a *Home Alone* scenario. That would have the most appeal, of course. All would be tragedies. But each offered pretty decent story possibilities.

There were at least ten squad cars, two crime scene wagons, and that RV, which I took to be a mobile command center, parked in the street near the Haydens' home. Without question, this was a heater case. I was out of time.

I tried Rudy Esperanza's cellular again. It rang three times before a gruff voice answered.

"Esperanza."

"Espy, it's Reno McCarthy."

"Shit. Hold on."

I waited for about five minutes, listening to what sounded like an angry conversation muted by a hand over the mouthpiece. Then a door closed and Esperanza spoke again.

"Jesus Christ, Reno. Nice timing after what? Two years?"

"Things a little tense?"

He grunted a laugh but it didn't seem to contain much mirth. "Whadda you need?"

With some cops, you have to play a game. Ray Esperanza you hit straight on.

"Who's dead?"

"Trey Hayden. That's T-R-E-Y, like in cards. The TV lawyer's son."

I hadn't realized I'd been holding my breath until I blew it out. For me, confirming a hot story is better than winning the Powerball.

"When and how?"

"If I was gonna guess, I'd say the middle of the night. Two to the chest, looks like."

"Parents been notified?"

"Beats me. You'll have to get that from the locals. In fact, I should keep my trap shut."

"Just tell me this. What are you guys doing out here? Wihega's got its own ETs."

"Yeah, I trained some of them. Supposedly they wanted our laser kit. But it's a screwy situation."

"How so?"

"They had me bust a nut to get here. Now they're saying they don't need us after all. Like they think I'm going to try and take over, make 'em look bad or something. Fucking politicians."

"Politicians?"

"You better believe they were all over this from the git go. That's who's running the show, my friend. First, when we got here, I talked to a patrol commander named Duvall who seemed to have his shit together. Since then, I've had face time with a detective commander named Teague and the chief of police, okay? They had a cell phone going the whole time so somebody backstage could listen. Law enforcement isn't in charge of this. No way."

We nailed the exclusive. Just barely, right before we went to network at nine.

Chucky and Florbus insisted I use Trey Hayden's name. I could have but I refused. Florbus called me an asshole. They both tried to convince me the police must have told Croix and Margo Hayden of their son's death by now. "Must have" wasn't good enough justification.

There's good reason why a reporter says, "Police are withholding the name until family has been notified." Most people wouldn't want to find out from watching local TV that their loved one has been murdered. Guessing that an official notification has been made doesn't cut it with me. I confirmed there had been a murder in Croix Hayden's home. Period. Not perfect, but better than any of the other stations managed to do. We broke the story.

Jody motioned to me as I got off the air.

"The coroner is a woman named Perkins . . ."

"Johnnie Perkins? Used to be an assistant ME in Cook County?"

53

"I dunno. Why? You know her?"

I grinned. Things were looking up. "Sure do. Go on."

"She's the only one in the office who talks to media and she's 'in the field.' I told her assistant that we've all but confirmed the victim's name. He tells me, off the record, his people are having a 'communication' problem with the cops. He wouldn't explain but he wasn't happy."

The sound of a helicopter approaching washed away my reply. I looked up to see Channel 2 taking a pass over the house while another bird orbited a few miles out.

As the rotor noise from the helicopter diminished, Al tapped me on the shoulder and jerked his head toward the police line. "Company."

I looked up in time to watch a white-shirted uniform duck under the yellow tape and stalk toward us. He wore one of those expressions I'm accustomed to seeing on cops ready to get in my face. Wonderful. Al drifted toward his camera. I waited for the cop.

"You McCarty?" he asked. The mispronunciation seemed deliberate. Dark hair, deep five-o'clock shadow, bags under the eyes. His nameplate read "Cmdr. Gary Duvall." He was the officer we'd seen arguing on the stringer's video.

I smiled. "Reno McCarthy, Commander." Nobody offered to shake hands. He made a wide gesture that took in the live truck.

"We need you to shut this thing down and move out of the area."

"Excuse me?"

"You're done here. The homeowner called us. He wants you out of his driveway."

The live shot, I thought. Duvall had seen the live shot, seen the quick hits of video from the mast-cam and from the stringer. And he was pissed. I couldn't blame him. The cops had tried to keep us back, but our video made it look like we were right up next to them. Along with the argument, a couple of Al's long-range shots even caught a glimpse of people moving around one of the rooms on the second floor of the Hayden home.

"Was there something inaccurate about our report?"

He was looking off over my shoulder now, avoiding eye contact. Easier to pretend he hadn't heard me.

"As you can see, there's no other parking available. We'll give you ten minutes before we start writing tickets. Have a nice day." He turned to leave and noticed Al behind the camera.

"You taping me?"

Al said nothing but the glowing red light above the lens told the story. The commander's condescending look vanished. "Hey, asshole, I didn't give you people permission to tape me before, and you don't have it now."

"Commander, the homeowner told us we could park here," I said. Always use the title. Sometimes deference alone defuses things. "I'm sure if you speak with her she'll confirm it."

"And *she's* a widow," Al added. So much for defusing.

"Turn that fuckin' thing off," Duvall said, jabbing a finger at the camera. Al kept rolling. Duvall took a step toward him. "I said I want it off or I'm going to seize it as evidence."

That was my cue. "The helicopters are all feeding live shots to the networks, Commander. A good portion of the country is watching everything you guys do. Just a thought."

I kept my voice as relaxed as a social worker's counseling a patient. We were at a point where this could turn sour in a hurry and I didn't want to say or do anything the commander could take as a threat.

Even so, my words sent a red flush up Duvall's neck. I wondered if he was a poker player and if that tell of frustration ever cost him. He muttered something to me in a low voice then brushed past Al, jostling him with his shoulder, and headed back toward the police line. As he snapped it up to pass underneath, the crime scene tape broke. He shoved it away, strode to the nearest patrol car, and got in. Al's lens followed him the whole way.

I heard laughter from inside the truck and then brief applause from Jody.

"You're my hero," she said. "Both of you."

Al swiveled the camera so it pointed back toward the Hayden house. "Who stuck the pipe bomb up his rectal orifice?"

"Was calling him a liar the best way to go, partner?" I didn't like the sarcasm in my voice but there it was. Al just looked surprised but Jody stared at me, her grin fading.

"Hey, are you okay? What did he say to you?"

"Nothing."

But she was still in pushy-producer mode. "Your face doesn't look like it was nothing."

"Leave it alone, Jody." I snapped open my cell and turned away from her.

For the next fifteen minutes I wandered up and down the sidewalk near the live truck and called old contacts, trying to find a cell phone number for JohnElla Perkins. I'd forgotten that she'd moved to Falcon Ridge, her hometown, and gotten herself elected coroner. We'd always had a decent relationship when she was in the Cook County ME's office.

A half-block down from where Al was parked in the driveway, a Channel 7 remote truck was nosing in to the curb and a News-Star satellite unit arrived right behind it. That meant one of the networks. When they don't have one of their own handy, they rent. I walked past, giving a wave to the crew from 7.

A buddy called to give me Johnnie Perkins's cell number. I left her a message.

I slipped the phone back into my jacket but it rang almost immediately. Yogi.

"What the hell did you do to piss off those Wihega County

people, dude? You haven't even been there an hour. Some commander just ran you for warrants."

"Once the rest of the stations and the networks show, they're going to have their hands so full they'll forget about us."

"I don't think so, dude. When the guy ran your name? He sounded like he knew all about . . ." He stopped and seemed embarrassed when he continued. "You know."

Yeah, I knew. Yogi meant the cops knew my history. No surprise.

What Duvall muttered to me before walking away was, "See ya, killer."

CHAPTER SIX

Ray Fong called before I got back to the live truck.

Not only Vinnie's doc, he's mine, too. And a close friend. One of four people, including Vinnie, with whom I shared all the particulars after I killed the Russian gangster who was gunning for me.

"Sorry as hell about this morning, buddy. Had a patient relapse." He's first-generation American but has a Chicago accent stronger than any you'll hear in Bridgeport.

I didn't have time for anything but facts. "How bad is Vinnie?"

"He's in what we call cardiogenic shock, secondary to a massive heart attack. The big ones like that, they knock off enough heart muscle that the rest of the organs don't get enough blood. Basically, everything goes to shit. We've inserted a balloon pump."

"Bottom line?"

"Drugs to elevate his pressure, bypass surgery to save the remaining heart muscle. The best bet is angioplasty. We can put in a stent, open the main artery that feeds the heart . . ."

"I said bottom line, Ray. I meant what are his chances?"

He cleared his throat. As a teenager, the throat clearing routine usually came right before he started throwing punches.

"It depends on just how badly the heart muscle is damaged. Based on what we know now, I'd say he's got about a thirty percent chance of recovery. Even then he'll likely have post-op congestive heart failure and arrhythmias."

He had no siblings. No children. For all intents, we had been his kids. Ray and I.

"Christ," I said. Guilt fought for supremacy with feelings of betrayal. I wanted to sit down on the curb and bury my head in my hands. Or go back and pick a fight with that cop.

"I know you're angry as hell about . . ."

"Don't go there." I snapped. One of the techs in the satellite truck glanced up. I turned away and lowered my voice. "Listen, Ray. Vinnie's a user. First, he dangled me as bait, and I had to kill a guy. Then he tried to cover up that whole Russian nightmare just to keep a U.S. senator happy. I don't know what I am, but 'angry' doesn't even come close."

"You gotta get over it, Reno. For him and for you, too. The man could die. You turn your back on him now, you'll have him on your conscience forever."

I opened my mouth. Nothing came out.

"Another thing. You know about his health care power of attorney, right?"

Only a portion of my brain was paying attention to him. The rest kept showing me Vinnie's hands flat on the bed, like they would be if he were laid out on a morgue table.

"No."

"He didn't go over this with you?"

"No. Why would he?"

Ray hesitated. "Because you're the one he chose to make the decision, buddy. If there's one to be made."

I didn't get it right away. I heard the words, but from ear to brain took a nanosecond or two longer than usual.

"Jesus Christ." My voice came out hoarse. "He wants *me* to pull the plug?"

"Everybody he respected on the Job is dead or retired to some nursing home somewhere. We're the last of a pretty select group. Who else was he going to ask? The law says I can't do it for him. Not alone anyway."

"The point is, he didn't ask. He just assumed I'd kill him when the time came. The son of a bitch. When did he sign this thing?"

"Reno . . ."

"When? Sometime in the last three months?"

"Yeah."

"God damn it! Did he know this was going to happen? Was he sick?"

"Not as far as I know. We had lunch back in, what? July, I think it was. He mentioned he'd signed a power of attorney naming you as his agent. I didn't ask him if he'd talked to you about it. I guess I assumed . . . shit, I don't know! He sent me a copy a few weeks later to add to his chart."

"Son of a bitch." I ended the call. My hand was shaking so hard I nearly dropped the phone. As I stowed it away, it rang again. I ignored it. The ringing stopped.

Another setup. Just like with the Russians.

Well, pick another sucker, old man. I'm not killing you.

I've bagged my limit for this lifetime.

As I came around the corner, I saw Peter and Al visiting with two senior-looking gentlemen and a woman in her youthful fifties. Everyone was laughing at something Al had said. Several feet away from them, however, and peering into the back of the truck, stood another sort of individual.

He was slender, with lank, dark hair that hung to his collar in back. About twenty or so. Jeans, the type prison inmates wear, and a lightweight jean jacket that also could have been prison issue. Trendy. Except his outfit only mimicked convict wear. Even a state legislature on crack wouldn't allow the Department of Corrections a budget high enough to pay for designer label jackets and jeans. He seemed to sense my approach and

60

backed away from the truck to turn and greet me. The knuckles on his left hand were abraded and swollen. He saw me notice and stuffed his hands into his jacket pockets.

Some women would have described his narrow features and the little squib of hair hanging down on his forehead as sensual. Girls his age and younger probably called him "thug" or maybe "edgy." His grin was slow and mocking and curled the edges of his mouth but never made it to his eyes, which seemed to have their own agenda. He was floating somewhere around Pluto.

I moved into his space, making him step back. "Can I help you?"

"Hey, I was just talking to the pretty lady here. Checking out all the electronics. Nice setup, man." He breathed beer fumes in my face.

I looked into the truck. Jody was frowning, arms crossed.

"When are you gonna be on again, Reno?" Jean Jacket asked. "I'll hang and watch. I dig all this live TV shit."

"You live around here?"

He rocked back and forth while he considered how to answer. "Yeah, in fact. I do. Want to interview me? Five hundred bucks, you get everything. Exclusive." Another glance into the truck, as though to be sure he still had his audience.

"Everything about . . . what?"

"Duh. What are you here for, man? I can tell you what happened to ol' Trey. Scoop like that's got to be worth five hundred bucks. Even if he was my, sob, best friend." He rubbed a knuckle into his eye in a theatrical way.

"Beat it," I snapped.

He glanced over his shoulder at Jody, smile faltering. "Come on. You know I'm worth it, baby."

"Reno . . ." Jody said.

I put a hand on his chest and leaned into him. His back hit the truck's sliding door. I had four inches and probably eighty pounds on him. The smartass grin rippled like the ground radiating from a fault line.

"Hey! Get your hands . . ."

"There's a young man dead inside that house. Show a little respect."

Jody spoke up again, more insistent this time. "Reno, I think . . ."

"We don't pay for information. You have something to say, say it. Or take a hike."

Jean Jacket wasn't expecting someone to call his bluff. His stare lasted about ten seconds before he decided to bail.

"Fuck you, man!"

He slithered out from under my hand and walked to where a girl in a tank top and short skirt waited on the parkway across the street. She said something to him. He kept walking. She hurried to catch up. I noticed the big guy who had been squatting there earlier now leaning against a tree, still eating jelly beans. While the girl made a wide arc to avoid walking near him, Jean Jacket stopped for a moment and said something that caused the big guy to suddenly reach out and clamp a hand on his arm. I smiled. Apparently someone else didn't appreciate Jean Jacket's attitude.

From inside the truck, Jody said, "Damn it, Reno. He told me some things."

I turned away from the action across the street. "Yeah? Like what?"

She slapped her notepad down on the counter in front of the rack of monitors. My first thought was that Jean Jacket had been trying to come on to her but I realized her anger was directed at me.

"He's just a little high. He said he had good stuff to tell me."

"It's all good when you're high."

"He knows the victim was Trey Hayden."

62

"Everybody knows that by now. What else?"

"He said he beat Trey up last night."

I flashed back to the swollen knuckles I'd seen on his left hand. "Why?"

"An argument over a girl. If you hadn't scared him off, I think he was about to tell me more. He seemed like he wanted to get something off his chest."

"Christ." I glanced across the street. The big guy was alone. Jean Jacket was nowhere in sight.

"Reno, I don't know if it was what that cop said to you earlier that put you in this snit or whether you're always so obnoxious, but your attitude isn't helping us."

She had a fierce look in her eyes. Pit-viper was right. No one would walk over this gal when she was in story-getting mode.

Was he getting ready to confess? The idea panicked me. Had I just let a killer walk away? And why had I come down so hard on the kid anyway?

"You're right," I said. My neck felt tight.

"Good. Now you want to go fetch my witness and bring him back here."

I went looking but he and his girlfriend had disappeared.

The Hulk with the bone dome still leaned against a tree on the parkway, but he'd put away his bag of jellybeans and folded his arms across his chest. He watched me with a faint smile as I approached. Closer to him, I smelled coffee and corrosive body odor.

"Where did your buddy in the jean jacket go?" I asked.

He kept looking but stopped smiling. When he did that, his mouth hung slightly open. He didn't respond.

"Thanks anyway," I said.

"He's a big liar," he said in the cartoon voice you get after sucking helium. Or using steroids.

"What's he lying about?"

That furrowed his brow. After a moment he said, "Every-thing."

"Want to be a little more specific?"

Silence.

"What's his name?"

More silence.

I walked on, more aware of the tightness in my neck.

The sidewalk turned into a cedar-mulch path after less than thirty yards. I followed it for another thirty before stopping to listen. Birds sang and sunlight sparkled through breaks in the trees near me but up ahead, as the path curved out of sight, it became almost subway tunnel dark. I continued a few yards farther. Had there been gravel underfoot, I might have been able to hear Jean Jacket and his friend walking but the mulch muffled footfalls much like thick carpet. Should I lie down and put my ear to the ground or did that only work when listening for the thunder of horses' hooves? Since I didn't think they'd ridden off on a pair of stallions, I didn't try it. Maybe I should have. I chose not to follow them any farther, either.

Someone, probably a park or forest preserve district, had put some money into the trail's upkeep. Railroad ties, to prevent the rich-looking mulch from washing away in a downpour, bordered the path and the underbrush on either side was neatly trimmed back to allow for unobstructed walking. Before I turned to head back, I glanced at a slanted notice board tacked to a cedar post. A map under plastic showed how the trail meandered through the neighborhood. Up ahead, I would find Falcon Ridge High School West Campus on my left. A little farther along, the path curved into something called Mandy's Meadow. No individual residences were identified, but I assumed that if I walked back the way I'd come, I'd pass the rear of the Hayden's home. I was tempted but decided not to risk pissing off the cops again.

I turned to head back to the truck. Startled, I found myself facing the giant. I hadn't heard him approach. He still had his arms folded but the little smile was missing.

"Small world," I said. He said nothing. I started to walk around him.

He stepped sideways to block me.

I stopped. A chill tickled my spine. I'm not a small guy, but he had three inches on me and the density of the Bears' front line. If shit hit the fan, I was going to get hurt. Then I felt the adrenaline kick in and a perverse little voice whispered in my brain: *I will hurt him worse.*

"You have something you wanted to tell me? Your buddy's name maybe?"

He unfolded his arms and put one hand into his pocket. I watched his eyes. He came out with his white bag of goodies.

"Thanks anyway. Sugar makes me jumpy," I said.

Nothing.

"Excuse me."

Whether he read something in my expression or just decided to end his game, this time he didn't get in my way.

As I stepped into the street from the trail, my cell phone rang. Loud enough to punch my pulse into overdrive. Caller ID said the number was blocked. I glanced over my shoulder to be sure my new buddy hadn't crept up behind me. I was a little disappointed when I saw he had not.

"McCarthy."

"Just when I thought I was safe from the media," Johnnie Perkins said. There's something about her voice that always suggests she's about to chuckle.

"You can run but you can't hide. Not even in the sticks."

And there came the chuckle. The sound reminded me enough of my mother that it brought to mind a vivid image of her and me sitting on the screen porch with Vinnie a year or so after my father's death. Vinnie could always make her laugh.

"Why, I do believe I hear verbal banter. You do not know how much I miss that with our local press corps, Reno. How are you?"

I jousted with her for a few moments, and then she asked what she could do for me.

"For starters, confirm there's been a murder here at the Hayden's house and that Trey Hayden was the victim."

"You do know the right things to say to a girl. All right. Your information is correct. If you need his age, he was nineteen. He lived at this address."

"Shot?"

"That is correct."

"Once or more?"

"You know how I have to handle that, Reno. Pending autopsy."

"Is there some conflict between your office and the county police?"

"Whatever leads you to think so? Off the record? The county police asked us to remain outside the crime scene until the evidence technicians finished their preliminary work."

"Asked or ordered?"

"Let me put it this way. We have some . . . authority issues . . . to work out."

"Call me crazy but that sounds like a story to me." In Illinois, coroners have absolute jurisdiction over the deceased. No one can keep them from a homicide scene.

"It might very well be. For now, I would appreciate it if you would keep it between us. Until I speak to the state's attorney."

Give and take. It's how sources learn to trust you. "One question on background. This dispute didn't just pop up in a vacuum. What's going on?"

She chuckled again. "That is a discussion we could have over lunch sometime. Suffice to say, the police administration and I do not play golf together."

I hurried back to the truck.

Peter and Al's group of admirers had thinned down to one of the seniors in gray slacks and a light blue windbreaker. He held a portable police scanner in one hand and a baseball hat in the other. Jody was back inside, typing and talking on the phone at the same time. She waved me quiet before I could say anything. From the tone of her conversation, she seemed to be talking to a cop. I shut up and went over to Al and Peter.

I smiled at the older man, spoke to Al. "I need to do an update if Jody can get us time."

"Reno this is Mr. Moulet," Peter said with enthusiasm, rhyming the name with "roulette." "He lives down the street. He's been telling us a little about the Haydens. How they aren't his favorite neighbors. You'll want to hear this."

The man fumbled his scanner into his jacket pocket and gripped my hand. "Ernie Moulet." Eyes the color of his windbreaker probed mine. His hair was on crooked, a bad rug of parchment yellow settled just enough off center to be noticeable.

"I was just telling your people here. I live on the other side of the Prairie Trail three doors down. Close enough to the Haydens' to hear their damn dogs barking all the damn time." He wiggled his fingers vaguely in the direction of the Hayden home.

"Real nuisance, huh?" I was eager to get on the air with Johnnie's confirmation.

"You better believe it was! Nobody in the vicinity could go outside, even in the middle of the night, without those dogs sounding like they wanted to tear us apart. German shepherds. Skinny little things, poor beasts. Looked like coyotes. So I got a petition together. My son's a lawyer. It was his suggestion. About walked my feet down to the bone, taking it around for everyone to sign."

"Did it work?"

"You don't hear any barking, do you? Thing was, city hall loves those Haydens. Would have let them slide, except we got the local paper interested. The high and mighty Haydens and their media empire were scared to death. They didn't want to look bad in their own neighborhood. They agreed to sit down with a group of us and 'negotiate the dog issue face to face.' Damn white of them," he snickered.

"What about the Haydens' son and daughter?"

Ernie Moulet looked like he'd swallowed musk oil. "What's the word the shrinks use? Dysfunctional. I've lived in my house for close to forty years. And my house is between their place and the school. By the way, both of the kids're his, you know. Her being his second wife."

I nodded.

"They're not much different than the dogs. Out of control. Parents let them do any damn thing they want to do, including drink." He held up a hand. "I know I'm speaking ill of the dead but so be it. The boy, Trey, was the worst. It was in the paper, maybe two weeks ago? Arrested for DUI."

That got my attention. I wrote it down. "What was his relationship with his parents?"

"With his father, I couldn't really say. Probably not good. I know Margo wouldn't let him drive after the arrest. Heard that argument loud and clear. Saw him walking quite a bit recently along the path, too. Smoking. You can always tell when he's around. I find cigarette butts. And not just tobacco, either."

"Did you see him last night?"

"Oh, he was back there at some point. Sure. Saw a car parked in the school lot. Looked like one of the driver's ed cars, but it wasn't. They had some vandalism awhile back and I've been keeping an eye on things. That's what they taught us at the

Citizens' Police Academy. They keep two driver's ed cars back there and last night there were three. Third one didn't belong. Gonna write that down?"

He stared at my notebook. I dutifully scribbled, "3 cars—school lot."

I had to fight the temptation to look at my watch. "Anything else?"

"Saw a flashlight along the path a couple of times, too. And just now, when I was walking over here, there were more cigarette butts. I'd say to Trey, 'You want to start a fire? Burn all our houses down?' He ignored me. You know those kinda kids. I pick up the butts, throw them in the trash. I complain to the park district but they get tired of hearing from an obnoxious old fart." He grinned, as though pleased he had made a nuisance of himself.

"Mr. Moulet, speaking of his friends, do you happen to know the young guy I was just talking to . . . ?"

"You bet I do. Awhile ago, I made it my business to get his name. Lucas Bremmer. He comes around sometimes, him and that girl. If anything, he's worse than the Haydens. Always plays the radio in that damn Jeep of his so loud it shakes the walls. I told him to turn it down once and he gave me the finger."

"Bremmer claims he beat Trey up last night."

"Doesn't come as any surprise but I didn't hear anything and I pay attention. Mopes are what they are. That's what the cops around here call them, you know. Learned that in class, too."

"Does Bremmer live nearby?"

"No. But if you need to know his address, I could ask my grandson. He knew him in high school." He dug a cell phone out of an inside jacket pocket. A moment later, he recited the address so I could copy it down. Jody called my name. I excused myself.

"Five minutes until you go live."

I nodded and turned back to thank Ernie Moulet. He was already halfway down the street, using both hands to arrange his hat atop that awful hairpiece.

A public information guy with sergeant's stripes on his arm came over about a half hour later and stripped down the tape, allowing us to move closer to the scene. As crisp in his tailored uniform as a Marine in dress blues, he had a craggy face, mustache trimmed to exact regulation length, brush-cut blond hair, and the ripped upper body of a weightlifter. His smile crinkled the corners of his mouth but didn't reach his eyes, like an expression he dusted off only when it was expected of him. He offered a hand.

"Reno. Sergeant Callahan. I'm just getting here myself, but I heard you and Commander Duvall had a little disagreement. Figured I'd try to set things straight."

So smooth you'd think he drew a six-figure salary from one of the top five PR firms.

"The commander is just coming off midnights. He had his hands full with the situation until the detectives showed up to help him out."

"The way I hear it, the operative word was *throw* not help."

"That's harsh, Reno. Nobody threw anybody out. I'd take into consideration that your witness was about twenty-five yards away before you put anything so inflammatory on the air."

"What was the disagreement?"

"Oh, you know how it goes after a long shift. Probably just a lot of stress talking." He glanced past me and seemed to go on point. I looked and saw Jody stepping out of the truck.

"Hi there. I'm Ben Callahan." A business card appeared in his hand and he passed it to her. I wondered if it was a maneuver that worked well for him at his favorite watering hole. From the expression on Jody's face, she wasn't charmed.

Callahan said, "I was just about to tell Reno that as soon as I get up to speed I'll pull everybody together for a briefing."

Jody put the card in her pocket. "Any secrets you'd like to share beforehand?"

"Well, I'm a pretty good dancer . . ."

"Of course. You're a police spokesman."

CHAPTER SEVEN

The buzz of the vibrating cellular phone distracted Pike Wescott from the complicated electronic diagram he'd been drawing. Perhaps "drawing" was the wrong word. He laid his Cross pencil on the leather blotter and stared at what had taken him nearly an hour to produce. The cellular continued to buzz against his chest. Briefly, he wondered what his caller might do when he failed to answer. *Would it make him angry?* A flutter of fear in his chest told him yes. *Good.*

He'd been scribble-scrabbling, the childhood name he'd given the savant-like doodling he used whenever he wanted to take his mind off something that troubled him. Nine times over the years his apparently mindless but creative scribbling led to patents for electronic devices or circuitry, the first when he was only eleven years old.

Wescott folded the Scotch-taped pages. He'd used the flip side of his embossed stationery because it was the only unlined paper he could find in his office. He liked the way thoughts flowed from his hand to paper. Liked the low-tech approach to creating high-tech ideas. The focus required. Anyone could draw schematics on the computer nowadays, even children. He preferred the old-fashioned way. What Eldon Forge would have called "old school." He kept Eldon's chalkboard in his lab. Real scientists always used chalkboards. He remembered Eldon claiming he had "chalk dust in my blood."

Eldon. His broken heart took eight years to kill him.

The cellular stopped buzzing. Wescott imagined the caller punching disconnect and crushing the redial key under his thumb. As if on cue, the cellular came alive again.

Locking his scribble scrabble away in the safe, he took his time answering.

"Yes?"

"Am I interrupting something important, Robert?" Annoyed. *Good.*

"Paperwork."

"The item you were concerned about was retrieved."

Twenty-four hours ago that news might have put him in a good mood. Not now. Relief was no longer possible.

"You can speak English for God's sake. The phones are encrypted."

"I'm quite certain they're the best and most expensive the Pentagon ever purchased but as my favorite newspaper columnist once wrote about me, I wear caution like a treasured old suit. If you're not going to thank me for my assistance with your little problem, may I continue?"

"Go ahead."

"My specialist feels it's in his best interests to retain the item temporarily."

Wescott closed his eyes. A part of him, the most fearful part, had anticipated this.

"How much does he want?"

"It's not blackmail, Robert. He's concerned that he'll become collateral damage."

"Then convince him he's safe. Manipulate him. That is your *raison d'etre,* isn't it? 'For every soul, a lever.' Aren't those your words?"

"Yes. However, I think it would be better if we accede to his wishes for the time being."

"His wishes? What about my wishes?"

Abruptly, the caller switched topics. "Robert, what prompted you to take that little drive this morning? I taught you better than that."

Wescott felt like a teenager caught doing something shameful. Then realized that was his caller's intent. *Always manipulating.*

"I thought it would be wise to . . . show some interest."

"Ah. Because of your well-publicized concern for your fellow human beings?"

"As a neighbor . . ."

"As you no doubt noticed, your appearance attracted the attention of the media. Most especially a reporter named Reno McCarthy. The others are manageable. Even CNN. But if McCarthy hasn't discovered it by now, I'm sure he'll find out soon enough that your sense of community fellowship and goodwill couldn't fill a shot glass. If anything, his curiosity about your presence will be more dangerous to you, to *us,* than any questions asked by the police. That makes him another problem to handle."

A part of Wescott, left over from when he'd had a working conscience, cringed.

"I've said this to you before," the voice continued. "You have a tendency to try and snatch defeat from the jaws of victory. I can protect you against everything but yourself. You'd do well to remember that."

Wescott's right hand curled into a fist and, not for the first time, he wondered what it would be like to smash his caller's face and watch him die in agony.

CHAPTER EIGHT

Over the next couple of hours, the camp that invariably springs up at the perimeter of a major story swelled in size. We broke into programming so I could identify the victim as Croix Hayden's son. By then, I'd talked to a handful of other neighbors who confirmed Moulet's assessment of the teenager as, charitably put, troubled. Even better, Jody found the facts of his DUI arrest in online court documents. She sweet-talked somebody into bringing us a copy of the Falcon Ridge High School yearbook, too, which featured several pictures of him. We slapped everything into the piece, making it look like we truly had all the angles covered.

Chucky was waiting when I got off the air. Jody made a face as she handed me the phone.

"Nice work, Reno!" he boomed. "I knew you were the right guy to send. The network picked up your live shot. You watch the others? None of them have anything except helicopter video. We *own* this story, man."

I sensed what was coming next. He couldn't keep hands off.

"We're going to need another crew out there, don't you think? For backup and sidebars? How would it be if I sent Caroline?"

It would suck, I thought. Blond, perky, and charming in front of the camera, Caroline Levings's off-air life was a train wreck. With jobs at two other Chicago stations in flames behind her, everyone in the newsroom agreed Channel 14 would be only a whistle-stop. She was headed out of the market for sure. The predictions about where seemed to be split between serious time in rehab and a network correspondent's job.

"You're the boss." No use debating. Word in the newsroom was that Caroline and Chucky shared an appreciation for the same recreational chemicals.

"Good. I'll get her doing neighborhood reaction. Maybe the kid's background. People open up to her. It'll be a natural."

"Why don't you have her anchor the coverage on site? I'll follow what the cops are doing."

"Sure. Great. Thumbs up, buddy. We're out in front. Let's stay that way."

"Yeah." I clicked off, sighed, and looked at Jody. "So let's find out what happened to Trey Hayden and why."

Grabbing a worn map book out of the truck, I laid it across the hood and looked up the address Ernie Moulet provided for Lucas Bremmer. Two miles away, more or less. Worth going over there if we could get a confession to murder.

Al had driven a station Crown Victoria to the scene. He's an ex-Chicago cop who had fifteen years on the Job when he decided to combine his background and camera skills and jump to TV. I told him to bring a camera and come with me. Peter set his camera up on the tripod facing the Haydens' house as we left. You never want to leave a scene uncovered. Every news photographer has at least one hard luck story about things they watched happen when their cameras were turned off, turned away, or not even out of their trunk. In a famous case from several years ago, a state official back east called a news conference after being indicted for a variety of crimes. Reporters figured he was going to make a statement defending himself. A number of photographers slow to set up their equipment were horrified, perhaps a little more than the rest of the crowd, when the guy yanked a .44 magnum out of a thick manila envelope and blew his brains all over the most eager reporters sitting in the front row.

In the car Al said, "I heard about Vinnie. How's he doing?"

I had to clear my throat to speak. "Hanging in."

He nodded. "Worked a couple cases with him when I was starting out and he was a burglary dick on the West Side. Good copper."

No need to ask how he'd heard. Like Vinnie, Al is a walking hard drive of police intelligence and information.

Only a couple of miles away from the Haydens', Lucas Bremmer's place was a drop of several levels in social strata: a long 1950s ranch with a mostly browned out lawn and substantial cracks in its blacktop driveway. What made it stand out among its neighbors was that, while other houses nearby featured at least small gardens or hanging flowers under their eaves, it lacked any touch of color or brightness. A round clay pot with withered stalks of something that could have been the same vintage as the house sat next to the front door but that was it for landscaping. No car in the drive. The sheer curtains in a wide bay window hung lank and dispirited.

I told Al I'd go to the door alone and signal him if I needed him to come up with the camera. The neighborhood looked closed, awaiting the end of the workday. Nobody answered either the bell or my knock. I peered in the front window and caught a glimpse of old people's furniture thirty years out of style, a couch and two occasional chairs draped in clear plastic, and a row of framed snapshots on a round table.

I was in the middle of wondering just who Lucas Bremmer lived with, parents or grandparents, when a nearly new Volkswagen Jetta burbled down the street and swung up into the driveway next door. The woman who emerged gave me a curious glance before leaning into the back seat. She drew out a grocery bag and bumped the door closed with a pudgy hip. I walked into the Bremmers' driveway.

"Excuse me?"

Clutching the bag like a shield, she turned her head in my direction and offered a questioning smile.

"You know where I can find Lucas Bremmer?"

She could have been forty or a washed-out thirty, her hair with some gray in it pulled back into a bun. She wore a man's work shirt over jeans, and there was a Rorschach splotch of blue and green paint across her chest, visible around the sides of the bag. She checked out the Crown Vic idling at the curb and brought her eyes back to me, smile faltering.

"What's he done now?"

The car often gets people to thinking we're cops. "We're TV, not police. We're doing a story here in town. His name came up."

"What kind of story? You're not putting *me* on TV are you? Not looking like this . . ."

"No worries. What's Lucas drive?"

"A two-year-old Jeep Sahara. My ex sold it to him, right before we got divorced. We had to give up one of our cars and I told Pond Scum I didn't care what he did with his but I was keeping mine."

"You know Lucas pretty well?"

"I know he's got a cute butt." She hoisted the grocery sack into the crook of one elbow and dug into her jeans pocket, bringing out a set of keys. "You never did say what kind of story."

"One of his friends was killed last night."

"Oh Jesus." The bag wobbled. "Who?"

I watched her eyes. "Trey Hayden."

"Dear God. Did Lucas . . . do the police know what happened?"

"The police aren't talking. What were you about to say?"

She stared, lips parted, looking ready to speak. Then

78

something seemed to click behind her eyes. She moved toward her house again. "I really shouldn't talk to you about this."

"It might help your friend if you do."

"Oh yeah, right. Like you TV people are all about helping."

"Lucas has been in trouble before, right? Guys like him are the first ones the cops go after when something like this happens."

"What do you mean?"

"He's Trey's friend. He's got a record, a little attitude. Cops don't like attitude." I thought of Commander Duvall. "You don't cooperate when they question you or you act the fool, it's like spitting on the flag. They remember that stuff. You better believe, when they find out about the beating he gave Trey last night, he'll be their number one 'Person of Interest.' "

She dropped the shopping bag at her feet while she unlocked her front door.

"On the other hand," I continued, "I don't have to solve Trey's murder. I don't have any preconceptions about Lucas. I just want to do a story that's fair to both sides."

I wondered if I should swear on a copy of the First Amendment.

Not looking at me, she said, "What if I told you the fight was nothing? That Trey walked away from it?"

"I'm listening."

"I don't want you using my name or anything."

"No need. Go on."

She turned. "The fight happened at Megan McGarrity's house. I was there. It was a party. I guess what happened was, Trey walked in on Lucas getting some head."

"So?"

"It was Trey's girlfriend, Lindsey, who was doing him. Kinda freaky but it's not like they're in love or nothing. It was just a blow job! Trey walked into the middle of it and took a swing at

Lucas. That's what Lucas told me, anyway. But after Lucas punched him, he left."

"What kind of shape was he in?"

"It wasn't like he was gonna die or nothin' if that's what you're asking." She shrugged. "He was plenty upset, though. Shouting and shit. I offered to give him a ride home. He told me it was no big deal and he'd walk."

"How about Lucas?"

"Yeah, he came downstairs after. I saw him, too. Yelled at him, the stupid ass. He kept claiming it wasn't his fault. That's what he always says when stuff happens, but Lindsey backed him up. She said Trey was, like, in this rage or something."

I waited.

"He's not that bad a guy. Lucas. Maybe a little goofy. He gets blamed for a lot of things but I think you're right. It's because he talks back. I know some of the cops in this town. They have it in for him because of . . ."

She stopped as though she'd suddenly run up against a hard thought she couldn't get past. She yanked open the screen door. "I'm not talking anymore."

"What do the cops have against him?"

"Why don't you go talk to Gramma Bremmer? She's hiding over there. Her and her cigarettes and her Johnny Carson videos. Go around back. See what she tells you about Lucas." I heard a thump and her door slammed as though she'd kicked it.

You meet such fascinating people in this business. I followed the Bremmers' drive up toward the two-car garage. At this rate, even if Gramma took a shot at me I'd feel more welcome.

The Bremmers' backyard was tucked into the midst of so many evergreens it could have been in the Pacific Northwest. A screen and glass all-weather room extended halfway toward the tree line, its low-rise profile the reason I'd seen no hint of it from out front. Ed McMahon grinned at me from behind the glass facing the driveway. The sidekick from the old Carson show had his hand raised, holding what looked like a check. Beyond that life-size cardboard cutout, seated with her back to me on a couch, was a gray-haired woman watching a television. It was set up against the glass on the opposite side of the room. Sixty-inch screen at least. Made it easy for me to see Johnny wearing a turban and robe and holding an envelope to his forehead.

I crossed a flagstone patio to the door. The check Ed held was for a cool million and made out to "Mr. and Mrs. USA Homeowner."

My knock startled the woman. Her head snapped up and she looked everywhere except behind her for the source of the sound. A gray tabby cat exploded from the couch, streaked across the room, and disappeared. I knocked again. This time the woman whipped around and, when she saw me, lifted a remote control and fiddled with the buttons before getting to her feet and darting toward the door like a small bird anxious to snatch up a morsel of food and get back to its tree. Her purple sweat suit matched purple running shoes but not the blood-red frames of a pair of narrow glasses that hung on a chain around her thin neck. As she approached, she fingered them to her eyes, staring at me. Another cat, this one marmalade colored and probably about twenty pounds, swirled around her legs.

"Yes?" She called through the glass.

"I'm a reporter, Mrs. Bremmer. From Channel 14 News."

"Say it again?"

I took out my Chicago Police media credential with my photo on the front. I held it up.

"Channel 14 News. Is Lucas here?"

Spindly fingers yellowed by nicotine snapped back the lock

and drew the door inward three inches. She peered cautiously around it. Her grandson wasn't the only one in the family with eyes the color of ball bearings.

"Why? Whattya want with him?"

"I'd like to talk to him about one of his friends."

I looked for signs of surprise. Instead, I saw anger settling into the creases of her face the way water finds familiar crevices through rock.

"Yes, yes. The Hayden boy. I watch the news. What's that have to do with Lucas?"

"He came by our live truck a little while ago bragging about getting into a fight with Trey over a girl last night. I'd like to hear the whole story."

"So, my Lucas beat up little Richie Rich, eh?" Her other hand came up from behind her back and she took a hit off an unfiltered cigarette. The cat flopped next to the door and stared at me, tail going.

"It couldn't have been the other way around?"

"You think you're funny? One thing my grandson knows how to do is fight. Started him early. No man in his life, he needed to learn. I found him a good trainer, taught him to box years ago. Like his grandfather. Now there was a man who could box. Who were they fighting over? That Lindsey Sears girl?"

"From what I understand."

"Trash. Like mother like daughter you ask me. He could do better."

"Does he spend time with any other girls?"

She glanced toward the driveway and then back at me. "You've been talking to that one next door, haven't you? Did you ask her why a woman in her thirties has to spend all her time messing with teenage boys? Why she goes to their parties? Ask her that!"

She nodded as though agreeing with herself. Behind her,

Johnny wound up the monologue. The camera closed in on Doc Severinson, frowning. I knew how he felt.

"Mrs. Bremmer, where's your grandson now?"

More nodding. Suddenly she snapped her head up and stared at me with accusing eyes. "It wasn't my choice for him to live here. My daughter-in-law ran off when he was five. His father drove his car into a tree. Drunk, naturally. That's all he knew how to do was drink. I'm his only blood relative. Family court decided it was in his best interests to live with his grandmother. Did they give one iota's thought to *my* best interests? Not a one. I raised one child. Then just like that, I had to raise another. In my fifties and him in grade school."

She swept her arm back. Startled, the cat jumped to its feet. "I added this room. To have enough space to make those court people happy. Rearranged my life. Then he turns out to be a little . . . pervert. He's almost twenty. I threw him out. Little pervert."

I wondered if the big TV had been for Lucas, too. "Why do you call him that?"

"None of your business!"

I made a mental note to ask Jody to check out Lucas Bremmer's criminal history.

"If he's not living here, do you know where I can find him?"

" 'If?' You think I'm *lying?*" She gave me a sly look. "I should sue that one next door. I could, you know. Sticking her nose into confidential family business. If you live next door to someone you shouldn't be making googly eyes at their grandson. Hmm? Speaking of perverts. There's a story for you."

The Nextel in my pocket chirped, saving me from having to respond.

"Reno?" Al said. "Heads up. Cops are here. Couple headed your way."

CHAPTER NINE

Two cops rounded the corner. The older one, salt-and-pepper-haired, with a hand under his sports jacket toward his right hip, the other, younger and wearing a black tactical outfit and Kevlar vest, an H&K MP5 automatic rifle strapped across his chest. Heavy artillery. When they saw us, the older one pulled up short, but his hand remained on the butt of his pistol in its hi-rise holster. The cop with the MP5 spread out a good ten feet from his partner, weapon up, barrel pointed in my direction. His finger caressed the trigger guard.

"Freeze!"

The older cop glared at me. "Who the hell are you?"

I've been in on plenty of arrests and drug raids. Guns in the hands of cops, even jittery cops going after a possibly armed suspect, don't bother me. Guns pointed at me, however, are a different matter. These two Wihega County officers put me on edge. Their flat expressions reminded me of pictures I'd seen of Marines kicking down doors in Iraq after snipers attacked their unit. Cold. Intent. My presence seemed to startle them. The guy with the MP5 eyed the plainclothes as though waiting for instruction. I kept my hands very still.

"Reno McCarthy. Channel 14. ID is in my coat pocket."

A uniform with a red face and large belly appeared in the driveway, walkie-talkie crackling from the speaker-microphone clipped to his left shoulder. He was breathing in short gasps. He, too, had his hand on the butt of his still-holstered gun.

84

The rifleman dropped his aim. The plainclothes took his hand out from under his jacket.

"Mrs. Bremmer, I'm Commander Bill Teague with the county police. You remember?"

Her lips were set so hard they seemed bloodless. She nodded once. Didn't speak. He glanced my way again.

"Mr. McCarthy, nothing against the press, but you need to go back out front and wait for us to finish." His eyes roamed behind me, checking the house and the yard, alert. Looking for Lucas, no doubt. I opened my mouth, ready with an objection. Mrs. Bremmer saved me from myself.

"I want him to stay."

"That's not open to negotiation. We—"

She stood up straighter. "You're on my property. You have paper that says you can search my house, like the last time, that's fine. But I want this man here while you do it."

Teague appeared as surprised as I was.

"In that case, you both remain outside with Officer Fritts."

Mrs. Bremmer squeezed through the door. "Don't you dare hurt my cats."

Teague said, "Ma'am, if Lucas is here, it'll be easier on everybody if you ask him to step out and talk to us."

"He is not here."

"Is anyone else in the house?"

"No, there is not!"

Teague motioned the rifleman to precede him and both of them stepped through the door, weapons raised. The fat uniform turned his head slightly and keyed up his microphone.

"Detectives entering from the rear."

I heard Teague call, "County police! Step out where we can see you!" A moment later there was the rush of several sets of feet moving in fast from the front. I hoped Al was taping.

"Bastards best not break anything," Mrs. Bremmer muttered.

She sucked nervously on her cigarette. "Why can't they just leave him alone?"

"This happened before?"

She bobbed her head.

"What was the charge the last time?"

She sighed and closed her eyes, waving off my question with the hand that held her cigarette. She smoked in silence, stubbing out one with the toe of her house slipper and lighting another, until Teague came back alone less than five minutes later.

"Martha, was Lucas here earlier this morning?"

"Mrs. Bremmer to you." She eyed him. "What if he was?"

"The law says I can arrest you if you don't tell me the truth. I don't want to do that, believe me. So I need to know when you last saw Lucas and where you think he might be."

She dropped the butt of her cigarette on the concrete and did the grinding out thing again. Slow and deliberate. I hoped her slippers had leather soles. She folded her arms.

"He may have come in this morning. I can't say for sure because I didn't see him. I thought I heard something, but I was still trying to sleep."

"Someone in your house and you didn't get up to check?"

"I don't sleep so good any more. I don't like to get up when I don't have to. Besides, what's a burglar going to do? Walk off with my big TV over there?"

He patted the air with both hands. "Take it easy. Does Lucas still live here with you?"

"What is it you think he's done now? Do you think he killed that Hayden boy? Is that it? Because when I call his lawyer, I want to give her some kind of reason for all this crap."

"Martha, Mrs. Bremmer. This will go a lot easier if you let me ask the questions, okay? Now, to your knowledge, does Lucas own a handgun?"

"I never seen him with one."

Teague pinched the bridge of his nose with two fingers and appeared ready to ask another question when the uniform's radio crackled.

"House is clear. Evidence tech to the basement."

Teague excused himself and slipped back through the door. At the same moment, my Nextel went off again.

"Reno?" Jody said. "Cops say news conference in fifteen minutes here at the scene. Are you close by?"

I stepped away from Martha Bremmer and switched to the earpiece speaker so we could talk privately. Keeping my voice low, I said, "We're watching the cops search Bremmer's grandmother's place right now. I need you to pull his record. He did something nasty not so long ago that energized the cops to go after him hard this time."

"What are you going to do?"

"If he's the triggerman, he may still have the gun. You saw how goofy he was. I want to stick with this."

"Do you know where he is?"

"Not yet." I glanced at the neighbor's house. "I may be able to find out."

When Teague returned fifteen minutes later, he carried a large paper shopping bag with the top rolled closed under his arm. It bulged with the shape of shoes or boots.

"What'd you find?" I asked.

"Evidence." He kept walking toward the driveway.

"What kind?"

He shook his head, even as one of the techs was handing Mrs. Bremmer a piece of paper and explaining in a low voice that it was a receipt for items seized pursuant to a search warrant.

"What made you come looking for Lucas?"

"If I said good investigative work, would you leave it at that?"

"To get a search warrant this fast I'd say somebody must've pointed you in his direction."

He nodded to the two e-techs who slipped past us and headed back down the driveway. The uniformed Officer Friendly had already disappeared. Quick search, I thought. Almost like they knew exactly where to look.

"When a murder victim has a friend like Lucas Bremmer it's a no-brainer to check him out first. Standard procedure."

"Must be cool to work in a county where the judges give out search warrants based on known associations and hunches."

Teague smiled. "We have a little more than that," he said. Before I could press him he shook his head and walked away.

Mrs. Bremmer stood next to the door to her all-season room clutching the piece of paper the evidence technician had given her. For the first time, fear joined the anger in her pinched features.

"What did they find?"

Her hand shook as she held out the paper.

"He didn't do this. They can say whatever they want. I raised him to fight. To take care of himself. He's wild kid, that's true. I admit it. But killing . . ." Her voice trailed off hopelessly.

I read what was on the receipt. Boots. Okay. They'd apparently found a footprint in or around the scene. Even if they matched it to Lucas's boots, however, that alone wouldn't be enough to indict him. It was reasonable to assume that, since the two were friends, Lucas had visited Trey Hayden's home on other occasions.

Unless they'd found the footprint in blood or near the body. Or both.

"It's exactly like the last time," Mrs. Bremmer said. "God-damn cops have their minds made up. All I can do is call his lawyer." She held my eyes for a moment. "I didn't raise a monster, Mr. McCarthy. I didn't."

She shuffled back inside. I watched for a moment as she went over to the couch where I'd first seen her and picked up the TV remote control.

There was Johnny, I thought. But wherrrrre's Lucas?

Maybe somebody who liked his butt would know.

I crossed into the neighbor's yard and rapped on her back door. She answered it immediately, like she'd been just out of sight, listening. I noted an open window into what appeared to be a kitchen.

"We haven't been formally introduced," I said. "But I couldn't bear to leave without saying goodbye."

Her eyes were bright and I could've gotten high just from being near her.

"Jana Kirkendoll. What the hell happened over there, anyway?" Casual, like we were buddies sharing the good gossip.

"Surprise. The cops are after Lucas. You think he's gonna turn himself in?"

"Are you nuts? He's a flake. No way will he give it up. No waaayyyy."

If I'd been talking to her on the phone I would have sworn she was fourteen.

"Then tell me how to find him before the cops do. He have a girlfriend? How about this Lindsey Sears?"

"She ain't his girlfriend. You want to look for him at his girlfriend's, you'll be goin' door to door for a long ass while! I could tell you a secret, though. You wanna hear a secret, Mr. TV Man? He hangs out at Wiley's. It's a crummy beer and brat place down along the river. Won't be open now but Wiley lives upstairs." She winked. "He and Lucas do a little business."

"What kind of business?"

She mimicked holding a cigarette to her mouth, inhaling sharply and rolling her eyes. "Ganja. Some X, too, but you didn't hear it from me."

"Which one is the distributor? Lucas or Wiley?"

"Uh-uh." She waggled her finger at me. "That's for me and you to know and find out. You to know and me . . . whatever!" Maybe she'd smoked more than one.

I headed back to the Crown Vic. Al was across the street, leaning in the window of an unmarked but obviously police-issue Chevy. I knew better than to join him when he was schmoozing. Instead, I shucked my jacket, climbed into the car, and began updating my notes.

Sharp news photographers, when they put their cameras away, can become information magnets. I think it has something to do with threat-perception. People figure reporters are always working, laying verbal traps for the unwary. But when a camera guy puts away the box, cops, firefighters, and even regular folks see him as off-duty and safe to talk to. Al more than most. With his cop background and his big, friendly bulldog's face, he's instantly trustworthy.

He stuffed himself behind the wheel a moment later and grinned at me.

"I'm so fuckin' good I amaze myself sometimes."

"You can amaze *me* while you drive us down by the river." I read him the directions Helpful Jana had provided. He turned around in the Bremmers' driveway.

"Patrol cops. I tell ya. They know everything. When the dicks blow you off, count on the district car guys. They always have the skinny. The Hayden kid got popped twice in the chest with a nine mil from close range. Second floor hallway. And the sister is their eyewitness. Claims she came home and saw 'ol buddy Lucas bopping out the front door."

"With the gun?"

"That'd be something, wouldn't it? No. And, just so you know, back there, I got some good shots of them rushing the

Bremmers' place and then bringing out that bag of whatever he had. One bag. Shortest damn search I've ever seen." He scowled. To his way of thinking, suburban cops never got it right.

I briefed him on what I'd learned about Lucas's background. He lit up while I was talking and extended his arm to hold the cigarette outside the car. When I finished, he took one long drag then flicked it away. His version of cutting back.

"So what you're saying is that we probably have a better chance of finding this Lucas character than the cops do."

"With any luck."

He snorted. "Get my ass shot and you'll need more than luck."

Wiley's looked like it had been lifted out of the North Woods and dropped alongside the Wauconda River on the north side of Falcon Ridge. It lost some of its charm in the transition, however. A two-story expanded log cabin, the first floor was painted white and the second floor in green. The tamarack logs in the walls of the first floor, tightly meshed together during construction, appeared to have settled slightly out of position, as though the foundation had shifted one way and the logs hadn't followed the shift. A sagging screened porch protruded from one end and two chimneys badly in need of tuckpointing popped up along either side of a slanted roof. A hand-lettered sign hung from one of them that said, "Wiley's North Country Tap."

The parking lot held no cars but looked like the mother of all tailgate parties had just ended. Beer cans and wine bottles littered the gravel near the screen porch and a trail of garbage led down to the water's edge.

"Classy," I said.

"Groundskeeper's day off?"

"He's probably buried under some of it."

I glanced at a long shed with a garage off to the side of the lot. The garage doors stood open. A brown Chevrolet van sat inside. Lettering across the back spelled out "Wileys." Next to it was a Jeep Sahara. Al reached over the seat to lift his camera out of its secure restraint and put it on the seat between us.

"That Jeep is probably Bremmer's." I started to get out of the car.

The Nextel hauled me back. Jody sounded out of breath.

"Couple things from Callahan's newser. Number one, you were mostly right. They are looking for Lucas Bremmer, but they call him a witness, not a suspect. They won't even admit he's a Person of Interest. They say he has important information and they want to talk to him, he should make himself available, all the usual."

"They did a five-minute search of his house and seized a pair of boots. He's no witness. They're not calling him a suspect because they don't want him to get scared and blow town."

"Number two," she continued, "Bremmer's record. You remember the girl, maybe a year or so ago, claimed that a boy raped her at a party, took nasty video, and put it on the Internet? That would have been Lucas."

"That's the one where they let two guys go?"

"Didn't even get to trial. This Bremmer got certified as an adult but then something happened to the evidence. The judge threw the case out. In fact, that case resulted in a . . . quote . . . realignment of the county police detective division. Sounds like it was a huge embarrassment."

"Good reason for the cops to want to blowtorch him."

"It might be one reason they gave you and Al a rough time, too. The media made the Wihega County cops look like bozos. And get this. That guy, Commander Duvall? Guess who used to be chief of detectives and got sent to the midnight shift after all the stories ran about the lost evidence?"

I told Jody I'd get back to her. I stared at the bar.

"Not trying to spoil your fun or nothin', boss, but you sure you want to go up and knock on that door?" Al asked. "Especially after what Jody just said? We could call in the locals, lay back, and roll some tape. Let them do the heavy lifting. If they have a hard-on for the press, that might even get us some decent PR."

I didn't respond. There was no sound from inside the place and no movement. If Lucas was in there, he might be asleep by now. If the cops handled it right, arrived quietly, slipped a Hostage Barricade team inside, they might be able to take him before he woke up enough to resist. The logical thing to do was exactly what Al suggested. We'd even get an exclusive.

"I hate to admit this," I began.

Al's face split into a grin. I checked my notebook for the Wihega County Police main number and began punching it into the phone.

That's when we heard the scream.

Closely followed by the *kapow* of a single gunshot.

I knew Al kept a Sig-Sauer P226 in a custom-built, spring-clip holster under the driver's seat. I'd just never seen it appear in his hand so fast.

I scrambled out the passenger-side door to drop to my knees behind the engine compartment. He joined me there a couple of seconds later, head up, eyes scanning the building. His camera was on his shoulder and he'd stuffed the Sig into his belt.

"Sounded muffled. Like it came from the other side," he said, his voice low.

"By the water?"

"Nah, it was indoors."

I was trying to finish dialing the cops when a girl clutching an orange cat burst through Wiley's front door and ran, howling, to a point halfway between the building and our car. She was topless, the same sweater I'd seen her wearing earlier as she waited for Lucas near the live truck knotted around her waist.

"Fucking bastard!" she screamed, facing the bar. The effort seemed to exhaust her, however. She sank to her knees. In doing so, she let go of the cat. It hit the ground moving and tore off into the trees.

Al came up to a crouch, knees crackling, and leaned against the car. Both hands were on the camera. "Miss. Miss!"

She fought her way back into the sweater as though she hadn't heard him, muttering, "Goddamn asshole. Goddamn asshole."

"Lindsey," I said. That turned her head. She did a double take.

"What the fuck . . ."

"Lindsey, get over here. Now."

She hesitated, then crawled around the car to us on her hands and knees. Tears welling up, she said, "He tried . . . he tried to shoot the cat. The asshole. I woke up and he was pointing . . . right at it while it was sleeping. I screamed and . . . it jumped away. Right before he shot."

"Lucas?" I said.

"Yeah. He hates cats. I didn't know Wiley had one or I would've . . ."

Al interrupted her. "Where is he now?"

"He's . . . I don't know. I just grabbed the cat and got out." Her hair looked like she'd been running dirty hands through it, and her sweater was covered in cat hair. Suddenly she was holding a switchblade knife, blade extended, down close to her leg. "I'll cut his balls off, the miserable son of a bitch . . ."

I touched her arm. Carefully. "Put that away. Is anybody with him?"

94

Lindsey shook her head miserably. "I thought we were going to sleep. He kept talking about how he wanted to kill himself. I . . . gave him some head, you know? I thought that would help him calm down. We both started to doze off. I kept telling him things would work out. The cops think he killed Trey. He says he'll kill himself before he lets them take him to jail."

I heard sirens in the distance. I hadn't managed to get a call through to Dispatch but there were plenty of houses across the river and on the other side of the parking lot. Someone could have heard the shot and seen Lindsey's wailing exit from the bar.

"Lynn!" The shout came from just inside the same door she'd used. "Shit, Lynn, where'd you go?"

She started to rise but I touched a hand to her shoulder. A form moved in the shadows.

"Hey Lucas," I said. "It's Reno McCarthy from Channel 14."

Silence for a moment. Then, "Hah! I thought you were cops. What are you doing here?"

"Why don't you come on out and I'll tell you? I'm not big on yelling."

"Now you want to talk to me, huh? I'm doing okay right where I am."

"Yeah but my legs are killing me and I want to stand up. I can't do that while you have a gun in your hand. See my predicament?"

Unexpectedly, the screen door slapped back against the wall and he stepped outside. Disheveled, barefoot, blinking, his right hand up across his face to block the sun, his left held a Glock pistol pointed at the side of his head.

Lindsey gasped. I heard Al mutter, "Ah, Christ," and felt him shift position.

"Hey, reporter dude!" Lucas called. "Whatsamatter? See? You

can stand up. I ain't gonna hurt you."

I tried to ignore the fact that he had the hammer fully cocked. All it would take for him to shift targets would be a simple hand movement. Then again, he'd have to be pretty damn good to make a snap shot like that. I got to my feet.

"Reno, goddamn it," Al muttered.

"You started to tell my producer a story this morning. Care to finish it?"

"Gonna put me on TV this time?"

"Sure. Lay the gun on the ground and step away from it. We'll do an interview with you."

"As if! I can hear the cops coming just like you can. They got issues with me, man. You think I want to go back to their jail, let 'em beat on me until I give it up for killing Trey?"

"Did you kill him?"

"Duh? No."

"And you think shooting yourself is the way to prove that?"

"Whattaya mean?"

"You pull that trigger, partner, you'll give the cops just what they want. A suspect who can't defend himself. They'll put the blame on you and let the real killer walk."

He let his left hand drop to his side and stared at me. Maybe this was an angle he hadn't considered. I pressed the point.

"Tell us what happened. We'll tape them arresting you. The Wihega County cops may be mean but they're not stupid. TV tape of you healthy should keep them off you."

"I know you didn't do it, baby!" Lindsey scrambled to her feet. Wonderful. Our little tableau now provided what the hostage negotiators would call the perfect suicide audience. The camera, the girlfriend, the reporter. If the demons were really after him, this was when he'd pull the trigger.

The sirens, now a couple of blocks away, abruptly shut down. They'd cruise in quietly from there. I guessed I had less than thirty seconds before all of this was out of my hands.

Lucas suddenly brought the gun to his waist, ejected the round in the chamber, and slipped out the clip. Then, leaving gun and clip on the ground, he walked over, leaned across the car's trunk, and flipped the round he'd removed into my palm.

He grinned. "I get to be on TV now?"

It was one of the quickest interviews I've done. One, because he smelled like a brewery. Two, because a bunch of uniformed cops, not totally aware of what was going on, showed up and watched, dumbfounded, until one of them noticed there was a gun lying on the ground a few feet from us. Simultaneously, their radios crackled with an order that they take Lucas into custody. Al taped the action that followed as they put him up against a car, searched and handcuffed him, and deposited him in back of one of their squads. They couldn't seem to figure out what to do with Lindsey until a female officer arrived and took charge of her.

After all that, the late-to-arrive Commander Teague gave Al and me attitude.

"You call this responsible reporting?"

"I'm not a suspect and I'm not under arrest. So take a step back, Commander."

Our eyes seemed to fuse together but he gave ground.

"You knew where a man wanted for questioning in a homicide was hiding and didn't report it. That's a crime . . ."

"Bullshit. You could have questioned the same people I did."

"The first officers to the scene say Bremmer was talking to you on camera. He won't give us a statement without his lawyer present."

"He thinks you're going to beat him up the minute you get him alone."

"I want a copy of that tape."

97

"That's why God created subpoenas."

We went back and forth like that, creating our own version of a bad Abbott and Costello routine. It could have lasted all afternoon. Fortunately, his cellular phone rang. When he stalked off to answer it, Al and I left. As he drove back to the Haydens' house, I used the monitor between the seats to watch the interview.

"Me n' Lindsey was supposed to meet Trey at this party at Megan's place. Her parents are outta town. So we're upstairs and there's a room empty and we started fooling around. We've always sorta . . . well you know how it is, right? What is it, forbidden fruit, like?"

"What happened then?"

"So then Trey walks in and freaks. He jumps all over me. I had to do something, man. He doesn't know how to hit, but he's a big guy. I'm getting whacked all over. So I smacked him."

"Did you knock him unconscious?"

"Nah, nothing like that. He goes downstairs and when we come down he's gone. So, later Lindsey gets to feeling guilty and we go over to his house, like, to check on him? And he's layin' out there on the floor dead, man. That shook me up."

"Did you shoot him, Lucas?"

"Hell no. I didn't even have a gun!"

"You had a gun just now."

"Hey, Trey was my friend, man. I mean, I beat him up a little but he needed it. He was trying to hurt me so I was just, you know, defending myself."

The way Al had the shot framed, we could see the cop cars pulling into the lot behind Lucas. "Did you see anyone else?"

"What's that? Well, shit, it was like two o'clock in the morning, dude."

"So you didn't see his sister? She saw you."

"Oh well, later, yeah. Yeah. The second time. See, we went and

slept in the car for awhile. Smoked a little bowl, trying to decide what to do? I mean, I've never seen anybody dead before and Lindsey was, like, his girlfriend and she was totally bummed. So then I got to thinking, 'maybe he's not really dead.' You know? So we went back, and I went inside alone. He was still real dead, dude."

"There's brilliance for you," Al chuckled as the interview ended. " 'He was still real dead.' "

"Go back to where I asked if he'd seen anyone else."

Lucas reappeared on the screen. *"What's that? Well, shit, it was like two o'clock in the morning, dude."*

Al left Lucas in freeze frame. "His eyes were dancin' all over the place. My money says he's covering for somebody."

The Hulk had called Lucas a liar. Had Lucas seen *him* at the Haydens' the night before? Was he worried Lucas had ratted him out?

Al said, "As nuts as he sounded about gettin' locked up, you gotta wonder why he'd keep his trap shut about somebody else bein' there. Unless the two of them offed the kid."

I wondered.

When we got back to the crime scene, we found the media encampment had grown and now stretched for four blocks with satellite trucks from *America's Most Wanted* and Court TV salted in amongst the locals. Channel 14 now had two minicam vehicles amidst the throng, including the one that brought Caroline Levings to aid and assist.

I found her in the back of the truck, watching tape of the police news conference and frowning at her photographer, Ed Cibulski. Eddie wore the same expression he always does around her, brow furrowed and eyes mystified, as though he's trying to understand why he consistently draws the short straw and ends up shooting Caroline Levings's stories. What he will never figure out, because management is sworn to secrecy, is that she wrote a promise of his services into her contract.

Eddie's big enough to play in the NFL. Being a size zero, with a doll's fragile beauty and a knack for wearing outfits designed to be memorable, Caroline's biggest fear is that some day on some story, someone is going to assault or, worse, kidnap her. After all, she is, she once told a clueless cop, "an important Chicago celebrity." Eddie's supposed to be her insurance against anything bad ever happening to her while she's working. Her best insurance is herself. Kidnapping her would be "The Ransom of Red Chief" all over again.

"Why didn't you get a reporter cutaway of me taking notes?" she asked Eddie, oblivious to me standing in the truck's doorway.

"You weren't taking notes. You didn't even have a notebook in your hands. You were just licking your lips and staring at the cop doing the briefing."

"Then why didn't you give me a notebook to hold? I'm not in any one of these shots. How will people even know I was really there?"

"I don't know, Caroline. Maybe from the way you asked the same question three times."

She made an exasperated noise and swiveled in her chair, finally noticing me. I smiled and gave her a little wave. She scowled.

"Well look who finally showed up. I'm the main reporter on this story and you make me wait forty-five minutes to get information from you? Leave me covering a news conference I know nothing about . . ."

"Always nice to work with you, Caroline," I said. "You look lovely today, as usual. What is it you'd like to know?"

That stopped her as effectively as if I'd cracked her across the face. After a short hesitation, she smiled. Eddie rolled his eyes and went back to what he'd been doing.

I gave her the facts but held back my guesses. Too much

input and Caroline tends to mix up what's off the record with what she can say on the air. She, with help from Eddie, gave me nuts and bolts from the newser. By the time we finished, Jody was at my elbow, all but jumping up and down to get our attention.

"Al says the Haydens are in the command center."

Crap. I left Caroline and Eddie to resume their bickering and fast-walked, trying not to look concerned, past several other live trucks to where the yellow tape was stretched across the street, a half block south of the Haydens' house.

Along the tape, lined up like soldiers summoned to firing squad duty, were twelve tripod-mounted TV cameras, some leveled at the RV I'd seen earlier, some aimed at the house. Several photographers milled about talking, a couple of them eating sandwiches, others were seated on the ground or in their trucks several feet away. Only Al looked ready to shoot. He leaned on his Beta SX drinking from a Styrofoam cup, but every so often he'd glance in the direction of the RV.

"How long ago did they go in?"

"Right after we got back, so, maybe, fifteen minutes? Guy from CNN tipped me off."

Why bring the parents here, I wondered? Surely it would have been better to question them at the courthouse or some neutral location away from the crime scene.

The RV's door popped open. Croix Hayden appeared at the top of the little flight of steps, Robert Redford good looks wearing chinos and an aqua polo shirt, trademark blond hair mussed and ready for a woman's smoothing touch. He swiveled his head as though searching the crowd. When he raised his hand, I thought he was going to wave at us. Instead, the hand suddenly clapped over his mouth and he stumbled down the steps like his legs had given way. If he hadn't grabbed the railing at the last second he would have landed on his knees.

All around me, photographers lunged for their cameras. I was aware of Al already shooting, eye at the viewfinder, hand on the focus bevel. But Hayden spun away from the lenses and disappeared around the back of the RV.

That's when he howled.

It was as harsh and as mournful a sound as I've ever heard, the bellow of an animal being dragged down by wolves. I thought of my mother when the cops told her my dad had shot himself to death. I remembered a friend from high school who awakened after a devastating car crash to find the doctors had amputated his leg. I thought of Vinnie and shards of glass ripped into my heart.

One of the cops standing nearby spun around, hand on the butt of his holstered sidearm. Another deputy burst from the same door Hayden had come through and vaulted the stair railing to go to his aid.

Two other deputies ran behind the RV. Radios began to squawk. Teague came to the RV's door and pointed at one of the squads parked along the curb. Another deputy hustled over to it, jumped inside, and screeched into a U-turn to place it in front of the mobile command center.

A couple of moments later the three deputies who had gone to Hayden's aid emerged. Much as they tried to place themselves between Hayden and the cameras, he was a large man and it was evident they were supporting him. One of them opened a back door of the waiting squad and helped him climb inside. His knees buckled at the last moment and the cops nearly lost him.

Somewhere in the distance, a leaf blower ground to life. It was so quiet all around us, though, I could hear the lens mechanism move as Al zoomed for a closeup. A moment later the RV door opened again. Margo Malveaux marched down the steps in shorts and a flower print blouse. One of the deputies who had helped her husband stepped forward. She waved him off as though annoyed and climbed into the squad's front passenger seat. The driver made a three-point turn and rocketed away. A moment later he hit his siren.

The next sound from our side of the police line was a collective sigh as everyone realized we now had the video that would lead all of our live shots that evening.

Al leaned back from the camera.

"That was a scum ass thing for the coppers to do. Bringing them here. No need. Shows a real lack of class. Fucking suburban weenies."

"Maybe the Haydens insisted."

He lowered his voice. "Nah. Some pinhead wanted to shake them up. What do you want to bet they showed 'em pictures of the crime scene? Tells me either the guy running the investigation has his head up his ass or it was some kind of a power play."

I remembered what Esperanza had said about politicians being involved. I thought about Theo Zak. Sucker-punching the famous lawyer parents of a murdered kid to make sure they kept their clout out of the investigation was just the sort of aggressive offense Zak might play.

I stepped away from Al and the other crews and took out my phone. This time Rudy Esperanza answered on the first ring.

"Am I to deduce from not seeing you running back and forth into the house wearing your crime scene booties that you've packed up your toys and are heading back to a friendlier neighborhood?"

"You *deduce* pretty well for a reporter."

"What happened?"

"First boss I talked to wanted us to run the laser for 'em. That was damn odd in itself."

"Why?"

"Guy named Duvall. He took the classes. Hell, he used to run the detective division. He knows the laser won't do what he wanted it to do. I got the feeling he wanted us there for something else. I'm thinking it was to witness all the political crap."

"Theo Zak's name get mentioned?"

"No but it was obvious the suits were running the show and he's still el jefe around here."

"Heard anything about Zak lately otherwise?"

He grunted. If he had the same habit I remembered, he'd be chewing the plastic tip of a Swisher Sweet.

"Nah. I know the Intelligence guys did a work up on him back when he was pushing for that casino but I haven't heard his name since."

"One more question?"

"Good ol' 'One More Question' McCarthy. What is it?"

"Have they recovered the slugs?"

"They will, yeah. One was in the wall, the other's in the boy."

"That doesn't make sense. If the slugs are accounted for and it was close quarters in a hallway . . . why did they want the laser?"

"That would be two more questions. But, you're right. It's not my case anymore and I'm easy. So here's a little surprise for you. That Duvall claimed he wanted the laser because the killer wasn't the only one who fired a gun."

CHAPTER TEN

I stepped out of earshot of the other reporters. "There was a gunfight?"

"I wouldn't call it that but you're the one in show business. We found some gun-cleaning oil in the bedroom and there's a bathroom window with a bullet hole through it. If they run a nitrate test on the victim's hands, I'm betting it comes back positive for gunshot residue."

"What kind of gun was it?"

"We couldn't find it."

I stopped scribbling. "It's gone? As in the killer took it with him?"

"You got me. But the window doesn't figure any other way than in the victim got off a shot. Probably just one. Like he was surprised and fired by reflex."

"The killer couldn't have fired a stray shot?"

"Unlikely. The angle would be all wrong."

"So with the gun missing and the slug out the window, you don't know . . . wait a minute. You got the caliber from the rod in the cleaning kit, didn't you?"

"The kit was for a .38 or nine millimeter and we found a box of .38 ammo in the kid's closet."

"Do we have any idea why the kid was armed?"

"Not a clue. Nobody in the house signed up for a FOID card. First thing I checked." FOID is the state-issued firearm owner identification card. Illinois registers owners, not their weapons. I gave that a little thought.

"Speaking of guns, do the Wihega cops know if the killer was right- or left-handed?"

"From the blowback residue on the wall near where the boy fell I'd say right-handed." He hesitated. "Should I ask why you want to know?"

I thought about the way Lucas held the gun to his head stepping out of Wiley's. And which knuckles were torn up from his fight with Trey.

"Their favorite suspect is a lefty."

He made a sound like a cat with a hairball. "Sorry, didn't hear you. Lousy connection."

I closed the phone thinking that, on its face, this case had the appearance of a one-day wonder. TV execs hate it when the cops catch the bad guy. A good manhunt, especially a hot pursuit a la O.J., now that's what sells ad time. Once the state filed charges against Lucas Bremmer, there would be some limited lawyer play-by-play, pretty ironic given who Trey Hayden's parents were, and then we'd all move on to the next Story of The Week.

Unless they charged Bremmer and he was the wrong guy.

And where was the missing .38? Better yet, why did the kid have a gun in the first place?

Jody was rewinding the tape of Hayden's breakdown when I got back to the truck.

"Got a minute?"

That brought a smile and she turned to face me, brushing hair off her forehead. I noticed she had Scotch-taped the small picture of her daughter to the side of the editing console.

"What else did you find on Bremmer and that rape case?"

She clicked a window on her computer and a screen with the masthead of the Wihega County *Examiner* popped into view. She looked at her watch. "You want to read through it here, I'll run back to the car for a few. It's about time I call home to check on my kid, anyway. But take a look at who his partner was. Oh and here . . ."

She handed me a sheaf of papers, all with Internet headings.

"I printed it so you'd have some light reading for later. Stuff about Wescott."

She slipped past me and I took her place in the cramped chair in front of the truck's electronics console. I scrolled down and began to scan the articles about Bremmer.

According to the *Examiner,* it all started with an unsupervised backyard pool party not far from Hayden's Falcon Ridge home in July, two years ago. Sometime after midnight, a party guest stumbled into an attic bedroom to discover Lucas and a guy named Duane Grum having sex with an underage girl in front of a poorly hidden video camera.

A week later, the video popped up for sale on the Internet. Though the boys' faces never appeared and the girl claimed she didn't know them, police found the witness, searched Lucas's grandmother's home, and turned up a camera, the original video, and several vials of Ecstasy. They didn't, however, find a computer. Officers arrested Grum on the street.

Prosecutors filed charges against Bremmer and Grum. Both refused to talk. Police held a news conference, crowing about their quick success in solving the crime. A judge set bail high enough both seemed destined to sit behind bars until trial.

Unfortunately, a week later, it all went to hell. When a detective went to fetch the box containing the tape and vials so they could be examined by the defense on a discovery motion, he found a soggy mess. Not only had the vials broken open, they had soaked inside the videotape. It didn't really matter at that point, however, because a quick viewing revealed the tape was blank. "Sloppy Storage Sacks Sex Case!" the *Examiner* crowed.

A fast shuffle resulted. Chief of Detectives Duvall took the first hit. He ended up with a transfer to Special Details monitoring traffic at construction sites, sporting events and funerals. Two Evidence Unit officers were fired. A secretary resigned.

Bremmer and Grum, a previously convicted sex offender, walked. Photos from the day of their release were included. I had to look closely and then enlarge the shot, but Grum was unmistakable. He was the same guy with the shaved head who'd been watching us and eating jelly beans. The guy I encountered on the path.

I glanced at the people milling around the other live trucks. Got out to peer around one truck that was in the way. Checked the parkway where he'd been seated earlier. Grum was gone. I went back to the computer disappointed. Another face-off with him might have been interesting.

I scrolled to the next article. The girl's family threatened a lawsuit, but I could find no stories indicating one had ever been filed.

A year later, the police board refused to reinstate Duvall as chief of detectives but agreed, without comment, to restore his prior rank of commander. A later story mentioned he'd been permanently assigned to the midnight shift. It didn't take a journalism degree to figure out why he had been so pissed at us for running the tape of him outside the crime scene. Two public humiliations in one police career would be enough to turn anyone bitter.

Sorry, buddy. No way could we have known.

A polite cough brought my thoughts back to the present and I glanced outside.

Sunny DeAngelis stood next to the truck, smiling in at me.

"Hey," I said and promptly smacked my head on the ceiling as I stood to greet her.

"As smooth as ever," she laughed, accepting a hug when I managed to clamber gingerly outside.

Sunny is one of my closest friends and a former colleague who occasionally filled in for me during my TV-exile job as news director of one of Chicago's more popular FM stations. Her real career, however, is about as far from broadcasting as a politician from the truth. She's the owner of DeAngelis Consulting, a private detective agency that specializes in bail recovery, a fancy word for chasing down people charged with crimes who are dumb enough to skip out on their friendly local bondsman. Other services DeAngelis Consulting provides include body-guarding and security assessments. Sunny doesn't run the show from behind her desk, either. The semiautomatic on her hip attests to the fact she's made a few enemies, just like her client list underscores the relationships she's developed with an impressive array of Chicago notables.

I grinned at her. It had been a month since she persuaded me to join her and a small group of friends in one of the Wrigley Field mezzanine suites for an evening of Cubs and cocktails. I'm not a baseball fan, per se, but anyone who grew up in Chicago listening to Vince Lloyd, Lou Boudreau, and Jack Brickhouse would have to possess a heart of stone not to feel a little awed by the "friendly confines."

She pointed at the computer screen. "Big story like this and the best you can do is sit around and read the paper?"

"Trying to find the damn cartoons. What brings you out to the sticks?"

"Doing a security audit. An interview with the big boss got postponed until tomorrow. Saw your noon piece as I was leaving, and I thought I'd come by and see if you needed somebody to put up bail yet."

"Let's take a walk," I said.

She dismisses me with a whack on the arm, when I compare her in looks and feisty attitude to Holly Hunter, an actress we both admire, albeit in different roles. Sunny gives thumbs up to the *Raising Arizona* Holly Hunter while I preferred her as the detective in *Copycat*. Sunny is taller and more athletic in build and movement than Hunter, but she wears her moxie and charm right up front.

She's single, tends to intimidate the guys she dates, and lives for her work. As well as I know her, however, there's a huge part of her history she keeps hidden. She's an ex-Marine and tells funny stories about being a drill instructor, but beyond that I don't ask, she doesn't offer, and I don't speculate. You'd never make her as a bounty hunter until she kicked down your door.

I'd planned to call her at the end of the day to get her take on the Hayden story. This was easier. And it was fun watching the well-coiffed male and female TV talent do double takes when we walked past, no doubt wondering if the hot redhead was new competition.

"Do you think this Bremmer kid pulled the trigger?"

"Esperanza says the shooter was right-handed. Bremmer's a lefty."

"That should make his lawyer happy."

"I don't know, Sunshine. I get the feeling Wihega County's the old West and Zak is Judge Roy Bean. If he really wants him to go down for it, Bremmer could be a double amputee and it won't make any difference." We walked past a pizza delivery guy unloading at the CNN truck. The smell reminded me I hadn't eaten since downing a doughnut in the newsroom.

"Have the cops suggested a motive?" Sunny asked.

"Not in front of a microphone."

"Have you talked to this Lindsey? Or what about this Grum character?" Her memory and ability to assimilate facts has always astonished me. I was paging through my notebook trying to remember what I'd written down fifteen minutes before, and she was coming up with the names off the top of her head.

"The girl's my first priority. I get the feeling she and Bremmer might have seen something or someone he wasn't willing to tell me about."

We kept going, in silence, until we were out of the forest of news vehicles. Then she stopped and turned toward me, putting a hand on my arm.

"Ray Fong called me about Vinnie. I was surprised not to hear it from you."

"Yeah, well, I had kind of a busy morning."

"Ray said . . ." She saw the look on my face and shook her head. "I told him you'd either come around or wait until after he dies and beat yourself up over not saying goodbye."

"Goodbyes aren't the problem. He set me up again. Or didn't Ray tell you I'm the one who's supposed to pull the plug when the time comes?"

"He told me." She put her hands in her jacket pockets. The fabric pulled tight, showing the outline of the holstered automatic at her hip. "What would it hurt to sit with him a while?"

"Goddamnit Sunny . . ." She was with me the day Vinnie told me he would feed me to the federal wolves if I didn't back off my investigation that touched on the Russian mob.

"All I'm saying is think about it, Reno."

My ringing cell phone saved me from having to reply.

Johnnie Perkins.

"Reno. Do you have your pen ready?" I propped the phone against my shoulder as I found a blank page in my notebook. She went on to confirm what Esperanza had told me about the manner of Trey Hayden's death. Shot twice, at close range.

"How about a gunshot residue test on the victim?"

"You will have to ask the police about that. I cannot comment on their evidence."

I sighed. Even without that, I now had enough official information to put on the air. Something else bothered me.

111

"What about the police initially locking you out of the crime scene?"

"Are we still off the record? I have to admit, that is puzzling, yes. These are all seasoned police officers, not rookies. They are familiar with the death investigation process. The chief tells me it was the 'confusion of the moment' and delays in getting some equipment. He apologized profusely. Any kind of apology, from him, is quite unusual. However, I have made it clear to the state's attorney this cannot occur again. I am not sure I will ever know exactly why it happened, but I do not choose to pursue it while the case is pending."

"Tell me something. Is there anything your people have found that could suggest the investigating officers might have used the extra time to tamper with the body? Or the scene?"

"Oh my goodness, no. No, of course not. Why do you ask?"

"A hunch from talking to some other people. That's all."

"No. If anything, keeping us from the scene was a . . . a political slap at me by the county's powers that be."

"So the word would have come down from somebody outside the cops? Theo Zak, perhaps?"

She chuckled. Unlike earlier, though, it sounded strained.

"Reno? I am not going there with you. As I said earlier, some day, if you are still interested, I will be happy to give you my views on the county's political structure. Now is not the time. If there is nothing else from a medico-legal standpoint . . . ?"

I checked my watch as I hung up. Forty-five minutes before we went into a two-and-a-half hour block of news beginning at four.

I looked at Sunny. "I've got to—"

"I know." She was smiling again. "I have an idea. You want me to track down that Grum character for you?"

"I thought you had a security audit to do."

"I told you. My appointment got rescheduled to tomorrow.

Now, I could drive all the way into the office and sit on my butt, or I could get a room, hang around here, and use my extensive investigative experience to run down Mr. Jelly Bean. What do you think I'd rather be doing?"

"Did you mean to say 'extensive' or 'expensive'?" I asked.

"Both. My experience is extensive so dinner tonight will be expensive."

They gave me two minutes' worth of the "live team coverage" of Trey Hayden's murder.

I opened with the cause of death, including the part about the missing gun, segued to the interview, or what TV-heads call sound-on-tape or SOT, of Bremmer admitting to the fight and the discovery of Trey's body. We used his claim of innocence. We ran the video Al had shot of the searches of both the Bremmer house and the bar, showing officers leaving from both places with bags under their arms. We ran a bite from the news conference in which spit and polished Sergeant Ben Callahan made it sound as though the Wihega County Sheriff's Police would be moving earth, moon, sun, and sky along with several of the major planets, to find the "offender or offenders responsible for taking the life of this young boy," and then revealing Lucas Bremmer was "not a suspect at this time." Tsk, tsk. Saying that at virtually the same moment a team was searching Bremmer's house suggested a certain lack of candor to me, but then I'm a born cynic.

I stepped away from the camera after my live shot, thinking I might get enough of a break to grab a snack. Wrong. As competitive as Chicago's television stations are, if the cops announce a news conference everyone passes the information along. So, when Nicole Henderson, the Fox reporter, asked if I was aware that Lucas Bremmer's first court appearance was in less than thirty minutes, I ditched the food idea and grabbed Al and his car.

The courthouse was a stern, six-story slab of brick and concrete that looked out of place among the newer, trendy storefronts just down the street. Funky reflective windows surrounded the top two floors, making them stand out dark against a very blue sky. Low-rising brick steps in front of the entrance led to a two-tiered brick pool with a fountain bubbling at the center. Beyond it, opposite the glass front doors of the building, a semicircular slate wall had names listed in several rows. An old man in a white shirt and Bermuda shorts past his knees sat on a stone bench facing the wall, head down as if praying.

Three other stations beat us there. They had their cameras pointed at the main entrance and the old man. He seemed oblivious. I left Al and trotted inside. After the obligatory trip through a metal detector, I got directions from an oversized deputy in an ill-fitting uniform.

The courtroom was small and made even smaller by a floor to ceiling Plexiglas security barrier that separated spectators from the action. I settled into a seat in the front row of the gallery, next to the dark-haired reporter who'd identified Pike Wescott for me outside the Hayden house. He'd picked a spot right in front of one of the two speakers mounted on the barrier like he knew from experience that it was the best place to be. Local newspaper, I guessed. He glanced at me but said nothing. I nodded at reporters I knew from Channel 7 and ChicagoLand TV and a producer from CNN. There were other people in the seats as well, but they looked like courthouse hangers-on come to kibitz.

The lawyers, a slim athletic blonde in an expensive-looking suit for the defense and a polyester-clad assistant state's attorney, were already in place. Two deputies hustled Lucas into the courtroom ten minutes later. He wore the same clothes from earlier, the jail-look denims ironically appropriate now. He scowled and rubbed his wrists as though too-tight handcuffs had just been removed. When he looked up and saw us watching him, though, a cocky grin replaced the irritation. He offered a little wave and double thumbs up before his lawyer put her arm around his shoulders and guided him to a seat. There, she leaned close and I could see tension ripple her back as she spoke to him.

Once Judge Debra Cassens heard the prosecutor allege that Lucas had gone to the Haydens' house with the intention of killing Trey and, after shooting him twice, stole an iPod and a laptop computer, both of which were found in Lucas's Jeep, it took Her Honor all of five seconds to deny bail and order Lucas jailed until trial. Going out, his smile and the thumbs up were nowhere to be seen. In fact, it looked to me as though he'd aged about ten years.

Out on the courthouse steps, the other news buzzards circled the prosecutor. Never one to follow the flock, I wandered around to a parking lot in the rear of the building. The guy I'd sat next to in the courtroom was already there, leaning casually on a light pole and smoking an unfiltered cigarette. He smiled, showing very square, white teeth.

"I wondered if any of you Chicago people would be smart enough to join me back here. Tom Wozniak from the *Examiner*." He extended a hand. His byline had been on most of the articles Jody pulled up on the computer.

"You're McCarthy, right? Hell of a series on those Russians. You waiting for the Pulitzer people to call?"

I smiled. "I'm just enjoying the regular paycheck."

"Whattya think? Any early predictions on where this is going?" I shook my head. He lit a second cigarette off his first.

"Word upstairs is Charlie Marcus is gonna handle it himself. The state's attorney. It's his name on the ballot so he only takes the slam-bangs."

"They think the evidence is that solid?"

He smiled and blew a smoke ring. I hadn't seen anyone do that in years.

"You ever watch an animal control officer working a dog he thinks may be rabid? The long pole he uses with the loop of rope at the end? The better officers, they can drop that loop in their sleep, get it cinched, and slip the dog into the back of their truck before you can even blink. That's just what's going to happen here, my Chicago media friend. Evidence or not."

"In other words, you think they're going to frame him."

"In squeaky clean Wihega County, Home of Good Government? Of course not." He took another hit from his cigarette. "You got any interest in working this as a joint project? Since you're from out of town, I figure you can use some local insight. Maybe a little, what do the play-by-play guys call it? Color commentary."

"What did you have in mind?"

"Well, you know you're not gonna get any more from the cops after using that tape of Teague handing Duvall his ass at the scene, right? Especially not any," he made quotation marks in the air, "exclusives. Teague's chief of detectives. He'll queer your action for sure. Duvall's a prick, especially when he thinks somebody's screwing with him. And Duvall and Callahan, the PIO, are like brothers, so you're even kinda screwed there, too."

"Damn, you mean when they hand out news releases to everyone else, they might run short before they get to me? I think I can live with that."

"Joke all you want, but what if they cut off all your access? From the state's attorney to the lowest deputy? What if the word goes out that nobody talks to Channel 14? What about that? I could be your conduit. Anything I find, I tip you to it. Goes both ways a'course, with outside sources. If you got any."

His smugness and air of being one of the courthouse good 'ol boys grated on my nerves.

"Sorry. That's not the way I work."

"C'mon, man, you know it would . . ." He looked past me.

I turned and saw Lucas Bremmer's blond lawyer coming toward us down the sidewalk from the courthouse. Wozniak didn't finish his sentence.

"It's nice to see you Mr. McCarthy. Moira Cullen," she said, ignoring Wozniak. She shook with a firm grip. In the courtroom, separated from her by thick Plexiglas, I'd guessed her to be in her late twenties. Now, I revised my estimate upward by a dime, taking in the tiny wrinkles around her mouth and weariness in her eyes. She had her suit jacket over her shoulder and wore a short-sleeved white blouse that showed tanned arms with a good cut at the biceps.

Wozniak gestured with his notebook. "The usual?"

"You know I don't try my cases in the press." Her voice was as sharp as it had been in court. Wozniak just shrugged.

"Got to ask."

She shifted her eyes to me. "You, on the other hand . . . walk me to my car?"

"Hey," Wozniak said.

"If it's any of your business, Mr. McCarthy and I have some mutual friends to discuss."

She touched my arm and we moved away from him. He stood there, whacking the notebook against the outside of his thigh, dark eyes staring lasers at her.

"You don't feel the need to humor the local press corps?" I asked.

"The *Examiner*'s little weasel?" she asked. "I made a mistake my first year here, with the public defender. Woz knows quite a bit about crime scene investigation from all the stories he's written. I said more than I should have to him about one of my first cases. Later I find out he passed the state's attorney the name of a witness the state didn't know about. I should have known. His mother used to work in the state's attorney's office. His stories always slant the state's way."

"What happened to your case?"

The wry grin again. She had nice cheekbones. "My guy went to jail. Of course, he was guilty as hell but I haven't given Wozniak the time of day since. The sleazy worm."

"And you're willing to consort with another reporter? I'm flattered."

"I'd hardly call you a worm." She squeezed my arm. "And we do have a mutual friend."

"Who?"

"Let me put it this way. The cops have done two searches, one at the Bremmer house and the other at Wiley's. The only gun they've found is one Wiley swears Lucas stole from under the bar this morning. If I'm counting correctly, that leaves two guns still missing, the murder weapon and a mystery piece. Is that enough ID for you?"

"Esperanza is being mighty generous today."

"I handled the intake logs for the state's attorney while I was in law school. Espy and I used to *habla español* when he brought in evidence. We talked enough to realize we're both purists. Neither of us likes the way some people play games with the system for their own ends."

"Isn't that a little like saying you think the sun shines too brightly?"

We reached her car, a black Beemer. She let the question hang while she stored her briefcase and jacket inside and turned to face me. I noted her legs had the same taut musculature of her arms and shoulders.

"Espy told me what he told you, about how his team was treated when they got here. I also watched the tape on your station of Teague throwing Duvall out of the scene. I put that together with seven years practicing criminal law in this courthouse, and it fits as tightly as a pair of jeans I bought in college that I've been trying to wear for six months. This building runs on games."

"It's a courthouse."

"I said games not politics. I plan to run for state's attorney next year. Politics I can live with. I mean cases manipulated by individuals for their own purposes."

"Like?"

"Get in. I'll tell you a story."

For being a black car with black leather upholstery, the air conditioning made it comfortable quickly enough. Moira offered me water and, when I accepted, withdrew a bottle of Dasani from a small cooler on the back seat. As I drank, she put both hands on the steering wheel and seemed to lose herself in the breeze coming from the vents.

"You know about Theo Zak, right?"

"Sure."

"He has three children. All of them are attorneys. They're best known for two things: burying the titles of all his property in trusts so when he sells some to the county he's not named in the deal. And defending his image."

"This is sounding familiar. Wasn't there some county official . . . ?"

She gave a brisk nod. "The finance director, a nice fellow named Edgar Whitehall. He's one of those older fellows who could wear a bow tie and still look dignified. Like everybody's grandpa. Zak was county board president. He ordered a review of the county's pension funds. When it was over, he said there were discrepancies and wanted to hire a new fund manager. Edgar did some research and gave information to the county board showing that the firm Zak thought was so tremendous was, in fact, mob connected."

"I remember the stories now. He claimed Zak was mobbed up, too. Zak sued him."

"That case ran through the system like cra . . . like water through a goose. Not much of a surprise when you consider Zak raises money for all the judges. Not much of a surprise when he won, either. Edgar couldn't pay the judgment so Zak's kids said 'Fine. We'll take his house.' Just like that, Edgar was homeless."

"I suppose the county board moved the funds to the new firm?"

"Of course. But it gets better. A month or so later, a manager from the *old* firm comes forward swearing he'd bribed Edgar way back when to get the county's business."

"Nothing like kicking a guy when he's down."

"Hang on. Edgar was fired but they never charged him. Of course, if they'd taken him to court he would have had the chance to defend himself. Zak certainly didn't want that. I hear they let him keep his pension as a hedge against him bringing some sort of civil action of his own, but he was out and that satisfied Zak."

I drank some water. "In that indirect way you lawyers sometimes have, are you telling me all this because you think Zak is sticking his thumb into your case?"

"I think there's something odd going on, yes."

"Why Zak?"

"The cops wouldn't let the medical examiner get close to the body for almost an hour. They kicked Duvall out of the scene . . ."

"I hear he used to be chief of detectives?"

"Yes he was. He's a hell of a cop. Used to be commander of the Western Counties Major Crimes Task Force, too. I think he still teaches Techniques of Investigation at Northwestern."

She went back to ticking things off her fingers. "And then

there's this rush to file. A case of this magnitude, to be in court within a couple of hours is just too weird. Somebody has to be pushing it for that to happen. Only Zak's got that kind of clout. I've never had a first appearance in a murder on the same day the body was discovered. Maybe in some counties but not here, where the state's attorney usually moves like a little old man taking a dump." She glanced at me as a blush started on her neck.

"Sorry. I've always had a potty mouth. Comes from growing up in a family of boys."

"I grew up with a cop. Is Zak tight with the Haydens? That would explain a lot."

A dismissive shake of the head. "Absolutely no indication. In fact, it's pretty well known that while Hayden was in the U.S. attorney's office, he tried to initiate a RICO case against Theo. He never made it to the grand jury."

"Hayden isn't a prosecutor now. Maybe they kissed and made up."

"Highly unlikely."

"So you're saying Hayden tried to burn Zak in the old days but kindly 'ol Uncle Theo is willing to turn the other cheek for no apparent reason? I have a different idea."

She started to smile, waiting for the punch line. "What's that?"

"You have a guilty client."

Her smile vanished.

"What happened to reporters keeping open minds?"

"It's wide open. But before you throw Zak into the mix, let's hear what else you've got."

"Okay hotshot, first of all there's no motive. Lucas and Trey were the best of friends *despite* the fight. Lucas feels horrible about that. Second, he's not into guns. Doesn't own one."

"Had one when I found him."

"I told you. He got it from under the bar. Wiley will back him up. And then there's the matter of blood. Shooting someone at close range, you'll wind up with blood all over you. Where are his bloody clothes? He left the boots at his grandmother's house. Why would he do that if he ditched the rest of his clothes somewhere else?"

"Maybe he wanted to keep them. Maybe he was high. On second thought, he *was* high."

"I believe that. So high, in fact, that Trey threw beer on him before the fight and he never changed his shirt. Don't tell me you didn't notice the smell when you interviewed him. He was wearing the same clothes when they booked him that he had on at the party, right down to the beer and the salsa stains on his pocket."

"That part I'll buy. For the moment. So tell me why you think Zak's on Hayden's side."

This time when her smile appeared it was wry.

"If he wouldn't do it for Hayden, he's doing it to help himself. I just don't understand why. If I can prove he's working against my client's interests and manipulating the police, I can ask for a change of venue."

"Sounds like you have your work cut out for you." I toasted her with my nearly empty water bottle. "Good luck."

She turned in her seat to face me. Her eyes were a very rich brown and as angry as the worst kind of Lake Michigan summer storm.

"Instead of jousting like this I thought we might be able to help each other. Within all ethical guidelines on both sides, of course."

Beware of lawyers bearing offers, I thought. But what eyes she had.

"What kind of help did you have in mind?"

"From what Espy tells me, you get a chubby from working

the unique angles. I just gave you one. An angle, not a chubby that is." She winked. "As quid pro quo, I'd appreciate you letting me know if you come up with anything exculpatory."

"Your idea about Zak only becomes a story if it's true. What if I don't feel obligated to return the favor?"

She gave me a look that probably turned hostile witnesses into babbling children.

"Then don't."

Silence settled around us. I considered her offer. I'd turned down Wozniak because he seemed greasy. Even so, I wasn't supposed to have any wiggle room. You learn early in the news business that getting too involved with one side or the other in a story you're covering is a big no-no. As one of my first bosses liked to say, "We only take the side of Truth." Problem is, I've always found Truth to be perched atop a long slippery slope that's tough to climb without churning up some ethical muck.

What the hell.

"So we put altruism aside," I said. "What's Mr. Zak been involved in lately?"

She spread her hands. "That's part of the problem. Because his kids are so ready to file lawsuits, people don't like to talk openly about him. And the extent of my personal knowledge of the man is that I see him around the courthouse. Usually at lunchtime. He likes the cafeteria manager. Someone he hired, naturally. His old cronies from the building come in to kiss his ring but the ones who know him best aren't in my circle of friends."

"How about Bremmer? He ever come into contact with Zak and Company?"

She sighed, as though testing the muck with her shoe. "Not that he's expressed to me."

"I suppose you wouldn't need my help if he had. But let's assume for a second that not every client tells his lawyer the whole truth and nothing but. Who else might know if there's a connection? Who are his friends?"

I could see her weigh her answer. "Lindsey," she said. "I sent her home to get some sleep. She's due back in my office tonight."

"Think you could persuade her to talk to me?"

She nodded. "I can try. She's pretty impressed with how you kept Lucas from killing himself."

"I didn't keep him from doing anything. He came out of that bar expecting to be on TV. The minute he realized we weren't rolling tape he started looking for a way to back it all down. I just gave him one. He pull this Johnnie Depp-*Pirates-of-the-Caribbean* routine very often?"

"The rogue all the girls love. What do you think? That's part of the reason he's in trouble now."

"Why? Don't tell me Theo Zak has a daughter?" I joked.

She smiled wanly. "Worse than that, I'm afraid. Among a few others, Lucas says he used to screw Ellie Hayden."

"The sister?"

"The *little* sister. The one who can place him coming out of the house after the murder."

CHAPTER ELEVEN

Focus.

He handled his afternoon meetings without significant incident, glancing at cable news between visitors. He caught a glimpse of his neighborhood on CNN. Missed the story by moments.

Discussing expansion plans with his banker and reviewing software enhancements with his management team, he asked and answered questions with precision, even laughed at their jokes. Once, when his hand began to tremble as he held a set of blueprints, he laid them on his desk and slipped the hand into his pocket.

Otherwise, he carried it off well. Why wouldn't he? Wescott thought. Practice. Years of practice.

Sophomore year in college his "Uncle Theo" showed up in the lab on campus one afternoon when he'd been working alone. Three-piece suit complete with a watch fob, a cop/bodyguard trailing behind. Wescott hadn't seen the Wihega County state's attorney for three years. Theo Zak had added a few pounds.

"You can't hide in this Science building forever. You damn well better start inventing a human personality for yourself. Eldon's designated you to run the company when he dies."

"How do you know?"

"Sneer at me like that again and I'll take your head off. I worked for him. I wrote his will. Remember? After graduate school, you become president of Forge Technologies. You have four years to learn to act the part. If I were you, I'd get started. I can help but I can't do it for you."

Wescott remembered sliding his eyes away. "I don't have to accept the job. I'll turn it down."

"You don't want to do that, Robert."

"You can't tell me what to do."

"You may be a genius, but you aren't very bright where it counts. You want to break his heart? He took you in when your parents died. Don't you think you've done enough to ruin him?"

Wescott knew he owed it to Eldon to follow his plan. So he spent summer nights over the next few years listening to the old man's goals for the future of the company and discussing strategies to accomplish them. Offering his own suggestions.

He studied movies on the side. Every chance he got he watched Stewart and Fonda, Wayne and Mitchum. "Learn to act the part," Zak ordered.

He did.

Wescott stepped into the bathroom to wash his hands. Mockingly turned on his Jimmy Stewart smile for the mirror. Couldn't hold it. Saw *her* face, behind him. He almost spun around.

Jesus, that wouldn't do. He couldn't deal with the memory. She appeared enough in his dreams. Twisting away. Falling. Mouth curved into sometimes fear, sometimes disappointment. Sometimes . . . rage? Rage for what he'd done to her.

He needed a drink.

CHAPTER TWELVE

Al fed me the gist of the news conference as he miked me up for the six in front of the courthouse. I barely had my intercom earpiece in place when one of the producers in the control room began snarling that we were two minutes to air, where the hell had I been, and wasn't I enough of a professional to show up on camera in a timely manner?

I couldn't listen to him and Al simultaneously, so I yanked out the earpiece and let it dangle from my shirt collar by its coiled cord.

"Prosecutor wouldn't comment on whether they'll make this a death penalty case, but you could tell he was drooling at the idea," Al said. "The broad from Channel Two got to where she was almost begging him to confirm our story about the Hayden kid having a gun. He wouldn't do it. In fact, he says it was irresponsible for anyone to report such a thing in the first place."

"He didn't deny it, did he?"

"Nope." Al finished attaching the microphone to the front of my shirt and stepped back behind the camera where he donned a headset. We were off and running.

"Lucas Bremmer faces a first-degree murder charge this evening, and Judge Debra Cassens has ordered that he remain in the Wihega County jail without bond until he goes to trial.

"Several sources have provided a look at some of the evidence against the twenty-three-year-old Bremmer. A witness claims to have seen him leaving the Hayden house soon after the murder was com-

mitted. Sources also tell us that police seized a pair of bloody boots from Lucas Bremmer's home. Bremmer told Channel 14 in an exclusive interview this afternoon that he and Trey Hayden fought over a girl at a party last night and that Hayden lost that fight. Bremmer, however, denies prosecutor's allegations that he later shot and killed Hayden in a fit of rage."

As tape of my interview with Lucas ran, I looked out at the small crowd in front of the courthouse and my eye caught a familiar, well-filled T-shirt. Duane Grum. I quickly scanned the crowd for any sign of Sunny but couldn't find her. I went back on the air.

"There are many questions about this case which prosecutors and police have yet to address. Number one is information we've received that Trey Hayden may have confronted his killer with a gun in the second floor hallway of his parents' home . . . and may even have gotten a shot off . . . before being fatally wounded himself. Sources tell us the Hayden boy was shot twice at close range. Police found no firearms at the scene. Other evidence, however, leads investigators to conclude that an additional shot was fired, possibly from a second gun. Police lab technicians are doing tests to determine if Trey Hayden fired a handgun immediately prior to his death. Though results can be quick from such tests, police have not chosen to share those results with us."

I closed as quickly as I could after that and, as soon as Al signaled I was clear, popped out the earpiece, disentangled myself from the microphone and walked quickly into the crowd toward the last place I'd seen Grum standing. Naturally, he wasn't there and no one in the vicinity could offer any more information than that they'd seen a big hulking guy who smelled like a coffee house. And that he'd been staring at a group of teenage girls in half-tees and shorts who were also watching us do our live shots.

I asked the girls about him. Got nothing but odd looks and

laughter. Trudged back to the live truck.

I found Jody as she was getting off the phone. She looked like she wanted to run over it with the truck. When I asked her what the problem was, she sighed.

"We're stuck here. Chucky says the four of us are supposed to handle the ten o'clock and then find a place to stay. I'm glad I stopped by the dry cleaners before work. Gonna miss my kid, though. First night away since she was born. Damn."

For an instant, I wondered how it would feel to have a family awaiting my return. As it was, my cat, Socks, would be fine with the next door neighbor's kid checking on him.

I told Jody, "There's no reason for you to stay. Why don't you sneak home for a couple of hours?"

She gave me a sad smile. "Thanks for the offer, but no way am I running out on my first assignment in Chicago. Eric and I knew this might happen sooner or later. It's not the end of the world. So what have you got up your sleeve for the ten, anyway?"

I told her I was working on getting an interview with Bremmer's girlfriend. That widened her eyes. "Are you always this good?"

"Aw shucks, ma'am."

But in the back of my mind, one thought resonated. *Grum.*

Sunny arrived to remind me about dinner while Al and Peter were packing up the live truck. I offered to bring them food, but they told me Caroline and Eddie were headed out to eat, too, and had them covered.

The restaurant Sunny chose was a fern-and-flower-filled joint on the ground floor of the renovated River Traders Bank building in downtown Falcon Ridge. A political fundraiser for a guy named Allen Droot was being held upstairs, and people wearing "Root for Droot" stickers and little elephants on their lapels kept passing us as we waited to be shown a table. I wondered how he was related to the chief of police.

We put in a drink order and I told her about spotting Grum outside the courthouse and the way he had disappeared by the time I finished my live shot.

"Why wouldn't he stop by? The boy probably had time on his hands since he was a no-show at work today." She grinned at my reaction and gave me innocent in return. "What?"

"Yeah, yeah. You know what. Go on."

"There's DUI history on his driver's license and he's due in court this week on another DUI from June. His license was suspended about six years ago. He got it back but there aren't any vehicles registered in his name. Did six months in County for sexual battery. A health club trainer complained that he groped her during a weight-lifting session. If he's got credit cards, they're in another name."

"Does he have a job?"

"Yep. He's a full-time laborer with something called Dee-Bree, Inc. It's one of those outfits that does pre-construction demolition work and light hauling. The county funds it so they have a lot of guys who are on probation and work release. Just the sort of folks you want hanging around your house. Grum took a sick day today, according to his foreman."

"Sounds like an ideal spot for some ghost payrolling."

"Here's something else. Hayden had been working off his own DUI conviction there for the past month. And Bremmer used to work there."

"The foreman say whether they hung out together? The three of them?"

"Bremmer didn't last. Fell asleep on the job. The foreman thinks he's a serious pothead. Hayden was on a work-release crew. Grum rotated with a bunch of the full-timers. The only contact they might have had was when the trucks picked them up to take them to their job sites in the morning. If you're thinking they argued, fought, whatever, the foreman says no way. With a roster like that, the supervisors keep a pretty close eye on them. Fighting means you're fired. No exceptions."

"This foreman sounds like a regular font of information. Think he'd go on camera?"

"Not a chance. The only reason he talked to me is that he's a jarhead, too. We served in some of the same places." She winked. "We compared tattoos."

Our waitress put my iced tea on the table. I toasted Sunny with it. Smiling, she raised her glass of Guinness Stout. Before she took a sip, however, I saw her eyes narrow at something she saw behind me. When I looked, Moira Cullen was threading her way through the room to our table.

"You aren't stalking me are you, Mr. McCarthy?" she asked. The grin was back but it looked a little strained as she glanced from Sunny to me and back again. She didn't introduce herself and neither did Sunny.

"I could ask you the same question, Ms. Cullen," I said.

"Actually, I have to spend a few moments at a dreadfully dull fundraiser for a colleague who's running for state representative."

"Allen Droot? Is he related to the chief?"

"Of course. Father and son. Care to join me? I'm sure they'd love to have some media coverage."

"Politics with my meal gives me gas."

Her grin widened. "When I saw you here I thought I'd save myself a phone call. Lindsey's agreed to talk to us tonight in my office."

"Will she go on camera?"

"I told her that you would treat her gently. And that it could help Lucas. You will, won't you? Be gentle, I mean?" Those eyes, how they sparkled. Man.

"He's every bit the gentleman," Sunny assured her.

"Fine. Eight-thirty, then. You have my cell if anything comes up."

I watched her walk away. When I turned back to Sunny the smile was back, and she was shaking her head. "They sure come out of the woodwork when you're around, don't they?"

"Lawyers?"

"Right."

"She thinks Theo Zak's involved." I sketched out Moira's reasoning. Sunny reached out and tapped my forehead.

"Hello? She's feeding you tidbits of her case because you can get her message out to all those good citizens who might serve on Bremmer's murder-one jury."

"If that's what she wants, wouldn't it make more sense to say it at a news conference?"

"You're such a manly man, but when blood rushes from your brain to other parts of your body it makes you just as dense as the rest. By telling you, Bimbo Lawyer gets the help of the only reporter covering this story who has the credentials to do an actual investigation. She's not after what's in your pants. She's after your credibility, bucko. You come out with proof Theo Zak's trying to run up the charges against this kid, you'll muck up the waters to the point she can probably get the case dismissed."

"And if Zak is pulling the strings?"

"Well, then congratulations. You've got a damn good story, don't you?"

We looked at menus and ordered. Just as the meals arrived, my Nextel beeped.

Then Al said, "Reno? Eddie C's truck's been firebombed. He's hurt bad."

CHAPTER THIRTEEN

The smell of scorched metal, especially copper wire, makes me think of fresh blood.

I didn't share my observation with anyone gathered in the parking lot near where the live truck sat charred and smoking. Didn't share what I was feeling, either. If there's anything I've learned in twenty years of watching the grief and rage of others, it's how to keep mine in check. But it was present, all right. And growing.

Al and Jody made it there before we did. About a dozen civilians gawked. Some of them had been inside the Steer and Squawk with Eddie and Caroline when they noticed the truck in flames.

Eddie and Caroline, however, were on their way to the hospital.

While Sunny took off to canvass nearby businesses, I talked to four witnesses.

The Steer and Squawk Family Restaurant sat on a wooded hillside overlooking Main Street as it sloped into downtown Falcon Ridge. The parking lot was spread out; the back part of it abutted a thick stand of brush and evergreen trees. No doubt so they wouldn't be bothered by curious passersby, Eddie left the truck where the Steer and Squawk's lot met the woods.

A couple named Von Hertzen told me they noticed the smoke when a muted "Whump!" drew their attention out the window next to their table. A cook rushed into the dining room at almost

133

the same moment shouting that the television truck had exploded.

I asked the Von Hertzens if they'd seen anyone suspicious in the parking lot before the blast. Both shook their heads.

Eddie sprinted through the kitchen and out the back door. At that point, the Von Hertzens said, flames were shooting out of the driver's window. Eddie headed for the sliding panel on the opposite side intending, I suppose, to try to grab the $70,000 camera he'd left secured in a floor mount. The manager and the cook said they saw him jam a key into the lock, grab the handle, and then, while crying out in pain from contact with the superheated metal, wrestle the door aside.

To meet a fireball that exploded in his face.

"Wrong place, and piss-poor timing," the arson investigator told me. A couple of inches taller than my six-one and with a thicker, grayer beard, he had college professor's eyes peering out from behind wire-rim glasses. A fire department badge was clipped to the utility belt outside his coveralls. The name on the business card he'd handed me was Briggs.

"It's a damn shame. If your boy had waited even fifteen seconds longer, there would have been flames blowing out all the windows. No way he would have risked going in close like he did. As it was, he opened that door just as the second bottle ignited. Sure makes a different kind of case for us."

"Bottle?" I asked.

"You're not quoting me, right? Yeah, plastic pop bottles do the trick real nicely. He probably used a center punch to take out the driver's side window. He'd have some cover while he worked that way and a center punch doesn't make the noise a rock would. Had gasoline in two bottles, okay? Poured some out from the first bottle to saturate the seat, threw in the second container to really grease things up and then probably stood back a ways and used a road flare to torch it all. Fire got a nice start but when it melted the plastic of the second bottle that's when it really took off. Not really an explosion, you understand. But if you've ever seen gasoline burn, you know what happened. Just sort of jumps out. That's when your friend opened the door. He caught the full force of the ignition."

"You know anybody around here who would pull this kind of stunt?"

"I'd better start asking you the questions now. Whose cage did you folks rattle today?"

"Hard to say. Probably a few viewers, as usual. Maybe a couple of Wihega County cops."

"Cops huh? That's all I need. Then again, most of 'em would probably just lock you up if you pissed 'em off bad enough. Any specific civilians you can think of might have taken a disliking to you or your station?"

If Briggs could have read my thoughts, he would have seen the name Grum floating front and center.

"Not that I can think of."

He brought a hand up and squeezed the back of his neck. It left a soot smudge on the skin.

"Guess I'll ask the gas stations, see if anybody remembers seeing a guy filling up pop bottles. Process the scene. See if we can't scare up a few more witnesses. You want to hang around for a few minutes, I'll call the hospital and get a condition report on your buddy."

"You working this alone or do the cops pitch in?"

"I need investigative help, I call the state fire marshal or ATF. I need a ticket written, that's when I call the cops."

Sunny joined me as he walked off. "Ringing endorsement of the Wihega County Police."

"Yeah. You find anything?"

She nodded toward the trees. "Couple kids riding their bikes two streets over say they saw a motorcycle sitting in the bushes on the other side of this hill. They wanted to take a closer look but a guy came out of the woods and shouted at them to beat it."

"They describe him?"

"Yeah." She hesitated. "I was thinking I'd pass the information to Briggs so he could talk to them, maybe get a composite drawn up."

"Tell me first," I said.

"Bald, big as a house, and looked like a farmer."

Duane Grum in his overalls. I stared hard at the truck's remains.

"When you checked out Grum, did you get his address?"

"Reno . . ."

Little wisps of smoke rose from the interior of the live truck. The front of the metal cabinet holding the monitors and the gear that raised and lowered the microwave mast had melted. I still smelled blood. It wasn't a stretch to imagine the scent of burned flesh floating on the air alongside it.

"You want to give me his address and loan me your keys?" Heat had cracked the paint in some places on the truck's exterior and left it bubbled in others. The tires were globs of mud, welded to the ground.

Sunny stepped in front of me. She wasn't tall enough to block my view but the steel in her tone forced my attention away from the truck.

"No keys. I'll drive. But you're not gonna wig out if we find him."

"Sunshine, this guy . . ."

"Don't! I understand what you're feeling right now. I've been there myself. Doesn't make it right. If this guy's the whack job he sounds like, you go after him planning to whup his ass and you're gonna get both of us in a world of hurt." She paused.

"Do I have your promise or do I give Grum to the inspector?"

I nodded but my shoulders felt tight. It didn't get any better when Briggs came back to tell us Eddie was in critical condition with second and third degree burns on his neck and face.

Before we left, I checked our remaining live truck. Jody, as usual, was scrunched up in back on her Nextel. I couldn't tell in the shadows of the rear compartment, but she might have been crying. Al leaned against the engine compartment, also talking on the phone. He held up a hand as I approached. I heard him say something about making arrangements to get Eddie's parents from their home in the Ukrainian Village neighborhood to the hospital. When he hung up he looked more morose than usual.

"Eddie's old man has a bad ticker. Now he's gotta hear his kid's face was nearly burned off." His expression turned him back into the street cop he'd been for fifteen years. "That mope who's been hanging around. Grum. Is he the son of a bitch who did this?"

"We're headed over to his place right now to ask him that very question."

He nodded in the direction of Investigator Briggs. "You're not passing along his name?"

"Not yet. He could be just a goofy fan."

"You got the goofy part right. You want me to take a ride with you?"

I glanced at my watch.

"We have about an hour before we need to be at Moira Cullen's office to interview Lindsey Sears." I gave him the address. "If we don't make it back in time, have Jody do the questioning. She knows what to ask."

Al nodded. "You know the other really crappy thing? Chucky's the one should be getting somebody to take care of

Eddie's parents, right? But the suits are all tied up in some dinner meeting. Chucky told the desk, if the Cibulskis really need to see their son tonight, have 'em call a cab. He's not authorizing overtime for anybody to play taxi service."

TV news bosses. Gotta love 'em.

Falcon Ridge's Main Street slides north to south until it passes under a rusted iron railroad overpass and then swings west as a county road toward the river. Grum's last known address ended up being about a mile from Wiley's bar. It was an area where I would have expected to see houses the size of those in the Haydens' neighborhood and backyards capitalizing on grand views.

What we found was a miscellaneous collection of clapboard, Craftsman, and Cape Cod homes staggering haphazardly up a bluff overlooking the water. Some were in varying stages of renovation. Others showed gray, weathered exteriors and sagging porches that would have sucked up gallons of fresh paint. At the crest was a Victorian, looking as haughty as a wealthy old woman who's lost her pocketbook but not her dignity. It was perched on a lot overgrown with brush featuring a couple of dying crabapple trees and a locust that wore a "Rooms for Rent" sign.

I matched the street numbers on the sign to the ones from Sunny's notebook. She frowned and turned up a gravel drive that passed the house and turned into a blacktopped parking lot. A big Ford F-150 pickup shared the space with a rusted but serviceable Volvo station wagon. Back there as well, we found a single-story wood frame building that could have been chopped out of a 1940s L.A. motor court. Four units fronted the little parking lot. All along the bluff, a surly wall of arborvitae and other evergreens blocked any view of the river beyond. They had solid, mature growth but were nowhere near the age of the house or the motor court building.

Sunny leaned forward with her arms embracing the steering wheel and stared. "I always wondered what happened to the Bates Motel."

"Maybe we'll catch Grum in the shower."

I looked up to see a man step out on the porch of the Victorian. Elderly and stooped, wearing chinos that bagged out on him and a heavy cardigan over a white shirt, he came to the railing and placed both hands on it as he watched us climb from the Expedition. He had an aluminum cane hooked over his left forearm.

"Help you, folks?" He might've looked frail but his voice was strong.

"Does Duane Grum live here?"

He studied my face for a moment and then pointed a finger. "I just saw you on TV."

"Good to know somebody's watching." I reached up to shake. His hand felt like a skeleton's.

"I'm Leon Griffin. You're covering the Hayden murder, aren't you? Grum do it?"

"You say that like it wouldn't surprise you."

"Wouldn't. Not for a minute. But he moved out, oh, six months ago anyway."

I felt a pang of disappointment.

"You could ask the neighbors, though. Martha Corbett there, in Four, and Gordy Armstrong over in One. They weren't really friends of his, but they talked to him more than I ever did."

"Not the ideal renter?"

"About the only good thing I can say about him was that he was all paid up when he left. Didn't skip. Now *that* was a surprise."

Griffin coughed with enough force that, had he not been gripping the railing, he might have fallen. I moved toward the porch steps but he waved me off.

"Nah, nah. That wasn't a bad one. Got 'em where I can't stop long enough to breathe." He cleared his throat.

"Smoked for almost fifty years. Goddamn cigarettes. What I was saying, the problem wasn't him skipping on the rent. It was the women. Hookers! He'd go for a couple weeks without them and then it'd be like a revolving door over there. Sometimes he'd see three or four a day for a couple of days. The last straw was when he hurt one of them. I heard her screaming so I called the police. Lot of good that did."

He made a disgusted sound that turned into another rasping cough. When it ended, he wiped his mouth with a dark-colored handkerchief.

"By the time the cops got here, everything was copasetic. She told them she just got carried away in passion. Not too damned likely. She had a bloody nose and a good start on a shiner. The next morning, I told Grum to find a new place. He left."

"Any forwarding address?"

"No need for it. Never got any mail. You want to ask my other tenants about him? Here, I'll walk over with you. Need some exercise, anyway. Sitting in a damn easy chair all day, I'm all cramped up." He held tight to the railing as he limped across the porch and down the stairs. Once to the blacktop, he pointed at the outbuilding with his cane and smiled.

"You're wondering about my little motel, aren't you?"

"It's unusual."

"It was the only structure up on this bluff back in the forties. Full size, then, twelve units. President of the bank holding the paper on it wanted the land for a house so what did he do? Had the bank foreclose and force the owners out. Place was torn down except for these units. The banker figured it might keep anyone else from building up here and be cheap housing for his maid and a yard man."

He wheezed a short laugh. "When we moved in, my wife and

I, we sure as hell didn't have any servants. We added Pullman kitchens and turned the four units into three small apartments. That was twenty-five years ago. Corbett and Armstrong have lived here the whole time. Twenty-five damn years."

"It's so peaceful up here," Sunny said, staring at the tree line in the gathering dusk. "You must have had a wonderful view before you added the arborvitae."

"It was a spectacular view," Griffin's voice hardened. "We used to see a stable, horses, nice pasture land. Up to about a year and a half ago when . . . all this casino crap started."

"I thought the state rejected Falcon Ridge's casino application," I said. "They started construction anyway?"

He looked skyward and sighed. "I misspoke a little. What you see is *officially* a Marriott and a couple of restaurants. And a building the developer says is going to be a warehouse. You tell me. Who builds a warehouse that looks like a big log cabin right on the water? The Wihega Leadership Council! First, the stables burn, then the owner drives his car into the river. His daughter sells and, just like that, the bulldozers appear. You watch. The state will approve the license and that warehouse will turn into a gambling hall."

Sunny and I exchanged glances. "What's that about a fire?"

"Sure. Burned the stable to the ground. One night, two years ago. I woke up at two, two-thirty in the morning. Flames everywhere. Quite a show from up here. Fire, horses running. We watched it all."

"Did the fire department ever establish the cause?"

"The paper said a firebomb. Arson. Killed four horses that night."

"Was there an arrest?" Sunny asked.

"If there was one, I never heard about it. But then I left for Mayo's the next morning. Hip replacement, all the good it's done me."

We stopped in front of the first of the small units in the old motel. Someone had set out a canvas-backed chair and a small barbecue grill. The coals still glowed. I could hear country music playing inside. A woman flipped on an orange porch light and looked at us through her screen door.

"Is Leo giving you nice people a lecture along with your tour? I often tell him he should come speak to one of my history classes." She was well into her sixties but wore her gray hair with bangs and long past her shoulders. She marked a place in the Linda Mickey novel she held and stepped outside.

Leo said, "They're TV reporters. They think your buddy Duane might have something to do with that Hayden boy's death."

"Actually, we're just asking questions," I said. "The cops make the accusations."

Martha Corbett looked stricken. "My God! Who was killed? I'm sorry. I don't pay much attention to the news these days . . ."

I summarized the events of the day for her. Her hand moved up to her mouth.

"I'm not sure what to say. I always felt some responsibility for Duane. Did Leo tell you I used to teach high school? Duane was one of the students my last year. He came to me after he graduated. I helped him get a custodian's job at the community college. Of course, the school fired him when those rape charges were filed."

She gave Leo a look of contrition.

"He came to me again when they dropped the charges. Said the school wouldn't hire him back and he had nowhere to live. Leo and I talked it over and he allowed Duane to move in here."

"Reluctantly," Leo said. She glanced at him.

"Yes. Reluctantly. As a favor to me. Lord knows, I've always rooted for the underdog." She sighed. "A poor decision on my part in Duane's case, I'm afraid."

142

"No. My fault," Leo said. "Letting him stay as long as I did."

"Did he ever threaten either of you?" Sunny asked.

Corbett shook her head. "We seldom saw him. You should understand that Duane wasn't the most social animal. Nor the brightest. Until Leo told me about the girl he hurt, I always thought of him as just kind of . . . big and shy. I believe he was rather frightened of me. He was always very respectful. That probably came from living with his mother all those years."

"Is she still alive?"

"No. She died . . . around the time he was arrested, I believe. I'm sure it broke his heart."

I asked, "Any other family in the area?"

"Yes. He has an older brother. Come to think of it, the brother was in trouble with the police, too, at one point. When Duane was very young. The mother sent him away to school. I never knew him."

"I tried to overlook the hookers," Leo said suddenly. "Mostly, he had them coming over during the day when Martha and Gordy were gone and I figured, a guy like that, it just wouldn't pay to get into it with him. Big mistake."

"So you thought he could be violent?"

A short nod. "I had boys like him working for me at the store. You don't hire stock clerks for their brains. Some of 'em were big and just slow. Others, you had to walk softly around them. I read Grum like that. Quiet one minute, flare up on you the next."

"How did he react to the eviction?" I asked.

"Now there he surprised me. I was expecting him to go off, so we all three told him together. But he just nodded, sort of mumbled 'okay' and that was that."

"Did he have a car?" I asked.

"Not while he lived here."

"How about when he moved?"

"Somebody picked him up. Fellow in a truck like mine, in fact. He came around a few times." He gestured to the heavy-duty Ford pickup. "It wasn't like Duane had much to pack. Just clothes and those dumbbells of his."

Corbett spoke up. "I think he has a motorcycle now. I saw him in the mall parking lot last week. He was standing next to a bike and putting on a helmet."

Sunny stirred beside me. "Did you notice the make?"

"A black Harley Davidson Softail Classic," she said, smiling. "Custom paint, windshield and fenders. I'm sorry but I didn't think to look for a license plate."

Leo's mouth dropped open. "How would you . . . ?"

She patted his arm. "I keep telling you, I had a wild youth. I grew up in Cicero, remember?"

"What kind of job did he have that he could afford a Softail?" Sunny asked.

The man and woman exchanged blank looks. "He worked for the county, didn't he?" Corbett asked Leo.

"Some kind of laborer, I think." He motioned toward the Victorian. "I have all that with the tax stuff. I can go get it . . ."

"No need," I said. We chatted a few minutes longer, and then I looked at my watch and realized we'd have to hustle to get back to Moira Cullen's office for the interview with Lindsey Sears.

"One thing," I said. "The Leadership Council you mentioned. Is that a civic organization?"

Leo cleared his throat and used the handkerchief again. "Civic? Ruling cabal is what it is. You want the long version or the short one?"

"Oh Lord." Martha Corbett rolled her eyes. "The short one, please. Your blood pressure, remember?"

" 'Leadership Council.' Sounds harmless, doesn't it? Think of it like Daley's Chicago Machine. They control every political office, every major project in Wihega County."

"Theo Zak behind it?"

"Of course not. Paper says he's retired. Takes the grandkids fishing." He snorted. "Leadership Council scholarships paid for law school for his children. When he was board president, I know two realtors on the council who paid for his vacations to Jamaica."

"Anybody ever look into any of that? The paper or . . ."

In the light from the yellow insect bulb next to the door, his face was the color of parchment.

"The publisher is a past president of the council. See, Mr. McCarthy, I was a grocer. The Leadership Council ran me out of a store I owned for twenty years so they could bring a super-duper Wal-Mart to town. Everything totally legal and above-board, but you know how easy that is to fake when you own the local government? So I watch them now. This casino operation is Zak's way of paying back some of his mobster friends. You watch, too. That permit's not dead down in Springfield any more than Theo Zak's retired."

Back in Sunny's Expedition, I said, "You make Grum for a world-class planner?"

"Enough of one to find 'Escorts' in the yellow pages."

"Here's a guy, when he's not tearing down buildings on a county program, he's sitting home in a low-profile, out-of-the-way place, lifting weights and calling up escort services. And his criminal record is for overtly sexual stuff. The rape and the groping. What would motivate him to set a barn and a television truck on fire?"

"He had to get the money to pay the hookers somewhere. Contract muscle?"

"So, if he did the barn, and Zak profited, it stands to reason he's working for Zak. Or this Leadership Council Leo mentioned. But what's the sense in doing our truck? Even if Moira's right and Zak's part of the Hayden case somehow, he's been around a long time. He's a fairly sophisticated guy for a crook. He's got to know reporters don't spook so easily."

"How long has he run Wihega County, Reno? Leo says he's got the local publisher in his pocket. Maybe the reporters he's dealt with are wimps."

"Or maybe Grum's freelancing."

"Could be. When I get the chance, I'll try to find out who he hangs with."

Downtown Falcon Ridge after dark has an old-timey feel, due mainly to lighting provided by turn-of-the-century gas-style lamps hung from posts rather than the harsh glare of the carbon-arcs popular in the city. Much like Geneva and Richmond, other Chicago suburbs that play off their colorful histories, Falcon Ridge continues to attract visitors to its business district by encouraging quaint shops selling everything from antiques to ice cream and river memorabilia. Brick-paved sidewalks are bordered by slanted curbside parking and planters thick with bouquets of perennials line the center median.

Moira Cullen's office was in a brick, four-story office building about six blocks from the hotel where she'd found us having dinner. Al's Crown Vic was parked in front next to the live truck. Peter sat in the back of the truck reading the paper.

"What's up?" I asked.

"Nada. Al says the girl didn't show."

I took the stairs two at a time. Moira Cullen sat at her secretary's desk frowning at Jody on the couch across the room. When I came in, she turned the frown on me.

"Lindsey was supposed to be here forty-five minutes ago. This really has me worried, Reno. Her mother says she left home at seven-thirty but she's not answering her cell."

"Is she facing any charges? Conspiracy, or aiding and abetting?" I asked.

"I can't imagine why. If she'd held back anything, maybe, but even the assistant state's attorney who sat in when the cops questioned her told me she was very forthcoming."

"Did she have any drugs on her when they brought her in?"

"I asked. If there was anything I would have advised her to get an attorney of her own. The cops said no worries."

"Maybe she saw it differently," Sunny drawled.

Moira's frown gave way to irritation. "How's that?"

"Look at it from her point of view. She knows her boyfriend isn't the killer but she sees the cops have stuck him in jail anyway. Maybe she figures they're going to lock her up, too. It's a pretty frightening thought. I've seen people take off with less motivation."

"Oh, really," Moira came back, heavy on the scorn. "She's seventeen years old. Where's she going to go? Her family and friends are all in this area."

Sunny jangled her keys in her hand. "What kind of car does she drive and what route would she normally take to get here?"

We waited an hour in Moira Cullen's comfortable outer office for Lindsey Sears to show or for Sunny to call in and say she had found her. Neither happened.

With a ten o'clock live shot staring me in the face, and the likelihood of a big fat hole where my exclusive interview was supposed to run, I spent the time rewriting my script and munching on three incredibly thick chocolate chip creations I'd taken from a bag labeled "Park Place Cookies" that Moira placed on the coffee table in front of me. I was covertly eyeing the bag, my hand twitching to reach for a fourth, when my Nextel buzzed and Sunny announced she had come up empty. Now I felt a faint tickle of dread.

"She's driving Bremmer's Jeep Sahara, not her own car. No

sign of it along the road. Her mother doesn't have a clue where she might have gone. Actually, her mother doesn't seem to have much of a clue, period. Lindsey didn't seem upset or angry or depressed. In fact, she was excited about getting to be on TV. Her mom wanted to know if she was getting paid for it."

"Angling for a chunk of the pie?"

"Of course. She has expenses, after all. And she's been letting her daughter live with her for free."

"I guess it's safe to say she's not panicked that Lindsey never joined us?"

"According to her mother, Lindsey is well known for making plans and then changing them on a whim. Usually because some boy calls and asks her to stop by."

"Was Mom able to supply you with the names of any of those boys?"

"Nope. I'm on my way back over there to see if she'll let me take a look at her room. Don't hold your breath."

I glanced at the clock as I hung up. We were twenty minutes away from show time. Now I was nervous. Al and Peter had moved the camera outside since we had no interview to do. Moira was in her office doing paperwork. I leaned in the doorway to give her Sunny's update.

She threw her pen down on her desk and frowned. "Goddamn it. I don't need the girl off on a goddamn booty call. I have to get her statement if I'm going to reapply for bail."

"If you have the names of any of Lucas's friends, Sunny and I can go looking for her after the news." Another thought struck me. "Speaking of his buddies, what do you know about a guy named Duane Grum?"

She looked like I'd slapped her. "He's a cretin. Is he involved here?"

"I'm not sure."

"He's been hanging around the live truck all day. Watching

148

everything we do." Jody shuddered. "Creepy."

I described my encounter with him on the trail and what we'd learned from Leo Griffith and Martha Corbett.

By the time I finished, Moira was shaking her head.

"I'm assuming you know about the bogus rape a couple of years ago? I represented both of them. The day the state's attorney dropped the charges, I told Lucas he should look up the word 'lucky' in the dictionary and he'd see his picture. But I also said he wouldn't hold onto that luck for long if he insisted on hanging out with Duane Grum. Your producer is right. He's about as creepy as they come."

"You agreed to represent him."

"Just to keep Lucas happy. I don't like to represent multiple defendants in the same case. Too many different angles and if one of them decides to give up the other you have a real headache. I explained all that to Grum. I even told him I'd find him another attorney. He wears that stupid smile that suggests he's a simpleton but I really don't think he is. He understands. He said he didn't want another lawyer. He claimed I was, 'The *best.*' But the way he said it always made me feel uncomfortable. He'd leer and smirk and stare at my chest. But Lucas insisted."

"Why would Lucas insist?"

"Got me on that one. He never said."

"Why didn't you withdraw when you saw Grum was a fruitcake?"

"All my clients are supposed to be altar boys? I can handle myself. I always made sure there was someone else in the room when I met with him. I've defended other men like him in sexual assault cases. Guys where there was no question in anybody's mind about their guilt. I didn't like it then either, but that's the job. What bothered me most about Grum was his attitude."

"What kind of attitude?"

She hesitated, as though considering the propriety of talking about a former client in front of a witness. Then she ran a hand through her hair.

"We established that the girl, the victim, wanted to have sex with Lucas, okay? We didn't put that out there but, trust me, it's true. To Grum, that made her a whore. So to him, everything he did after that point was perfectly fine. His joining in. The video. Uploading to the Internet. Every time we talked he referred to her as 'the whore.' And you've heard how he deals with whores."

"Have there been other incidents like the one Leo told us about?"

"Since? You'd have to ask the police. It wouldn't surprise me. A shrink would probably say he lacks impulse control. As far as I'm concerned, he's a nut job."

"Nice. You have a current address for him?"

"If he's not still at Leo's, nope. Once the cops dropped the charges, I told him to take a hike. Put it this way, Reno. He's so toxic, if he moved in next door to you, your lawn would die."

CHAPTER FOURTEEN

Without our planned interview for the ten, Jody decided to move my live shot to the front of the Steer and Squawk where, as fortunate timing would have it, a flatbed tow truck was maneuvering into position to load the carcass of our minicam unit and haul it wherever the fire department directed.

The lighting in the parking lot, along with an additional fill-light Al decided to use, gave the action a movie-set quality. Whether he was working at his normal speed or had slowed down because he knew he would be in the shot, the tow-driver managed to futz in the background and make sure the sign on his door stayed visible throughout my report. It annoyed me. The smell of grease from the restaurant annoyed me. Lindsey's going missing annoyed me. Worried me, too. And that just served to piss me off more.

I began by reviewing the case and the charges against Lucas then segued to the truck fire. Instinct told me the coincidence of the vandalism was far too great not to link it, if only gently, to the Hayden murder. I felt my insides clench as I described the fire and the injuries sustained by Eddie Cibulski. Injuries, I noted, that would require unbelievably painful facial surgery and skin grafts followed by months of rehabilitation.

I was supposed to stop there. The time constraints on the producers of any ten o'clock news program are incredible as they try to include all of the day's important local and national stories. I was already beyond the limits they'd set for me. I'd been formulating a couple of additional sentences as I spoke, however, and just went right on with them, ignoring a burst of sudden angry chatter from the director in my earpiece.

"Authorities believe the truck was purposely set ablaze, but have not connected the fire to the murder." I said. "We, however, are working on leads that suggest a link between the two incidents, and hope to have more information on that for you in our reports tomorrow."

The director was still cursing as I stepped off camera and unplugged my earpiece. Not more than a minute later, my Nextel chirped and I heard Chucky's voice. I lowered the volume as far as it would go and stuffed the phone into the bottom of my briefcase. No doubt he wanted to chew me out for mentioning unexplained "leads." I didn't want to try and explain. Hell, I thought I'd used great restraint in not naming Grum and suggesting he be shot on sight.

Sunny was parked in the lot of a shuttered service station next door. I trotted over.

"Let's vamoose," I said.

"Nice finish," she said, indicating the TV monitor built into the dash of her Expedition. "Setting yourself up as the arsonist's next target?"

"It gives him something to worry about."

"Oh, he's all tied up in knots, I'm sure. Meanwhile, you plan to sleep in a Nomex suit and keep a fire extinguisher under your pillow?"

"I'm touched by your concern."

"Back home we pronounce the word 'tetched.' As in 'the old feller's a bit tetched in the haid.' "

"I want to go by the hospital . . ." Out of the corner of my eye I saw her swing her gaze my way. "To see Eddie," I added.

"Oh," she said. "Eddie."

"Don't start, Sunshine."

"What is it you think I'm starting?"

"There's not a damn thing I can do for Vinnie except watch him die."

"And what?You're going to walk into your cameraman's room and heal him by your presence? The docs aren't going to let you near him. You're a walking germ factory, and his burns make him especially susceptible to infection. He won't even know you're there."

"You think Vinnie will?"

"Yeah. I think so." She seemed to want to take it further but then focused on her driving.

"You feel like explaining?"

"If I do, will it persuade you to go see him?"

My turn to sit in silence. I wanted to say something smartass. No, that's not right. I really wanted to punch the safety glass out of the window beside me. Not my usual reaction to stress but what the hell. I was having a bad year.

"That's what I thought," Sunny said. "Pigheaded."

As Sunny suspected, hospital security wouldn't let me onto the unit where Eddie was being treated. I stalked the halls until I cornered a nurse who told me it wouldn't be worth it for us to stick around. No time for visits. The plan was to do as much as they could for him locally and then ship him to the burn unit at Loyola Medical Center, in Maywood, by trauma helicopter.

"Take a run out to Wiley's?" I asked when I got back into the Expedition. Tension had turned the tops of my shoulders into boards. I squeezed one and then the other. The knotted muscles refused to release.

"The place where you found Bremmer? Who are we looking for? Lindsey or Grum?"

"With any luck, maybe both."

Sunny took two slow passes through the jammed parking lot at Wiley's, then crammed the Expedition into a space close to the road where we had a decent view of foot and vehicle traffic. No black Jeep Sahara.

Sunny's memory for faces is close to photographic. For backup, she keeps a detailed computerized record of every mope she and her team have tracked down over the years, along with those nabbed by a dozen or so of her bounty hunter colleagues. And she has Wi-Fi access to a slew of private databases with names like Seisint and ChoicePoint in case she needs to run a license plate or do a fast background check for criminal history. They're the same private intelligence-gathering services the Feds use.

She consulted the laptop mounted between the front seats.

"Jack Teasdale has an entry that he picked a guy up here a year ago. A car thief. His notes say it's a lowlife joint and they keep a pharmacy under the bar. Names a few mopes he recognized who hang out here."

Inside my briefcase, the phone began to ring. I unburied it and looked at Caller ID. Ray Fong's home number.

"How is he?" I asked.

"We're going to try the stent. Tomorrow morning. Can you get in to see him tonight?"

"Is he awake?"

"Not yet."

I didn't say anything.

"Look, Reno. Whatever you're thinking, get over it. You know how I grew up. Not like I was exactly writing myself a ticket to med school with all my good works. If Vinnie hadn't smacked some sense into me, I'd probably be sticking a hype in *my* arm instead of into other people. I got a responsibility to him. You do, too. How many times did he come between you and your old man? Save you from a beating?"

"As far as I'm concerned, he lost the right to ask me to do anything for him three months ago."

"My ass! That tune don't play here. You made the choice to go after those Russian assholes. The goof you shot was trying to kill you, wasn't he? You put yourself in that situation, Reno. Not Vinnie. Didn't you tell me he took your back afterward? He loves you, man."

I stared through the windshield. A layer of dust hung above the graveled parking lot. The party under way inside the bar spilled outside; people were drinking from both bottles and plastic cups as they leaned up against their vehicles and a mix of music played from a variety of car stereos. With my free hand I squeezed the back of my neck, trying to relieve the tightness that spread from my shoulders.

"I gotta go," I said. "What time's the operation?"

"Christ you're a stubborn bastard. You don't want to listen to me as a friend, take this as advice from your doc. There's no way to tell how it's going to go tomorrow. Get in here and spend some time talking to him. Patients come back from coma and give me almost word for word of conversations that went on around them. It won't do him any harm and it might do you some good."

"What am I supposed to tell him? 'Come back home. All is forgiven?' "

"Forgiveness? Now *there's* a concept you might want to learn something about."

A row away from us, a man humped a woman on the hood of an old Cadillac, heedless of the traffic swirling around them. I put the phone into my pocket.

The breath I sucked in brought with it dust from the parking lot, acrid at the back of my throat. I watched the couple on the hood of the Cadillac as they disentangled from each other. They glanced around as though startled at where they found themselves and got a brief smattering of applause from a group standing nearby. They were both on the downhill slide towards sixty and not slender. The woman turned away from him to smooth her skirt and duck into the passenger side of the Cadillac. The guy, on the other hand, shagged up his shorts, accepted a beer from one of the kids in the group, high-fived him, and climbed behind the wheel.

I repeated Ray's side of the conversation for Sunny.

She took my hand. Gripped it hard.

"I'm okay, Sunshine," I said.

"No, Reno. You're a long way from all right. I saw that when I first walked up on you this afternoon in the back of the truck, even before things started going crazy. We leave now, we can be back in the city by midnight."

I had a brief vision of Vinnie on the hospital bed, motionless except for the swelling and dropping of his chest, the timing determined by a machine that would keep to the same rhythm for days or weeks, whether or not it mattered. I imagined Eddie with half his face burned away.

"I want to find Lindsey," I said with a calm I didn't feel.

"You want to find Grum and shoot him in the forehead."

"That, too. But Lindsey could be in trouble and nobody else is looking for her."

"If we find Grum, we call Briggs. Deal?"

I squeezed her hand and nodded.

She reached into the console, coming up with what looked like a short flashlight. It was actually an ASP baton that, at the flick of a wrist, snapped out to twenty-one inches. Great nonlethal defense weapon. Slipping it in her pocket she got out of the Expedition.

Many of the cars in the lot looked like their owners came from neighborhoods like the Haydens'. An armload of Mercedes and Lexus and BMWs. A couple of Hummers. A few Cadillac Escalades, both in the SUV and spiffier pickup truck version. They were outnumbered by workingman vehicles, but the groups doing the roughhousing were gathered around the upscale rides. The same with the discarded bottles, cans, and red plastic bar cups strewn on the ground. Upper-crust suburbia, I thought. Where it's okay to make a mess because you know somebody else is always around to clean it up for you.

We sidestepped the outdoor parties and their trash and went through Wiley's front door. I saw immediately the reason for the midweek crowd of revelers. A banner stretched between cross-beams in the lobby read "$10 Cover, All Drinks $1.00." Two smiling, bikini-clad girls stood next to a metal bin filled with ice and bottles of a popular beer, taking the cover charge, while two guys, as clean cut as frat boys, waited in the background to check IDs.

We paid the cover, waited while they stamped our hands, and then walked into the bar.

The place was jammed and as loud as standing in an airplane hangar while a 777 revs up its engines. Three or four times bigger than any Wisconsin roadhouse I'd ever been in. There was barely room to move across the wood plank floor into a just-as-tightly-packed screened porch. Sunny and I split up and started at the perimeter of the room, working our way toward the center and then shoving through to the porch. Once in there, I could see the crowd extended into an outside deck as well. I was surprised to recognize three people at a table off to the side: a loud, blond producer I knew from Channel 2 making out with the sheriff's office public information guy, Callahan. And next to them, turning to talk to a woman as I looked his way was the local reporter Moira disliked so much, Wozniak. The woman looked like one of the deputies I'd seen in the courtroom during Bremmer's hearing. Two happy couples. Interesting.

It took us a half-hour to figure out that Lindsey wasn't part of the throng, another ten minutes to get back to the entrance.

"Saw some dealing," Sunny said. We stood near the door, watching the frat boys stare vacantly into space between doing ID checks. "Some hand to hand in the crowd. A little less obvious from behind the bar, but the brunette in the spandex top down at the end is doing a pretty good business."

"X, weed, rock? What?"

"Don't know what's for sale at the bar. Weed in the crowd. Kid dropped a sampler next to me. Little balloons like they package heroin and coke. If it's just straight weed, you'd probably get more of a high off the paper you roll it in. I bet it's laced with crystal meth. The chick at the bar, about every fifth order she fills comes with a chaser. Watch for a few minutes and you'll see the customer put a palm over the top of it or take it in his lap. Kinda odd way to handle a shot."

"First the orgy in the parking lot and now this in here. And with a couple of cops sitting in the crowd." I pointed out Sergeant Callahan and the other deputy. "I wonder if the cops are in Wiley's pocket or he's in theirs."

"We could ask him." She grinned. "I always like talking to the dealers who try to widen their customer base by selling meth-spiked grass."

We walked outside and strolled the length of the building. I remembered seeing a flight of stairs just inside the door where Lucas came into the parking lot earlier. The door was closed now. A shade was pulled down behind a dirty pane of glass, but dim light showed behind the shade. I tried the knob. It turned in my hand. I pushed it open.

We went in to a narrow hallway with knotty pine walls and ceiling and more of the plank flooring. A commercial icemaker occupied most of the right side of the hall next to a tired-looking Coke machine. The stairs were ahead. On the left was a kitchen where two Hispanic men in white pants and shirts washed dishes. One of them looked up, saw us, and ducked back to work without changing expression. See no evil. A swinging door to our right past the machines presumably led to the bar. The hallway smelled of spilled beer, smoke, and soap.

Sunny took the lead up the stairs. She was the one packing heat. I noticed that, like an old-time gunfighter, she swept her jacket back to clear her holster. I followed, staying on the balls of my feet. Halfway up, I heard voices with either a radio or TV playing in the background. Sunny hesitated at the top of the steps, her hand on the grip of her 9mm as she peeked around the corner. Turning slightly she held up two fingers to me. I nodded.

We emerged in the middle of another hallway with rooms on one side facing the river and on the other, the parking lot. On the river side, the two men Sunny had seen were seated in a large office. The one behind the desk was round and fifty-ish. He yanked something off his desk with one hand and with the other lifted a remote control. The TV voices died. Whatever he said to the other guy prompted him to rise and turn to face us as we stepped across the threshold. He was a couple of inches taller than me, broad shoulders barely fitting into his T-shirt and a matte of blond chest hair poking out at the neck. For a moment I thought it might be Grum but then I saw his face. It was red, splotchy with zits, and had a thick W.C. Fields nose. The frown he wore looked sandblasted into place.

The guy behind the desk got up slowly, his right hand behind his back. I felt Sunny stiffen beside me.

"Y'all need to go back downstairs. This ain't a public area." He was short, with oily gray hair that started halfway back on his scalp and dark framed glasses. His white polo shirt had sweat stains at the armpits.

"We're just so impressed at the way you run your establishment we thought we'd come up and compliment you," I said.

"The crowd control, the way the entertainment carries out into the parking lot. The clean rest rooms."

"Yeah? You health inspectors or something?" His voice was hoarse. The nameplate on the edge of his desk read "Jack Wiley."

"Actually, we're looking for a young lady."

"Plenty of them downstairs."

"A particular young lady. Lindsey Sears."

"Hey, I seen you before," the big guy said. I glanced at him but he was staring past me at Sunny. So much for the big-time TV reporter.

"You're that bounty hunter. The one who busted down the door and took Kinky Alice to jail last month over in Elgin."

She nodded and smiled as though we were guests at a cocktail party and he had complimented her on her outfit.

Wiley raised his voice. "Hey! One chick at a time, okay? Who's this Lindsey Whatsis?"

"She's friends with Lucas Bremmer."

"Oh. Right." Like it made no difference. "Yeah, I told Lukie boy he could stay here. He had a broad with him. So what? She ain't here now. Who the fuck are you, anyway?"

The big guy spoke up. "She's a bounty hunter, Wile . . ."

"Shut up, Boner. I was talkin' to him."

I grinned. " 'Boner'?"

Wiley pointed the remote like he wanted to make me disappear. "You're trespassing. Bounty hunter or not, you got no right to be in here."

"She's the bounty hunter. I'm a TV reporter, Wiley. Channel 14. Don't you know we go everywhere? Hidden cameras and all that? Catch people selling drugs in bars. From behind the bar even. Do big specials on sweetheart deals between bar owners and the cops they pay off? Maybe their mob connections, too."

He looked from Sunny to me and back again. Blinked. Jerked his head at the big guy.

"Ah fuck it. Get rid of 'em."

I had my left shoulder to Boner. Before he could reach for me, I shifted my weight, pivoted slightly in a move that would have had my physical trainer clapping, and snapped my elbow into his face. The hit was so hard the electrical impulse shot all the way to my fingers. Boner was a big strong guy and no doubt used to bullying people with his bulk, but he reacted like anyone else to the sudden screaming pain of a shattered nose. As his hands automatically shot up toward his proboscis, I continued my left pivot and swung all the way around. With all the fury from my day and the full weight of my 210 pounds behind it, I drove my right fist solidly into his balls. Followed through as though I wanted to smash them up into his intestines. His breath exploded in a strangled, "Haw!" and he took one step before his leg pretzled under him and he toppled face first to the floor.

At the same moment, Sunny took two steps toward Wiley and snapped her Sig-Sauer up to eye-level in a two-fisted grip.

"Whatever's in that hand drop it! Do it now!"

Wiley stiffened. I heard something hit the hardwood floor. Her automatic still pointed at his face, Sunny used her free hand to grab his shoulder and haul him out in front of the desk. His hands were empty.

Boner wheezed out pained breaths but, surprisingly, stayed conscious. Not a blessing for him. I knew how he felt. I've taken a few shots to the nose and to the nether regions, too. I turned his head so he wouldn't have trouble getting air if he passed out. His eyes were huge. He groaned.

Wiley stared at both of us. Sunny lowered her 9mm. I pushed between them. Smiled.

"Dumb move like that, she could have shot you."

"Fuck you pal," he blustered. "I make a phone call, you're both dead."

161

I slapped him. He stumbled backward. Sunny said my name and touched my shoulder. I ignored her. I wrapped my left fist into Wiley's shirtfront and jerked him away from his desk. Slapped him again. Resisted the urge to break his nose, too.

"Let's consider that phone call. What's Uncle Theo gonna say when you tell him you let a TV reporter walk in off the street and kick your ass? First, he's gonna think you're a pansy. Then, he'll wonder if you spilled your guts."

His face, scarlet from the slaps, suddenly took on the kind of knotted-up look a middle manager gets when he knows he's about to get crossways with the boss.

I shook him. "I'll ask again. Watch my lips this time. Where's Lindsey Sears?" Eyes locked on his, I became aware of a seething fury I could feel clear to my toes.

"Christ. You think I'm lying? I ain't lying. I don't know the broad! Luke said he was bringing somebody when he called me this morning. Didn't say who. I never saw her. He needed a place to stay. I wasn't here when I talked to him and I didn't know what happened until the cops got hold of me."

"Go on."

"He . . . he said he found his friend shot up, dead, and he and some chick needed a place to crash. He knew the cops would be coming for him even though he didn't do nuthin'. He wanted to know if anybody else was here. I told him the joint would be empty 'til we started setting up for tonight."

"What else?"

He licked his lips, and I got a whiff of his breath. I've been around better-smelling Dumpsters.

"He wanted to know if I had a gun he could borrow. He was afraid the cops were going to waste him. He had a history with them that wasn't so good, you know? I'm not crazy. I told him no, but he uh . . . found the one we keep behind the bar."

I tried a curveball. "Why did he need another gun when he

162

took one off Trey Hayden?"

"He took that piece of shit? He didn't tell me that!"

"Then how do you know it was a piece of shit?"

"It was a .38 Smith, right? They're not worth nuthin' nowadays. Like a week or two ago, Luke says the Hayden kid dug one up somewhere, and could I get him a box of ammo for it? I found one for him. Doin' him a favor."

"Yeah, anyone could tell you're a charitable kind of guy. Bremmer say where Hayden got the .38?"

He shook his head.

"Why did he need a gun?"

"What the fuck do I care? He wasn't my kid."

Wiley's face was the color of spaghetti sauce. I worried he was going to stroke out on me. I shoved him away. He fell sideways against the desk and clawed at it to stay upright.

"Was Duane Grum with Lucas this morning?"

"That freak asshole? Lukie knows better than to bring him around here."

"Where's Grum live?"

"Why're you askin' me? I don't know."

TV evangelists are more convincing. I took a step intending to slap him again, but this time Sunny gripped my shoulder with more authority.

"No more," she said. I lowered my arm.

"Damn right," Wiley muttered. He touched his face, eyes going to Boner. "Whattya think you're doin, barging in here, waving guns, pushing me and my people around? Cops are gonna nail your ass . . ."

I pointed at the phone on his desk. "Call 'em. Or better yet, just go downstairs and yell. I saw a couple deputies I recognized. I bet you've got a few more down there, don't you? Taking Zak's money to protect your operation?"

Wiley looked at the floor, bluster fading. "Go fuck yourself. I run a bar. That's all."

Sunny went around the back of his desk looking for what he dropped. It wasn't a gun as I'd thought. She held up a fist-sized baggie full of weed.

"After you call the po-leece . . ." Her fingers, inside a pair of black leather gloves, kneaded the bag like putty. As a hole appeared in the side of it, she began sprinkling the contents across the top of his desk. "You better get out the vacuum if you know what I mean. Because I'll make sure my DEA friends show up for the party, too."

I kept an eye on Wiley. Sunny checked the other rooms on the second floor. Empty. We left, watching our backs.

If anything, the parking lot crowd had grown both in size and rowdiness while we were inside. Sunny gripped the ASP baton as we navigated through the throng back to the Expedition. When she gunned the engine, people moved out of our way as slowly as a herd of sleepy cows.

When we were out on the street she asked, "You satisfied now?"

"That Grum and Lindsey aren't back there? As satisfied as I can be without pulling the fire alarm and checking everybody as they run out the door."

"Fire alarm? I'm not sure a mortar attack would be enough to empty that shithole." She paused. "This .38 Wiley says he found ammo for. You sure that state cop isn't woofin' you when he says the locals didn't find it at the scene?"

"Esperanza would have told me."

"What the hell would the killer want with it?"

Al beeped my Nextel, forestalling an answer. Which was fine because I didn't have one to offer.

"Reno? Chucky says if you don't call him tonight, he's sending Stoddard out to pick up the story in the morning."

Chucky answered the phone already ranting.

"Why didn't you give me the heads up I asked for on these alleged leads you claim to have?"

"Didn't have time."

"Take time now."

I outlined my suspicions about Duane Grum. Now that the adrenaline that had been goosing me all evening was wearing off, I realized how thin my case against him sounded. A kid had seen him nearby when the truck was torched. He'd been keeping an eye on us, knew both suspect and victim, and had a history of violent behavior including, possibly, fire-setting. Entirely circumstantial evidence, your honor, I thought.

Chucky surprised me. After taking a couple of moments to consider my summation, he gave me a partial green light to keep digging into Grum.

"Hear me on this, Reno! You listening? I'm backing you only with the understanding you stay in touch. If you haven't established a hard connection between the murder and the truck fire by the 6 o'clock show tomorrow night, I want you off that angle. You hear me? Then you hand your information over to the arson team. All we need is this schmuck claiming we're stalking and harassing him."

"That's not likely to happen."

"Yeah, that's what Marcia Clark and her people said when somebody suggested O.J. would beat the charges, too." Ice cubes tinkled against glass. "What are the cops like?"

I chose my words carefully. "There are some indications they aren't operating entirely . . . independently."

"I read some of our previous stories on Wihega County. The name Theo Zak keeps showing up. Is he still running the show out there? And is there any way he's connected to all of this?"

I began to wonder if Chucky wasn't one of those rare guys who function more efficiently when they're half in the bag.

"He's the one who spearheaded the drive for consolidated law enforcement so his thumb may be pretty deeply embedded in the county police pie."

"Well, hey, I'll have Stoddard do a sidebar on this combined law enforcement operation. But be that as it may. This is why you and I need to communicate, Reno. Team effort." He was still telling me what a terrific reporter I was when I clicked off.

I took a deep breath and slowly let it out. I could still feel my heart thumping against my ribs but the cadence seemed to be getting back to normal. My elbow felt like I'd rammed it into a wall.

For the next hour, we chased down three leads to places where Lindsey might have gone. No success. It was closing in on midnight when Sunny drove us to the motel Al and Peter had selected. After she checked into a room near mine, she went around to the back of the Expedition and returned to hand me a Sig-Sauer P245 and two six-round clips.

"I can't help you with the fire-retardant suit," she said.

"That's okay. I'll fill the ice bucket with water and keep it next to the bed."

She nodded without smiling. Preoccupied. "I've got to go do my real job tomorrow, but if I get a minute I'll run Grum a little more thoroughly. See if I can come up with any of his associates or maybe an address."

"Thanks."

"Why not call Briggs now? Tonight? He could probably put out an alert and have him in custody by morning."

I slipped the Sig-Sauer into my belt and dropped the clips into my jacket pocket. "Then he'd be everybody's meat," I said. "I want a chance to talk to him first."

"Right. Talk." Her eyes in the pale light of the motel parking lot were troubled. Off in the distance, I thought I heard a rumble of thunder.

166

"Speaking of talk, you never called that shrink I recommended last summer, did you?"

"Oh, c'mon, Sunshine. I told you I'd go. I went. Once."

"Stay for the whole hour?"

I grinned. "The guy collects teddy bears and plays Yanni CDs."

"The Feds don't seem to mind. The Department of Justice keeps him on retainer. So does CPD. He specializes in counseling officers involved in shootings."

"I'm not a cop. We've been through this . . ."

"No, we really haven't. Thank God it's never happened, but if one of my people capped a fugitive and refused counseling afterward, I'd fire 'em."

"Good thing I don't work for you then, huh?"

"Ah, Jesus, Reno."

She lowered her voice but it didn't lessen the impact of her words. "You shot and killed a man and watched another one die. Do you really think you're such a stone cold operator you can walk away from something like that without it marking you? What do you know about post-traumatic stress?"

I held out both hands. "No shakes. No blurred vision. No headaches or hallucinations. No crying jags . . ."

"No nightmares?"

I let that pass but felt my heart racing. Jesus, was I sweating?

"Reno." She touched my hands gently. I dropped them back to my sides. "You've obviously been reading up on the subject so you have to know those symptoms don't begin to cover the whole list. Everybody reacts differently after they pull a trigger. Since June, I've seen this ferocious anger building in you. It blew tonight."

"Being thrown out of that bar was an option?"

"No, it wasn't. But don't tell me you haven't been itching for a fight. For months! Vinnie being in the hospital . . . don't tell me that's not affecting you. You need to take a step back, Reno. Report the story. Don't become part of it. Let me call Briggs."

"Tomorrow."

"What exactly do you accomplish if he pitches a firebomb through your window tonight?"

"Look at the story possibilities."

She stared at me and gave an exasperated sigh. "No, I was wrong. It's not post-traumatic stress. What was I thinking? It's just typical Reno-boneheadedness. Give me a break."

With that, she put both palms up in surrender and trudged away toward her room. Two big fat drops of rain smacked the ground in her wake.

CHAPTER FIFTEEN

The rain changed to bullets thwacking against the window of my room. I tumbled from sleep about four-thirty the next morning. Liquid tension started in my chest and suffused my body. I sat up in darkness and clutched the .45 like a good luck charm. I couldn't remember grabbing it. From the bedside table to my hands. How did that happen? Some sort of sleepwalking? Sleep-grabbing? The hammer was back. I felt for the safety with trembling fingers and cringed when I found it in the "off" position. I eased the hammer down, re-engaged the safety, and placed the weapon back on the table.

Best not mention that one to Sunny.

I couldn't recall having a nightmare or even dreaming. Or could I? My waking thoughts were bizarre and fearful, like those that trail a fever or too much booze. Night terrors. I smelled gasoline fumes and, with that, the belly-twisting, nose-wrinkling odor of charred flesh. It propelled me off the bed and over to the window to make sure the Channel 14 truck wasn't in flames.

Nothing moved in the parking lot except the rain dripping from the gutters and sluicing across the sidewalk to the driveway blacktop. The truck sat undisturbed, touched only by shadows. I knew either Al or Peter was probably fighting to stay awake at the window of their room, keeping an eye on things.

The room's dreary morning chill ate through my skin. I spent a couple of moments trying to coax heat from an ancient HVAC unit under the window. While it shuddered to life, I went to make use of the coffeemaker kit on the bathroom counter.

I showered. Somewhere in the process, my hands stopped shaking. The coffee brewed. It was ready when I was. I poured the first of the two cups the yellowed carafe held and went to check the truck again, then sat on the bed, towel wrapped around my waist.

What the hell was happening to me?

The combination of steam from the shower and whatever gunk lived inside the HVAC unit made the room smell of wet cat food and old sweat pants but it was warm enough. I clicked on a lamp. My eye caught the sheaf of Internet articles Jody had printed out for me about Pike Wescott. I paged through them and sipped my coffee, wondering if the maid had washed the cup, the pot, or, more likely, both in embalming fluid.

The earliest piece on Wescott came from a 1976 *Fortune* magazine story about "The Midwest's Mod Prodigy." It described him as a sixteen-year-old genius spending summer vacation after early graduation from high school working in the Research and Development section of Forge Technologies. It noted Wescott's "wrinkled Nehru jacket," "serious expression," and even the "worn pocket protector." The article went on to mention his patent for some kind of improvement to Forge's line of two-way radios. He was quoted describing changes he'd make to the company were he the chief executive officer. The article described him as a "brainiac with attitude." It talked about his politics: his nickname came from boarding school where he once made a speech calling for then-President Richard Nixon's "head on a pike."

The next article came from the *Chicago Tribune* two months later. It struck a far more somber note. "Parents of Prodigy Die in Auto Crash," read the headline. Wescott had been orphaned, but not for long. Within weeks, a follow-up report told me, he became the ward of "Falcon Ridge Millionaire Eldon Forge, 57,

Chairman and CEO of Forge Technologies, and Forge's second wife, Elaine, 24." I looked to make sure I'd read the ages correctly.

I skipped ahead. Purdue, and then an MBA from Northwestern's Kellogg program. Named president of Forge Technologies at twenty-three. Steady growth of the company. Name change to Forge Global Technologies to reflect entry into the international market. Old man Forge dead. Two more patents in Wescott's name. Notation in a couple of stories that he was a hands-on boss, more at home doing R and D work in his private lab than behind a desk. Even so, voted CEO at twenty-eight.

The chirp of the Nextel startled me before I could finish reading and just as I was pouring my second cup of coffee. I took a quick taste. Worse than the first.

"I don't know if this has anything to do with your story, dude," Yogi Elfman said, "but Wihega County's talking about a crime scene somewhere. They sound just as tight-assed about this as they did yesterday about that murder." He sounded awake and happy to face the day. Probably hadn't poured his coffee from a piss-yellow pot.

"Location?"

"I just heard the tail end of whatever it is. I'm rewinding tape now."

I poured the rest of the coffee down the drain. Then, as an afterthought, I unplugged the coffee maker and threw the whole setup into the wastebasket, making a mental note to consider doing an investigative piece on the health considerations of motel room java. Where's Juan Valdez when you need him?

"Reno? They're at Riverfront Drive and County Highway 52. The fire department's got divers out and a tow truck on the way. Somebody reported a car in the river."

"What kind?" I grabbed for my notebook. I'd written down what Lindsey was driving.

171

"Hang on . . . ah . . ." I heard the stutter of police radio traffic as he rewound the tape. "No indication. I guess the witness who called in was a fisherman who saw a vehicle floating on the surface. By the time the cops made it over there, it had gone under."

I started to feel another chill. "Do me a favor," I said, leaning into the tub to crank on the shower and add some heat and humidity to the room. "Beep Al. Have him gear up and meet me at the car in ten minutes."

I used the time to shave, towel off, and dress. Focused my thoughts on inconsequentials until I could get out of that damned room. Casual day, today. Chinos and a polo shirt under blue blazer and all under a treasured old Willis and Geiger raincoat. Lace-up Ecco boots, which are always a part of my ready kit. You learn quickly in this business to dress for the story, not success. Tilley hat with a brim wide enough that it was like wearing an umbrella. I was ready for anything our late September weather could throw at me.

Al's face, more droopy hound dog than I could remember seeing, told me he hadn't slept. He moved as though each joint protested and the camera wrapped in plastic under his arm had never been heavier. His eyes, though, were alert.

"You're thinking it's the girl?"

I glanced at him. "You, too?"

"Yogi said they're talking like they got a crime scene out there. Simple crash, drunk drives off the road into the water, they aren't gonna call it that. Why make more trouble for themselves? We gotta check it out. Stupid to roll over and go back to sleep."

"Sleep, huh? That what you were doing?"

"Manner of speaking."

The Falcon Ridge map guided us north out of the city, along part of Wihega County's high-tech corridor. Chain-link fence guarded long buildings of metal and glass that reflected the dull, slowly breaking morning. It appeared, however, that more than a few of the parking lots had thick wedges of grass growing up through cracks in the cement and the kiosks at the gates where guards normally would be stationed were as empty as the saloons in a ghost town.

We stopped at a mini-mart for coffee and I filled a plastic thermos, thinking ahead. The rain continued its drone on the Crown Vic's roof when we pulled out of the driveway.

We found the scene easily enough. Two pieces of fire equipment, electronic sirens warbling, sped past us as we left the mini-mart and we kept them in sight for about a mile. Their red lights reflected off the light fog that had arrived with the rain. When they turned off the road, we were about a half-mile behind. Al slowed. We were in more rural country now, and the businesses alongside the road reflected that. A farmer's co-op, propane gas company, junkyard, and commercial nursery sat on one side and there were woods opposite. The turnoff was a two-lane blacktop leading through the trees.

"Cops're gonna have a block point set up," he said. "D'you want me to cruise by and try to find another way in?"

I shook my head. "We could drive around in the fog all morning. Let's see if they're going to play games."

A Wihega County squad was angled across the road, light bar kaleidoscopically bright in the gray dawn. The deputy standing beside it waved us past, marking the Crown Vic as official, but Al pulled up short and leaned out the window.

"Don't want to get in under false pretenses," he smiled. "We're from Channel 14. Al Greco. This is Reno McCarthy."

The deputy was tall and dark featured, with a slight widow's peak and hair just starting to go gray. He stepped away from his squad, returning Al's grin as he leaned down to look in the window. The two men shook hands.

"How you doing?" He nodded toward me. "You're the one who's getting all the exclusive reports on the Hayden murder, aren't you? Is this part of that?"

"You tell us," I said.

"Wish I knew. I'm just supposed to make sure all the fire units know where to go. I 'preciate you not trying to skunk me."

"Can we drive in?"

"Don't see why not. Park behind the emergency vehicles and leave room in case anybody else shows up. Stay away from the divers. It's around that bend, about a mile, under the bridge."

Al held up the thermos, which the young deputy accepted with a surprised smile, and then we eased forward, following the road. The trees to our right thinned to nothing almost immediately and then the river appeared, down a grassy slope. It looked muddy and unappealing as it swirled past. The fog thickened about halfway out so the buildings on the opposite bank appeared only as ghostly images. The thermometer on the Crown Vic's dash read fifty-three.

The place where the car had gone into the water was about fifty yards downriver from the suspension bridge that carried I-90 toward the Wisconsin border. More than a dozen pieces of equipment, including three Wihega County–marked squad cars, fire trucks and engines, and a dive master's van were parked along either side of the road, and a group of firefighters and dive gear was spread out along the sloping shoreline. As we pulled up, four men in wetsuits muscled a rubber Zodiac boat off the back of a fire department utility truck and walked into the water with it. I could see two tie lines strung out as well and a red-and-white-striped scuba flag bobbed on the waves about twenty feet from shore. Divers would be under the surface at or near that point.

A deputy in a white shirt with sergeant's stripes on the sleeve looked up from talking into the microphone of his portable radio and broke away from the group near the water to walk toward us. I got out and met him at the front of the car.

"Don't mind you being here, but I can't let you leave the road or go near the team," he said. "And before you ask, no, I don't know what we've got."

"How did you get the call?"

"A fisherman across the river saw something floating. Coming across the bridge, one of my units identified it as a vehicle and called for backup. By the time we got down here . . ." He shrugged. "What you see is pretty much what we found. Alotta water. It's up to the divers now."

"We're looking for a girl named Lindsey Sears, driving a Jeep Sahara . . ."

He nodded, unsmiling but not unfriendly. "Yeah, I figured that's what brought you out. I'm not saying what or who we think is in there. What I will say is we got the Major Case squad coming and, when they get here, they'll probably want you gone. So if you're going to get your footage, you best do it quick."

Al had drifted up while we were talking and, as the sergeant went back to where the fire guys and extra divers were huddled together, he began to shoot the action. I leaned against the Crown Vic and watched.

For fifteen minutes, nothing happened. Then a buoy popped to the surface about a dozen yards from shore, followed by another. The Zodiac boat stopped moving and hovered between the buoys. I heard the crackle of chatter from a radio. Although it was too far away to understand what was being said, I could imagine the message. An image of Lindsey Sears as I'd seen her holding the frightened cat yesterday in Wiley's parking lot came to mind.

When I was a young reporter working at a small television station in Kansas, a friend and I met a couple of underage girls in a bar one night when I was on call. We spent a couple of hours with them until they realized it was nearly curfew and they needed to get home. They took off, a little drunk and still laughing, in an old MG convertible. We went back inside. A half an hour later, the station paged me with the report of a fatal crash on the highway south of town. As I heard the message, an odd, empty feeling came over me. I was suddenly certain that our two new friends were the victims.

I was right.

That same kind of realization now sent a chill down my spine, a feeling as dark and frightening as if a spectral being had walked out of the river and beckoned to me.

A heavy-duty diesel tow truck that had been parked along the shoulder of the road in the cluster of emergency vehicles backed down the slight slope and parked close to the water's edge. Two divers emerged from the water, grabbed the wrecker's hook, and dragged it with them into the river. The wrecker driver put wooden chocks behind his back wheels. By that time, Al had his camera set on a tripod at the front of the car and was letting the tape roll without stopping. I looked at my watch, surprised to see that an hour and a half had passed since I'd awakened to the sound of the rain. It had fallen off to a fine mist and now a light breeze was spraying the moisture into my face. I pulled down my hat brim. Al hunched over his camera. The hood of his yellow rain slicker obscured his face.

The tow truck's engine rumbled and the line into the water drew taut. Everyone backed away, giving the driver room to maneuver.

I heard vehicles approaching and turned to see two unmarked squads followed by a black Chevy Suburban headed toward us. The Major Case squad. I immediately focused my attention back on the river's edge, willing the wrecker driver to reel his line in faster. As I heard car doors slam behind me, the water churned for a moment and the bumper and then the back section of a vehicle rose into view. I saw what I was looking for immediately. A tailgate with a spare tire racked across it. Out of the corner of my eye, I saw Al give a quick thumbs up. He could see through his telephoto lens what I couldn't from my angle.

The Jeep emblem.

Al kept rolling as the tow truck winched the black Jeep Sahara out of the river. It slid to shore with surprisingly little resistance, water draining from the undercarriage as mud drooled off its tires. Even before it came to rest on the grassy slope, three firefighters and a cop rushed forward with a tarp held high and the sergeant headed for Al, making the universal gesture for "cut" with the edge of his palm across his throat. I saw the small form sprawled sideways across the Jeep's front seats.

At the same moment, a hand grabbed my shoulder and hauled me around. I didn't resist. Until I saw who the hand belonged to.

". . . the fuck are you doing here?" My old friend, Commander Duvall, snarled, then shouted past me, "Sergeant Dombrowski! What's the media doing inside this crime scene?"

Dombrowski stepped away from where he'd been talking to Al. His expression carefully in neutral he said, "What's the problem, boss?"

"I want to know why you allowed the media to contaminate this scene."

Duvall was out of uniform in jeans and a Schaumburg Flyers T-shirt, his gold sheriff's star displayed in a leather holder that hung from a chain around his neck. I smelled alcohol on his breath.

"Technically, sir, they're not in the scene. I didn't see any harm in letting them get their pictures. They haven't strayed from where I put them."

Duvall didn't look appeased. "I may be off duty, Dombrowski, but this is still my watch, not yours. You want to be a TV star, transfer to days. Get these people out of here."

Dombrowski showed no reaction to the dressing down as he glanced in my direction. If anything, his tone was apologetic. "You heard the man."

"Something you don't want the public to see, Commander?" I asked.

"Will you hear better if I speak louder? Get outta here!" Boozy breath washed over me.

"I suppose now isn't the time to ask why you made the coroner wait an hour to get access to the body yesterday. Is that why you want us to leave? So you can pull the same stunt again?"

He looked as if I'd slapped him. "All right, that's it! You're under arrest." He stepped forward and grabbed for my arm, but I'd anticipated him and moved back out of range. He lunged at me again and, again, I dodged, keeping my hands visibly away from him and at shoulder height. This time he slipped on the wet grass and fell to his knees. By the time he scrambled up, Sergeant Dombrowski had inserted himself between us, facing Duvall.

"Hey, boss, this doesn't need to get out of hand. They're leaving. It's not a problem."

Duvall's eyes homed in on me. "Nobody accuses me of sabotaging an investigation and just walks away!" he bellowed. "That man is under arrest. I want him in handcuffs, Sergeant. That's an order."

More plainclothes guys were coming toward us now and a couple of them had their hands on their weapons. I glanced behind me. Two uniforms had scrambled up from where they'd been helping the firefighters secure the Jeep and were trotting

178

our way as well. I left my hands where everybody could see them.

"If it wasn't you who gave the order, who was it? Your chief? Or maybe it was Zak?"

"Goddamn it, McCarthy. Shut up and get in your car or I'll bust you myself," Dombrowski snapped. He had a forearm up on Duvall's chest and the other in his face, like he was playing frontcourt in basketball. I wondered what that was going to cost him.

The thought made me retreat, almost running into Al, who had his camera tucked under his arm but pointed right at us. "Can't leave you alone for a second," he said.

With Duvall still loudly demanding that someone take us into custody, I slipped into the Crown Vic's passenger seat and closed the door. Al joined me and fired up the engine to make a quick U-turn. Two detectives and Dombrowski had hold of Duvall's arms and a husky uniform guy was patting his back as we swept past them. His eyes never left mine.

"What was that all about? Was he lit or am I just imagining the Jack Daniels?" Al asked.

"Nope. Off duty and trashed. Dombrowski looked as surprised to see him as I was."

"So what the hell are they doing giving him access to a crime scene?"

I shook my head. No answer for that one.

"Goddamn hayseeds," Al said.

With ten minutes to go until airtime, we were set up on the other side of the river, opposite the scene. We could see the coroner's SUV backed up to the side of the Jeep, the tow truck still parked behind it and a smattering of vehicles beyond that. As soon as the Wihega County guys saw Peter putting up the microwave mast on the live truck, they scrambled to put the tarp back in place. It didn't matter. I don't like body shots any more than the management of most local TV stations, especially Channel 14. Elise Bascomb Hanratty, having seen enough when her husband and father were killed, despises the idea of showing even a body-bagged or blanket-covered corpse on the air. Body shots that made it on the air were a firing offense at Channel 14.

The tarp, however, gave the scene a nice, mysterious, what-are-you-hiding feel. Even better, we once again obtained permission of the landowner whose property we were on to use his waterfront yard. That easily deflected the two deputies sent to chase us off.

We opened our 6 a.m. piece with a steady close-up of the live action, and then Al drew back to me in stand-up at the water's edge with the scene over my shoulder. I described the action I'd observed while Al's video rolled of the Jeep being winched from the water. The body in the front seat wasn't visible.

By 6:30, as our competitors' helicopters hovered and other live crews began arriving, there was nothing left for them to shoot. Seeing us had apparently galvanized the recovery teams and the Major Cases detectives into completing their work in record time. They'd departed before the rest of the media arrived. Hooray for us.

Before my last live shot, I confirmed with Johnnie Perkins that the body in the Jeep was Lindsey's. She sounded sad.

"Her mother and I grew up together. She told me she did not worry when Lindsey failed to come home last night. She was a wild child. Spending time with the wrong crowd. The self-destructive triad: drinking, drugs, promiscuity. Sweet child but she just made so many poor choices." She paused.

"You are a good listener as always, Reno. I always find I am saying more than is prudent to you because I know you will be discreet."

I glanced at my watch. I had four minutes to my live shot. Al was waving and pointing to the camera. "I'd appreciate anything you can tell me about the investigation."

"I am a stubborn woman. I have leave under law to act independently of the police as long as I do not compromise their work. Obviously, I cannot tell you what caused her death until after the autopsy. You can quote me as saying our preliminary examination shows Lindsey suffered a broken neck. Off the record and for your information only, I think we are also going to find she was sexually assaulted."

"Broken neck from the crash or before she went into the water?" I was scribbling as fast as I could to get her direct quotes. "Off the record is fine on that, too."

"Reno McCarthy!" she chided and a little humor came back into her voice. "You know I cannot go there."

"Hey, it's a reasonable question. She was a witness in a murder case who disappeared on her way to talk to the suspect's lawyer."

"I do not dispute it is a reasonable question. It is just not appropriate for me to speculate, even off the record. Telling you what I observed this morning is one thing. You know we will have to get her on the table to determine the full nature of her injuries. Why not ask your police sources if they think she was kidnapped and assaulted last night and her body dumped this morning?"

"Are you telling me . . . ?"

"I am not telling you anything," she said.

Way to go, Johnnie.

CHAPTER SIXTEEN

In Pike Wescott's office, the plasma television in the cherry wood cabinet across from his desk displayed a picture of the Wauconda River where a tow truck hauled a black Jeep out of the water. A banner at the bottom of the screen read "Breaking News." Wescott stopped tapping computer keys and punched the TV remote instead.

"... *Wihega County Coroner JohnElla Perkins identifies the Jeep's driver as twenty-two-year-old Falcon Ridge resident Lindsey Sears . . .*" A small rectangle next to the banner identified the reporter as Reno McCarthy.

The river scene was replaced with video showing a young woman crying as she was led to a police cruiser. Wescott realized he'd seen the same shot on the news the night before. Ice clutched his heart.

"... *Sears is shown in this video shot yesterday during the arrest of Lucas Bremmer, a suspect in the Trey Hayden murder. Sears was a friend of both young men. In fact, Sears disappeared last night on her way to speak to Bremmer's lawyer and be interviewed by Channel 14 news. Sources tell us police are investigating the possibility she was kidnapped and killed sometime during the night. It's believed the Jeep, with her body inside, was dumped into the river early this morning . . .*"

Christ! Wescott glanced at the atomic clock on his desk then took out his cellular and auto-dialed a number that was never busy, and would never go to voice mail.

"Yes, Robert."

"Goddamn it. Why the girl?"

The briefest pause, followed by a sigh. "If you must discuss this over the phone—"

"The phone's encrypted. And, yes, you're goddamn right I *'must discuss this'!*"

"I presume it was caution. Elimination of potential risk. Unlike you, I try not to look over shoulders after I delegate authority."

"She was just a teenager!"

"As were you, remember? A teenager who caused a great deal of heartache," the voice reminded sharply. "She and Bremmer saw things they shouldn't have."

"What? What did they see that would justify—"

"We don't need to go there."

"Yes we do." Wescott stood up and began to pace. "I have a right to know just how much jeopardy your 'help' has caused me."

"Why's that, Robert? So you can decide whether to flee the jurisdiction? Going on the run in that Escalade of yours? Have some first-class tickets to Uganda stashed somewhere? Or are you going to hang out with the orphan kids in Cambodia in those nice new shelters you built for them? I doubt those have the five-star accommodations you're used to, do they?"

If his caller only knew, Wescott thought, how he detested his lifestyle. The parties. The *obligations*. The trappings of wealth were just that. Traps. As though to underline the thought he yanked open his shirt collar and loosened his tie. Too warm. Where was the goddamn air conditioning?

The voice continued. "She was going to speak to that reporter. McCarthy. He's quite the bulldog. Who do you think would have been harmed most by that?"

"Are others going to die?"

No answer. Silence now, so complete he could have been listening to a room with all of the air removed. The meaning couldn't have been clearer to him. He tried again. Tried to put the whipsaw of command into his voice, too.

"No! This stops now. You understand me? Tell your people. The killing has to stop. I never intended—"

"You buy your ticket and you take your chance. Beyond those ivy-covered walls around your house, out here in the world, we call that 'life'! Let me handle the details, Robert."

Wescott folded the phone and set it aside.

I can't let anyone else die because of me, he thought.

Chapter Seventeen

After telling Al and Jody about Johnnie Perkins's tip, I said it was time to give Grum to Briggs. I didn't voice my darker thought. Like, if we'd pointed him out for Briggs when he asked, would Lindsey Sears still be alive?

Jody picked up on what I failed to say, however.

"Do you think Grum killed her? To keep her from talking to the lawyer?"

"I don't know," I said. "I do know we had a whack job hanging out watching us yesterday, and last night our live truck got firebombed. A couple of kids may have seen the same whack job in the area right before the truck was torched. If Briggs is any good, and I suspect he is, he'll have talked to those kids, too. But I want to get on record with him that we're willing to help. Might turn out to be a two-way street."

"But shouldn't we be talking to the police?"

Al put a hand on her shoulder. "You've seen these bozos in action. What do you think? So far, we got a patrol commander who shows up half in the bag at a crime scene, a detective commander who's playing hard ass, and a public information guy who hit on you. You think Wihega County wants to cooperate with us? At most, they'll pat us on the head while they're kicking our ass out the door. Reno's right. This Briggs seems like the one to approach."

"Okay. But we need a fresh angle for the noon show. I say we go after Emily Hayden. She's the closest thing we have to a witness. Also," she pointed at me, "what about this second gun? You think you can find someone to confirm there was one and that Hayden fired it before we go live at twelve?"

While she called Briggs and worked on getting the Haydens to talk to us, I moved to the Crown Vic, checked my watch, and made a quick call of my own. Ray hadn't said what time they were going to install the stent. I wanted to see if the procedure was under way.

The call went to voice mail. I didn't leave a message.

Trey Hayden having a gun bugged me. Where had he gotten the damn thing? Was it for self-protection and, if so, who was he afraid of? Was he a gun buff? And finally, though it might seem trivial to anyone but me, why in hell a .38 and not a semiauto?

I come from a family background that scorned revolvers, even though that was what the Chicago Police Department required my dad to carry. He and Vinnie both preferred the heavy, military-issue, Colt .45 automatic, and each wore one as a backup to their issued weapon, gun belts perpetually sagging under the weight of all that firepower. They encouraged me to follow their lead from the very first time I held a handgun.

My dad taught me to shoot when I was nine years old, near the cabin we rented that summer near Eagle River, Wisconsin. Vinnie came up and stayed with us for a couple of days, and together they found a small garbage dump with a high berm of dirt all around that turned out to be a perfect pistol range. I'll always remember the thrill that first day of watching my dad snap the small brass .22 cartridges into the clip of a long-barreled Colt he bought from a store in town. He showed me how the clip fitted into the bottom of the grip and how to ratchet the slide back to seat the first round in the chamber. He pointed to the safety and insisted I keep it engaged unless the barrel was pointed at the target. Then, he very carefully handed the little automatic to me and helped me arrange my hands on the handle so one supported the other.

"Squeeze the trigger, son. Don't yank on it," he said.

My first shot clipped the side of the Folgers coffee can fifteen feet away and sent it spinning into the thick overhang of dirt behind it. Hands still outstretched, I glanced over my shoulder at Dad. He'd been in the process of uncapping the flask he carried in his coat whenever we left the cabin. For the moment, however, he appeared to have forgotten about lifting the whiskey to his mouth.

"Thatsa boy, pal!" he said, grin as wide as I'd ever seen. "That's my boy!"

Vinnie gave me thumbs up. He was smiling, too. My whole body radiated pride.

We went "plinking," as they called it, every day for the remainder of our vacation. When we got home, the two of them occasionally took me along to the old police range in the basement under the stands at Soldier Field where they shot every month. By the age of twelve, I'd fired every handgun both of them owned along with a variety of esoteric backup weapons carried by their fellow cops. I ended up preferring an automatic over a revolver the way most all of them did.

A blast of cool, moist air off the river brought me back to the present. With the proliferation of automatics on TV, in the movies and magazines, and their ready availability on the underground market, I suspected Trey would have had to specifically go looking for a revolver to find one. Sure they were out there, but any self-respecting black market gun dealer would not offer them as a first choice. Why would anybody want to limit themselves to six shots when everyone else had at least twelve or fourteen, sometimes more?

Then the final question. Where was the gun now?

I considered who might know all of the answers. Lucas? I could have Moira ask him on her jail visit. Emily Hayden, maybe, and we were working to find out. Other friends? Moira might have some information on that, and I needed to call her anyway.

She picked up on the first ring. "You don't check your messages very often, do you?" she snapped. "I've been trying to call you since seven."

"What's up?"

"You tell me. The one witness who might have gotten my client out of jail is dead, and the cops are telling all you media that it was probably related to her history of drug dealing. I could have used a heads up from you instead of having to find out by watching TV."

"I leave my cell off when I'm doing live shots. What's this about her dealing?"

"Callahan just appeared on Seven and one of my colleagues saw him on Two a few minutes ago."

Son of a bitch, I thought. The cops had done a briefing but hadn't included us. Jody started toward me. I held up a hand to stop her and turned away, hugging the phone to my ear.

"I thought you said Lindsey's record was clear?"

"The only thing I found was one misdemeanor pot bust two years ago when she was seventeen. C'mon, Reno, that wouldn't have been an extensive record even back in the fifties. Her mother confirms it was her only arrest, too."

"So the cops are manufacturing this?"

"They have to be. I take it they didn't give you the same information?"

"No. And I'll deal with that. But you need to lean on Lucas for a couple of things."

"What?"

"He got Wiley to give him ammunition for a .38 revolver and told him it was going to Trey. See if he knew where Trey got the gun and why he had it."

188

"Wait. You confirmed Trey Hayden had a gun and you didn't call me?"

"We found out about the ammo last night when we were looking for Lindsey—"

"As Lucas's attorney, that's a fairly important fact I should know, don't you think? Especially since the police and state's attorney's office both say no gun existed!"

"Moira, I'm not your errand boy. I said I'd share when I could. That's what I'm doing."

"So I'm your little errand-girl? I thought what's-her-name with the tits took care of that kind of thing for you."

There's a patch of skin on the back of my neck that gets warm when I'm angry. It felt as though someone had touched a match to it. "Will you talk to Lucas about this stuff or get me in so I can ask him?"

Her hesitation lasted for a three-count. "Fuck you, McCarthy." Click.

My anger exploded. Pinpricks of light flashed at the edges of my vision, and I had to resist the urge to slam the phone against the dash. I gripped the door handle instead and hung on until the fury receded.

Eyes closed, taking deep breaths, I thought about Trey Hayden's DeeBree coworkers. Maybe not friends, exactly, but they might have some idea what he had been thinking about in the days immediately prior to his death. Why he'd felt the need to have a gun and where he'd gotten it. It was a start. I went to get the keys to the Crown Vic from Al, intending to drive to the county building and ask some questions. Jody stopped me.

"Investigator Briggs wants you to meet him at police headquarters. Now."

The Wihega County Police had offices on the first three floors of an angular, seven-story building across a small quadrangle from the courthouse. The two structures were connected by an enclosed pedway three floors up that led into the jail and allowed deputies to bring prisoners into court without taking them outside. I went through the public entrance on the ground floor and presented myself to a uniformed receptionist. She nodded without speaking when I gave her my name and whom I had come to see and pointed to a row of interlocked plastic chairs up against a window that overlooked the street. I waited, standing and looking through the glass at nothing in particular until Briggs stepped out of an elevator and motioned to me.

He'd changed out of his coveralls and now wore scuffed work boots, jeans, a lightweight flannel shirt, and a sport coat that looked like it had seen a few years' worth of better days. We shook hands as the elevator doors closed and it began to rise. He looked and sounded uncomfortable.

"Thanks for coming in. When your producer called we were about to reach out to you."

"Is that right?"

He swiped a hand one way across his beard and then the other. "Couple things came up. Let's wait 'til we get upstairs."

We stepped off on the third floor and he led me down a corridor past a warren of cubbyhole offices to a door marked "Detective Division." I got a bad feeling from that. It got worse when Commander Teague appeared and pointed toward the open door of yet another room. This one had a sign that said "Interrogation 1." I stopped short, causing Briggs to bump into me.

I flashed back to a Vinnie-ism, this one from a ride-along during high school: when the bully comes after you, get in the first punch.

"No," I said.

"Sir?" Briggs said. "We need you to—"

I glanced from him to Teague. I raised my voice and addressed Teague.

"Am I here to offer a statement or be questioned as a suspect, Commander?" There were two men and a woman seated at the other desks, and they all paused in what they were doing to stare at me.

"Just step into the room, McCarthy. Don't make a federal case out of it," Teague said.

"If I'm a witness, talk to me in an office. Ask me if I want coffee. Make me feel welcome and we'll have a nice chat. You put me in there," I pointed at the sign. "I'm lawyering up. And I want to make the call right now."

Briggs cleared his throat. "There's really no problem. We just want to clear—"

"I'm happy to help you. If I'm sitting across a desk from you in somebody's office."

"For Christ's sake, it's an interview room, not the death house at Stateville," Teague said.

"I get claustrophobic in rooms without windows when I'm surrounded by guys wearing guns and hard ons," I said. I thought I heard a snicker.

Commander Teague pointed to another doorway, waved his hand like a maitre'd, and said, "Please, Mr. McCarthy. Join us for some conversation, won't you? Would you like coffee or do you prefer latte?"

We crowded into a space roughly the size of a double closet but with a nice window offering a limited view of downtown Falcon Ridge and the low clouds approaching from the west. The rain had started again. The drops formed into worm shapes as they hit the glass and squiggled down.

Teague went to his desk and sat behind a barrier of family pictures. Briggs leaned his big frame against the door, ensuring I wouldn't make a break for it. I got the seat of honor in front of the desk, where both of them could watch my every twitch, and I could better see Teague's photo collection. His wife was an attractive brunette with tightly coiffed hair who wore a sheriff's police uniform in one of the shots and stood in front of what looked like a school in another. His daughter looked like a serious ten- or eleven-year old. In several of the photos, the three of them were in church settings. In one, however, Teague and Theo Zak stood in front of a podium, shaking hands. Part of a banner behind them read ". . . hega Leadership Council."

"Just for the record, Mr. McCarthy," Teague began, "this is an informational interview, nothing more. The firebombing of your truck may be coincidental to the Hayden murder, so I asked Inspector Briggs to keep our Major Case Task Force in the loop of that investigation."

Briggs jumped right in. "Your producer, Miss Taggart, tells us you think a gentleman by the name of Duane Grum set fire to your remote truck. You have any thoughts as to why he might do something like that?"

"The why is for you guys to figure out. We saw him a couple of times yesterday. Morning, afternoon, and while I was doing my live shot at six. Given what people are telling us about him, I thought we should pass along his name."

He smiled. "And what are they telling you?"

"He has a history of violence, as you know. For another, he was seen in the immediate vicinity before the truck blew up."

"I see." Briggs's tone suggested none of this was new information. "Now, if you saw him at six, he would've had to have been prepared with the gasoline and bottles. Already decided what he was going to do, just looking for the right opportunity. Did you have any kind of conflict with him earlier in the day that might have set him off?"

I told him about our brief encounter on the path.

"But the truck that was targeted . . . you weren't in that one, were you?"

"No."

"Do all your mini-cam trucks look the same?"

"Yes."

Briggs consulted his notes. Teague took over.

"Was Leo Griffith one of the people who told you about Grum?" Briggs didn't quite scowl at the interruption but he sure wasn't pleased.

"No comment."

"What were you doing at Wiley's last night after you left Griffith's place?"

"Reporting."

He glanced up at Briggs.

"If you don't have any other questions for Mr. McCarthy, would you excuse us?" Briggs frowned and went out, closing the door behind him. Teague fastened his gaze on me, as though he was trying to figure out what approach might work best. I sat there and kept the smile.

After a moment, he made a V out of his hands and aimed it at me. "Cards on the table, all right? Everybody recognizes you have the right to report the news, Mr. McCarthy. I'm not about to tell you to stop. That wouldn't be constitutional, would it? But you don't have the right to interfere in my homicide case. We investigate. You report what we give you. That's how it works."

"Basic difference in definition. Reporting requires getting to the truth. One person's interference is another's fact-finding."

"You don't think we're telling the truth?"

"Do you really want me to answer that, Commander?"

He reddened. "You withheld crucial information about a suspect in this case until you felt like turning it over. You interviewed witnesses who gave you a suspect description, and you didn't bother to pass that on in a timely manner. In my book, that's interference."

I leaned forward. "Knock off the bullshit, Teague. If you know about the kids, you got the same information we did. If you know we went to Griffith's place last night it's because you did too. I'm guessing you were trying to hook up Grum because you think he had something to do with the Hayden murder. Or you're afraid he does."

"What the hell does that mean?"

"Are you sure you've got the right man in jail?"

It was Teague's turn to clam up. He and I traded "fuck you" stares, instead. After a moment of that, though, he reinvented his grin, eased back in his swivel chair, and clasped both hands at the top of his head. Like he'd just remembered something.

"Suppose I told you the guy you punched in the nose out there at Wiley's is ready to swear out a battery complaint against you. How would that affect your 'fact-finding'?"

"A threat like that is kind of bush, don't you think?"

"I don't know, McCarthy. Guy like you, the stuff you've gotten away with in the past, it could get pretty nasty if the right judge caught the case. If he knew your background, that is. And we've got some pretty tough judges. Work close with them, too."

If they slapped charges against me, with my recent history, Chucky would yank me off the story faster than the judge could set my bail. But Teague knew his threat had no teeth. Just like his crack about withholding information. Filing any kind of case against me would only cause more of a media spotlight to be focused on Wihega County. No way would he or his handlers want that.

I realized, then, what he'd intended to accomplish by drawing me into his office instead of letting Briggs ask his few questions over the phone. He wanted me to know that he was the Big Dog. And to growl a warning to back off.

I said, "Since you have such a close relationship with the courts and are so honest with the media, I'm surprised you're allowing your spokesman to make misstatements of fact about Lindsey Sears."

"What misstatements? She was dealing rock cocaine."

"And you can substantiate that with . . . what? Surveillance reports? Intelligence memos? Show me the paperwork."

He smiled. "Confidential informant."

"Callahan claims she had a record of drug arrests. She was busted once, for pot. You're doing a lot of spin to make a dead girl look bad. Makes me wonder why."

"One arrest, huh? Imagine that. Callahan is a little zealous. He must have misread the girl's file. I'll say something to him. Now, if there's nothing else?"

Imperious. As though this meeting was my idea and he had other things to do. Or, behind his bland stare, he was uncomfortable enough with my questions he wanted me gone. I rose.

"What was Hayden doing with a .38 revolver? Who's got it now?"

I thought I detected a slight hesitation before the condescending smile came back. "You know, you reporters always think you can do two things better than the experts. One is coach the Cubs. The other is solve murders. Whoever's spreading that second gun theory, and I think I know who it is, is a pinhead. You tell him that for me."

"Sure. But you didn't answer my question."

"Fuck you, McCarthy. Get out of here before I book your ass for interfering with my day."

I left the county police building and walked across the little square to the courthouse. The fountain burbled away happily despite the mist and my foul mood. The bench in front of the memorial wall was empty this morning. The cold snap now seemed ominous to me, a warning of winter while late summer flowers still bloomed. Few images are more depressing to a warm weather person than the sight of snow falling on roses while the lawn's still green. I still could smell the roses, however, as I stepped into the courthouse lobby. Maybe fall wasn't quite all gone.

The guards on the metal detectors ran me through twice, even though I turned out my pockets and hadn't beeped, and then one of them scanned me with a handheld wand before letting me pass. As I was stuffing billfold and notebook back where they belonged, I looked up to see Moira standing just outside the jury coordinator's office, briefcase in hand. Today she was the essence of lawyer chic in a conservative blue suit and just a touch of makeup. She offered a wry smile.

"Got your ego all safely tucked away?" she asked.

"Nope. I wear it proudly right out there for all to see."

"Hmm. I never noticed." She turned and began walking. I fell into step with her.

"If you show me where they keep the coffee, I'll buy," I said.

"You presume both that I'm willing to go with you and that it's wise for us to be seen together. Oh, and that I drink coffee. Which I don't. Nonetheless, I could use some iced tea."

She gestured toward the stairs. I followed her.

There was a chemical smell in the stairwell, and when we emerged into the courthouse basement we found it filled with workmen installing a new floor. Yellow tape surrounded five-gallon containers of adhesive that lined the wall and three guys in plastic facemasks were on their knees laying wood laminate. Farther away, two other men pulled up old squares of linoleum and junked them in plastic bags. We stepped gingerly around the roped-off areas, staying where they'd unrolled plastic sheeting over sections of exposed concrete. Even so, before we entered the snack bar, Moira reached out and grasped my shoulder for support as she stooped to flick something gooey off the bottom of her shoe. When she straightened, her right breast brushed against my arm. She didn't seem to notice. I did.

Arturo's Café was a wide, bright room with green tile floors and booths instead of tables. Serapes hung along one wall and mirrors the other. There were more people than I expected to see in the hour before noon, most in suits and with briefcases either resting on the floor or open on the table in front of them. Lawyers, undoubtedly fresh from the morning's docket calls or on early lunch recess, down here plotting plea agreements or working out settlement offers. The few courthouse worker bees I saw in shirtsleeves or business casual seemed to just be stopping by, grabbing a coffee and heading back out again. One group looking a little shell-shocked sat in a corner by themselves.

Moira told me to order for her and stopped to chat with them. I ordered her tea and a Dr Pepper for me from a smiling Hispanic man with a thick mustache and one wandering eye who asked if I wanted a sandwich or salad. His nametag identified him as Arturo. I'd noticed a basket of homemade chocolate chip cookies and selected two of them. I might not get to the bottom of Lindsey or Trey's murder while I was in Falcon Ridge, but by God I was going to enjoy all the fresh bakery I could get my hands on.

As I settled into an empty booth, I noticed Wozniak leaning against the wall near the soft drink machine in earnest conversation with a guy in hardhat and jeans. After a moment, they shook hands and parted. Wozniak ambled my way. I thought about asking if he'd had fun at Wiley's the night before, but when I saw his sly grin, I decided to wait.

"Heard somebody firebombed one of your trucks last night. Got a quote for me?"

"You know the local mopes. What's your take on it?"

"That's pretty easy. I'd say somebody doesn't want you here."

Brilliant, these newspaper guys. "Any idea who that might be?"

"I guess it could be anybody. Last time you TV people came in and muddled around, all the stories were about how Wihega County was going to become the Vegas of the Midwest with mobsters everywhere. Right afterward Springfield voted to hold up our casino project. Local businesses didn't like that."

"So you're saying the chamber of commerce put out a hit on our live truck? Seems a little extreme."

He made as if to slide into the booth but then stopped. I hadn't invited him to sit.

"I don't know. Lot of people feel this county needs that casino."

"Even if the mob moves in with it?"

Wozniak laughed. "Who's an angel these days? You TV people create these reality show heroes one week and tear them down the next. We beat up politicians for doing the same things in their bedrooms all of us do, or would if we could. So what if a guy's got friends who have other friends who get into trouble sometimes? That doesn't make him the Godfather."

"You talking about Theo Zak?"

"Whoever. If lowlifes move in with the casinos, you police 'em up afterward. You don't screw a whole county out of the revenue."

"Guess I know where you stand on the subject."

His hand went into a jacket pocket and came out with a cigarette. He stuck it in his mouth and glanced up at the No Smoking signs all over the room.

"Hey, I don't have opinions. I'm a journalist. You ask anybody in this room, they'll tell you all my stories about the casino were objective as hell. Pissed some people off, too."

"Anybody so pissed off they set fire to the paper?"

"We lost a few advertisers. But you people come to town, it stirs up everybody. Sometimes we get dinged, too. You people got it a little worse, that's all."

"Our photographer's in critical condition, Wozniak. That's a shade more than 'a little worse.' "

"Right, right. What I mean is usually after the Chicago media takes a swipe, the business community holds us responsible. Like it's our fault. Makes the job that much tougher."

"What was it Joe Pulitzer said? 'A newspaper has no friends'?"

His eyes skittered away to where Moira appeared to be winding up her conversation with the shell-shocked family. After another moment, he gave me a nod and wandered toward the exit, slapping his reporter's notebook against his leg.

I was two sips into my Dr Pepper when Moira slipped into the booth.

"Client's family," she said. "They just saw their kid for the first time since he's been in custody. They can't understand why the judge won't let him out on bail."

I nodded, pushed a cookie toward her. She touched it with a finger.

"He's a third-time DUI. Two nights ago, he swipes Daddy's car and runs a squad that was chasing him off the road. Nobody hurt but he was out on bail for his second DUI. Judge Slovak finally got the message."

"You sound like a prosecutor."

"That's because I'm not in court. In court, I said something like, 'Your Honor, this is a fine young man with a serious problem. He needs to be with his family and arranging for treatment of his illness, not in a jail cell.' " There was self-mocking humor in her eyes. She inclined her head in the direction Wozniak had gone and lifted her iced tea.

"What did The Worm want?"

"A quote for his story about the truck firebombing. Ended up telling me local businesses blame the Chicago media for killing the casino project."

"I don't know about that but the community was pretty bitter when Springfield tabled it." She took a sip of her tea. "A casino would solve a lot of our problems."

I thought about the empty-looking buildings and the grass-filled parking lots I'd seen on the way to that morning's crime scene. "What happened to Wihega County's magic formula that kept the economy cranking?"

She laughed. "It worked right up until our lovely county board decided playing lapdog to billion-dollar companies was going to bankrupt us. When Zak was board president they could afford to ease off on some of the zoning restrictions or maybe agree to go halfzies on infrastructure improvements in order to attract the business in the first place. Phase in property taxes gradually. Being paternal like that is great when you have money in the bank. When you don't . . ." She waggled her hand.

"Economy starts to slide and the good guy landlord has to up the rent?" I said.

"Exactly. Some folks say we held on a little longer than most. I think it was smoke and mirrors. Two of the companies out on Tech Row, when their incentives ran out and the county wouldn't negotiate a renewal? They just picked up and moved to Mexico. The ones that stayed seem to be doing okay, but they really cut their work forces. Except for FGT. You talk about a magic bullet, they seem to have it."

Forge Global Technologies. Wihega County's hometown answer to Motorola. A smaller yet very eager multinational, high-tech communications company.

Moira looked past me and lifted her chin. "Well. Speak of the devil. And I mean that literally." I craned my head around.

I remembered Theo Zak as a sharp-tongued old guy in his mid-sixties. I counted and realized he would be past seventy now, hair grayer and thinning yet stylishly cut. A deep tan showed on his scalp, face, and arms. White slacks and muted madras shirt played well against the dark skin and gave him a vibrant glow. He walked slowly into Arturo's using a rubber-tipped cane to guide his progress. His gait allowed him to see everyone and to glad-hand at virtually every table he passed. The closer he came, though, other waypoints of age became apparent. What had been an ascetic face was sunken in at the cheeks, as often happens when teeth are removed and not replaced. His laugh, once booming and forceful, now sounded like he was trying to clear his throat.

I saw no surreptitious handing over of documents or envelopes filled with cash. When he spoke to the men in the booth behind us, the conversation carried no undertones of scheming or devilish plots. All I overheard was the typical stuff older men say to younger acquaintances.

"How's business, Jeffery?"

"Just fine, sir."

"Give my regards to your wonderful dad. Michael, I saw your promotion in the paper. Full partner! I'm proud of you."

"Thank you, sir."

He reached our booth and gave Moira a serene smile. "Why, if it isn't the crusading defense attorney. How are you, my dear?" When he glanced at me, his smile seemed to dim for just a moment. I thought he was about to say something but, at that moment, Arturo swept out from behind the counter and greeted him in Spanish. Zak responded and they moved away.

Moira finished emptying a packet of sugar into her tea. " 'Crusading defense attorney' my ass. You watch now. The lemmings will start to flock."

Arturo led Zak to a booth and helped him sit down. Zak slid in with his back to the wall.

"Speaking of lemmings, fill me in on Jack Wiley."

"Um, let's see. He was a bailiff when I was a law student. By the time I started practicing, he'd become a gopher for Zak in the state's attorney's office. He drove for him when Zak became board president. Why?"

"Now he fronts the bar for Zak?"

"You tell me. The county approved Wiley's expansion even though the place is a building code nightmare and the neighbors made a huge protest. As soon as the build-out was finished, Zak started holding fundraisers there."

"We saw some dealing last night. And the word is that Lucas and Wiley had a little drug thing going."

Frowning, she put her tea aside and took a legal-sized file folder from her briefcase. Bremmer's name was in the upper corner. Uncapping a roller-tip pen she began to scratch on a sheet of paper within.

"It's common knowledge you can get about anything you want at Wiley's. But Lucas a dealer? That halo I keep trying to hang over his head is looking more tilted by the minute, isn't it?"

"Is Wiley's wide open because the cops wink everything away?"

She didn't look up. "That's the rumor."

"Here's another one. It's a good bet Grum's on Wiley's payroll. Or has been. I'm not ready to say Lucas is innocent but in a scenario that included him and Grum, who would you see as more likely to pull a trigger?"

This time she met my eyes. "Dear God." She passed a hand through her hair. I thought she paled a bit as well but that could just have been the lighting.

"This is . . . great stuff, Reno. I'll ask him about Grum. And Zak. I'll ask him about the gun you mentioned, too. Sorry I went off on you this morning. I blew at one of my police contacts, too. When I saw my case going to hell on television . . ."

"Forget it."

"And while we're on the second gun theory," she made another note, "I'll check to see if anybody thought to swab

Trey's hands for GSR. Not that I don't believe Espy, but I'd rather not call him as a witness unless I have to."

I drank more of my Dr Pepper. As Moira predicted, a parade of supplicants was making its way to Zak's booth. I didn't see any ring kissing and that surprised me. Just an old man visiting with old friends. Occasionally, a white wall phone hanging above the booth rang and Zak would reach over and answer it. For a guy who claimed to be retired, it looked to me like Theo Zak still had an office in the courthouse.

"What are you going to do while I'm conferring with my client?" Moira asked.

"See if DeBree will give me a list of the other guys on Trey's crew."

"To what purpose?"

"If Lucas doesn't know where Trey got the gun, maybe they'll have some ideas."

She put down her pen. "That's the kind of thing I'd rather have my investigator do. I'm not sure I want you talking to Trey's coworkers before we have a chance to take their statements."

"Too bad."

"You think I'm going to let you dredge up stuff that could negatively affect my case and run it on the news?"

" 'Let' doesn't apply. Check your Constitution. You don't have any more right to tell me how to put together my story than Teague does. I agreed to tip you to anything that might help your client. That doesn't mean if I find something that points the finger at him, I'm going to ignore it. If it's really bad, and I have time before I go on the air, I'll give you a heads up. That's all I can promise."

She pursed her lips as though fighting the urge to explode the way she had earlier. But then she surprised me by nodding.

"Fine. I'll live with that. With the understanding that, if it's really bad, I get the chance to try and persuade you to hold off."

"If there's time," I said.

"If there's time." Unsmiling, she held out her hand. We shook. Her palm was smooth and warm. Her fingers curled hard against the back of my hand.

"We seem to fight a lot, don't we?"

"We do."

"So we'll talk?"

"We will."

I watched her depart, wondering if entire juries ever fantasized about her.

As she started into the hall, she almost ran into Ben Callahan coming the other way. He gave her a broad smile and paused to talk. They spoke for a moment before his smile faltered and she brushed past him out the door. Callahan glanced around the room and headed for me.

"I hear you didn't get the word about our briefing this morning. Sorry about that."

"If insincerity were gold, Sergeant, you'd be a wealthy man."

I saw the beginnings of a smug smile. "If you'd stay in the media containment area you'd have more accurate information."

"Really? Care to point out what's inaccurate about what I've been reporting?"

He leaned toward me as though to reply in confidence and his hand flashed out. He was rat-quick but I was faster. I caught his wrist before he could flip my Dr Pepper into my lap.

"Tell your buddies their cover-up isn't any more convincing than you are."

He yanked free. "You son of a bitch."

Across the room, Theo Zak's eyes met mine.

CHAPTER EIGHTEEN

I found the DeeBree office on the third floor, five steps from the county board meeting room. As I pushed through the glass door, a bell tingled overhead. There was no one in the small waiting area. Behind a secretary's desk, a plaque on the wall showed the county logo and a small sign underneath announced, "DeeBree Inc—Progress Through Employment." The nameplate on the desk read "Jan Daken." From the sticker attached following her name, I saw that she'd been "Serving Wihega County: 12 years."

Voices from the inner office stopped and a tall, narrow woman in gray slacks and a seriously formal white blouse peered out.

"Oh." She did a little double take and brought one hand up to touch the small cross at her neck. "You startled me. I wasn't expecting . . . sometimes the door does that by itself. Rings the bell I mean."

I smiled. "Ghosts of politicians still blowing hot air?"

"In this building, anything's possible. How can I help you?"

"Reno McCarthy from Channel 14. I'm looking for some information about—"

As if on cue, a woman's voice called from the inner sanctum. "Send him in, Jan."

Jan touched the cross again, as though fearing the worst and trying to indemnify herself. She ushered me into the office.

It was a typical bureaucrat's domain, a cold space with two worn throw rugs on the floor and Starving Artists prints hung in the spaces you'd expect to see filled on the institutional green walls. The desk was interesting, though. Gunmetal gray, it featured three small stuffed Pooh bears, a jar of malted milk balls, a jar of swizzle sticks, and several uneven stacks of paperwork. Behind it all sat a smiling, bonus-sized woman with too-tight blond curls and indelicate makeup liberally applied. Tiny, wire-rimmed glasses made her a facial match for Ben Franklin and she wore enough wooden bracelets that she clacked every time she moved.

"Sit, sit!" she cried, gesturing at the visitors' chairs in front of the desk. Plain, military style with worn cushions.

She smiled so brightly I worried about the melting point of her eye shadow.

"I'm so pleased to meet you! I've been watching your reports on this terrible murder. I feel as though I've been with you every step of the way. It's just an awful, awful thing. The poor boy. Do you think Lucas Bremmer really did it?"

"The police apparently do, Ms. . . ." Her name wasn't on anything I could see.

"Oh, for heaven's sake! Where are my manners? I'm Mrs. Shottlehauser. Just call me Verna. I'm the director of the Dee-Bree program." She sounded like the female cop from the movie *Fargo.* Her hand clacked across her desk and she shook mine with a grip strong enough she could have yanked me out of my shoes.

"Did you know Hayden and Bremmer?" I asked.

"Of course I knew them. You look surprised. I'm the first person my workers see after they fill out their application and the last one they see when they leave. If they have problems working for us, they come to me, too. I consider myself a sort of den mother, you could say."

"Was Bremmer on probation like Hayden?"

"No, no. Our Work Experience Program is only part of what

we do here. We hire from the public at large, too. About forty percent of our crews are full timers. Honest citizens seeking honest labor." From her expression, she liked the way that sounded.

"We serve two masters, Mr. McCarthy. One is the court system, specifically the probation department. If they feel one of their clients could use a supervised work experience, they send them here. Of course, I have to approve each and every one of them. We also provide a useful service for Refuse. Any lunkhead can tear out a wall or demolish a room when they're going to rebuild, but most people don't have the damnedest idea how to get rid of the mess. They pile it all on the curb, wood, flooring, nails, heck, sometimes even asbestos tiles. The County Refuse crews end up having to break it all down, sort it, that kind of thing. Our crews go in, do a job that's neat as you please, and zip! Package up everything and cart it all away."

She reached into the jar of swizzle sticks and extracted one, then winked at me. "We work cheap, too. Contractors love us. Homeowners think we're the cat's behind."

"How do you determine if an applicant will be a good fit?"

"Why I'd just call it instinct, I guess. I was a social worker in the Chicago public schools for fifteen years. I've been here for almost five now. These old eyes don't miss much. I'm pretty good at spotting the problem children."

"Was Lucas Bremmer a problem child?"

"Oh yes, I'm afraid so. Total lack of respect for authority. From his posture to his words. I worried he would be a troublemaker. Mean-spirited, that one. I gave him a chance, though. First time he got caught fighting, I fired him. And from what you've been telling us on TV, I made a good call, don'tcha know."

"You fired him for fighting?"

"Absolutely. I can't afford trouble on my crews. That's why

we don't accept anyone who has known gang affiliation. No one prone to violence."

"Duane Grum has a history of violence doesn't he?"

Her smile faltered. "I don't believe I know that name. Grum you say?"

"Isn't he on your current roster of full timers?"

"I . . ." She held up a hand. "Let me check just to be sure. We're up to sixty employees now." She clicked keys and looked at her computer screen.

"No, no Grum listed. Did someone tell you he worked for us, Mr. McCarthy?"

I dodged her question with one of my own. "How did Trey differ from Lucas?"

Beaming once more, she shook a sausage-link finger at me. "There you go now! Spoiling a perfectly nice chat by asking a question I can't answer."

"Seems like a pretty innocuous one." I threw a smile back at her. Couldn't let her corner all the sunshine.

"My heavens. All information about our personnel is confidential, of course."

"Ms. Shottlehauser, Trey was an adult. His arrest, conviction, and sentencing are public record."

"Oh yes, but he became an employee of Wihega County the instant he went to work for us, you see? And we sure can't be talking about our employees to just anyone who asks."

"Didn't you have to send regular reports on his progress to a probation officer or to the court?"

"Certainly."

"Then it's part of a public record. Besides, he's dead. Privacy doesn't apply."

"Oh Mr. McCarthy, now you sound just like a lawyer. Are you an attorney? If you are, you might be more comfortable talking to the probation department or even our chief judge. All

I can really say is that we've recently updated our privacy policy and my hands are tied."

" 'Recently' wouldn't mean in the past twenty-four hours, would it?"

Glancing away, she wiggled her hand. Clackclackclack. "Recently."

"OK. Suppose I ask for the names of the other guys on Trey's crew?"

"I'm afraid the answer is still no, Mr. McCarthy. If it's any comfort, I've told all of the other reporters the same thing. It's out of my hands. Protecting privacy has to come first."

"Oh, there's a whole lot of protecting going on," I said and got to my feet. "But I'm not so sure it's all about the privacy of your workers."

She put a finger to her lips.

"You know, before you go, the social worker part of me has a question. I'm fascinated that you went back to work so soon after your"—she clacked again as she waved one hand—"violent interactions during the summer. How did all of that make you feel?"

Her chins quivered slightly and she sat forward in her chair in anticipation of the story. I wondered if she questioned her "applicants" the same way.

"I'm fine."

Her narrowed eyes revealed her annoyance. "Really? I hope I haven't upset you by asking."

I put a confidential tone in my voice. "Actually, I should say I'm fine as long as I'm not around sharp objects. It's an odd thing, really. Guns aren't a problem. But knives, letter openers . . . the shrinks don't know what to make of it."

"Well then!" She slid her drawer open and put something I couldn't see inside. "You know, you really should talk to Judge Castle. He's the administrative judge. Upstairs on Six."

I grinned as I let myself out. Jan, the secretary, wasn't at her desk. Probably taking a break from all the happiness in Verna's office. I looked at my watch. Edging up on lunch hour. I would not have anything for the noon news. I beeped Jody on the Nextel. She told me Caroline was back and had a profile on the Haydens she could run instead. I crossed the hall to the stairs and considered my options.

I would do as Verna suggested, certainly. Visit the county board and the Probation Department. Go to the chief judge's office. Flash my media credentials, dance a First Amendment jig. Would anyone give me the list I wanted? Doubtful. Then again, half the job of reporting, like cop work, is following the routine. Knocking on doors. Making the phone calls you know will never be returned. Talking to people who would sooner gnaw off their arm than give a reporter anything.

Under state law, we could also file a motion requesting that Wihega County open its records. I called Chucky. His response to my request sounded a little like Verna Shottlehauser's. Four other news directors in town, along with the Associated Press, had asked that Channel 14 join them in court. He'd refused.

"The station's lawyers want us to keep our nose out of court. Besides, if the AP is in on the motion, they'll get all the relevant information anyway. We can go find the people when it's on the wires."

I considered what calling him a gutless wimp would get me. "You say you like being out in front of the pack. To stay there, I need to find somebody who knew what Trey was up to—"

"You're telling me the only friends this kid had were the other losers he worked with? Come on, Reno. I'm not buying that. His dad is a famous rich guy. Try some of the other rich kids. They all hang together. Go over to the country club and ask there, why don't you?"

The country club. I closed the Nextel, pissed at myself for

expecting backup from management. As I slipped the phone into my jacket, Jan from the DeeBree office rounded the stairs at the landing below. She carried a can of Coke and a salad wrapped in plastic. When she saw me, she gave a little start. She'd done that earlier, too. I wondered if she was always this jumpy or if something had her on edge.

"You again," she said, smiling a proper, secretarial smile. "Did Verna give you everything you needed?"

"Afraid not. Wihega County one, Freedom of the Press zero."

"Well. I'm sure you understand how those things work."

"Actually, I'm not sure I do," I said.

"Well . . ." She took another tentative step. I could see her checking to see how she might dodge by me. I leaned against the wall to let her pass, offering the most inoffensive smile I could produce.

"Did you ever meet Trey Hayden, Jan?"

She ducked her head. "I'm not allowed to make any comment . . ."

"I'm just curious about your personal reaction to him. As a mother."

She didn't look up. If she twisted her hand any more on the stair rail she'd leave a shiny spot.

"I only saw him once, when he came in for his interview. I never made the connection . . . to his parents. I don't watch their program. He seemed nice. Maybe a little quieter than some of the others."

"Did he seem afraid?"

"Afraid?"

I spread my hands. "Of anything. Starting the program. Particular people."

"Not really. He was just quiet. Some people are that way, you know."

211

"How about Lucas Bremmer? Did he seem like a violent kid to you?"

"Stop." She shook her head, looking everywhere but at me. "I can't do this. Verna would fire me if she found out I was even talking to you. I'm raising three boys on my own, Mr. McCarthy. I need to keep my job. Excuse me." She continued up the stairs.

"The plaque on your desk says you've worked here a long time. Twelve years? You know the way things play out in this building. You deal with people in the court system. Just tell me this. What are the chances Trey Hayden's death is getting a righteous investigation?"

She went so rigid I thought she might turn and pitch her Coke into my face.

"I don't know."

"Well," I said to her back. "That makes two of us."

The president of the county board, a whiny-voiced guy with a used car salesman's manner and a shiny suit that probably set him back eight hundred dollars, pumped my hand, told me Verna Shottlehauser was dead-on about the county's privacy rules, and then insisted I pose with him for a picture quickly snapped by a secretary wielding an ancient Polaroid.

In Probation, a college-girl intern shuttled my question to someone in authority who refused to see me. When I asked his name, the girl, now petulant from her run back and forth, snapped, "No comment."

Who says they don't teach interns useful stuff?

Judge Castle had a Porky the Pig thing going. Short, perfectly bald, and with narrow suspicious eyes, he made me wait while he arranged a tee-time, signed a half-dozen documents on his desk, and then slipped out of his robes, revealing a lime green golf shirt and khaki pants.

"Why would you even imagine we'd grant you access to crew

lists or employment records?" he asked. Irritable. "And Mr. Hayden's court file is sealed because the sheriff's police feel they may find investigative leads in there. As such, it's what we call evidence. Something else you people in the media have absolutely no right to see."

"I always thought judges needed more than bullshit to seal files."

"You know, there's a bumper sticker I like because it's simple enough for even morons to understand. It says, 'I'm the Mommy, that's why.' Hell, McCarthy. I'm the judge. That's why."

"The court of appeals may not agree."

He consulted the Rolex on his skinny wrist. "And in exactly one hour, if the traffic between here and Highland Park cooperates, I'll be drinking a Bloody Mary with three of those august souls in the bar up at Old Elm Club."

"Are they members of the Leadership Council, too?"

His face did a fast shift through surprise and worry and then settled on grim.

"As I said. The files are sealed. You want to have your attorneys try and get at them, good luck to you. Otherwise, you'll have to excuse me. I have other engagements."

Back in the hall once more, I found a bench by one of the windows that overlooked the police building and downtown Falcon Ridge. There was a copy of the Wihega County *Examiner* on the bench next to me. The sub-headline caught my eye: "Perkins Says Dead Files, Not Bodies, A Problem." I realized I should take some time and read up on what was going on in the coroner's office.

I checked in with Jody.

"Between Al, Peter, and I, we managed to keep Caroline on track for the noon." She gave a halfhearted laugh. "Is she really that dumb?"

"Dumber. You get anywhere with the Haydens?"

"I called their producer. The family refuses to do any interviews, even with us. Al is trying to find out where they're staying. Do you have anything?"

"Nobody wants to talk about Hayden or Grum. Bremmer's another story. The DeeBree foreman told Sunny yesterday Bremmer was terminated for falling asleep on the job. Verna claims she fired him for fighting."

"Why would she lie like that?"

"Somebody wants him to look like a tough guy."

"Somebody? You mean Theo Zak?"

It was time to call for an expert opinion on that.

John Gennaro is what *Chicago Magazine* calls a "colorful Chicago character." Once an FBI agent with some of the best contacts inside the Outfit that the Bureau had ever seen, John ostensibly retired a few years ago to write articles for *Playboy,* pen true-crime books, and consult with Hollywood insiders and documentary producers when they make movies about the Chicago mob. I learned over the summer, however, that his retirement, like him, isn't quite what it seems. On the days when he's not hunched over his laptop or fielding calls from Willis, DeNiro, and crew, he's back at his old post, keeping an eye on the Chicago mob as an unofficial/official watcher and go-between for the Bureau. He plays golf a couple of times a month with Polo Tony LaMotta, one of the scariest guys I've ever met. With all the Feds assigned to various terrorist task forces, he's often the only one doing OC-related work in a city where the prevailing opinion among many in law enforcement and politics is that the mob is dead. Gennaro heatedly disagrees.

I called John from a pay phone near the elevators. Cellular calls can be tracked and monitored covertly with equipment anybody can buy on eBay. If the county bugged its payphones near the courtrooms, John's electronics would catch it. He loves to talk, but years of working the Outfit have made him ultracautious.

Before I even had a chance to identify myself he growled, "I'm on with Tom Hanks. The call waiting beeps me. I tell him, Tommy, my friend Reno McCarthy is sticking his nose where it doesn't belong again, and I need to take this call. So you're out in the world of Theo Zak. How you like it out there, Reno?"

I took the receiver off my ear, looked at it, and then put it back. "You have ESP?"

"Prefixes, my good man. I memorize area codes and prefixes and pay phone telephone numbers. Old habit, from before goddamn cellular. When people knew how to be polite in restaurants and talk to each other, not some *sciocco* halfway across the country, you know? And, I've been watching you on the tube. Who the hell else is going to call me from a courthouse pay phone in Wihega County?"

"You've got to admit, it's a little creepy, even for you, John."

"After twenty-five years with the Bureau I gotta right to be a little *bizzaro,* don't you think? Eh? So answer my question. You having fun out there with my old friend Uncle Theo? That cocksucker."

I smiled. Talking to Gennaro is like reaching back through time. He was a street agent under Hoover.

"OK, I'll bite," I said. "What did Zak ever do to you?"

"I'll tell you something, Reno. This man is a very, very lucky man. This man has made some influential friends over the years. He keeps them happy. Why? Not only for the money. You know kids these days, how they're all wannabe thugs? Gang bangers? Even the white boys? Theo was born in the wrong part of the Mediterranean. This man wants to be a made guy so bad he pops a chubby thinking about it. Far as I'm concerned he's a sleazy, phony, son of a bitch."

"How tight are his Outfit connections?"

"Ehh, as long as he does for them, they do for him. Like hands washing each other, no?"

"He use mob muscle?"

"Understand this, Reno. Theo has built his own very subtle operation out there. He's learned finesse. You're his friend, he might take you to Vegas on the private jet he keeps at the DuPage Airport. You cross him, maybe all of a sudden you find your credit cards have all dried up and your car gets repossessed. Maybe the cops find some drugs in your pockets. I'm not saying legs don't get broken or heads don't get busted. Shit happens. What I'm saying is, Theo likes to keep his problems *his* problems. You get the idea?"

"Clearly."

"Thing is," John said, "there's talk he's maybe a little overextended with this casino project of his. Some people he plays golf with, occasionally has dinner with, people he maybe did some business with in the past, are getting their names in the paper. These people don't like the attention. Now, that all may be fine for the moment and they'll let it pass if Theo comes through for 'em, you know what I mean? But he can't let this casino go the way Rosemont's did a few years ago. All that noise and nothing to show for it? That would piss off the wrong fellas."

I glanced over my shoulder. Talking to John always makes me paranoid. "Would they clip him?"

"Let's just say Theo needs to get Springfield in his corner."

"I thought the casino project was dead."

"The state gaming board technically just tabled Wihega County's plan on the attorney general's recommendation. Tabled, did not kill. It's presumed dead because they don't have the votes to resurrect it. One member changes his mind? The right board member leaves? Maybe it comes off the table."

"Is that likely?"

"One of the anti-casino board members is a physician. He has notified the governor he plans to move out of state within the month."

"Don't tell me. Somebody's waiting to replace him?"

"Ah, Reno. This is an election year, is it not? If he loses, the governor wants to leave as many of his people in power positions as he can. He's asked Leighton Bruss."

"Bruss. The former Boeing chairman? Quit to design golf courses or something? Are you saying he's in Zak's pocket?"

"How he'll vote is anyone's guess. Bruss has no connection to Zak. Nor to the Outfit."

"So says the gaming board?"

"So says me," John chuckled. "The board asked me to take a preliminary look at him. I'll do a full background when the governor is ready to actually make his choice. No telling how Bruss would vote, but background, family ties, finances all tell me he's clean. Where you going with all this casino stuff anyway, Reno? I thought you were there to cover the kid's murder."

"Lucas Bremmer's lawyer thinks Zak's behind the push to nail her client."

"Watching your stories, I thought Bremmer was just some punk. No?"

"That's what he appears to be."

"Then no way, Reno. Zak's not gonna get involved with something like that. Especially not right now. If the kid pissed him off somehow, that's another story. The two of them got a history?"

"The lawyer's on her way over to question him." I gave him a quick rundown on what we'd learned about Lucas so far, finishing with Lindsey's seemingly all-too-convenient murder. I could almost see Gennaro shaking his head.

"I've gotta be honest. Your truck getting blown up? It don't wash for me. Okay, Zak may have primed his people, 'Deal with this and get these reporters outta here post haste before they start looking around at other stuff.' That kinda thing. That makes some sense. Media people being in town probably scares the crap outta him. But the people he's beholden to have a motto: 'Never make *unna brutta figura.'* A bad showing. Torching your truck, eh, I can't see him ordering that. I told you, he's a sneaky little shit. Comin' down on Bremmer with real weight, killing the girl, out of the question! He'd have to be nuts with what's on his mind about that casino."

"Unless there's some overlap."

"The casino and this Bremmer?" He grunted, always on the alert for new information. Like Vinnie, I thought. "How you figure?"

"That's why I called you."

"My friend, I'm happy to run the Bremmer boy's name by some people, but it sounds to me like that lawyer's reaching for a little *distrazione.* A little distraction to help her case. Wait a minute. She some kinda hot piece? She got you thinking with your other head now?"

I was saved from having to answer by the loud blast of a siren outside the courthouse. I told Gennaro to hold on and pulled the receiver away from my ear. People stepped from their offices looking puzzled. Louder than a car alarm.

"What's happening?" someone asked.

"It's the jail siren. Maybe somebody escaped!"

I told Gennaro I'd get back to him and joined two women at one of the windows that overlooked the police building and jail. As we watched, a handful of clerical-looking types stumbled out the front door and began milling around, pointing at the upper floors and acting as though they were waiting for something to happen. Within a couple of minutes it did. Two squads, light bars blazing, pulled up over the curb and into the plaza. One uniform jumped from each; one cradled a shotgun and the other what looked like an MP-5. Both ran through the front door. Within a moment, both were back and, from their hand gestures, it was obvious they were telling the people near the doors to clear the area.

I called Al.

"Something's going down at the jail. Got squads coming in and guys deploying into the building with automatic weapons."

"We're back at the Haydens' and two squads just took off from here. I'm on it."

I was just slipping the phone back into my pocket when I saw glass fall from one of the gun-port size windows on the jail level of the police building, one story below where we were standing. A spurt of greenish-gray smoke followed, dissipating almost as soon as it hit the air.

Fire? Unlikely. Tear gas probably. What the hell was going on in there? A nasty feeling started to gnaw into the middle of my stomach.

More people jostled me as they rushed up to watch the action. I felt torn between holding where I was and going down to the street. I don't like having any barrier between me and a story I'm covering. At the same time, I realized the high ground might be an advantage. If the cops were pushing employees away from the front of the building, they wouldn't want the media any closer. Up here I could see most everything that was happening. I grabbed the Nextel again and told Al to come into the courthouse. Then I called the station. Florbus answered.

"What do you need, Reno?"

"Smoke or tear gas coming from a window of the Wihega County jail. I think—"

She swept away the rest of what I was going to say. "Anyone dead? Building burning to the ground?"

"No, but with Trey Hayden's killer locked up in there, I

219

thought you might want to put it on the air. You know. Breaking news?"

"If there are fatalities, call me back. Otherwise, we'll use it for the top at four."

"Let me talk to Chucky."

"He's in a meeting. Goodbye, Reno."

The phone rang again the moment I put it away.

"Reno, it's Ray Fong."

I glanced out the window. A fire department ambulance and engine rolled up in front and disgorged four men in turnout gear and helmets. The two guys from the ambulance carried paramedic packs. All four shrugged air tanks and facemasks into place before charging inside. What the hell was going on?

"Ray, I can't talk—"

He didn't wait for my excuse. "The stent's in. He could wake up tomorrow or a week from tomorrow. I just thought you'd want to know."

For a moment I couldn't think what to ask. "How did it go? I mean . . ."

"Fine. Just come see him, okay?" He clicked off.

"That's the maximum security pod." Arson Investigator Briggs stood near a group of women who had walked over from the court clerk's office. He peered out the window. "Have a fight there once in awhile. Never saw 'em break a window."

"It looks like there was a fire, too," one of the women said. "We saw smoke . . ."

"Could be. They're allowed books and magazines. They could be burning those. But none of the furniture or bedding is flammable."

"Tempered glass isn't supposed to break, either," I said.

Briggs grunted. "Low bid materials, don't forget. Anything can happen when you build on the cheap. The bedding and the plastic chairs have an ISO rating but the glass . . . what can I tell you? We suggested some changes in the plans. Nobody paid attention."

He walked over to me.

"Just so you know, it wasn't my idea to sandbag you this morning. Teague's always been a horse's ass. The Hayden case put him in overdrive. I've been looking for your buddy Grum since last night. I don't know about the murders, but I like him for doing your truck."

"I hear he might have been a suspect in the stable fire down by the river awhile back."

"Severn Stables. Off the record, you wouldn't be wrong."

"Get anywhere?"

"Nope. He was there watching so we took him into custody. Had to release him."

"Any thought as to why he'd want to kill horses and a TV truck?"

He turned back to the window. "Somebody told him to."

Three squads pulled up. The drivers jumped out in black fatigues and began strapping on body armor.

A sudden thought flashed across my brain. *Moira's in there.* I punched her number into the Nextel. It rang six times and went to voice mail. Crap.

"Can you check something for me?" I asked Briggs. "Moira Cullen may be in the middle of whatever's going on. She was going up to meet with Bremmer."

He flipped open his phone and moved away from the crowd around the windows.

My Nextel beeped. Al spoke in my ear. "Cops have about a three-block perimeter around the courthouse. A coupla state troopers just passed me, headed in. What the hell's happening?"

I described what I'd seen. Briggs motioned to me. He produced a set of keys and unlocked the door to an empty office with two desks, several comfortable-looking chairs, and a gun locker in one corner. "Ready room so cops going to court don't have to wait in the hall with the mopes." It had a window facing the action that wasn't obstructed by other curious onlookers. I told Al where we were.

The fire marshal's face was grim and he chewed a toothpick, rolling it back and forth with his tongue. When he talked it drooped from the corner of his mouth.

"If Cullen was in there, she's fine. She wouldn't have been anywhere beyond the lawyers' room. But it's a cluster fuck. Dispatch says they've got a fight in progress in Pod C's dayroom. At least one officer down. Probably got about twenty guys in there. SWAT hit 'em with tear gas and went in right on top of it."

I heard more sirens. The warbling tone coming from the other building had ceased.

Three ambulances jammed into the little plaza between the buildings and a fourth rolled down a ramp on the south side of the building and out of sight. I counted two cops with rifles at the building entrance and several others who had taken up positions on the side in view of my window.

Al, cherry red from humping his camera and a tripod up six flights of stairs, burst into the ready room and declared the window glass too grimy to shoot through. He used his pocket-knife blade to free the lock and levered the window open. Our angle on the action proved so worthwhile I wished we could get a signal back to the truck so it could be used for a live shot. No way to make that happen. Al said he'd barely made it through the back door of the building before he heard the order given to lock down the entrances.

I tried Moira's phone again. After three rings a muffled voice answered, fumbled, muttered a curse, and then said, "Cal?"

"No, it's Reno. What's going on up there?"

"Oh, I thought . . ." Flustered. "Hey. Hey it's crazy. Are you here somewhere?"

"Courthouse. You okay?"

"Whoa," she said and took a breath like she'd been running. Then her voice firmed up a little. "Scared shitless for a bit. I'd just come from seeing another client and was on my way to meet Lucas. They'd just led me into C section, the outer hall, when this buzzer went off. Almost like a truck backing up. Next thing . . . Jesus! The officer escorting me shoved me into the attorneys' room and locked the door. I thought she'd gone nuts until I saw other officers running past in the hall." She coughed.

"Sorry. I took in some of the tear gas. It's all over the place in there. I saw them bring a big canister of it, almost the size of one of those propane things you use with a barbecue grill."

"What happened?"

"I'm not . . . sure. A fight, I know that much. I could hear it. The paramedics are here so I know people were hurt . . ."

"Lucas?"

"I don't know. I've asked everybody. Nobody seems to know or want to say. They've tried to get me into an ambulance, but I need to know if Lucas is okay first. So far they haven't made an issue of it, but I have a feeling they're going to pretty soon."

"Don't be a goof. Lucas is either okay or he's not. Get out of there."

"Goddamn it, he's my client!"

"You're going to end up as somebody's patient if you get a face full of tear gas or a nightstick upside the head. That going to do Lucas any good?"

"Wait," she said and I heard the scratchy sound of a hand being placed over the mouthpiece or the phone rubbing against something. Then she was back.

"The jail director's here. I gotta go."

I started to respond but heard only dead air. I looked back out on the plaza. It looked like the parking lot of a police convention. I stared, counting. Eight squads, nine . . . another ambulance . . . state police . . .

My Nextel rang, startling me. This time I turned back toward the window to answer. I knew who it would be and what I was going to hear, even without looking at Caller ID.

"Reno?" Moira's voice cracked along the edges. She sucked in a big gulp of air and blew out the words, "Lucas is dead."

CHAPTER NINETEEN

The rain had stopped and the sun was reasserting itself by the time I got outside. The fire department's heavy apparatus was gone, leaving only a red Crown Vic parked at the curb. A police Ford Expedition remained on the plaza, doors open to catch the breeze, and several officers stood near it, occasionally glancing over at what was an impressive array of television cameras set up in a semicircle in front of the door to the police building. I saw all of the local stations represented along with a couple of networks.

Ben Callahan was there, too. He stood a little off to the side, head ducked, getting instructions from an older uniformed guy with a pasty face and thinning gray hair. One glance at the stars on his shoulders and gold braid on his hat told me this was Gerald Droot, the chief of police. Making sure the cover-up was nice and tight?

Droot squeezed Callahan's shoulder. Spin one for the Gipper. Callahan began scribbling on a clipboard and the chief turned and went inside the building.

Callahan began right on time. As before, he was so smooth he could have been reading from a teleprompter. Though he kept his tone somber, speaking about "the regrettable nature of the incident" and the fact that Lucas was "sentenced to death by his fellow inmates before he could be tried by a jury of his peers," I could see he was enjoying himself. His gestures were expansive, like a politician trying to convince you the tax increase really won't hurt, even a little bit. He moved in quick bursts of energy, acknowledging each question with a nod and a smile.

It started, he explained, when one inmate saw another bending the corner of a page in his Bible and called him on it. The two argued. Others joined in. Other books were thrown. Someone punched out the female correctional officer. Someone else hefted and then threw a plastic chair into another group of inmates. A fight broke out.

During the melee, probably right before a squad of officers stormed the pod and emptied an entire canister of tear gas, "an unknown suspect" stuck a homemade plastic shiv into Lucas Bremmer's left eye.

Callahan grinned at the cameras. "Questions?"

"Where was Bremmer killed?"

"Where?" he cocked his head at me and produced a puzzled look. "In Pod-C of the Wihega County jail. That's why we're all here, Reno."

His wry response brought a few titters. I followed up over them. "Where in the pod? In the dayroom? Or in his cell?"

"I believe he was in his cell—"

"Inmates are allowed to go back and forth during the day? Visit each other's cells?"

The way his eyes narrowed told me I was onto something. "In some of the pods, inmates are allowed to come and go, yes."

"Was he lying down or standing up when he was stabbed?"

"That's unknown at this time—"

Three other reporters tried to ask their questions simultaneously and overrode any chance to follow up. I'd started a trend, however. They wanted to know if somebody started the fight to cover the murder and wondered why, given his notoriety, Lucas hadn't been kept out of the main jail population. Then

226

another questioner, a woman from Channel 2 whom I'd once accused of having all the emotional depth and sensitivity of a Number Two pencil, threw Callahan a curve ball.

"How do you respond to allegations that your officers contaminated the crime scene at the Hayden home yesterday?"

Callahan's slight double take looked phony. "Contaminated it in what way?"

"You know." She gestured with one hand. "Walking all over. Touching things. Whatever."

Now came amusement. "Who's making those allegations? You, Holly?" After the laughter subsided he cleared his throat.

"Well, since we haven't learned to levitate, investigating a crime scene requires the officers to move through it and, eventually, they seize evidence they find by doing so. If that's what you mean by walking all over and touching things . . ." He shrugged.

"No. I mean tracking tile paste from the courthouse basement into the house."

Callahan smiled and shook his head. "Better hold onto your exclusive, Holly. It's doubtful, but I'll check on that and get back to you."

He answered a few more speculative questions with no-comments but, before he could end the briefing, a tall reporter with wire-framed glasses from Channel 7 asked in a loud voice, "I'd think it would take pretty good aim to stab someone in the eye while they're standing up, wouldn't you?"

Callahan bowed out without answering, looking a little less confident than when he started. I headed for him, but he moved as though his exit had been rehearsed. Two steps and inside the building. Two grim-faced guys in response team fatigues locked the door behind him.

"All you do when you ask questions like that is piss 'im off you know." I glanced around. Wozniak was just slipping his notebook into his pocket.

"So?"

"Cal is an okay guy. I've known him since he was just a grunt evidence tech. Sometimes when the bosses don't want to let the cat out of the bag, he still gives us stuff. He's worked all over the department. Even used to be Officer Friendly at one of the high schools . . ."

"I don't care if he helps crippled nuns cross the street. He was feeding us crap."

"What I'm saying is, if you don't try to embarrass him he might slip you something. Then again, maybe you big-time city TV boys don't need friends like that."

I swiveled all the way around. "You don't think we should try to punch holes in their story? It stinks."

" 'Course it does. They're covering their asses against a lawsuit."

"Beyond that."

"You're thinking the cops nailed Bremmer themselves?" He laughed. "If they did it was just through stupidity. You know who they put him in there with? It's the super-max pod for Chrissakes. Two of those Aryan Nation skinheads being held for the Feds and Diego Rodriguez, the boy who shot up the bar and killed those people in Four Oaks last winter! Bremmer liked to run his mouth, didn't he? How patient you think stone killers are gonna be with somebody like him?"

When the crowd of reporters and photographers covering Callahan's newser broke up, I headed toward where Peter parked the truck in the circle drive in front of the police building/courts complex. Halfway there, I heard my name called and turned to see a gangly kid of about fifteen in a Bulls T-shirt and ultralong shorts loping my way.

"Mr. McCarthy?" I expected him to ask for an autograph but he thrust a black plastic folder into my hands.

"My name's Chad? Daken? My mom says you dropped this when you were in her office. She figured you'd want it back."

I opened the cover, saw what it was, and thanked the kid.

Seven in the evening, four live shots, and a quart of coffee later, I sat with my feet up on the dashboard in the front seat of the Channel 14 truck going through what Chad handed me. Peter had bought the largest bucket of the Colonel's chicken he could find. We reduced it to bones within minutes.

Tucked inside the folder, which still bore a Wal-Mart price sticker, were two sheets of paper. The first was a list of Trey Hayden's DeeBree crew members, including the file numbers of their criminal cases and their addresses. The second was a memo from the chief judge to all of his people plus the director of Probation and my buddy Verna Shottlehauser. It ordered in no uncertain terms that no information be provided to the media regarding Trey Hayden or Duane Grum. The memo also reviewed the law on slander before adding that there should be no lip-flapping to reporters about any current or former county board members, either.

Scrawled on a yellow sticky attached to the first page was a note.

"I've thought about your question all afternoon. My answer is 'no.' "

With darkness approaching and a light breeze blowing through the truck's open windows and doors, I gave half the list to Jody and Peter and kept three names for Al and me to try and interview. I figured if we broke into two groups and really hustled, we might find one of Trey's crewmates willing to talk about him on camera and, maybe, explain why he'd had a gun. It would be a fresh piece for the ten o'clock show and give us a new angle to pursue into Day Three. I'd just gotten off the phone with Chucky, who had made it abundantly clear that he saw Bremmer's death as a conclusion to the Hayden case rather than a reason to commit more resources. At the very least, I needed to find a way to prove Trey didn't have the gun as protection against Lucas. Otherwise, despite the huge questions that remained, Chucky wanted to scale back our on-scene coverage in Falcon Ridge. Even interest in national stories wanes for TV's bosses when the sparks aren't flying and the video isn't easy to get.

"Back off? Now? Bremmer is killed in maximum security custody about twenty-four hours after he told me he was afraid of the cops in this county. I've got other sources suggesting the whole Hayden investigation is being purposely skewed. Not to mention the very convenient death of Bremmer's girlfriend. And, in case you've forgotten, one of our own is in the hospital with most of his face burned off."

He chewed in my ear and then slurped something liquid.

"During the show at six," he said, and chewed some more, "you took us out on an almost nonexistent limb. You virtually accused Wihega County of murder based on the paranoia of a suspect who, even you admitted to me yesterday, wasn't the most reliable source. Christ, people get killed in jail all the time. And I thought the cops explained the girl's death pretty well."

"You trying to do Callahan's job here? If you watched the entire report, I factually refuted him on her arrest record. She was no more a major player in the drug world than I am. I think she knew something about Hayden's death that her killer didn't want us to find out."

"You think. Might have. Could have. Maybe. Possibly. These aren't compelling words to me, Reno. The fact is, you don't have anything but your suspicions at this point. That's not enough. We can't afford to have people accusing us of creating a conspiracy just for ratings."

"What if we're walking away from a conspiracy?"

"Who says we're walking away?" I heard the clink of ice

against glass. "Look. I'm not telling you to come home tonight or even tomorrow. You bring me something you can substantiate that says Bremmer didn't kill the Hayden boy or that the county cops arranged for Bremmer's murder, or even that aliens killed the girlfriend. I'll run with it. Until then, I'm down one live truck and one photographer and we could get another breaker any time."

It was a good thing I wasn't standing in front of him at that moment. If I'd gripped his scrawny neck as tightly as I had my fist wrapped around the phone his eyes would have popped out of their sockets.

"You got that list you wanted so badly, go see what those people have got to say."

I looked at my watch. Seven p.m. We had about two hours to do just that.

The sheet told me Luis Mendoza was on probation for burglary and theft. He lived on the northeast side of Falcon Ridge and we headed there after striking out with the first two names on the list. If either had been home they hadn't wanted to open their doors.

Al bumped the Crown Vic over two sets of train tracks, past the dark hulks of boxcars on a siding, and then down a street where two- and three-flats were crammed together with gangways between. A bodega with its doors boarded up. The offices of an immigration lawyer advertised above. On another corner a taqueria, dirty windows spilling a sad yellow light into the early fall darkness. I'd seen pictures of street fighting in Iraq where the buildings were in better shape.

Luis lived in a rectangular box painted nut brown, on a street filled with other rectangular boxes. A couple of them, including his, had cars not only in the driveway but up on the postage-stamp lawns. Just outside his garage, a guy had his head and shoulders poked inside the engine compartment of a late-nineties Trans-Am. He'd plugged in a light stack and the two halogens pointing at him threw shadows onto the scraggly trees in the yard next door. As we parked the Crown Vic and walked toward him, he straightened and looked at us without expression. His left hand was empty but he held a wrench in his right and didn't put it down. He was a squat, muscular little guy with a flat-top and even in the faint chill of evening wore oil-stained shorts and a T-shirt with the sleeves hacked off.

"Evening," I said, getting a nod in return. "Reno McCarthy from Channel 14. This is Al Greco. We're looking for Luis Mendoza."

"For what?"

"We'd like to talk to you about DeeBree."

"Shit," he let out a breath and turned back to his engine, moving a utility light hanging from the hood and worked the wrench in somewhere behind the fan.

"I don't know nuthin' about any of that shit, man. You can ask whatever you want but I just been doin' what they tell me."

I was confused. "What do they tell you?"

"They tell me to haul the trash and leave it someplace, I leave it there. Don't care where. They pay me to take orders not ask questions."

"Somewhere . . . other than the landfill?"

He gave me the look my question deserved. Illegal dumping.

"Actually, I wanted to ask about Trey Hayden."

"The kid who got himself killed? He was nuthin' to me. Just another guy."

"Did his work, didn't bitch or cop an attitude because he came from money?"

"Not around me he didn't. No more bitchin' than anybody else. Maybe less. Not the best job in the world, you know? Doesn't help we got a racist prick for a crew chief."

"How's that set up anyway? Your boss work for Refuse? Or for DeeBree?"

"DeeBree's only a cutesy name, man. That fat lady, she just sits in her office and eats her candy and plays shrink. It's all a front. The bosses work for Refuse. We all do."

"So Trey got along with everybody? One big happy family?"

He came out from under the hood, apparently satisfied with his work, and tossed the wrench into a toolbox at his feet.

"I wasn't trying to make friends with any of them guys, okay? I never figured that place out about shit like that. They tell us in court, that judge, he says to me one of the conditions of my probation is no contact with crooks, right? But then he sends me out on this work crew that's all crooks. I don't get it."

He picked up a rag and blotted his forehead. "Then they have us throwing the shit all over the place except at the dump 'cause they say it's getting full and they can't afford to go opening a new one. The crew chief says anybody comes around asking questions, we don't know squat."

"Was Hayden involved with the dumping?"

"Nah. Just me and Peron and Hargis and a couple guys from another crew."

"Why?"

"Our crew boss. He didn't trust Hayden. Said he was too quiet."

"Could Hayden have known what was going on anyway?"

"Don't see how. He wasn't buddies with Peron and Hargis any more'n he was with me."

"Was there anybody he was tight with? Or the other way around. Anybody hassle him?"

Luis began to answer then hesitated, as though thinking. "Now you mention it, there was something. Maybe like two weeks ago, we were on this job site. Tree fell on a greenhouse. Caved in the roof, really fucked it up. We was having to be real careful the place didn't collapse before we tore it down, you know? Middle of that, Hayden just up and leaves. Walks into the woods."

"What was that about?"

"Beats me. Said he got sick. I seen him holdin' his belly. We broke for lunch, he still wasn't back." His dark eyes brightened.

"That was when the owner of the place shows. Big Escalade drives up, he comes flying out, maybe just as we were finishing lunch break. Tells us he wants to go in and look around." Luis shook his head and smiled.

"So in he goes, no hard hat or nuthin'. Robinson, the crew chief? He about shits. Guy's inside there, down on his knees. In his suit, man! All the glass we hadn't got to yet coulda fallen on him and he's picking shit up, shoving stuff all around. He's not yelling or nothing but you can tell he's really pissed. Robinson tries to get him to calm himself, get him out of there so he doesn't get hurt, you know? Like, 'Hey, your wife told us to do this, we got a work order, and it's all legit.' He wasn't paying no attention to nothing! Robinson even told him we'd help him find whatever he was looking for. Guy picked up a shovel! We all were thinking he was gonna beat Robinson to death but he just started digging."

"Did he say what he was looking for?"

"No, man. He was just acting crazy."

"How long was he inside?"

"Fifteen minutes? And you gotta understand, there wasn't even anything in there to begin with 'cept some old tables and some pipes for the plumbing. The place was ready to fall down all around him and he's in there picking bricks out of the walls and shit. Crazy ass bastard."

"Where was Hayden while all this was going on?"

"Lemme think." He squinted. "I think he came back in the middle or right after. Maybe after. Yeah, after for sure. I remember because Robinson was pissed all to hell. First, he had this crazy guy in his face and then Hayden comes out of the woods looking like he just got laid or something. Stood there and smiled the whole time Robinson was screaming at his ass."

"Did he say where he went?"

Mendoza shrugged. "Said he was sick. Had to go puke."

"Was the homeowner still there when Hayden came back? Did he see him come out of the woods?"

"I dunno. By then we was all watching Robinson yelling, hoping he'd have a heart attack or something. No such luck."

Al and I exchanged glances. "Where was this job site?"

"You got me. Someplace up in the Heights where they got all the mansions."

"Think you'd remember it if we drove you through the neighborhood?"

"No, man. I wasn't paying attention. I just know the street had about three houses on it and bigass lawns, that's all I remember. Houses big as banks."

Suspicion clouded his features. "Why you asking about all this anyway?"

I closed my notebook. "You tell me. Guy walks off a job site into the woods. A few minutes later the homeowner shows up and goes nuts because he can't find something inside the building you're tearing down. What's that say to you?"

"Oh man, I dunno . . ." He looked away.

"C'mon Luis. The sheet says you're a thief. Give me your professional opinion."

His jaw tightened, like maybe I'd pushed him too far, but then the corners of his mouth twitched.

"You really want to know? I think he stole something and went off to hide it, man. But what the fuck? What's there to steal from a place that's full a' bricks and dirt?"

Before we left, I asked Luis some questions on camera about the illegal dumping he'd done. Turned out the DeeBree crew regularly left trash in a half-dozen locations both inside the county and farther west, mostly in creeks and in remote places along the riverbank. He couldn't provide exact directions to any one spot but gave highway information that might put us in the right neighborhood.

Back in the car, Al said, "Whattya steal from a broken-down old greenhouse?"

"I wonder if any of the others saw what Hayden carried away from there."

"You're thinking it was the pistola, aren't you?"

I nodded. "Cash he could have just stuck in a pocket. And why go off in the woods?"

"Well, if it was a gun, you gotta wonder what it was doing in the greenhouse to begin with. Not exactly easy to grab if you got prowlers in the middle of the night."

I dialed Jody's phone. She picked up on the second ring. I quickly sketched what we'd gotten from Mendoza then asked if any of her people were saying the same thing.

"Peron refused to talk to us. Hargis, though, backs up Mendoza. He saw Trey take off, watched him get his butt chewed for it later. Dexter, the guy whose house we just left? He was sick the day the crew did the work at the greenhouse, okay? But the day he came back he says Trey began nagging him, asking if he could get ammunition for a .38 revolver. Dexter says he took offense, the white guy trying to get the black guy to run an errand for him. That shut Trey right up."

"No way Hargis and Dexter would go on camera with this?"

"No. They say they'll deny they talked to us. Each of them has six months of probation left. They were told any kind of screwup means jail. They're terrified the county's going to lock them up."

When we got back to our spot in front of the police building, David from CNN handed me a news release. The cops claimed they were setting up a special task force to investigate the jail fight and the death of Lucas Bremmer. Chief Droot even named a well-known former U.S. attorney to lead the probe.

I began my ten o'clock live shot with more of Al's high-angle video, included a comment that Callahan had made early in his news conference that "we see no immediate connection to the murder of Trey Hayden," and mixed in some video of a group of teenagers placing flowers outside the Hayden home. Maybe I'm just a cynic but it seems like, no matter what happens nowadays, if someone dies, there's always somebody around to lay flowers. And to cry on cue for the cameras.

But, compared to what we had been airing since we hit the ground in Falcon Ridge, all of that was schlock. Nothing I could do about it, either. If just one DeeBree crew member had been willing to back up Mendoza's version of what happened at the greenhouse we would have been golden. Their refusal left us without any new information to stir into the mix.

I expected Chucky to call as soon as I was off the air. He didn't disappoint. He railed at me about the lack of a fresh lead.

"And what's this crap Channel Two is leading with? Source close to the investigation says one of the officers tracked floor tile glue or something into the Hayden house?"

Crap. The reporter's off-the-wall question at the news conference. "They got a tip and we didn't."

"If you can't come up with more than a rehash of what people already know by tomorrow afternoon, I want you people back here. I can't afford to have a full crew out of town for another day."

Three other stories were already vying to take over the top spot in our newscasts. A nurse, her physician husband, and four kids from Chicago had gone missing in the Philippines, likely kidnapped by terrorists. A crusty former governor, who just barely managed to avoid prison for his misdeeds a couple of years ago, hovered at death's door. And the cops were investigating reports that a local female contestant on one of the more popular reality shows was pregnant by a twelve-year-old boy. Unless we could compete with those headline grabbers, the Hayden story was toast. This time I sucked in my anger. It was useless.

Sunny called me a couple of minutes after I hung up with Chucky.

"Just got back to the motel in time to watch you. Those kids with the flowers crying for their dead friend sort of choked me up."

"If all the tears on TV had to be heartfelt, we'd be out of business in about three days," I said.

"Golly, a cynical reporter. Now there's something you don't see every day."

I smiled for the first time in hours. "How did your consulting thing go?"

"Actually, it was a little weird. They gave me a full walk around and full access, no problem there. But the CEO . . ."

She sighed. "He's an odd duck. He smiles, nods, asks questions all in the right places. But tonight there was something . . . I don't know. Something off. He was preoccupied."

"Maybe the country club reconfigured his handicap."

"The forensic accountant who audited them says their books are clean. So why would the CEO sweat a routine interview with me?"

I grinned. "Because it was with you?"

"Right. So what happened today besides what I saw on TV?"

I told her about my visit with Briggs and what Mendoza had given us that we hadn't been able to use. "Problem is," I said, "Wihega County—"

"Doesn't post those kind of records online so you have no way of knowing where the house was," she finished. "Yeah, what a surprise. I'll see if I can track that down for you before I go to bed."

Hanging up with her, I sank back in the seat and closed my eyes. Sleep sounded like an excellent option. I tried to think if there was any reason I shouldn't go back to the motel.

Then Al wrenched open the driver's door and slid in behind the wheel.

CHAPTER TWENTY

Wescott paced between his lab and office, tie undone, shirt open at the neck, suit jacket draped over the back of his chair.

She knew, he thought.

The private investigator doing the audit for Forge Global's insurance company was charming, attractive, and possessed the information processing skills of a Cray supercomputer. When, after a two-day casual inspection of the Forge facilities, she sat across from his desk and reported her findings, he wanted to offer her a full-time job.

"I've found nineteen breaches, sir. Cameras out of service, access codes not kept private, confidential and top secret files being mishandled. That sort of thing. In addition, there are at least three secretaries who know far more about projects than I suspect they are cleared for. Oh, and one of the workers on your loading dock either has a terminal cold or is snorting cocaine on company time. I'm guessing the latter."

Sunny DeAngelis.

She knew. He had watched her eyes. Saw her notice his sweat, his trembling hand. She knew something was wrong with him.

His desk phone buzzed. His wife. "Are you coming home tonight?"

"Why on earth would you care?"

"The girls saw you on television. They want to ask about what happened. Kelly knew the Hayden boy. He was in her class."

His daughters. How would he have reacted if someone had . . . ?

"No. I have an early board meeting. I have to prepare my notes." Lies came easily and he told them well. For an instant, he wondered if Elaine Forge had ever lied to him.

So long ago.

"How could you allow something like that to happen?" his wife asked.

The timing of her question startled him. My God, he thought. Did she know? It had happened thirty years ago. How could she . . . ?

He realized she was just taking her usual potshots at him. He let the taunt pass.

"Good night, Olivia."

Chapter Twenty-One

Al said, "Thank God for cell phones. You know I don't hang out on mine like you and Jody do but damn, sometimes they come in real handy. I got a location on the Hayden family."

"Where?" Maybe sleep could wait.

He fired up the engine but didn't put the car into gear. "Here's the deal. I called this guy I used to partner with when I was in the Second District, Bernie Lazar. He runs a security company that's got the contract with a bunch of hotels out this way. Helluva guy and he owes me. He just called. The Haydens are staying at the Briarcliff. You know the joint?"

I shook my head.

"It's a couple miles downriver. Bernie says it used to be a flophouse for railroad workers back in the old days. Group of businessmen bought it as a retreat, blew their wad remodeling it, and now it's this nice, upscale hotel. The Haydens have three rooms on the top floor."

"Can we reach out to them?"

"No legit way. Bernie says nobody's even 'spozed to know the family's on the premises. But get this. Emily, the daughter? Bernie says she booked out of there last night to hook up with some guy she's bangin'. He says her parents don't know she went out. The rent-a-cop told Bernie he expects she'll pull the same stunt tonight. Apparently, she was a real little charmer at five a.m. when she dragged back in. Cried, claimed the boyfriend was 'comforting' her, begged the hotel guy not to rat her out."

"Of course, being a gentleman . . ."

"Of course. The hotel guy reported it to Bernie. It gets better, though. I buried the lead of the story like you reporters say. The boyfriend is twice her age."

"I don't care if she's sleeping with her grandpa. Can we get the hotel guy to tip us if she leaves?"

"I set it up already. Last night she took off about midnight. But get this. Hotel Boy ran the friend's plate. So we can either wait for her at the hotel or show up at the dude's house."

We cruised the hotel, Al driving and working the phone with his security buddy, me watching for outside police surveillance. Had to cover the idea that they'd assign at least a token car in case Trey Hayden's parents had been the real targets of the home invasion. I saw nothing.

The Briarcliff had a look of subtle elegance. Vine-covered brick walls and a riverfront cocktail lounge that appeared to be doing a brisk business. Balconies set up with tables for two overlooking a swimming pool. A brick front courtyard with colored lights done up in a Spanish motif. From where Al turned around in the driveway, I could hear the soft strains of a guitar. Not the kind of place I'd associate with hiding from tragedy, but it was small and out of the way. And best of all for the Haydens, not surrounded by TV trucks.

Al slapped his cell closed and nosed the Crown Vic between two trucks parked at a loading dock across the street from the Briarcliff's back door.

"The boyfriend's car is registered to a Max Gambrel. Bernie ran him on the computer. He's a math teacher at the high school. Bernie's guy just showed for work. That was him on the phone. He sees this Emily on the move, he'll let us know. That's the door she came out of last night. The family's rooms are on the other side of the building so he figures, if she's going, she'll come out this way again."

"How's he know she's still in there?"

"He called up to their room to see if there was anything they needed. She answered."

"Then we wait."

He ratcheted the seat back, opened a bag of M&M's and settled his head on the headrest.

I said, "You want to offer any thoughts about where we take this story?"

"Well." He offered me the M&M's. I shook my head. "You heard what that Mendoza character had to say. Personally, I think the kid found a pistol and took it."

"The one the cops say never existed."

He snorted. "Right. And they've been so up front with everything else there's no reason to think they'd mislead us about that."

"And they don't want us thinking about a gun that came out of the greenhouse because, being the topflight journalists we are, pretty quickly we'll be asking why it was in there in the first place."

He rattled the bag. This time I let him pour a handful into my palm.

"OK. So, Trey comes across the gun. People say he was a pretty smart kid so he starts thinking the way we are: it's hidden in a weird place, chances are the owner isn't going to call the cops if it turns up missing. Trey wants a gun, for whatever reason, maybe just 'cause he's a teenager. Who knows? He walks off the job to hide it, or maybe take it home."

"And the owner doesn't call the cops. Instead, he sends a gopher to get it back." Al stopped with two M&M's at his mouth. "Wait. How's he know the Hayden kid is the one who took it?"

"Mendoza said he could have seen Trey come out of the woods. He's panicked, suspicious, so he asks the crew chief who the kid was."

The door to the hotel opened and two young Hispanic women in blue maid's uniforms walked out, followed by an older Hispanic man in hospital scrubs. A moment later a ten-year-old black Cadillac nosed out of the parking lot and glided off down the street.

I closed my eyes for a moment, drifting . . .

Vinnie sat up in front of me. His skin, usually a deep ebony, was gray, his face almost the color of dust. He was gasping for air. One hand at his throat, he yanked at the IVs attached to his arms with the other. The lines wouldn't come free. He pointed a nearly fleshless finger at my face. I moved forward and stepped into my own field of vision. I was hunched over as though in pain, both of my arms curled around my midsection. In the next instant, however, I withdrew a handgun. Vinnie's mouth opened. I realized he was trying to scream. I reached out and tried to grab the figure of myself but the .38 revolver came up anyway, traversing Vinnie's chest. And then I was back in my own body with the gun heavy in my hand and my finger squeezing back the trigger . . .

"No!"

I jerked awake as Al touched my arm.

"Whoa," he said. "Nightmare?"

I looked down, expecting to see the .38. When it wasn't there, I lifted my hand to my scalp. I was sweating. Flashbacks and nightmares. Wasn't this fun?

The smell of Vinnie's hospital room lingered. Had I said anything? I started to ask but Al gestured across the street. A dark Ford Thunderbird convertible was parked at the curb. Al grinned.

"Math Max and his Thunderbird," he quipped. Then, as if suddenly thinking of it, "Shit. Did you want me to shoot this?"

I coughed, cleared my throat. "I don't want her on camera at all."

Emily Hayden stepped through the Briarcliff's door. I caught a quick glimpse of jeans and a T-shirt, a bag over her arm, and then she got in on the passenger side of the sporty Ford and the car accelerated away. Al waited until we saw her turn in her seat to stow her bag and look forward again before pulling out into the street and following.

The ride took about ten minutes. With hardly any traffic on the roads, Al stayed well back leaving me to track where we were going on the Crown Vic's GPS map system. About two blocks from the address on the Thunderbird's plate, Al took a parallel street and gunned it so we arrived at the boyfriend's digs just ahead of them. I was out of the car and crossing the dark street as they pulled to the curb. I could feel the tension of imminent confrontation all the way up my back and into my neck. I shrugged, trying to release it.

I stopped where I could easily be seen in the throw from a streetlight. "Ms. Hayden? Emily?" I said as they opened their doors.

"Oh Christ." The driver seemed to shrink into his seat. He had tight, dark, curly hair, glasses and a hooked nose. His left foot was on the pavement and he kept one hand on the open door but didn't move.

"Who are you?" Emily Hayden had a throaty voice that might turn sexy in a few years. Now it just sounded harsh, on the edge of petulance.

Walking up, I'd decided her reaction would tell me how to play it, gentle or . . . not so gentle. But it was the boyfriend's shock that gave me a third option.

"Sorry if I took you by surprise, Max." I leaned down as

though I was checking him out. "Max Gambrel, right? You teach at Falcon Ridge North?"

"Christ," he repeated. "This isn't happening . . ."

"God, Max! Shut *up!*" Emily threw an evil glare at me. "I'm here because I want to be so there's nothing you can do to him."

"I don't care why you're here. I'm a reporter, not a cop. I'm sorry about your brother. And I'm sorry to approach you this way, but there are a couple of things we need to talk about."

At that, Max lunged from the car and started around to the passenger side, arms flapping. He wore black baggy pants and a white, open-front shirt and looked like a puffed up penguin with improbable eyebrows. I took a step back out of range and turned a shoulder toward him.

"Em, get in the house," he said in a tone he probably used on his students when they weren't up to speed on the Pythagorean theorem. "You don't have to say anything to him. Just go in the house. It's private property, they can't do anything . . . they don't have any proof . . ."

As he reached for her, she grabbed his arm with both hands and gave it a little shake, leaning into him. "Hey! Max! Shut. Up." Voice lowered to a hiss with some desperation in it. "Just be quiet. Nothing's going to happen, okay? You go in the house if you want but chill." She patted his arm before letting it go.

"I can't let you . . ." he began.

"Dude, chill. Chill. We're cool. We are." She glanced at me. Almost like a mother asking me not to hurt her child. I nodded.

"I have some questions for Emily," I said to him. "No pressure. If she chooses to answer, fine. If not, there's no downside. I was never here."

He was shaking his head. Under the streetlamp I could see his movie star cleft chin but he was sweating through his cologne. "You're here to fuck with us. That's all you TV people do. And it's my life you're going to fuck up." His right hand curled into a fist.

I settled into a nice balanced posture, knees slightly bent, hands down at my sides. I had height and reach on him and the advantage of having been in probably two zillion more fights than he had. Even so, I kept my eyes on his. It's the ones you underestimate who will hurt you.

I said, "I don't give a rat's ass about what you guys have going. Not my business. But, Max, if you take a swing at me, that all will change."

Emily reached out again, took his fist in both hands. "Nothing bad is going to happen. You know how I told you I can sense things? It's cool, dude. It is."

It took him a minute while his mathematician's brain figured the odds that he'd be able to land a good first punch. When he realized the equation wasn't going to come out the way he wanted, he let out a sigh.

"Go up to the house. I'll be up in a minute," she said.

He stalked up to the front porch and settled into a chair, watching us.

"You handled that well," I said.

She gave me a sidelong glance. "I know boys. He may be older but that's all he really is. That's all most men are."

"How does he compare to Lucas?"

No hesitation. No asking how I knew. No embarrassment. "Lucas was just a fuck buddy. Actually, it was sweet doing a friend of my brother's. Max . . . he might be different. Long term maybe. We'll have to see."

Part of me wanted to tell her she was trodding a dangerous path, but I needed her on my side. Besides, I was no social worker.

"Did Trey know about Lucas?"

"I don't know. Lucas was really into creating drama. Trey

and I don't . . ." She stopped, took a breath. "We didn't talk much. He used to always try to be the 'older brother' when I was a kid but in the last couple of years, he's been so whacked on weed he couldn't even tie his shoes."

She leaned back on the Thunderbird and crossed her arms under her breasts. "And your next question is going to be do I think Lucas could have killed my brother? No. Not possible."

"Why do you say that?"

"Lucas liked sex real physical, okay? Even painful. But I never saw him pick a fight with anybody. Plus, Trey was like this *follower.* Lucas needed his audience. Plus . . . when I saw him coming out of our house? He was totally zoned and crying. I can't really explain it." She shuddered and leaned her head back, drawing in a lungful of air.

"Take it easy . . ."

It was a couple of minutes before she could speak again and only after she ground the heels of both hands into her eyes.

"It's so fucking strange, you know? Trey being . . . gone. Like, I'd go for days not thinking about him at all, and he was still right there in the house. He wouldn't usually talk to me. I mean, it's not like I wanted him to or anything. Now, I can't stop thinking about him. And then I wonder, like, what if it had been me there . . . alone . . . when that guy came? Instead of him."

Her words sent a tremor of guilt through the center of my chest. *I can't stop thinking about him.* I had tried to put Vinnie out of my mind all summer.

To get us both back on track, I asked, "Did you notice anything odd lately about your brother's behavior?"

"Yeah. I heard him and Margo arguing. He screamed something about wanting to be the only one to clean his room. That was so not like him."

"They argued about him cleaning his room?"

"Yeah. Come on. He was a slob. But, like, two weeks ago he acted like a real dick to Ivana. She's the maid. He liked her. But he, like, *ordered* her to stay out of his stuff. Margo heard it and went off on him. So, yeah. I figured he was worried she'd find his stash or something."

"We think Trey stole a handgun he found on a job site about two weeks ago. Could that be what he was hiding?"

She lifted her head as though listening for a faint sound.

"I don't know," she said finally, "but I was in the downstairs hall a couple of nights ago? Getting ready to go out? I asked him for the five dollars he owed me. When he pulled out his wallet, something fell on the floor. I looked. You know how you do when somebody drops something? It was a bullet."

"He say anything about it?"

"No. I didn't ask."

"It didn't surprise you?"

"Come on, dude. It was a bullet, not a machine gun, okay? He always liked guns. I just figured, you know, he found it somewhere or something."

"Let me put it this way. If he'd found a gun and didn't think anyone knew about it, would he take it?"

She nodded. "Prob'ly. Why not?"

Two cars passed and she seemed to cringe, the way I'd seen street people do at the sight of a patrolling squad. The night air was cool and she had her arms wrapped around herself now, huddled against the side of the Ford and looking miserable.

"Can I ask you something?" she said.

"Sure."

"Do you think the police really want to, like, solve my brother's murder?"

"The fact you ask tells me you have your doubts."

"Well, yeah. I guess." She hesitated. "They made my dad look at the video of, you know, the whole thing. The crime

250

scene. That just wasn't right. He told me he felt himself dead there on the floor when he saw Trey. Said it was like everything around him stopped and there was no sound, no nothing. He thought he was having a heart attack. And then he wished he was."

Nice thought to share with your daughter.

"Emily, has your dad ever mentioned the name Theo Zacharias? Or maybe Theo Zak?"

Her body went utterly still. "Is that the guy who killed my brother?"

"Do you know who he is?"

"Isn't he like . . . the mayor or something? Lucas used to take me out to Wiley's. There was a party once that he was at. He's a nasty old man."

"Did Lucas know him? Talk to him?"

"No. I don't know. Wait. Wait. So do you think he like, came here looking for Lucas and Trey was just . . . in the way or something?"

I felt like she'd smacked me with a shovel. From her expression, she noticed my surprise.

"What?" Emily asked. "Is that what happened . . . ?"

"I don't know. I need to check on something, though." I wanted to talk to Al and Sunny. "Do me a favor. Keep that name to yourself. For the time being, anyway. Okay?"

Emily put her hand on my arm.

"OK, but can I ask you something? Even if the cops don't care, you're going to find my brother's killer, aren't you?"

"I'm going to try."

CHAPTER TWENTY-TWO

"Talk about feeling stupid," I said.

Al and I were in Sunny's room at the motel. She sat on the bed with her computer in front of her. Al had his feet up on a little desk in the corner while I leaned in the open doorway, glancing every so often at raindrops that looked like ice crystals exploding when they hit the hood of Sunny's Expedition.

"It was the way Emily said it that finally got to me. All along, I've been thinking Lucas had to be part of this. He was a player and he knew the other players. He sold dope with Wiley; Wiley's in bed with Zak. But what if there *is* no direct connection? What if Zak sent the killer in there and, by blundering in afterward, Lucas set himself up as a very convenient fall guy?"

"You're saying it was Zak's gun Hayden stole?" Sunny asked.

"Pretty easy to tell. Did he just lose a greenhouse in a storm?" Al asked.

I handed that off to Sunny. "What's Zak's address? Does he live in The Heights?"

"Checking," she said. Computer keys clicked. "The only listing for Zak is on Old County Road B. That's west. Nowhere near Falcon Ridge Heights."

"Anything on any of his kids?"

"A Zak law office, downtown Falcon Ridge. No residential listings."

"How about the demolition permit? Tax records?"

"Like you thought. Wihega County doesn't keep any records

online. Their site is all news releases and pretty pictures."

I grunted. "Crap."

Al said, "Off the subject but something I got to ask. Which cops are fucking with the case?"

Remembering the Leadership Council banner in the picture in Teague's office I said, "Teague did a couple of questionable things at the house. First, he booted Duvall, and second, he kept the coroner's people at bay for no apparent reason. And, he's denying any possibility Trey had a gun when it's pretty obvious he did."

"He wouldn't have been in the house by himself," Al said. "Teague, I mean. So if you're thinking he might have messed with the scene that means he's got somebody else working with him."

"That's another thing. What exactly happened in there? Duvall calls Esperanza for help, but once Teague arrives he countermands the order and gives Espy the old, 'Don't let the door hit you in the butt on your way out.' "

Without warning, the steady rain escalated into a blitzing downpour. The lights seemed to be out in Jody's room across the courtyard and in the one Al and Peter were sharing. For several moments we were silent, listening to the storm surge and then diminish.

"Feels like the temperature's dropped about ten degrees," I said.

Al got up from his chair and joined me in the doorway. He sniffed the ozone-scented air. "Talking about crooked cops depresses me. I'm going to bed. Don't stay up all night talking, kiddies."

When he shambled off, closing the door behind him, Sunny said, "There's another scenario, you know. Emily seems to have her share of boys. Her stepmother is young, attractive, and on TV. What if our guy is a predator? Went in there looking for one of them? Or both?"

"And ran into Trey by mistake? And he just happened to have a gun and decided to *Home Alone* it?"

"Tell me you don't think that's plausible."

"Sure. But it doesn't explain the cops' goofy behavior at the scene. And since."

"Cops don't like reporters. So what else is new?"

I remembered the way the cop with the H&K at Grandma Bremmer's house had looked at me. Teague's threats.

"No. This goes beyond cop hostility toward the media, Sunshine." Another thought struck me. "You finished with your security audit?"

She shrugged. "I have to write the report. What's on your mind?"

"Crimes with a handgun in Wihega County where they never found the gun. Any way to check? Say going back ten, fifteen years?"

"Maybe. You're hanging a whole lot on this phantom pistol, you know?"

"Won't be a phantom if you find it." I was starting to get a headache. I rubbed the back of my neck.

Sunny grinned and got to her feet. She wore jeans and a dark, short-sleeved polo shirt. Her 9mm automatic rode in a high-rise holster on her right hip.

"Come on, sailor," she said and hooked my arm with her hand. "I'll walk you back to your room. Al isn't the only one who needs some shut-eye."

The motel's parking lot was quiet in the downpour's afterglow. As we passed the door to Jody's room, however, a scream bristled the hairs on the back of my neck.

Sunny moved a fraction of a second before I did. As she tried the knob, it spun in her hand, broken, and the door sprung inward. She barreled forward, right hand coming up with the

9mm. I was a step behind and in perfect position to see her track the gun to the two figures, one large one small, struggling against the wall next to the bed.

Jody's attacker was half-again as wide across the shoulders as me and perhaps two or three inches taller. In the dim light of a bedside lamp at its lowest setting, I saw his face as he twisted our way. Duane Grum. He had one arm across Jody's throat, the other hand on her chest. She wore only panties and a sweat-shirt that was pushed above her breasts. As Grum spun away from her, she shoved him. The move forced Grum to take his first step toward us off balance and his foot caught in the tumbled bedclothes. It gave Sunny just enough time to re-holster her gun.

I saw Grum's eyes shift from me to Sunny and knew he was going to blitz. When he charged, trying to get past us and through the door, she tore into him. Punched chest, throat, and eyes, turned, elbowed the side of his thick neck. Rolled behind him, smashed kidneys, ducked a massive, flailing arm, levered him upright with a fist thrust somewhere near his armpit and with a move as subtle and quick as a hunter snapping the neck of a wounded bird, brought him to his knees. She bent with him, hand splayed across his back, as he went down. He made no sound.

"A girl says no," she said into his ear, "she means no."

He wanted another shot. Braced on the knuckles of his right hand, in a clumsy variation of a three-pointed stance, he tried to shake her off. She brought out her Sig-Sauer again and jammed it in under his eye.

"No," she said. "Remember?" She thumbed the hammer back. No threats, no pronouncements, just a double click. No emotion whatsoever and that's what made it work. He was as convinced as I was that, if he kept trying to get back in the game, she would blow his brains out the back of his skull.

"Down on your face. Do it now."

He hesitated. I was about to step over and force the issue when I heard a gasping wheeze from behind us. Jody, bent double, was holding the end of the bed for support as she tried to suck in oxygen. Her free hand flailed at me and when she lifted her head for a moment, her expression was red from the effort of trying to breathe.

"Where's your inhaler? Bathroom?"

She gave a grateful nod.

I found it next to the sink. When I came back, I saw Sunny squatted on the floor, out of Grum's reach, one hand holding her cell phone to her ear. She had the other rock solid around the grip of her Sig pointed at the back of his head. She ordered an ambulance and the cops.

Jody put the inhaler in her mouth and squeezed it. I could tell from the relief in her eyes that she'd gotten at least a partial puff of the medication.

I said, "Paramedics will be here in a few minutes, kiddo. Just take it slow." I glanced back to check on Sunny . . . and was just in time to see Grum gather his feet under him, hear her shout, "Don't!" and then see him lunge toward the door.

The Sig barked once as she uncoiled from her squat. Part of the doorframe disintegrated but his wide body was already through it. A ninety-degree jig to his left and he disappeared.

Sunny took three steps with the Sig in a combat grip, turned, and leveled it down the passageway in front of the other rooms. Before she could fire, however, I heard the crack of another weapon and the *thwack* of a bullet striking something solid. Sunny dropped to her belly.

"Shit!"

For a moment, I thought she'd accidentally squeezed off a second round from the Sig. Then the room's front window imploded and I heard a second gunshot and then a third.

"Get down!" Sunny snapped. I was already in motion, though, lunging for a kneeling Jody, getting one arm around her and carrying her with me into the bathroom.

"Get into the tub!" I snapped and charged back into the room. Through the open door I could see Sunny had come up into a squat in front of Jody's SUV. Movement outside the window caught my eye and Al appeared in a crouch next to her, pistol in his hand as well.

Sunny pointed across the courtyard. "Shooter's on the roof above those rooms. All I saw was a dark shape."

"I'll try to draw his fire." Al moved to his right. The warble of an electronic siren from about a block away stopped him. As a civilian, it's never good to be running around with a gun when the cops show up.

And show up they did. A black, unmarked Crown Vic, red and blue lights flashing behind the grill, roared into the courtyard from the street. As its siren died, I heard others coming from farther away. I saw Al slide his gun under his shirt. Sunny stowed hers back in her hip holster. Neither came up from their crouch. When Ray Duvall emerged from the driver's side of the Vic, Sunny shouted, "Gun!" and gestured toward where she'd seen the sniper. Duvall dodged behind his car, pistol in hand, and began jabbering into a hand-held radio.

There was no more shooting.

"Thirty cents worth of lock," Duvall said, examining the knob on the door to Jody's room. He fell silent, watching a pair of young female paramedics check a bruise on Jody's arm. Sunny was talking to a couple of deputies outside, giving them what little description she could of the shooter. The courtyard was crowded with county squads, fire equipment, and nervous motel guests in various degrees of clothing.

I could still smell gunpowder from the shot Sunny had fired.

Mixed with the vehicle exhaust it was turning my earlier headache into a pounding drum.

"I heard the door bang against the wall as I was getting into bed," Jody said, voice a little shaky. "Then he was all over me."

The paramedics asked us to step out so they could finish their work. I pulled the door closed behind me and stood in front of it.

Duvall grunted. "I was a block away when the 'shots fired' call came out. On my way here to warn you people we made Grum for firebombing your truck and to keep your heads down."

"Yeah and if you hadn't eaten that last donut, you might have gotten here in time to do some good," I said.

He stared at me. "You love all this banging around where you don't belong, don't you? Steven Seagal meets Woodward and Bernstein?"

"Bullshit, Commander. I'm not the problem."

"You see any other media people getting their shit blown up? Anybody else with a target on his back?" He snapped, face reddening the way it had outside the Hayden crime scene.

Sunny turned toward us. "Boys? How about instead of comparing the size of your dingalings you zip 'em up and just try to have a nice conversation? Think you can accomplish that?" Her smile could have tamed a herd of raging rhinoceros.

The door behind me opened and the paramedics stepped out.

"How's our girl?" Sunny asked.

They said they'd like to take her to their unit for a more complete exam. As Jody followed them into the parking lot, Duvall took a slow breath. I leaned against the wall, my foot finding some of the glass from the broken window. Neither of us said anything for a moment. The radio on his belt murmured something and lights off one of the ambulances winked a pattern against the doors of rooms across the courtyard.

Duvall grunted. "That fuckin' Grum. Maybe now, with the ISPERN alert, we'll be able to snatch him up. Doubtful but, maybe."

"Why doubtful?" I made sure I used a neutral tone.

"You know his history?"

I nodded. Stayed neutral. "The rape, the screwed-up video tape in your evidence vault?"

"Twice since then he's been a suspect in other rapes. Both times he split before anybody could question him. When the victims suddenly refused to press charges, he reappeared."

"So you're telling me somebody's tipping him off and then getting to your victims."

"Draw whatever conclusions you like."

I gestured at the roof across the way. "Well it's pretty obvious he's not working alone."

As if on cue, a voice on Duvall's radio said, *"There's roof access from a maintenance closet on the third floor. Looks like that's what the shooter used. Probably had a car waiting out back. He's long gone."*

Just as that voice finished, another said, *"All units. Heads up. Wozniak is here."*

At that, Duvall sighed and said, "Shit. Is he teleporting himself like on *Star Trek* now?" He keyed up the microphone attached to his shoulder. "I don't care what he says, keep him outside the tape. I'm on my way." He got to his feet.

"One question before you go," I said. He glanced at Sunny, still standing in the doorway, and then looked back at me.

"What?"

"Did you really think you needed help from the state at the Hayden murder scene? Or did you just want an impartial witness there to back you up?"

"Aren't you the one who accused me of misdirecting the investigation?"

"Maybe I was wrong."

"Imagine that." He stared unblinking for a moment. "Maybe I was wrong getting in your face down by the river, too."

The cops took another hour getting out of there. Jody agreed with the paramedics that she should go home and see her own doc in the morning. Peter drove her in her Jeep with Al following. Sunny set up shop in Al and Peter's room next to mine. A precaution, she said, though neither of us expected Grum to return with a county squad now parked in front of the motel.

I went to bed and awoke, not to the alarm I'd set for four-thirty, but to the Nextel's annoying chirp and Chucky's voice snarling, "Reno. Reno! Goddamn it, answer me." It was slightly after four by the bedside clock. I'd slept for about three hours. I wondered if this was just a dream.

I thumbed the unit off and had just started to drift again when the room phone rang. I gave up and answered it.

"What the *hell* are you people doing out there?" Chucky snapped.

I thought he was talking about Jody. He threw cold water on that right away.

"I just got a call from Margo Hayden. Her daughter claims you confronted her in the middle of the night, threatened her, God knows what else. What on earth were you thinking, McCarthy? The *sister* of a murder victim and she's not even an adult. For Chrissakes . . . we'll be lucky if the Haydens don't file a lawsuit as soon as the courthouse opens—"

"Give me a minute." I put the phone on the bed while I went into the bathroom to throw some water on my face. It didn't make any sense for Emily to have told her stepmother about our conversation unless . . .

Unless the security guard snitched her off and she was covering her assignation.

260

I sat on the bed. Picked up the phone again. "You finished?"

"You're the one who's finished. I told you—"

"What's she say I did?"

"Bushwhacked her. She's getting some air. You stuck a camera in her face . . ."

I explained what really happened. "She's trying to keep her boyfriend clear. There's no video. Al never got out of the car. I questioned her alone."

"You don't get it, do you? It doesn't matter. Mama Hayden wants to file a restraining order against us. How's that going to look in the *Sun-Times*? Hell it'll probably be the headline story on the News-Blues site."

Disgusted I said, "For Christ's sake, Chucky."

"You're suspended. I'm sending Caroline out to meet with Al and Peter. She'll do the morning live shot. You're going to be looking for another job if you're not sitting in front of my desk at ten a.m."

I threw the phone across the room. The ringer chimed once as it bounced on the carpet.

The alarm didn't wake me and neither did the sun streaming through drapes I had forgotten to close. Al succeeded where the clock and Mother Nature failed. He pounded on the door until I got up and unlatched it for him. A snippet of the morning chill followed him inside. He handed me a cup of Starbucks coffee. I took it in both hands, grateful for its warmth, and went back to sit on the bed.

"You look like shit and you got four hours more sleep than I did," he said.

"Caroline show up in time?"

"Yeah. Had to do makeup though. If I had to wake up next to that in the morning I'd shoot myself. Chucky or somebody wrote the piece for her and dictated it to Peter over the phone."

"Probably a good thing. She mention any of the new stuff?"

He made a rude noise. "Total rehash of yesterday's five o'clock. Made it sound like we took the night off."

I sipped the coffee. Took a tentative swallow. It burned. "Is Chucky pulling you out?"

"Yeah. Says he thinks we've done all we can do, the story's pretty much over with. Doesn't think the Grum angle is worth pursuing. I even tried to get him interested in what Channel Two was chasing last night, the 'cops screwed up the scene' crap. No go."

"You tell him about the greenhouse? Or what Emily gave us?"

"He didn't wanna hear any of that. Especially anything about the girl."

More coffee. Despite the warmth, I felt numb. "Have you seen Sunny yet?"

"I was just over there. She's working on the computer. Said to come over when you're done playing Rip Van Winkle."

I showered, called Sunny's room, and told her I'd meet her in the motel's sad excuse for a coffee shop. When I walked over there, blinking in the fall sunshine, she was already in a booth. Two guys in rumpled business suits were sitting two booths away and the one with his back to her kept turning around to glance her direction. I slid in across the table and caught the guy frowning at me. I stared at him until he swiveled to face his friend.

"You're just a bucket of cheerful this morning," Sunny said.

I signaled the waitress for coffee. "Always wanted to settle down with a siding salesman, have you?"

"You know it. A little trailer in the country, college football Saturdays, and NASCAR after church Sunday." She winked at me. The waitress showed up. As she poured she asked if I wanted breakfast or if I was going to be a cheap date. Cheap date, I told her. The way my stomach was rolling I didn't want to chance food.

"You find anything on the gun?"

"I ran some keyword checks through the newspaper and came up with eight hits, all from the last ten years. Lowlife stuff, mostly domestic homicides. Google couldn't do any better."

"Go back further."

"Would you ingest a chill pill? I tried. The *Examiner*'s online archives only go back as far as 1986. Nothing helpful in the *Tribune* or the *Sun-Times*. I can call a buddy at ATF later this morning, see if they have anything."

"While you're doing that, mind if I borrow your wheels? I need to run an errand."

Her head tipped as she slid her keys across the table. "I thought you had an appointment at the station."

"Chucky can wait."

I left Sunny's Expedition in the parking lot behind the courthouse and followed a group of high school kids through the metal detector. The county board's anteroom where I'd posed for the photo was jammed with people and another dozen lingered in the hall outside. I passed them and pushed through into the DeeBree offices.

No sign of Jan. I peered around the corner, expecting to see Verna Shottlehauser hidden away behind her paperwork and collection of candy jars, ripping big gouging bites out of a turkey leg. She wasn't there either. I settled into a plastic chair in the outer office to wait. A moment later, a connecting door to the county board chamber pushed open, and she waddled through carrying a plaque. Today she wore a blue caftan and outrageous red lipstick with a string of pearls so snug around her neck they could have been a tattoo. She blinked once when she saw me and then flashed the phony smile.

"Mr. McCarthy. What a nice surprise. Are you here to cover the Good Government Awards?" She brandished the object she was holding. "Or are you back with more questions I won't be able to answer?"

"Just one."

"Well, you'll have to excuse me if the phone rings. My secretary called in sick. The poor girl sounded awful. Come, come." She swept past me, trailing a fragrance that was at once too sweet and too much. Settled behind her desk, she asked, "So, what are we investigating today?"

"Two weeks ago, one of your crews cleaned up a collapsed greenhouse on some property in Falcon Ridge Heights. I'd like the name of the client."

Her smile compressed to a thin, smug line as she tapped the space bar on her computer. "I can do that for you."

A view of sea surf and California's Point Sur lighthouse disappeared. She talked while she entered data.

"I imagine Wihega County must seem like a very obstinate place to you by now."

"No worse than most dictatorships."

"Goodness, I don't think we're quite that bad. Two weeks ago you say?"

"Somewhere around there."

"We'll try the week of September eleventh then." She clicked more keys and looked at a calendar page.

"Hmmm. No. No greenhouses down in rainstorms. Let's go to the first of the month." Another series of clicks, some more peering at the screen and then she glanced up. "I'm so sorry. I don't have a record of that. It must not have been our crew."

"Shall we cut the crap, Verna?"

My tone and words killed her smile. "Do you need to curse? I was just trying to be helpful—"

"You're acting helpful. There's a difference. I didn't say

anything about a rainstorm.""

"Well, we've had a lot of rain—"

"Give me the owner's name, and I'm out of here. Nobody ever needs to know it crossed your lips. Hold back and my lead story at noon will be how DeeBree is helping the County Refuse Department keep its landfill open by dumping your loads all over creation, including in neighboring counties. You think that'll win you another Good Government Award?"

I suspect if she'd been able to spring to her feet, she would have done so. Instead, a red flush started where the pearls were imbedded at the base of her throat.

"That's preposterous!"

"Is it? We'll see what the EPA thinks. Given that the trash we shot video of is along the river, I expect the Coast Guard will want in on the game, too. You know how the Feds love to pile on if they see a chance to make the locals squirm."

"People always dump trash where they shouldn't. You can't prove it came from a DeeBree crew."

"I don't have to. How long you think it'll take for an investigator to come up with a name on a scrap of paper? 'Mr. Jones, does that wood look like it came from your basement? Oh, you say you hired someone to do the demolition work for you? Was that DeeBree by chance?' "

"But I didn't . . ." She struggled.

"It's going to get ugly, Verna. Lawsuits. Maybe indictments. Of course, the regular refuse crews have probably been doing the same thing so it may take awhile to get around to you. But, maybe not. And telling your people you'd get their probation yanked if they didn't play along? Nasty. Justice Department Office of Civil Rights will love you for that."

I was posturing, of course. I had no idea if she was directly involved. I was swatting her with fabrications that popped from my imagination like the yellow orbs whipping out of a tennis ball machine. The probation bit seemed likely enough, though. At least it was what Mendoza had claimed the night before. And that's what nailed her. I saw it in her eyes. She got redder and redder until I began to worry she might pop the Big One right in front of me. I hoped not. No way I was doing mouth-to-mouth on those wormy red lips.

Eventually the hands she'd pressed into the desk pushed her back into her chair. "Don't do this. Please."

"Then tell me who owns the greenhouse."

Eyes wide open, she shook her head back and forth sharply several times like a terrified little girl and reached into the jelly-bean jar. She came out with a fistful and tried to stuff them all in her mouth at once. She shook so badly that half the beans cascaded down her front like the broken pieces of a colorful life.

"Let me guess," I pressed. "It was a routine request for a crew. A day or so later somebody told you to keep it off the books."

Her hand flashed back to the candy jars. This time she opted for a swizzle stick. She bit into it viciously. Had her addiction been whiskey and not sweets, she'd be in the bag by now.

I had to choose: good guy or bad. I sighed. What the hell. I didn't like doing it, but it had gotten us past the initial bullshit. I lifted each of her goodie jars off the desk and placed them on the floor. Tough love, baby. Replaced them with my notebook and pen, which I slid across the desk to her.

"Eat yourself to death after I leave. Write the name if you don't want to say it. Draw a picture. I don't care. Otherwise, I'll make sure the next person to sit in this chair has a federal badge in their pocket." The reporter makes The Big Threat.

She kept chewing and staring, chewing and staring. It went on so long I figured she'd swallowed the jelly beans and was gnawing on the inside of her cheeks or maybe her tongue. When she snatched up my pen, I was surprised. She scrawled something on the pad then shoved it away from her so hard it flew into my lap.

I let her keep the pen.

CHAPTER TWENTY-THREE

That morning, after he ushered the plant's security chief out of his office, his secretary asked him if he was feeling okay.

"You're a little pale and your eyes . . ."

Wescott summoned a smile. "I may have a touch of the flu. Thanks for your concern."

He closed his door and leaned on it. If his secretary could see the way he looked, so had Marks the security man. Jesus Christ, he was falling apart.

Control. Focus.

In truth, he had slept little the night before, uncomfortable on the couch but even more so with the scenarios that played out whenever he closed his eyes. Not nightmares. Familiar paranoid fantasies of a police detective (it was always Frank Duvall, the one who investigated Elaine's death) confronting him in his office. The feel of handcuffs slipped around his wrists. Visions of being led into the Wihega County jail amidst a crowd of television cameras. The cell where he would be confined.

He would never survive a night behind bars. Of that he was certain.

A charity fundraiser in the newly constructed Wihega County jail fifteen years ago had convinced him. It was held the week before the jail received actual prisoners and offered contributors the opportunity to spend the night locked up. Then president of the Wihega Leadership Council, urged by his "mentor" to do the politically correct thing, Wescott foolishly accepted the invitation.

He would never forget the sensations. The blood-red nightlighting that seemed to squeeze in all around him. His short, panicked breaths. The isolation that made him want to scream. He lasted fifteen minutes before demanding his freedom. Even as he fled into the dark parking lot, he remembered glancing over his shoulder, terrified they were chasing him.

He felt that terror again now.

Isolation. He realized that's what was causing him to panic. Other than the voice on the phone and the blather of TV news, he had no way of knowing how close they were to him. To his secret. He was cut off from the investigation. But he didn't have to be.

He hurried into his lab. Scanned shelves that contained various models of Forge-produced two-way radios and beta-test versions of others. Selected the unit he wanted, carried it to his workbench, and booted up the computer. Felt stupid he hadn't thought of this before.

He knew the Wihega County Police encrypted its surveillance and investigations channels to avoid monitoring by crooks, reporters, and nosey scanner buffs.

He also knew how to decode the encryption so he could listen as he pleased.

So he could hear them coming.

Chapter Twenty-Four

I drove back to the motel. Sunny had her room door propped open to catch what was now a warming breeze and sat cross-legged on the bed, frowning down at her laptop. She glanced at her watch as I came in.

"You've been gone so long, I thought they'd arrested you."

"Robert Wescott owned our collapsed greenhouse. He's . . ."

Her face went gray. She leaned back from the computer. "I know who he is."

"What's the matter?"

"Let's just say I now have a huge conflict of interest."

It took a moment for her meaning to sink in. "The security audit. He's your client? Forge Global?"

She didn't answer. I dropped into the closest chair.

"Shit," I said. "Can you withdraw?"

"No. I'm too far in. I've seen some of their proprietary stuff and interviewed people. I interviewed *him!* And I sure as hell can't work against his interests while I'm on his dime."

"For Chrissakes! He could be a killer, Sunshine."

"And he used your phantom gun?" No banter now.

"Trey sneaks something out of Wescott's greenhouse and within a couple of days he's asking a buddy to get .38 ammo for him. He drops a bullet in front of his sister. There's a hole in a window at the crime scene that can only be explained by a second gun, which, by the way, the cops are in a panic to deny they know about. Nobody wants to talk about the gunshot residue test. You don't believe that's all a coincidence any more than I do."

She slapped the computer closed. "Damn it."

"Based on what you told me about him yesterday, he could be cracking under the strain."

"I don't know about 'cracking.' Given my earlier impression of the guy, he's got a monkey on his back. About what, I don't know. I'm not going to assume he's responsible for a murder based on your theory. Your witness saw Hayden leave the greenhouse and disappear. He didn't *see* him take a gun. Even if he had, what's to say it was Wescott's? A groundskeeper could have hidden it there. Wescott's wife could have hidden it there."

I started to speak. She held up her hand.

"No more questions. I have to think about this."

"Think about it how?"

"Reno, he's my client."

This I didn't need. Not from her. Not now. "Right. Borrow the wheels again?"

"Put gas in it. What are you going to do?"

"I need more background on Wescott. Are you willing to help me with that right now?"

She shook her head. "Hang onto the truck. I saw a gym down the street. I'm going over there for a run."

I drove back to the center of town and parked near Moira Cullen's office building. A crew was jackhammering a section of the street about a block away. I could feel the vibration in my teeth. It was annoying enough it made me want to go pick a fight with one of them. Since all three looked like they worked out by bench-pressing freight cars, I figured I'd end up with more than my teeth vibrating. Might be a good thing. Get the brain cells moving, too. Flash of insight during beating solves murder mystery. Details at 10.

Moira's perky secretary told me she was with a client but not for much longer. I asked if there were any cookies left. She laughed and pointed me toward the conference room. The bag looked deflated but two nestled at the bottom. I sat at the end of the long table and stared out a window, thinking dark thoughts about Sunny's conflict of interest.

I heard movement and voices in the hall. A moment later Moira appeared in the doorway. This morning she wore a gray suit and had her hair up and clipped. She carried a mug of coffee and looked crisp, focused, ready to take on the worst Wihega County's prosecutors could throw at her.

"Reno? When I saw that bimbo doing the morning news, I was worried . . ."

Caroline wins over another viewer. "I'm off the story."

Her face crinkled in surprise. She refreshed her mug from the coffee pot in the corner and sat down across from me. "Why? Tell me."

I described the attack on Jody, the revelation about Wescott. My theory about the greenhouse, Trey taking the gun, the killing. She kept her expression neutral, the way a good lawyer does when the opposition comes up with an unexpected piece of evidence, but her coffee mug hit the table with a thump.

"Reno, that's so left field. Pike Wescott isn't the warmest of men but a murderer?"

"Give me a thumbnail picture of him. Not warm and fuzzy. What else?"

She turned the mug in a complete circle on the table, inspecting all sides before picking it up again.

"Dick Cheney, after nine-eleven. The way he disappeared, locked himself away from the press? Pike's always been like that. He's friendly when I run into him, but it's the kind of friendly you see on the Sunday news programs."

"He have any close friends?"

272

"He knows everyone. Close? I have no idea."

"How about Zak?"

"Well. They attend some of the same social functions. I'd hardly say they're bosom buddies."

I thought about that. Zak and Wescott. Wescott and Zak.

She drank some coffee. "By the way. The gunshot residue test on Trey came back positive. He fired a gun."

"The cops tell you that?"

A wink and an un-lawyerly grin. "I have my sources."

"So, where do they think he got the gun?"

"Lucas."

"That makes no sense." Restless, I moved to the window behind her. Peered through the blinds. "Lucas beats and humiliates Trey, but that isn't enough. So Lucas sneaks into Trey's house in the dark, knowing Trey's armed. To what? Finish the job by shooting him with a gun Wiley says Lucas didn't even have until after the murder?"

She held up a placating hand. "I didn't say I bought the idea."

"How about this? Wescott is hiding the piece for some reason. He finds out Trey helped himself to it as a little souvenir. He sends somebody in to fetch it. Trey defends himself, takes a shot at the guy, and the guy shoots back."

"Why on earth would Wescott be hiding a gun in his green-house?"

"Good question, Counselor. You tell me."

"Jesus, Reno! He's a multimillionaire. His company has solid government contracts. They keep announcing record earnings. He's an inventor, too, did you know that? I think he has something like sixteen patents in his name for electronic technology. Along with running the company he keeps designing new stuff."

"That's quite an answer but not what I'd call responsive to

the gun-in-the-greenhouse question."

"Sue me. I'm a stockholder." She joined me at the window, gently poking my shoulder. "Most business people in Wihega County have a piece of FGT. The lucky ones got in years ago with the IPO. Two-for-one split a year ago. My *point* is, I don't see Pike Wescott as a murderer. If anything, I think it's more likely Trey Hayden hid *his* gun in that greenhouse and wanted to get to it before anyone else did."

I didn't move. Felt aroused by her perfume, her shape, her proximity. "He lived four blocks away. Don't you suppose he could have found a hidey hole a little closer to home?"

"Not if he wanted it far enough away his family wouldn't find it."

"His sister told me the kid loved guns. He ordered the maid out of his room, beginning about two weeks ago. He would have wanted it nearby, believe me. To clean it, play with it . . ."

She lowered her voice. "Sounds like you have some personal experience in this area, Mr. Reporter. Did you have a gun you played with when you were a teenager?" I could smell Starbucks on her breath.

"Loaded question," I said.

She leaned forward and kissed me. It might have turned into quite a bit more, her arms coming up to my shoulders as she tucked herself into me. A knock on the conference room door killed the mood. She hitched back, straightening and blushing like a teenager caught with her shirt off in a parked car.

The perky secretary poked her head inside. If she registered anything amiss, she didn't show it.

"Excuse me, Moira. Mr. Formiss is on line three. He has a question about the plea agreement in the Duckworth case . . ."

Moira scooted away and scooped up the phone. Her blush faded.

There were some framed photos hanging on the wall near the

windows. I glanced absently at them. Moira on the tennis court. Moira on the front page of the Wihega *Examiner,* winning acquittal for a client in a murder case. Another clip from the newspaper showing Moira at a golf match. Moira in a group of women at a picnic. Moira winning an award. I looked at that one more closely.

She ended her call. The girl with the soft lips was gone, replaced by the lawyer who was all business.

"I have to go hold a newbie prosecutor's hand while he writes a plea agreement."

"One thing before you leave?"

She gave me a long-suffering smile. I get those from women a lot. "What?"

"Point me to somebody who'd know about unsolved homicides in Wihega County going back thirty years or more."

"Thirty years? Why so far back?"

"If I counted right, that's about as long as Pike Wescott's been in the public eye. I'm wondering what he might have been up to before that."

"Before that he was child! For Christ's sake, Reno, do you think he was a . . . a *hit* boy in grade school or something? Maybe he snuck off the playground to assassinate world leaders?"

"Never hurts to ask."

"No. That's where you're wrong. It could destroy this county. Do you have any idea what Forge Global is doing for us? With the war in Iraq, their government contracts alone mean new jobs. Expansion of their facility—"

"You'd let a murderer walk so commerce can thrive?"

"That's not what I meant. Wescott . . . the idea of him as a murderer is absurd."

"Then what's the harm in taking a look? It's not my intent to smear him. If it's a wrong turn, we won't do the story."

Her eyes flashed. "You can't just go digging up the man's past like that."

"It's not just his past I want to research. Zak was here then, wasn't he?"

She considered, biting her lip as she did so.

"You won't do any kind of story until you have proof we can take to court?"

"I won't do a story until I can substantiate the facts."

"Reno, god*damn* it . . ."

"Moira I'll put this together with, or without, your help. Without will take longer and more people will probably figure out what I'm trying to do."

She stood up again, mouth a tight line, and shook her head.

"I'll think about it. That's the best I can do."

Right. I was on my own.

Moira's reference to Wescott as an inventor sent me off on a little tangent.

Grabbing a hot dog and fries, I went back to the Expedition and paged through the articles about him that Jody pulled off the Internet. I was curious. Why would Eldon Forge promote a callow techie to president of the company that he had founded and obviously cared a great deal about? Sure young Pike Wescott had been exceptionally bright, even possibly a genius if I chose to believe the puffery some reporters wrote about him. But come on. Wouldn't Forge have had his own seasoned managers and even top-flight execs from other firms all angling to make the step up? Why would Forge take the risk on a kid right out of grad school even if he was a kind of surrogate son?

I finally found a *Fortune* article written to mark Wescott's promotion in 1983 that gave a sly hint. It referred to Forge's "delicate emotional state." What was that about? It wasn't until I reached the middle of the third page of a mind-numbingly geeky piece in *Technology Journal* that anything clicked. Throwaway mention of the death of Forge's second wife. His *second* wife? I knew the first one was dead. The young one, too? I rifled back through the previous articles I'd read. Yep, there it was. A 1977 piece in the *Tribune*'s business section put Elaine Forge's age as twenty-four. She died at twenty-four? Why? Or better yet, how? *Technology Journal* didn't tell me. The final two articles in the Internet bunch failed to enlighten me, too.

Johnnie Perkins was in conference and unable to come to the phone. I left a voice mail asking if she could check her office's historical files and find out what killed Elaine Forge. Then, being the impatient guy I am, I took a ride to see if I could discover the answer for myself.

The Hester Browne Memorial Library was, like many in the Chicago suburbs, so brand new the stacks sparkled and the front desk hummed with the high-tech efficiency of an airline check-in counter. Without the wait. As soon as I stepped up a smiling, gray-haired lady with granny glasses hanging from a chain around her neck pointed me to the right computer terminal and gave me a temporary password to access back issues of the Wihega County *Examiner* past the twenty-year buffer Sunny had found online.

Thirty seconds after I sat down, I wanted to leap to my feet and high five the guy with the oxygen bottle two tables over. I restrained myself.

"Forge Founder's Wife Murdered," the headline proclaimed.

Hooray for computer technology and newspaper archives. And libraries.

Four articles appeared on successive days after Elaine Forge's death. Heart hammering so fast I thought I might need to ask the old guy for a hit off his bottle, I devoured every word looking for mention of what killed her.

Chief of Police Lucca Fischer, the only source quoted by

name, said she had been shot by an unknown intruder, perhaps someone with a gripe against Forge Technologies or even gunning for Forge himself. The murder weapon had not been found. Fischer claimed his officers were interviewing several recently fired workers, as well as groundskeepers from the Forge estate, and following up a number of promising leads.

In cop speak that meant, "We have diddly."

By the fifth day, the paper dropped its coverage of the murder to an inside page. None of the articles mentioned Pike Wescott.

Then came a surprise. Instead of challenging Chief Fischer to provide more information or building out the story by interviewing family or neighbors the way most papers and other media would have, the *Examiner* gave up. The only other mention of Elaine Forge came in a two-paragraph obituary a week after she was killed.

A heater case involving a prominent local family and they blew it off.

I searched using all the keywords I could think of to find any more coverage. Nothing.

I thought of the quote I'd used on Wozniak. "A newspaper has no friends." On the contrary, the Wihega County *Examiner* seemed to have had quite a few buddies in the old boy network back in 1977, but didn't seem willing to offend any of them by asking tough questions.

I walked up to the reference desk. The smiley lady was gone, replaced by a woman the people in front of me called Marge. The name fit in a wizened, wrinkled, senior-with-savvy sort of way. White hair in cloud-like tufts and the eyes of a debt collector who thinks she's getting stiffed.

When it was my turn, she looked at me for a couple of seconds and then said, "Well? What do you need? Speak up. Sign says 'reference.' That's what we do here."

"Were any local newspapers other than the *Examiner* covering

Falcon Ridge or Wihega County in the mid-seventies?"

"Ha. Not unless a scandal sheet is your idea of a newspaper."

"A scandal sheet?"

She pointed to a glass-enclosed room behind her, "In there, along the south wall you'll see the microfiche section. Yes, we still use microfiche. Check the drawers on the right for the Falcon Ridge *Pictorial Times*. It was a weekly. One of those one-man operations run by a paranoid little fellow named Bert Palmer. Nowadays you would probably call him a conspiracy theorist. My husband, rest his soul, used to read the thing front to back." She sniffed.

I thanked her and turned to walk away. She stopped me.

"Please leave everything on the table when you're finished."

"Suppose I just take out one spool at a time and put it right back?"

"Oh, please. You're a man. Trust me, you'll screw it up."

Palmer's first story contained few details amidst a three-paragraph rant about how police, on the order of State's Attorney Theo Zak, refused to even allow him to enter the "neighborhood of Falcon Ridge's rich and famous residents." The story in the next week's issue featured "no comments" from virtually every official from the chief of police to the county coroner but plenty of speculation. Palmer described how State's Attorney Theo Zak had ordered him "forcefully extracted and banned" from the police building after "I confronted him about lack of progress in the case."

Two weeks after the killing, Palmer crowed that he had again "confronted" State's Attorney Theo Zak at a Rotary luncheon about the lack of progress and, this time, "received thin assurances" that Eldon Forge was not a suspect in his wife's murder. Neither was seventeen-year-old Robert Wescott, described as Forge's "brilliant ward." But Palmer also mentioned that Zak had been Forge's personal attorney for five years before his election. Palmer wondered in an editorial, "Is this an unbiased investigation or a case of one hand washing the other?"

Palmer's rants against Zak and the Falcon Ridge police continued for the next several weeks along the same theme: lack of progress, no arrests, no further information being released. And then, two months after Elaine Forge's death, it seemed that time ran out for the *Pictorial Times*. Without a single mention in print that it was going to stop publication, the paper disappeared. I checked the next spool drawer. I was viewing the last one.

How peculiar. Or was it? The fact the Chicago papers hadn't picked up the story didn't surprise me. I hadn't been working in the market then, but it was reasonable to assume they just hadn't heard about it. It happens. Not so much today, but thirty years ago, before they set up bureaus in the suburbs, any number of interesting stories might have slipped through the cracks. What struck me as strange was that each of the local papers had covered the story for a time but then had stopped, either by apparent design or by circumstance.

I've felt the heavy hand of clout pressing down on me numerous times while covering stories in Chicago, in some of the Outfit-friendly suburbs out by O'Hare and even a couple of times on the publicity-sensitive North Shore. Never to the extent I'd experienced in the last couple of days in Wihega County, however. Had clout been at work thirty years ago?

I carefully loaded the spool I'd used back into its container and replaced it in its drawer, leaving the area around the microfiche machine in pristine condition. I thought of wiping the table with my coat sleeve but decided against it, sensing Marge would be disappointed if I didn't allow her some way of earning my five bucks. I waited for two teenagers to leave before approaching her. Her eyes probed me, no doubt searching for the telltale bulge of a microfiche spool under my jacket.

"Did you find everything you need?"

"I did, thank you. I have a question, though. Is Bert Palmer still alive?"

"Why, as of last week he was."

"That sounds like you know where I could find him."

"I certainly do. He's working for his daughter. Trish's Coffee Bar over on Fourth Street. I have to say he doesn't have quite the mouth on him that he did thirty years ago."

"One other thing. Do you recall why he stopped publishing the *Times*?"

She drummed fingers on the counter, thinking. "Don't think I ever knew. One day he was there and the next he wasn't. Good riddance, far as I was concerned. Drove my husband nuts, though. He loved the chaos almost as much as Bert liked creating it."

I thought about that as I walked back to the Expedition. Guys like Bert Palmer, whether they work for newspapers, television, or radio, are the little yappy dogs of the press, biting at the heels of those in positions of power. Sometimes the chaos they cause brings needed change. Sometimes it just brings all that power right down on their heads.

Trish's Coffee Bar had a great location next to the river and a large deck to capitalize on the view in nice weather. Because the menu offered sandwiches and soup to go along with a dozen different coffee drinks, there was nearly a full house inside and a couple of tables filled outside as well. I had an idea of what Bert Palmer looked like thirty years ago from a picture he'd run of himself on the editorial page. I've never been particularly skilled in doing mental age-progression, but as I stood in line waiting to place my order I saw two women and a guy in his twenties serving up the coffee and carrying the meals to the tables. A woman in her forties who I took to be Trish was smiling and laughing as she checked her customers out at the register. Two other guys were in a small back room putting the sandwiches together. One of them joined Trish, but the other just kept working. His head bobbed up when I ordered, however, and by the time I had my cup in one hand and a home-made chocolate chip cookie in the other, he'd moved out to the deck to begin bussing tables.

"Bert?" I asked as I settled in a chair as far from the other customers as I could get, and he began wiping down the next table over.

He straightened. "Figured you were here to see me."

He was a small man with narrow shoulders and the pinched features of a ferret. Physically he hadn't changed much from the guy in the editorial page photo except around the eyes. The fire, the reportorial zeal I'd seen was gone, replaced by a small animal's wariness and a slight tic. I guessed him to be in his early sixties, but he'd kept himself in shape and moved without any sign of the little holdbacks evident in those who suffer from chronic pain or the other vagaries of age. He watched me carefully.

"My name's Reno McCarthy—"

"I know who you are."

"Have time to join me for a cup?"

He looked past me. "I don't like to sit on the job. Looks bad to the customers. What can I do for you, McCarthy?"

"I was just looking through the *Pictorial-Times*. Why did you shut it down?"

"No offense, but if you read more than a few of the articles I wrote back then and still can't figure that out, you should turn in your press pass."

"Pressure from Theo Zak over the Forge murder?"

He gave a single nod.

"Must have been pretty heavy-handed."

"You could say that. He had the bank call the note on my

building and printing equipment. When I went to his office to tell him I'd keep after him if I had to rent a Xerox machine, he claimed I'd threatened him. I did thirty days in jail. While I was serving my time, his people searched my house and threatened my wife. She persuaded me to back off. Hadn't been for her, rest her soul, I'd probably be dead today. Zak was so angry, I think that's where he would have taken it."

"He had that kind of power back then?"

"I scared him into using it. The *Examiner*'s publisher was part of his campaign committee, but I felt obliged to keep asking questions. He didn't want me around." For the first time I saw something in his eyes other than suspicion and anger. It might have been shame.

"I don't much like talking about those days and I need to get back to work. Is that all you need?"

"There is one more thing," I said. "What do you think Zak was hiding?"

"Why is that relevant now?"

"Three kids are dead and one of my people is in the hospital."

I watched him consider the ramifications. And the possibilities they presented.

"I'm not the one you want to talk to about this," he said after a moment. "There's a guy, he was a detective on the Forge case. Went a little out of bounds and got shit-canned for it. He was my source, the one who started me asking the questions I asked. You need to talk to him."

"I can do that. What's his name?"

"Frank Duvall. From the coverage I watched on your station the other morning, I think you've already met his son."

CHAPTER TWENTY-FIVE

Johnnie Perkins called me back as I walked out of the rest room at Trish's.

"What are you trying to get me into now, Reno? My children need their mama to keep her job."

"You're an elected official, Dr. Perkins," I said. "You can't be fired."

"Do not even try to make a joke out of this. Why on earth are you asking for information about a thirty-year-old case? Much less one that has the name attached to it this one does?"

"It may have a direct bearing on the Hayden murder. It's a public record isn't it?"

"Reno . ." She let out a breath and started again. "Public or not . . . have you read anything that has been in the local paper this last week?"

I remembered the headline about dead bodies and dead files. "Tell me."

"Since I took office we have been scanning everything into the computer, all the old files. Some we have. Some we do not. Some are not complete. Upgrading our records is one of my priorities but, as I am sure you realize, it requires manpower, which is not always available. It is very slow going. That file may not exist."

"Shit."

"Let us reverse roles for a moment. Would you care to tell me *off the record* why you are interested in that case?"

"Trey Hayden may have stolen the gun used to kill Elaine Forge. I think he fired it in self-defense right before he was shot to death."

"Stolen? From where? The Forge murder took place thirty years ago."

I told her about the collapsed greenhouse. How Trey left what remained of the structure shortly before Wescott arrived. About Wescott's panicked search for something in the wreckage.

"Please tell me you are not thinking Robert Wescott killed the Forge woman and then killed Hayden to get the gun back."

"I think Wescott killed Forge, yes. I think Zak covered it up. I think Wescott asked Zak to have someone retrieve the gun from the Hayden house. Trey may have been an accident."

"My dear sweet Jesus."

"If you review the Forge file you might find a way to link the two cases."

"You give me far too much credit. Even if we were to find a file, we do not have the body and there is just so much the paperwork can tell us." She sighed. I waited.

"All right. I will do this. I will see if the Elaine Forge file has been computerized. If not, we would have to search the records in the old county building, and that could take forever. If it comes easily to hand, I will have a look. It is the best I can do."

"Actually, there is one more thing you could do . . ."

I asked Johnnie to look up Gary Duvall's home number in the county directory. It's best to go straight to the source for an interview, but a voice far back in my pea-sized brain told me if I wanted to talk to his father I should approach him first. We'd dissed him enough with the video outside the Hayden house. If I upset him with my request, what was the worst he could do? Get drunk and breathe on me again?

He answered with an annoyed, "What?"

Was I interrupting his version of Happy Hour? Maybe Happy Afternoon? When I identified myself, he said, "Yeah, what do *you* want?"

"Your father worked the Elaine Forge homicide in 1977. I'd like to talk to both of you about it."

I thought he'd hung up, but I could hear him breathing. Finally he made a sound that could have been a laugh and said, "You've got a set of 'em. I'll give you that."

"Will you ask him?"

"What's the Forge case got to do with anything?"

"Ask your father if they ever recovered the gun."

I met them for lunch at a joint called Zima's Market in downtown Falcon Ridge. A former grocery-turned-fern-restaurant with plank floors and rock walls, it still had a meat counter in the rear where two guys in long white butcher's coats stood at a carving table creating monstrous sandwiches and serving up soup in bowls the size of water troughs. The Duvalls sat side by side in a rear booth, backs to the wall.

I ordered roast beef very rare and went to join them. Gary stood up when I approached and motioned for me to follow him through a set of metal swinging doors into a back room. When we were out of sight of the other customers he said, "Hands against the wall."

A bearded guy wearing a bloodstained white apron came out of a cooler across the way. He carried a stack of hamburger patties, each sandwiched between pieces of wax paper.

"Hey Gary," he said.

Gary nodded back. "Joe."

Joe proceeded to the front of the restaurant, metal doors swinging in his wake. I assumed the position.

Frank Duvall was working on his sandwich when we returned

to the booth. He put it aside.

"He's clean. No wire," Gary said.

I slid in across from them. They could have been brothers. Frank had jowls and a little more gray in his hair. Cop-hard eyes made me feel like I was in an interrogation room.

"I made some calls. People I talked to say you're okay for a reporter. You got the floor."

They listened. When I finished Frank wiped his mouth with a napkin. Looked at his son. "Go ahead and tell him."

Gary Duvall's voice was flat. "Wiley'll deny he ever spoke to you. He's Zak's boy. Those DeeBree guys won't stand up, not with more county time staring at them if they draw any heat. Shottlehauser's gonna be indicted if you bring up the dumping so she won't fly as a witness, plus the odds are she's told you everything she knows. Who else? Oh the Hayden kid, the daughter. What she said is interesting but it doesn't point to Wescott."

Frank snapped off the end of a pickle. "My Jewish friends would say you got bupkis, McCarthy."

"Without your help, that is."

"My help. Why would I want to help you?"

"A former state trooper I know tells me most retired cops have at least one case that still drives 'em nuts. He calls them 'mind scrapers.' The fact you're here tells me your mind scraper is Elaine Forge."

Around us the lunchtime crowd swelled and the noise level increased. The Duvalls watched everything, the way cops do. Frank finished chewing.

"We don't go on the record."

"Agreed."

He nodded. Let his eyes roam some more. "What do you want to know?"

"It's your story to tell."

He said they'd been screwed from the start.

"I had a year in detectives. Hadn't worked anything major but I knew how to handle myself. The call came in, June seventeenth, nineteen seventy-seven. About two in the afternoon. Chief himself phones down, says Elaine Forge is dead in her pool, looks like she's been shot. I was up in the rotation, but we had this sergeant, Ernie Mueller. He'd transferred in from patrol about two weeks before. Right off, the chief makes him the lead."

He took a sip of beer and continued.

"We get to the scene and it's a cluster fuck. Ambulance guys had fished her out of the pool and she's lying on her back on the cement. Naked. There's blood in the pool water but all around her? It's pristine. No blood, no signs of a struggle, nothing. Right away, I'm suspicious. I tell Mueller it looks like somebody hosed down the place before we got there. What's he do? Instead of ordering everybody to back off so we can process the scene, he assumes she was shot *in the pool* and lets everybody who shows up wander all over."

"What kind of wounds did she have?"

"One to the head. But it was from an up angle. Grooved her from here"—he traced his finger along a diagonal line on the left side of his face from below his nose to up past his hairline—"to here. She was a little thing. Unless the shooter was a midget firing from under water, no way she was shot in the pool. There was a wrought iron table and chairs nearby. I always figured the shooter was sitting there and she was standing next to him when it happened. But Mueller stuck by his pool theory. Guess which one the chief bought?"

He leaned back while one of the butchers cleared our plates. I hadn't touched my sandwich. I asked them to bag it for me. Gary finished his burger and sat back, watching his father.

"We recovered the slug that hit her. That was entirely magic or karma or by the grace of God or Allah, depending on your preference. One of the crime scene guys suggested draining the pool. For some reason Mueller let 'em. Found the slug stuck in a drain. She had really thick long hair. Coroner said the slug probably came to rest close to the surface of her skull, maybe got stuck in her hair, and worked out when she was floating."

"A .38?"

"Looked like it."

"I suppose it's too much to hope that it's in a file someplace?" I asked.

Gary Duvall snorted. Frank just shook his head.

"What do you think? Oh, I got copies of some of the reports, a couple photos. But the file and the slug and the other physical evidence, such as it was? I rooted around a little when I got appointed chief of detectives. Couldn't find it. Started thinking about it a little more when I was ready to retire and looked again. Even asked Gary to look a year or so ago. Nothing."

"So even if the gun turns up . . ."

"There's no slug from the victim for a match, unless the file magically reappears. But here's something. Two days after the killing, my old partner from patrol got back from vacation and called me. Asks me if I knew Elaine had a little target range set up in the woods next to their place. He says Mueller, when he was still in patrol, went to check a 'shots fired' call once and found her screwing some guy back in there."

"Wescott?"

"Pearce didn't know. He said he backed Mueller up that morning but when he arrived, Mueller waved him off. Said it was taken care of. Mueller never told 'im who the guy was."

"And the target shooting?"

"I got curious after Pearce brought it up so I took a ride out there. Somebody had tried to sanitize the place, but I pried two slugs out of a couple shot-up trees. And yeah, they were .38s."

"Did they match the slug from the pool?"

"Mueller said he'd send them to the state police lab for comparison, and that was the last I heard. Last I heard about all of it."

"Why? You were part of the investigation . . ."

"Yeah I was . . . until I brought in those slugs." Duvall glanced at his son and got a knowing smile in return. "Mueller was plenty pissed that I went out there without him assigning me. Got more pissed when I asked him about catching Elaine in the woods. He denied it ever happened. Said I was nuts. Couple of hours later the chief accused me of 'conducting an unauthorized investigation' for nosing around in the woods and flopped me back to working midnights in the jail."

"Seems a little extreme after you turned up new evidence."

"I was a rookie dick who thought he was Dirty Harry." He smiled, as though remembering how it felt to be that young and brash. "What they were coming up with . . . none of it matched my take on what happened. So they booted me out."

"That's when you talked to Bert Palmer."

He shrugged. Smiled a tight smile.

"How did Wescott figure into all this?"

"He was the one who discovered her body and called it in."

I blinked. "Did you question him?"

"Tried, sure. When we got to the scene he was in the house, waiting for us. Get this. Zak was with him." Duvall rapped his knuckles on the table. "Son of a bitch was in his first term. Got the job because he'd been the Forge family lawyer. That was the problem. The whole time he acted like he was still working for the old man."

"How do you mean?"

"He wouldn't let us talk to the kid. Said he was too traumatized, under age, on medication for some emotional problem or other. Plus Forge wasn't home yet. His 'legal guardian.' In other words, ten pounds of lawyer bullshit. Instead, he says *he's* a law enforcement officer so he'll do the interview. Supply us with a transcript. I wasn't having any of that, but Zak called the chief and Fischer overruled me. That was how things were done in those days."

"Same crap today," Gary Duvall muttered.

His father resumed. "Zak talks to Wescott alone for an hour or so, then comes out and gives us the highlights. He says the boy went out for a run, came back and found Elaine floating in the pool. He called Zak and then called us. Panicked, not thinking straight. Claims he didn't see nuthin', hear nuthin', and knows nuthin' about nuthin'."

Frank shook his head.

"At this point, a head doctor gets there and goes in to tranquilize him. Not that he needed it. He was shitfaced. We found a broken wine bottle under a table near the pool so I asked about that. I remember Zak's answer. The boy was terrified by what he'd seen so he had a little nip to calm his nerves but dropped the bottle. This is the impartial turd we had questioning our murder suspect. Kid needs help to stay upright but all he'd had was a little fuckin 'nip.' "

Thinking of Hayden, I asked, "Did anybody check him for gunshot residue?"

"Have you been listening? The patrol guys saw him for two minutes, I maybe had a minute with him before Uncle Theo shot us down. Never even got close after that. The next day, Forge shipped him off to some nuthouse down in Kansas. Chief Fischer said that was that. Work with what we had. Funny thing. As soon as they decided it was a random killing by an unknown assailant and young Master Wescott was off the hook, he was back, all over being traumatized. I think he even finished the summer working at the Forge plant."

"And you never found the gun?"

291

"No gun. Your theory about him hiding it is as good as any. I remember clear as glass asking to have a look inside the house. Zak looked at me liked I'd farted in his punch bowl."

"Was there any physical evidence other than the slug?"

He shrugged. "Next to nothing. Some fibers on the chair where I thought the shooter was sitting. Crime scene report said they were strings like you'd find on a pair of cutoff jean shorts. Would have been great if the kid had been wearing cutoffs but he had on running shorts when I saw him. My guess was he got blood on the cutoffs and put 'em in the wash. With Zak stepping in like he did, we'll never know. The other evidence was nothing. Botched investigation, little or no evidence collected. Even the photos of the scene and the body were half-assed."

"What's your take on all that?"

"Hell." He rattled the ice in his glass of tea. "At first, I was naïve enough to think Mueller was just out of his league and Chief Fischer was covering up for him. When they transferred me, I realized what was really up. Zak wanted the kid to skate, and he arranged it so he could."

"To keep Forge from losing both his wife and his, what? Surrogate son?"

"If you'd seen Forge . . . I was the one they had notify the old man his wife was dead. He'd been out of town that day, came back and I met him at the door. I'll never forget it. You ever see one of those horror movies where they have a character who's alive one second turn into a skeleton and then into dust? When I gave Forge the word, I thought that was what I was seeing. He was a tough old bird but he just shriveled up in front of me. If he'd found out his wife was dead, and this kid he was raising had killed her, God knows what would have happened to him. I figured Zak knew he was a heart attack waiting to happen and was covering up to protect him."

"You still think so?"

His mouth twisted. "No chance in hell. Zak has no feelings. No remorse I've ever seen. Some people collect art, old cars, Pez dispensers. Whatever. He collects people. That's what he did with Wescott. Knew he'd be useful some day so he just . . . scooped him up to save for later."

"Whoa. Wescott was seventeen years old . . ."

Duvall leaned into the table, lowering his voice. "He was seventeen but he was a fucking genius at business. I found an article in *Fortune* magazine that said he worked up a complete reorganization plan for Forge as a class assignment his last year in boarding school. The article said he followed up on what he wrote, word for word, after he took over the company. Zak knew how bright he was. He'd been Forge's lawyer, for Chrissakes. He knew Wescott was bound to inherit the whole shootin' match."

He tapped the table.

"And that's just what happened, isn't it? Sure as shit, Zak turned an accident into a murder and then collected that kid and just waited for payday."

"An accident? What did I miss?"

"Surprised? Yeah, that's what I thought it was. Mueller didn't let me spend too long by the pool, and you can't really tell from the photos I got, but remember what I said about Elaine being a tiny little thing? The way the slug traveled, the gun had to be at about her waist. There was a tear on one of her hands, too. Like if you made a grab for the gun and got the web of your thumb caught under the hammer as it fell. And we found that wine bottle I mentioned. I always thought the pair of 'em might've been drunk, roughhousing, arguing. She grabbed for the gun. The gun goes boom. She goes into the pool."

"What'd the coroner have to say?"

"Ollie Gore." He snorted. "Hell of a name for a guy who

worked with corpses. You'd walk into his office and catch him reading porn."

"Defense lawyers called him Ollie Gore the Prosecutor's Whore," Gary interjected.

Frank Duvall said, "If you brought in a victim with an axe stuck in his head and needed old Ollie to say it was a gunshot wound? No problem. Ollie'd not only estimate caliber but make and model and put together a slide show to prove it. What's that tell you?"

"Zak wanted a murder so he got a murder," I said.

"Not that I got any respect for Wescott, leaving her in the water and running off to call good ol' Uncle Theo. But Zak . . . Forge had been good to him. Hell, he was state's attorney 'cause Forge made sure he got slated and then bought the vote. But Zak made it where Forge ended up a victim, too, not ever knowing what really happened. Unknown perpetrator my ass."

Frank reached for his beer and drained it.

"Let me be clear. I'm not saying I don't have a fault in this. I stayed with that department for eighteen more years and never lifted a finger to make things right."

Gary Duvall spoke up. "Christ, Dad, that's not—"

"I'm not saying I could have brought to light what they did. Fact is, I didn't try real hard. I got to liking the promotions they gave me a little too much. By the time I realized what a . . . a goddamn yes-man I'd become, I was sitting in the chief of detectives chair. And it was pretty darn comfortable."

He looked over at his son, and for the first time I saw the flint in his eyes replaced with a glimmer of pride.

"At least one of us tried to stand up to that bastard Zak a time or two. That's why Gary was the first to get busted out of there when they had that trouble with the evidence locker. He pissed Zak off by doing some real law enforcement."

Gary Duvall gripped his father's arm and gave me a stare

that could have cut diamonds. "We're done here."

I slid out of the booth. "You said you have photos?"

"I got a couple out in the car with my file, yeah," Frank said. "They're lousy but you're welcome to them."

"One other thing. Is Mueller still alive?"

"Yeah he is. Works security out at the Zavagno Arena. Mostly the wrestling matches."

"Security," Gary repeated in a derisive tone.

"What's that mean exactly?" I asked.

"He shows up about five, drinks with the manager until all the receipts are in, then drops the money bag off at the night deposit. Unless he's too hammered by then, in which case they give him a ride home and pour him into bed."

"Don't waste time on Mueller, McCarthy," Frank said. "I've tried. He says he doesn't remember anything about those days. Shape he's in, he's probably telling the truth."

Chapter Twenty-Six

I felt pretty good walking out of Zima's Market. Blue sky, birds singing, Indian summer in full progress. New information percolating.

Three things I knew. To my satisfaction, anyway. One, Lucas Bremmer wasn't a killer. Two, accident or not, Pike Wescott was. And three, I had support for my gun theory. That was the good news. The downside: I couldn't see any way to prove my allegations. And, given that I'd blown off Chucky's mandatory meeting at the station, I might be out of a job.

The photos Duvall gave me were grainy and out of focus. The first showed a naked woman with thick dark hair lying on her back next to a swimming pool. The two others were close-ups of the wound track leading from near her chin up past her hairline. In one, someone had pulled back her hair to show where the slug had penetrated her skull. I looked at her eyes. They were glazed and expressionless. No surprise, no horror. Just dead.

The Wihega County morgue turned out to be three blocks from the law enforcement–courthouse complex in a gray, one-story cement building with a few narrow windows and even fewer doors. Johnnie was in a meeting. I asked the dour-faced receptionist for an envelope and left the photos. I also left a message on her voice mail saying they were waiting for her. Getting distrustful in my old age.

Sunny wasn't in her room and didn't answer her cellular. I

drove back to the motel, passed it, and parked between a sky-blue Hummer and a Toyota Land Cruiser in the lot of a structure that was all glass, metal, and sharp angles that announced itself as the Wihega County Sports Complex. As I was getting out of the Expedition, my phone rang. It took me a moment to place the number since it was a station extension I didn't often see. Yogi usually just called me radio to radio on the Nextel. Which I wasn't carrying.

"Hey, dude, I picked up a message for you somebody left at the desk. You got your Sucks-tel turned off or something?"

"Yeah, something. What's up? Who called?"

Paper rattled. "Dude named . . . Ernie Moo-let? Moo-lay? Says he's a neighbor of the Haydens and met you at the crime scene?"

The senior citizen with the bad rug. "And?"

"He just said it's important you call him. I guess Florbus didn't think to try your cell."

Or figured I was road kill and why bother?

Ernie Moulet didn't answer his phone. I left a message with my number and started into the club. The cellular rang again before I hit the door.

"McCarthy? Ernie Moulet. You caught me on the crapper." A delightful old man. "Did you ever bother to check out that clue I gave you?"

"Clue?"

"Holy Maude in Saint Petersburg! Yes, a clue! Didn't write it down, did you? The extra car in the school parking lot. By the drivers' ed storage."

"Oh. Right. You said it was a . . . third drivers' ed car?"

"I said it *looked* like one. You don't listen so well. And it wasn't."

"It wasn't?"

"Follow along, son. The third car didn't belong to the school.

I asked in the main office. Turns out, I was right on the money. Only supposed to be two cars there. Inside the fence. Locked up. Two cars, not three. Brand new Impalas. One of the instructors has a cousin who works at the Chevrolet dealership. He got 'em a deal on the lease so the school lets them advertise on the cars. That's how I knew the third car had no business being there."

"No advertising?"

"Now you're with the program. Clean as the butt of a just-diapered baby. And it wasn't the same model year, either. I'd say maybe two years older. But close enough to pass if you weren't looking for it."

"You're sure the third car was parked inside the fence with the other two?"

"Sweet Jesus, McCarthy, I may be an old man, but I can see just fine. Our bathroom window looks down on that parking lot. I was looking at it the whole time I stood there pissing. I got prostate trouble. You know what that's like? You will. Means I was looking for quite awhile."

"Did you give your information to the police?"

"Fellow at the school assured me he'd take care of it. Then Sergeant Callahan called back."

That surprised me. "Callahan's the media spokesman."

"He also runs the Citizens' Police Academy. I suppose that's why they had him call, me being first in my class. He had me describe everything I saw. The pompous ass."

I tried to keep the smile out of my voice. "Why do you say that?"

"He is one! Said he appreciated the information but that being a graduate of the academy didn't give me the right to go snooping, and that's just what he called it, in an active case. Said I was a private citizen, and I had no business at the school asking questions. Said the car was an extra one from the other high school. Central."

"I see."

"Yeah, that's all dandy, but he's still full of crap. As a tax-paying *private citizen,* I called up Central this morning." He sniffed. "That's a different district with a different drivers' ed program. Plus, they use Fords."

I found Sunny running laps on a banked track that circled a fitness area roughly the size of side-by-side tennis courts. From the sweat stains on her shirt, she'd been pushing it hard. She held up five fingers and pointed me toward a small café tucked under a circular flight of stairs leading to the locker rooms. When she joined me, a guy who followed her from the track with a hopeful smile on his face veered off and made it look like he'd just come in to order a salad.

She plunked down across the table and gulped half a bottle of Dasani, paused, wiped her mouth with the back of her hand, closed her eyes, and drank the rest of the water.

"Want another?" I asked.

"Had three already." She looked at me.

"Most people go shower after they work out," I said. "Before they hang in the juice bar."

"What're you, my mother? C'mon, you look like you stuck your finger in an electrical outlet."

"You sure you should hear this? Ethically speaking, I mean."

She kicked my ankle under the table. "McCarthy, if you don't start talking, I'm going to break every bone in your body and push you through that wall over there."

Some of the tension flowed out of my neck. She wasn't shutting me down. I told her about Ernie Moulet first.

"You think he's a credible witness?" she asked.

"Parking at the school, the killer could've come up on the house from the hiking trail and left the same way. One thing

299

worries me, though. If Moulet really saw the killer's car . . ."

She picked up my thought. "Right. He might end up like Lindsey or Lucas. I'll arrange for Russ Traynor to come out and keep an eye on him." Russ is one of Sunny's sharper colleagues. An ex-SEAL, his biceps are as thick as my thighs.

"Now what's got you looking like you swallowed a happy pill?"

I walked her through my visit to the library and coffee with Bert Palmer. I told her about lunch with the Duvalls. We were quiet a moment. A woman in Spandex stepped up to the counter and ordered a strawberry smoothie with a shot of wheat grass on the side. I watched her as she waited for it. She stood very straight and tall.

Sunny cleared her throat. I shifted my gaze from the woman to her. "I was just thinking," I said.

"I could tell."

"Here's a guy, Wescott, who lives behind a wall of lawyers and friends in high places. He's as Teflon-coated as any CEO in America. But he still spooked when he realized the gun was gone. Do you find that odd?"

"No way. Anybody who chases bail skips sees a variation on that kind of behavior every day. Fugitives are some of the most paranoid people on the planet. It's one reason they're so unpredictable and dangerous. Wescott may not be a runner in the technical sense but, yeah, the way he was acting the other night, something's bugging him. Given what you're telling me about his history, why wouldn't he be looking over his shoulder?"

"Then spooking him again would be good. You up for helping?"

"Maybe."

"The ethics thing?"

"Put it this way," she said with a wry expression. "Would you help if you were me? But there's nothing wrong with watching and listening while you plot clever strategy."

"Great. Instead of a sidekick I get an audience." I pushed away from the table. "Just don't snicker. I hate that."

"Where are you going?"

"I figured I'd strategize my way over to the high school and look at those cars."

"Hang tight for a few minutes and I'll keep you company." She got up to go shower, then turned and looked down at me.

" 'Sidekick?' "

I suspected we might not be welcome on school property, public schools being about as media friendly as a teacher who's been impregnated by a student. So we left Sunny's Expedition in the cul-de-sac where I'd entered the trail the other day, walking in the back way like a couple of kids on the way to class.

The school was perched on a hill across a large open field that included two baseball diamonds packed with students and six tennis courts where another class seemed to be in progress. A lot of shouting and cheering came from both places.

A brick two-car garage with barn doors sat adjacent to the woods. There was a fenced security area next to it that could have been a large dog run but was roomy enough to park several cars. It was empty save for a spray of sand on one portion of the concrete slab. I walked over and looked in the window of the garage. Snow removal equipment, two Cushman carts, and a riding mower took up most of the space.

Sunny came up, peered over my shoulder. "They have a Medex Government lock on that gate. Short of an alarm system, that's pretty good security."

"Unless it wasn't locked."

"It's locked now."

Up through the trees behind us I could make out the second

floor of a couple of houses but didn't know which one belonged to Ernie Moulet. Both would have good sight lines down to the enclosure.

Sunny pointed at a lamppost about a hundred feet away across the parking lot. "Plenty of light. Easy access to the trail. Put your car behind that gate and lock it . . . no cop on routine patrol is going to bother checking a car inside a secure enclosure. It's in with the school cars, it must be another school car. Talk about hiding in plain sight."

"That means the killer had to not only scare up a car that matched the drivers' ed vehicles, he had to know this enclosure was here. And figure a way to get access to it. And I bet you're going to tell me he didn't pick the lock."

She snorted. "A Medex Government? Put it this way, the Secret Service uses them in the garage downtown where they keep one of the presidential limousines."

"And you know this fact how?"

"I read a lot." A tiny grin came and went. "My point is this guy had a key. No way around that."

"Good planning. Except he didn't figure on a cop buff with prostate trouble getting up to take a leak." I stared at the locked gate. "I wonder how many keys are floating around out there."

"No more than four. The key form is proprietary. Medex only issues four with each lock they ship."

"Can't get a copy made at the kiosk in the mall?"

"Nope."

I smiled. "Then I think one of those key holders might have some 'splainin' to do."

"Us, too." She lifted her chin toward the school buildings behind me. "Unless you want to run off into the woods before he gets here."

I turned to see a Cushman cart zipping toward us from the tennis courts. I stayed. I doubted school personnel were allowed to shoot trespassers, even in Wihega County.

The Cushman slid to a halt. The guy behind the wheel wore gray slacks and a blue windbreaker with a school district emblem and the word "Security Director" underneath it. Probably in his mid-sixties, he looked every bit the part, too, from the paunch to the square jaw to the iron gray hair shaved to drill instructor length. If you were a student, he wasn't the sort of fella you'd want to catch you smoking grass in the boys' bathroom.

"Afternoon, folks." He slid from the cart smiling, but with the watchful eyes of a cop who's seen too many routine encounters with citizens go south. "Out for a nice walk?"

"Actually, we came over to look at this lock," I said and gave it a flip.

His eyes settled on me. "And why's that, Mr. McCarthy? Is Channel 14 investigating our drivers' ed program now?"

Sneaky old buzzard.

"Maybe one of your instructors."

"Really?" He made a show of looking around. "Are we on camera right now?"

"Nope."

"Good. I hate TV news." His smile disappeared. "Get off school property and don't come back or you'll be arrested for trespassing."

He touched a radio clipped to his belt at just the spot where he'd probably worn a gun for more than a few years. "You're not a very popular guy with the sheriff's department. Those stories you've been doing. They'd probably love locking you up."

"No doubt. How long since you left the Job?"

"This isn't a coffee klatch, McCarthy." He pointed in the direction of the hiking trail with one hand, the other lifting the radio. "Two choices. Hit the road or take a trespassing bust."

"Reason I asked, if you're friendly with Frank Duvall, you might want to buzz him before you call the uniforms. Could save us both some hassle."

If I'd used the mayor's name, or Chief Droot's, he would have ignored me. Cops in every jurisdiction arrest "friends" of the mayor and the chief all the time. But mention one of their buddies, keep it casual and not a threat, and sometimes the older guys will give you wiggle room they wouldn't otherwise.

"Is that right? Best friends are you?" Noncommittal but he took his hand off the radio.

"We had lunch today."

It was a risk, of course. This guy could be wired into Zak's people. We waited while he considered the meaning behind my words then, without comment, he moved around to the back of his Cushman and withdrew a cell phone from the pocket of his windbreaker.

His conversation lasted a couple of minutes. As soon as he clicked off, he grabbed his radio but it was only to tell someone he'd be tied up for a while with a couple of visitors, and there was no problem. He motioned us over and settled sideways on the driver's side of the Cushman like he was glad to be off his feet. He stuck out a hand.

"Wayne Pritchard. Frank says you're a cocky SOB, and he doesn't know anything about you investigating my people. But he says I should listen before I bust you."

I introduced Sunny and explained the lead we were checking out. He acknowledged he'd talked to Ernie Moulet.

"As soon as I hung up, I asked the instructors about a third car in the enclosure. They didn't know beans about it. Now, if you're thinking either of them had anything to do with that boy's death, you're nuts. Marty Fawcett retired from the PD a year or so ago. He's worked this gig as off-duty employment for years. And I've known Rick Torrez since he took drivers' ed himself."

"The two of them carry keys for the Medex twenty-four seven?"

"Yep. So do I." A small smile said he wasn't worried if we suspected him.

"And the fourth key?"

"Key box in my office. Medex doesn't let us make copies so it's our backup."

"You the only one with access to the box?"

"My second in command can get in." Another smile. "Donna Teague. She used to work for the sheriff, too. Good people."

"Teague. As in—"

"His wife."

Interesting.

Sunny jumped in. "What if there's a problem? Your night people find one of the car's lights on, for instance."

"Night people?" He shook his head. "We used to have a night guy. He died a couple of months ago. The budget let me hire one person this year. That was Donna, and I need her during the day. But the sheriff's office has our home numbers if any of the deputies see anything."

"Are Mr. Torrez and Mr. Fawcett always conscientious about locking up?"

"It's not like I check on 'em but, yeah. Marty's real anal about the condition of those cars. And if the coppers ever found the gate unlocked, they didn't say anything to me."

He spread his hands. "Look guys, I'm not claiming the system is letter-perfect. We had a break-in to one of the cars awhile back, and this is all the school board let me do to keep it from happening again. But, if I was you, I'd consider my source. Ernie Moulet's not an unknown quantity around here. We got leagues using our ball diamonds after hours? You better believe, if they forget to kill the lights, Moulet's the one we'll get a call from. Same with the noise. Hey, he even came to a board meeting and tried to get them to reposition that sodium vapor over there because it's so bright he has to pull his bedroom shades. He likes to bitch."

"Seeing three cars instead of two doesn't sound like bitching," Sunny said.

"No. What it sounds like is, the man wasn't wearing his glasses and saw something that wasn't there. He tell you he graduated from the Citizens' Police Academy? He's just a cop buff."

I glanced at the enclosure. "You say Fawcett takes the condition of the cars seriously?"

"Marty's a perfectionist, yeah. Always was on the street, too."

I motioned him over to the fence. I pointed at the sandy spot I'd seen earlier.

Pritchard grunted. "Probably had an oil leak. So?"

"The rest of the concrete is so clean you could do surgery on it. Which says to me that leak was recent. Why don't we find out which car it came from?"

We waited a half-hour for Martin Fawcett to return from dropping off his last students of the day. His full red beard was the first thing I noticed through the windshield as he nosed the car up to the gate. Casually dressed in slacks and a golf shirt with the school's logo, he was tall, thin, and light skinned except for his tanned right arm. The price of riding shotgun beside a bunch of student drivers. He nodded at Pritchard, worry lines crinkling his pink forehead.

"What's up, Pritch?"

"These people are from Channel 14. Our good neighbor Mr. Moulet called them, too," Pritchard added. "They're wondering about that oil leak."

"What about it?"

"When did you first notice it?" I asked.

He glanced at the spot then back to me. "When I pulled in night before last. Put the sand down yesterday. Put more down this morning after the rain."

"You know which of your cars it came from?"

"Yeah. Had to be Number Two. Rick's. Yesterday was our busiest day so I told him to take it into Bernardi's today and get it checked. There a problem with that?"

"Did they find a leak?"

"I dunno. Probably. I haven't seen Rick to ask him. He got the car back or he woulda called and bitched. Why?"

"Is there a way to check?"

"Jesus Christ, Pritch, Callahan said Moulet's tip was bullshit. What's this now, we're working for the media?"

Pritchard sighed like he'd dealt with Fawcett's attitude before. "Why don't you call over to Bernardi's and ask 'em about the leak?"

With a grunt, Fawcett slid behind the wheel of the Chevy and snatched up a cell phone. We watched him talk, frown, talk some more. When he got out of the car, he looked surprised.

"Mechanic couldn't find anything. No sign of oil anywhere."

Sunny touched the Chevy's hood. "Could this be the one that leaked?"

"Nah. I always pull in first. This car is never parked that close to the gate."

Pritchard stared at Fawcett for a moment then he rubbed his forehead.

"Well, son of a bitch, Marty. Moulet might be right after all."

CHAPTER TWENTY-SEVEN

He was finishing lunch in his private dining room with a former chief of staff of the army when the cellular phone vibrated in his pocket. He had taken to carrying the unit everywhere he went, while at the same time praying it wouldn't ring.

The vibration against his chest felt like an irregular heartbeat. He began to cough and excused himself. He waved away the general's concern and rushed to his rest room.

"The reporter, McCarthy, just lunched with the Duvalls. You remember that name, don't you Robert? Father and son. If he didn't know your history before, he knows now."

The handcuffs. The jail cell. "Goddamn it!"

Wescott thought he heard a chuckle. The phone's echo gave it a malevolent edge.

"You find this funny? Three people have *died!*"

"Four to be precise. Let's not forget Elaine. Be that as it may, what I find intriguing is McCarthy's tenacity. Witnesses die, his coworker falls, and he blunders on. Then there's the matter of those times you made me delay taking profits from one of our ventures just so you could feel virtuous. I must admit, I'm enjoying your discomfort."

Wescott wanted to slam the phone against the sink and flush the pieces down the toilet. "You bastard."

"Name calling now? I thought I taught you to have more class." The voice hardened. "The matter will be resolved. Have patience for a few more hours. I'll let you know when your sphincter can relax. Haven't I always?"

"If you don't handle this, I will—" Wescott began.

"What will you do? I'm curious. Turn yourself in and try to ruin me? I wonder how your friends in the Department of Defense would feel if they knew you left 'murderer' off your curriculum vitae. Think you'll be invited to any more White House dinners? Any more junkets to Cuba with the governor? What will happen to your precious company if you go to prison?"

Breathe, Wescott thought.

CHAPTER TWENTY-EIGHT

I got us out of there while Pritchard called his buddies at the cop shop and before he could tell us to stick around. There wouldn't be any logical reason for us to wait until one of Teague's people showed, but Pritchard was still a cop, more or less, and cops know when the shit starts to fly, you haul everybody in and leave the sorting out until later. I didn't want to get stuck while someone else began running down Ernie Moulet's lead.

And run it down they would, I thought. Pritchard might not admit I was the one who put the oil stain together with the third vehicle, but I was sure he'd tell them I knew about it. With one TV station alleging the police had messed up inside the crime scene, they sure as hell wouldn't want another to be able to say they ignored an obvious lead outside.

"Moulet said the car he saw looked a couple of years old. Can you reverse-check the secretary of state's office for Impalas registered in Wihega County?" I asked Sunny as we reached her Expedition.

"Sure. And you can bet it'll be the first thing the cops do. What I'd try instead would be rental cars. It'll take them longer to get around to that and, personally, I think it's a better bet. Trust me, Reno, this guy didn't use his own wheels."

"What are the chances Hertz is going to have a two-year-old car in its fleet?"

"None of the majors will, but that's my point. We start looking at the rent-a-beaters. Since nine-eleven, cops can ask the Feds for access to the computers of the major rental companies. The smaller outfits aren't so tied together. Big Brother can't techno-peek at their records."

"That's good," I said, pleased by her idea as usual. "Really good."

"Of course it is. I'm a bright girl." She flipped me a grin as she punched a speed-dial number on her phone. "The bad guys we're usually after either steal their rides or go cheap. So we keep track of the mom-and-pop rental agencies."

Into the phone: "Hey, Eric it's Sunny. Run a check of the beater database for the last week on Chevy Impalas, would you? City and suburbs." She paused, then grimaced and rolled her eyes at me. Her tone of voice changed from laid-back to Boss.

"Yes I know, Eric, I've done this myself. I'd do it myself this time if I was in the office. I don't keep the list on my laptop. It should take about thirty minutes to make all the calls. When you're finished, I'll be on my cell."

She closed her phone and looked across the seat at me. "Half an hour."

I pointed to the computer mounted between the seats. "You have a printer connected to this?" She nodded. "Let's get a picture of the right model Impala to show the neighbors. If Emily Hayden's right, the killer watched the family a while. Seeing the car might jog a memory."

Most of the neighbors closed their doors in our faces once they realized we weren't the police. Of those who were willing to talk, one pointed out the obvious. The Impala was too vanilla. In addition to the two in the school fleet, everybody from cops to cabbies drove them. As we headed back to the Expedition, two unmarked Impalas turned down the other end of the street, parked, and disgorged one detective each to begin their own Q and A.

"Wonder if your buddy, Callahan, is going to get burned over this," Sunny remarked, unlocking her door. "Blowing off a witness like he did without even checking out the information can't win him any points with his bosses. Especially when a reporter comes by later and confirms the witness's story."

She was right.

Callahan wasn't a detective. Why was he acting like one?

Her phone rang. I hoped it was Eric. It had been more than an hour since she'd talked to him. I was antsy. She listened for a while, then said, "Nice work. Thanks." She grinned at me.

"There are twelve rent-a-beaters in the seven-county area and two more in Rockford. Eric called them all. Apparently the Impala is a popular vehicle for them, too. In the last three weeks there have been sixty rentals. In the last week, there were six."

"Okay. How do we get the lists? E-mail or—"

"We don't need no stinkin' lists," she growled. "Eric's a pain in the butt sometimes, but he has good instincts. He asked all the rental reps if there was anything that stood out in their minds about any customer who rented an Impala. These places don't do near the volume of the biggies so their clients are easier to remember. He got a hit from last Friday in Wheeling, by Pal-Waukee Airport. He ran the name and address for criminal record. Nothing. So he got curious and checked the driver's license number with the secretary of state. It was one of a batch stolen from their Libertyville facility last spring."

"Could the agency people remember what this guy looked like?"

"Better than that. The owner appreciated getting a heads up on the bogus DL so he can call it in and make points with the state. He told Eric the car was supposed to be back today. Didn't come in. The best part is, he has a surveillance camera photo of the renter. He's faxing it to us."

"What made him remember the guy?"

"You'll love this. He was, quote, as big as a Mac truck, unquote. When the girl behind the counter asked if she could help him with anything else he asked her for a blowjob."

"Duane Grum."

"Let's go back to the motel and see."

The fax showed a mountain with sloped shoulders and bullet-head wearing suspenders over a T-shirt and baggy shorts that hung to his knees. Duane Grum. The driver's license he'd presented was photocopied next to it. The ID picture could have been of him or one of a dozen other people wearing a baseball hat pulled low and sunglasses. The name listed was phony.

"Ol' Duane look like an 'Eddie Villarreal' to you?" I asked when we got back to her room.

"Hardly." She opened the small refrigerator and tossed a soda can to me, then got one for herself and sat on the edge of the bed. Dr Pepper. It's a shared addiction.

"OK," I said. "We both know Duane's a follower. So who's leading him by the nose?"

"I don't know, Reno. This is beginning to have a funny feel to it."

"Duvall thinks a pro did Hayden."

She made a face and said, "I don't think so. A professional burglar won't carry a gun. Why would he? If he does his homework, more often than not he won't get caught. On the off chance the cops do jump him up, there's an extra rap for carrying."

"A wannabe?"

"Maybe. Yeah. You know what makes me lean that way? The car. Why not just steal a car appropriate to the neighborhood, park a couple of blocks away, and walk in? The rental, the phony ID, it's too much. The pros keep it simple. Plus," she said, "why would a professional hook up with a flunky like Duane Grum?"

"The head office told him he had to work with local talent?"

She pushed that one away with both hands. "If you hired Spielberg to direct your movie, do you think he'd agree to let your plumber brother-in-law score the soundtrack?"

"You think it was one of Zak's people?"

"Had to be somebody local who knew how to get the key for the security area."

I smiled.

"What?"

"Who would know law enforcement can track the major car rental agencies but not the smaller ones?"

"Cops. Federal agents. Any of the official man hunters, probation, parole investigators, and what have you. Some of the people in my business."

"But it's a small club, right? Mostly people in or near the criminal justice system? For example, I've never seen any news stories about the Feds having that kind of access."

"Are you kidding? The G knows the Patriot Act has about worn out its welcome. They keep that kind of Big Brother stuff on the down low now."

"So the guy who had Duane rent the car either just lucked into a company that would be hard for the cops to canvass or he knew about the computer trace capability."

"You're thinking he's a cop?" She cocked her head. "Not just any cop. You're thinking it was your buddy. Whatsisname. Callahan."

I took out my phone and got the number to Falcon Ridge West High School. When the operator answered, I asked for Sergeant Callahan.

"Oh," she said in a cheerful voice. "Sergeant Callahan's not assigned here any longer. I mean, he's still our liaison officer but now you have to call him at the Wihega County Police Department. Do you want the number?"

I hung up with a smile on my face.

"Callahan's the PIO, but he's also the school liaison officer," I said slowly. "Moulet calls the school about the car, so Pritchard calls Callahan. Callahan tells him 'no problem.' Then he tells Moulet to forget it, too. But why?"

I tapped the can of Dr Pepper against my chin, thinking.

"See how this sounds to you. Callahan's one of Zak's cops. Wescott goes to Zak. Zak sends Callahan to get the gun. Callahan blows it. Both he and Uncle Theo get a break, though, because Hayden's sister spots Lucas leaving the scene. Dumb luck. They drop the hammer on him. But they're not happy with that as a permanent fix. How tough would it be for a cop to pay off one of the bikers?"

Sunny shook her head. "Be easier for Zak to make that call. The Outfit uses bikers as freelance leg breakers and couriers from time to time. If Zak put the word out to those guys . . . let them know they'd pick up a few bucks plus points with the mob for the help . . ."

"Callahan could have done Lindsey himself. Red lights in the rear view, she pulls over?" I swallowed some Dr Pepper. It tasted bitter. I put the can down. Felt a chill as I considered what to say next.

"Callahan had Grum torch the truck. Maybe he figured that would pressure the station to pull me off the story."

She raised an eyebrow. "The only problem I have with your theory is that Callahan's got to know if Grum gets busted he'll turn snitch in about twelve seconds."

"*If* he gets busted. Wihega County doesn't have much of a track record in that regard, does it? And doesn't that strike you as strange? Grum's just a thug but look at his history. First, the evidence against him in a major case gets messed up, pretty obviously not by accident. Since then, Duvall says they suspect him in a few other sexual assaults. Every time, he disappears

315

until the victims back down."

"Okay. A cop could screw with the evidence and probably talk a victim or two out of pressing charges. But why would he? You're talking about protection that goes back years. What makes a piece of trash like Grum worth protecting?"

"Now that," I said, "is the question of the day."

"And your answer?"

"Don't have one," I admitted. "How about we get the names of the women who filed against him? See what or who made them back off."

"Charges dropped, I bet the records would be locked in a file somewhere." She cocked her head, considering something, then reached over and tapped a couple of computer keys.

"But, never let it be said the little lady turned down a challenge. Let me look around."

While she was doing that, I went back to my room to clean up. I felt dirtied by the day.

I was stepping out of the shower when the cellular rang. Grabbing a towel off the rack, I wrapped it around my waist and answered.

"Reno, it's Ray Fong."

My heart began thumping so hard that if it burst out of my chest it would probably wind up a couple of blocks away. "What happened?"

I'd avoided thinking about Vinnie almost all day. Helps to have distractions.

"I thought you might've come to see him by now."

"Little tied up here, Ray." I realized how cold that sounded and softened my tone. "How is he?"

"You mean has he managed to defeat medical science and die even though we have him on a vent? No. We're still breathing for him. Keeping him as comfortable as possible. But . . ."

"But what?"

"We're going to start weaning him off the ventilator. The stent's doing its job. He has some heart function back."

The room tilted and I had to sit down. "Is he conscious?"

"No. Maybe not for a couple of days. Even then, we don't know the extent of brain anoxia . . ."

"What the hell does that mean?"

"There's a lot we don't know, Reno. What I do know is that you need to get in here, man. It can only help."

"I've got a murder case out here. I can't just walk away from it."

"Yeah." Pause. "Well, you do what you gotta."

Ray hung up. He hadn't called me a selfish prick but the words hung in the air.

By habit, I'd been dressing while I talked, pulling on slacks, a shirt, and reaching for my sport coat. A good thing, because Sunny knocked as I snapped the phone closed. When I let her in, she took note of the phone, still in my hand, and the look on my face.

"Now what?"

"He's still alive. Ray was playing the guilt card."

She nodded, eyes boring into mine. "He should know you better than that. It didn't work did it?"

"You're right. He should know me better than that." Was my voice a little hoarse? I cleared my throat.

"What have you got?"

"Come see."

Back in her room, she had me stand over her shoulder while she pointed at the screen. It was a backlit night photograph of a stable on fire, flames shooting out windows and through the roof. Near the building, I could make out fencing and a horse crumpled on the ground. In the foreground were the backs of several people apparently watching the scene. She tapped on one wide shoulder.

"Look familiar?"

Grum? I looked closer. "Maybe . . ."

She clicked her mouse and the shot disappeared, replaced by another. In this one, again artfully backlit by the flames, cops were leading a handcuffed figure toward a squad car. A large and familiar handcuffed figure. Duane Grum.

"Briggs told me they popped him at the scene—" I began.

Sunny nodded, hands moving over the keyboard. "I know. Just listen. Traynor e-mailed me to say he's in position on Moulet. As a by-the-way, he told me your minicam truck fire already made it to this Web site. It's for fire buffs and insurance investigators. Just for grins, I ran a search on the Severn Stables fire."

A headline appeared: "Arson Suspected in Stable Blaze." I read it as she scrolled down.

A twenty-six-year-old man arrested at the scene of the fire at Severn Stables had been released from custody. A witness had first identified him as the person she'd observed fleeing the scene moments after an explosion ripped through the building, then recanted after police questioned her further. The paper's source about the recantation was the man's lawyer: Moira Cullen.

"Son of a bitch," I said. "She said she only represented him the one time."

She flipped back to the second photo. "I'd say your honey held back part of the story."

"Let's go find out why."

She shook her head, gave me a smile. "I'll let you handle that on your own. I have a call in to the stable owner to try and find the name of this witness who recanted. And I still want to see if I can find any of those other old cases." She handed back the keys I'd given her.

"If I need to go someplace, I'll call you. Go get her, stud muffin."

As I drove to Moira's office, I tried to keep an open mind. Tough to do. The fact remained she had lied about representing Grum a second time. Why?

To say he'd been a client more recently might mean she had his current address. Saying she'd washed her hands of him meant she could deny knowing where he lived. Why?

She didn't want to give me his new address and, thus, accept responsibility for what I might do if I found him? Or what he might do to me?

I smiled to myself. Nope. Nice thought but that wasn't it.

She didn't want him found, period? She was protecting him? Why?

I thought back to our brief conversation about Grum. She said she had represented him only as a favor to Lucas because she didn't like representing multiple defendants in the same case. So why do your client a favor that might wind up being against his best interests?

I parked a block from her office but then sat for a moment, surveying the street. It was a comfortable evening. I could see two restaurants had their patios open and people were slowly filling them. What probably passed for late commuter traffic in downtown Falcon Ridge backed up five and six cars deep at the traffic lights then moved smoothly through, their tires rumbling ever so slightly on the cobblestones. Through a window of one of the cars that paused behind me I could hear the bridge music from Public Radio's *All Things Considered* and then a woman's calm voice cataloguing the death toll from an Israeli bus bombing.

What was Moira hiding?

I got out of the SUV and punched the button on the key fob

that would lock it, glancing around as I did so. I was taking my time because Duane Grum's face kept intruding on my thoughts. I didn't expect him to try anything as obvious as a drive-by but, hey, even Lex Luthor managed to sneak Superman a little Kryptonite surprise once in awhile.

Reaching Moira's building, I trudged up the stairs. The outer door stood open as it had earlier, but the perky secretary was missing. She'd left her desktop neatly arranged and her computer dark. The outer office's limestone walls and exposed ductwork seemed colder than when she inhabited the room. I realized she was the only person in Wihega County who had given me a genuine smile all day.

I looked into Moira's office. Empty. I peered down the hall. The door to the conference room was closed.

A wind chime tingled ever so softly.

"Moira?" I called.

I thought a chair creaked but couldn't be certain. I listened harder. Called her name again.

"One minute!" The terse response was followed by sounds of feet thudding on the hardwood floor. After a moment which I spent listening to the hum of the air conditioning and the filter unit in the corner, the door to the conference room opened and Moira stepped out, careful to pull it shut behind her. She wore the skirt and blazer combo I'd seen her in earlier but the collar of her jacket was turned up, as though she had just slipped it on.

"Reno. What are you doing here?" There was a chill in her voice.

"Hey. Have a couple of questions."

She frowned, did the hand through her hair thing, then moved past me into her office. I noticed her eyes hadn't quite focused on me yet.

"Hey, you okay? You're looking a little spacey."

"I'm fine," she said.

When she got behind her desk, she glanced over her shoulder out the window and then back at me. Waiting, probably, for me to turn tail and go. I leaned against the doorframe and folded my arms instead.

"You have questions?" she asked.

"You happen to know where Duane Grum lives?"

"You asked me that the other night. I told you he wasn't someone I'd represent again. So, no."

"After you defended him on the rape you mean."

She looked down, shifting papers. "Uh-huh."

"Moira, I know about the stable fire. Congratulations. You're two for two for Mr. Grum. Or were there other times you got witnesses to recant that we haven't discovered yet?"

Her jaw moved and a moment later she lifted her head and sighed. "It was hard enough sharing the information with you that I did. Do you know what happens to lawyers who tell reporters too much about their clients?"

"Let's see. Don't tell me. The Disciplinary Commission hangs you up by your thumbs and tickles you for an hour?"

"Reno . . ."

"If I recall correctly, at that point you and your ethical boundaries were in two separate counties. Why hide that you're still working for him?"

"There was no reason for you to know. Now if you don't mind? I have stuff to do here."

"You planning to have him turn himself in for blowing up our truck and putting my friend in the hospital?"

"I'm not having this conversation with you." Her eyes shifted away again.

My shoulders tightened to the point of pain. I stared at her.

"If this was a lawyer-client thing, I could buy it. But all you're doing is helping to hide this creep. Here's something you might not know. Grum rented the car the killer used to get to Trey Hayden's house."

"What? Who told you that?"

I took three steps and put a copy of the surveillance photo on her desk. The rental agency had faxed a copy of the photo with the phony driver's license included. She touched it with her index finger, as though testing its heat, but didn't pick it up right away. When she finally did, I went back to lean in the doorway. Giving her room.

A moment later she humphed. "This could be anyone."

"Anyone with a twenty-inch-neck and I-beams for shoulders. What's he got on you, for Chrissakes? Or is it his buddy who's jamming the foot down on your neck?"

From where I stood I couldn't tell for sure, but I thought she paled a little. She tossed the paper toward the desk. It fluttered like a bird that's just had a wing clipped. Her right hand went to the back of her chair and she froze, gazed fixed somewhere on the wall to my right.

"You can still walk away from this, Moira. I'll help you. If you don't trust the cops here we'll take everything we know to the FBI—"

"You'll *help?*" She made a rude sound, then crossed her arms and squeezed them tight against herself. A solitary tear leaked from her left eye.

"I don't need the FBI, damnit. I'm an attorney. I'm representing my client to the best of my ability. There's nothing wrong here. I'll talk to Duane about surrendering, okay? If I have to, I'll bring him to the courthouse myself. Are you happy now?"

"It's too late for that."

"Why?"

I gestured at the paper I'd brought. "I'm not buying the cover-up. You talk to the FBI or I will."

I wasn't about to mention that the FBI would laugh me out

of the federal building if I went to them with what I had.

"You think you can tell me what to do?"

I shrugged. Another tear appeared and seemed to race the first down her cheek. We stood there like that for probably five minutes, neither of us speaking. Finally, she heaved a sigh and sat down behind her desk.

"I want you to leave, Reno."

When I started to respond, she raised a hand. "There is nothing I can do to . . . alter my situation. There is nothing you can say or do that will change my mind. Nothing. So please go before I call the police."

"The police or a specific cop?" I asked.

She finally brought her eyes up to mine. "I'll say this once. No matter what you think you know about me, you're wrong. Now, do I make that call or not?"

I walked out of Moira's building, waited for a break in traffic, and headed into a joint called the Dog Breath Cantina across the street. Not to skulk and watch Moira's door like a good investigator should, waiting for her to leave so I could follow her to the killer, but so I could knock back one of the half-price *cervezas* advertised on the window and ponder my next brilliant move.

Twenty minutes later, I'd finished my second serving of chips and salsa, drained the Carta Blanca, but was zip in the pondering department. Blank wall.

Was Moira just lawyering or was there really something more personal in her relationship with Grum? It's not unheard of for the hottest, smartest chick to go after a loser bad boy. Perhaps, if I sat here long enough drinking *cerveza*, he would come tooling up on his motorcycle, Moira would skip out of her office, mount up behind him, and they'd go puttering off on a date.

I waved the redheaded bartender down and ordered another

beer. Blending in. Accepted more chips as camouflage. This time the salsa burned hot enough to open clogged drains. The crowd standing around the bar watching one of the last Cubs games of the season was getting so rowdy you'd think the boys had made it to the playoffs again. Hotshot big city reporter spends an early fall night drinking with the locals.

I decided to break into Moira's office to get Grum's address.

I'd burgled once or twice before, but those had been relatively low-risk situations. Going after a lawyer's files, especially in a county where I was already unpopular with the local criminal justice system and said lawyer seemed to have all sorts of connections, would be akin to skydiving with no reserve parachute. Even so, the thought of finding Grum made me smile. I glanced at my reflection in the back bar mirror. Maybe smile was a little too strong a word. The bartender saw the look and drifted back toward me with a worried expression.

"Did I add too much Tabasco to the salsa? Put some cayenne in there, too. Heh heh."

"Not a problem. Who needs enamel on their teeth?"

He gave another *heh heh.* "Well, just don't choke to death and sue us."

I opened my mouth to ask for the Tabasco bottle when the bartender looked past me and said casually, "Hey Woz. Checking the action?"

And then a hand slapped down on my shoulder. I glanced in the mirror to see who it belonged to as a loud voice said, "Don't you know this guy, Billy? Mr. McCarthy's from Channel 14. Maybe he's here to do an exposé on you."

The bartender grinned. "Got your exposé right here, Woz. What're you drinkin'?"

"Sober night tonight, Billy. Business to be done, stories breaking. But I'll pick up Reno's tab." He opened his wallet before I could protest. I saw the glint of a sheriff's star nestled inside. It surprised me.

"What's with the tin?"

"Special deputy. Women dig it. What can I say?"

"Your editor doesn't object to you being part of an agency you cover?"

"Oh, hell no. He's one, too. So's the publisher. Want another?" He nodded at my beer. Instead of the rumpled jacket and slacks I'd seen earlier, he wore jeans and a polo shirt tight enough to emphasize a muscled upper torso. He smelled of lime cologne. Reporter by day, gym rat and lounge lizard by night? Right down to his Doc Martens with no socks.

"I was just on my way out. Thanks anyway."

"I'm surprised you're alone. Especially since we're right across the street from . . ." He winked, gestured toward Moira's office.

"Are you winking at me or do you have something stuck in your eye?"

"Hey, hey. No offense. I just thought you and the counselor were pretty friendly."

"Why's that? Because she talks to me and wouldn't piss on you if you were on fire?"

He smiled. "I guess we all have our own way of getting information from sources. Whatever it takes. Hell, she screws most of the courthouse, why not you too, right?"

I didn't rise to the bait. People like him spend their lives goading others, either with their words or their behavior or both. Yell at them, even beat them bloody, and you'll get no more reaction than an infuriating smile.

I started to walk away.

In a low voice he said, "Cops are taking Grum down tonight."

I felt my heart rate zoom into the stratosphere. Son of a bitch. Keeping my expression absolutely bland, sure I was being played, I asked, "Where?"

"They just called me. I was getting ready to meet Teague and the others when I saw you sitting here. C'mon and ride along with me if you want."

"I'll follow you. Where is he?"

"So you can bring in a crew and a live truck and screw this all up? I don't think so. We don't need your cameras getting in the way."

" 'We?' I thought you were a reporter, not a police department flack."

He shrugged. "Getting pissed doesn't change anything. Besides, Teague won't let you within five miles of the place if you're not with me. You know that."

It burned me to admit he was right. But TV people tell stories with video. I needed to bring a cameraman.

As though reading my mind he said, "Hey, if it helps, I heard Teague talking to one of the freelance photographers. The video guy, Philke. I think he's going to be there, too."

He motioned toward the back of the restaurant. I waited a beat then thought, "What the hell?" We pushed through the crowd next to the bar and down a hallway with sports memorabilia on the walls that led to the restrooms and another door marked, "Wine Cellar." A fourth door had a crash bar and a sign warning that it was alarmed. Wozniak hit it with the palms of both hands and we went through. No alarm sounded. Gotta appreciate a guy who knows the territory.

It was a wide alley and so clean the brick pavement seemed to gleam. Just what I would've expected for downtown Falcon Ridge. The day's fading light showed me a black Ford F-150 pickup truck with a tarp stretched tightly across the bed parked in one of three reserved spaces behind the restaurant. Wozniak grabbed the handle on the driver's door and swung up and into the cab. I drew out my cell phone and headed for the passenger side, intending to call and brief Sunny.

I had just finished tapping in her number when I smelled coffee.

Duane Grum, sunglasses and all, reared up out of the shadows on the far side of the pickup and slammed the heel of his right hand into the center of my forehead.

The last sound I heard was the wet smack of a melon hitting the pavement.

CHAPTER TWENTY-NINE

In the make-believe world of special effects, guns that can shoot thirty or forty rounds before requiring a reload, and super-fit stunt men and women, the hero of the picture gets socked in the noggin, wakes up two minutes later, and flings himself back into the fray.

Doesn't *really* happen that way. It's just that moviemakers know showing some poor oaf barfing for five minutes won't sell many tickets. Even a mild concussion can make life really unpleasant for a couple of days.

I faded in slowly, made the mistake of trying to sit up, and had to swallow hard twice to avoid upchucking salsa, chips, and beer. It was a near thing. My throat burned. Dizziness overtook me, and I teetered for a moment on the edge of the world.

Disoriented, I lay on my back at an angle, feet elevated, pain in ridges from my hips to the back of my head. I was in the dark, terrified that I couldn't feel my feet or legs. I moved my right leg. My knee hurt. Moved my left leg and began to slide backward.

I was upside down at the bottom of a flight of steps.

From the sharp pain at the base of my spine, I gathered I'd been thrown down there. I spread my hands and reached for the walls on either side. Felt a banister to my right. Used it to push myself backward all the way down to a concrete floor. I straightened into a sitting position.

By the time I finished, little white lights blinked at the edge of my vision and I was inching toward a definite grumpy frown on the Faces of Pain Scale.

Quick assessment: No numbness. Both arms, both hands, both sets of fingers worked. Legs, ankles, feet, and toes all good too. Vision was still up for grabs. My head felt like someone had squeezed it with a giant nutcracker, stopping short of breaking the shell. Whether there was any serious damage was a question I couldn't answer. I reached up and touched the back of my skull. A couple of lumps. The stickiness told me I was bleeding.

I leaned against the wall and closed my eyes. From the floor above me, I could hear the murmur of either two people having a conversation or a television blaring. I deduced I was in a basement. I sniffed again.

I could still smell coffee. It mixed with the musty, yeasty odor I associate with places where men spend a lot of time sweating. Gyms, locker rooms, prison cells.

Didn't take much to figure out that, since it was Grum who had slugged me, these were probably his digs. For all I knew, I could be sitting in his living room. But what about Wozniak? How did he figure into this? Was he down here in the dark with me, maybe in worse shape?

Or Wozniak as the guy who killed Hayden? Wozniak as the guy bossing Grum?

A feeling of having been suckered started to seep in with the rest of my aches and pains. Along with it came the thought that there was no reason for me to just sit and wait for the next unpleasant thing to happen. I doubted the two of them were up there figuring ways to apologize.

Using the wall for support, I got up. Bit by bit.

The effort sent a spear rocketing through the center of my forehead where Grum had connected. My knees buckled and I made a grab for the banister. I didn't go down. I waited. The pain took as long to recede as the tide going out. Hand firmly anchored, I moved my head a bit. My stomach gurgled and acid filled my throat again but when I swallowed, the sensation disappeared.

First things first. Get some light. I searched the wall, touched a switch and clicked it. Nothing.

That left a couple of options for checking my surroundings. I could push straight out from the wall, hands in front of me like a blind man, and possibly stumble over, or into, something. Lousy choice. Or I could go with Vinnie's advice. He told me during one of my ride-alongs with him a century or so ago that, when you're alone and searching a dark room, keep your back to the wall and take a clockwise route, giving your night vision a chance to develop.

When I was certain I could move without having the pain jump into hyper-drive again, I pressed my back hard against the wall and started sliding to my left, careful to ascertain I always had solid floor underneath. Falling into a sub-basement or even a sump pump basin wouldn't be helpful. As I moved, I listened. Making sure the sound of voices upstairs stayed constant.

I reached a doorway. I slid around it and stopped. Went for the lights again. This time my fingers found a switch box and some wires but no switch. Was this going to be a pattern? The room offered old smells, but they were easily recognizable: bleach and detergent. Laundry room. My eyes were becoming more accustomed to the darkness and vague shapes began to appear. One was a sink I would have run into if I'd stayed on course. I skirted it, felt the side of my foot brush something that felt like a floor drain. At the same moment, the acidic smell of urine made my nose twitch. Why had somebody been pissing in the drain? There was a water heater and furnace, too, the sides of both warm to the touch and, farther along, a deep porcelain bathtub against the wall. No washer, no dryer, no furniture.

I encountered another doorway a moment later. Orienting

myself, I realized my circuit had taken me in a rough half circle and I was now directly opposite the stairs. The room was empty save for a threadbare rug I felt on the concrete floor. Light switch didn't work here, either. A pattern for sure. I kept up my clockwise baby steps until I reached what had to be an outside door. I thumped on it. Solid core, paneled in plywood. Dim light seeped from underneath, along with the barest hint of air movement. I sniffed. Fecund and wet, the good fresh smell of a pond on a summer evening. Made the basement seem all the more claustrophobic to me. I reached for the knob. It turned but the door wouldn't swing. I tried the lock. It snapped open after I played with it for a bit but the damned door still wouldn't budge. Jammed against the frame, I supposed, probably as the floor settled. Wrenching it loose would take more strength than I had at the moment and make too much noise. I left it unlocked for possible future use and continued exploring.

There weren't any more rooms. Right before I got back to the stairs, though, I passed an opening cut about shoulder height in the concrete wall. Deeper blackness than anything before. Crawlspace. If anything, the smell of coffee and body odor was stronger there, along with another indefinable smell that brought back a sense memory of Little League games in early summer. The hair rose on the back of my neck, and terror took control again. I imagined arms snaking out of the merciless dark to grip my shoulders and haul me up and into a netherworld of evil. My headache disappeared. My intestines clenched so tightly I nearly cried out.

The door at the top of the stairs crashed open.

"McCarthy. Duane doesn't like you being in his crib."

Wozniak's voice. It was different, more authoritative.

"You want to come up out of there?"

Anything was better than standing near that crawlspace, but I took each step slowly, assuring my legs would support me before putting any weight on them. Wozniak waited, watching. By the time I reached him, his expression had turned from amusement to exasperation. He held a Glock 9mm down alongside his right leg.

"You act like a wall fell on you. Duane only hit you the one time." He pressed a finger to my forehead. My knees gave way and I would have tumbled back down the stairs if he hadn't grabbed me under the arm. He guided me across the kitchen and shoved me into a straight-backed chair. The two ceiling lights turned into four and then back to two as the room swayed a bit.

"You're gonna have one hell of a bruise." Then, over his shoulder, he said, "Hey, bro, you almost caved in his skull. Is that what I told you to do?"

The doorway filled with Duane's bulk. Dark glasses hid his eyes but the way he kept biting his lower lip suggested Wozniak's words worried him. Between bites, though, he guzzled from a can of Schaefer beer that he held in one hand and jiggled a bunch of his black candies with the other. Not candy, I realized. Coffee beans. The guy chewed coffee beans. He showed no sign of residual pain, or even any stiffness, from the knocking around Sunny had given him at the motel. Maybe he was impervious to such things.

"I didn't mean to . . ." he whined in the strange high voice I remembered from outside the Hayden crime scene.

"Don't worry about it."

"So . . . I didn't fuck up?"

Wozniak rolled his eyes. "No, no. It's all good. Hey, why don't you check around outside and make sure we're alone here, okay?"

Grum took another swig, wiped the back of the hand holding the can across his mouth, and backed out of sight. Wozniak kept watching the spot where he'd been standing. For a long moment, nothing happened. Then Grum ducked into the doorway again. Wozniak sighed.

"If somebody's out there, you want me to kill 'em or what?" Grum's words were cold enough, but the tone was that of a kid asking if he should throw out the trash.

"Christ, how do you even manage to take a piss without asking me twenty questions? No, dummy, don't kill anybody. Come tell me. That's all."

Grum's face scrunched up as though he wanted to cry. He disappeared around the corner again. A moment later an outer door opened and closed.

"Must be like owning a pit bull," I said.

Wozniak swiveled his head to me. "What's that?"

"He always does what you tell him to do? Arson? Rape? Murder? Fetch?"

"Hey, he's a big guy. He has to let off steam somehow."

"Is that what he was doing when he killed Lindsey Sears?"

"That girl who went into the river? She was an accident, man. Didn't you read my piece in the paper?"

"Oh, I forgot. You call your mistakes 'accidents.' Was Hayden an accident, too?"

I thought I might get a rise out of him but he stayed with the smile.

"Hey, that kid scared the crap out of me. I had no idea he was even there. He popped out of his room and took a shot. What was I supposed to do? Clear self-defense, dude."

"Why did Bremmer have to die?"

"Call that self-defense, too! He saw me. I guess he and that Lindsey bitch were sitting in a car out in front of the house. I didn't see them. Couple hours later he's talking to you and then he goes up to Duane and asks how much he thinks I'd pay him to keep quiet. Can you imagine? His best friend murdered and he's looking for a payoff. What was I supposed to do? Wait 'til he spilled his guts all over TV?"

"How did you get to him in jail? Or did you leave that to Zak?"

He shrugged, hefted the Glock sideways like the TV gang-bangers do, and pointed it at my face. "All a matter of control. Like I got everything under control now."

"You think so?"

"Oh come on, Reno. You think you're gonna walk outta here a hero when we're done? You think Duane and I brought you here just so you could *interview* us or something?"

The meat grinder in my stomach cranked a notch or two. "You brought me here because you're so fucked-up-nuts you figure killing me clears the table for you. But you know what's funny? You weren't even on my radar."

"Ehh. You're a bright guy. You would've made the connection, eventually. You figured the car at the school. Yeah, I heard about that. I've got good sources. I overheard you talking to Moira tonight from the conference room. You interrupted us talking about my stupid brother's latest legal problems. You got family, McCarthy?"

"No."

"Trust me, you're better off. Moira didn't have a clue about any of this until you got her all riled up about Duane. Now we're going to have to deal with her, too. Probably be fun." He winked the way he had in the restaurant.

"I could tell you were getting closer to Duane. Most Chicago reporters just phone it in, you know? But you. You worried me from the start. You'd have found me out. Duane and I had different daddies, but I give you and the bitch bounty hunter credit. You would have gotten us. Hey, you want a beer?"

"Grum's your brother." No wonder he was willing to play errand boy.

"Sure is. All 250 pounds of him. Mama brought him from the hospital right to this house."

Without putting down the Glock, Wozniak grabbed two cans of the Schaefer out of an ancient white Westinghouse and held one out to me. I accepted it but didn't pop the tab. The full can would make a better weapon.

"See, Mama was foxy when she was younger. Big tits and all? She screwed around a lot. Duane's my half-brother. I figure she probably fucked one of those Russian weight-lifters to drop a kid as big as him. Don't you think? Twenty-six and has the mind of about a twelve-year-old, they say. That's why I have to keep him occupied. Permanent puberty. All those raging hormones."

"Doesn't look to me like you've done him any favors."

"You mean I was supposed to? Damn, Reno. We weren't big on reading Dr. Spock in this house. So how would I know? Being slow like he is, he messed up a lot when he was a kid. All Mama used to do was lock him in the basement. At least now I let him out to catch some sunlight once in awhile. And speaking of letting the dumb bunny out . . ."

He crossed to a window over the sink. For the first time, I took a look at the room. Bare walls and only essential elements: the metal table where I sat, two chairs, the refrigerator, a counter between the sink, and a four-burner-stove. The décor of a 1950's farmhouse. No sign of *feng shui*. I heard the muted hum of a generator.

Wozniak suddenly leaned across the sink and rapped on the window. "Get in here!"

Grum ducked through the kitchen door looking apprehensive. He held a cut-down pump shotgun by the handgrip, barrel over his shoulder. Hastily applied streaks of black cammo paint bisected his face.

"I said look around, not play soldier in the dark."

"There's somebody's car in the driveway," Grum said.

"The fuck there is!" Wozniak brushed past him and killed the kitchen lights. It was full dark outside. I could see nothing past the windows. Apparently he couldn't either.

"Bring 'em into the house. For Chrissakes don't hurt 'em!" Grum started outside. Wozniak grabbed his arm. "You hear me? Gentle, Duane. If it's cops just get back in here."

"Not cops," Grum muttered and disappeared into the gloom. "Not cops."

We waited, me in the chair, Wozniak by the back door, sighing often. He evidently hadn't counted on having more company. I thought about that. Focused as he was on what was happening outside, in two long steps I could hammerlock him, take his gun, and put him down. Of course, Duane would probably walk in during the middle of it all, rip my head off, and use it for a chips and dip tray.

I heard scuffling sounds and then a woman's voice. Not Sunny. Had it been, Grum wouldn't have returned, at least not upright.

Moira Cullen stumbled through the doorway, cursing, propelled by Grum who pushed in behind her.

"See? I told you there was somebody!"

"What the fuck do you people think you're doing?" Moira demanded. Wozniak turned on the light and showed her the gun. He was smiling.

"We were just talking about you and now here you are. See, Reno? Everything's under control." He pointed at the chair next to me. "Sit Moira."

"In a pig's eye—" she began. Wozniak backhanded her with his free hand. With a yelp, she crumpled against the wall. Grum yanked her to her feet and dropped her in the chair across from me.

"You will sit there and be quiet or I'll hurt you so bad you

336

won't be able to talk. You understand me, Moira?" The merry light that had been in his eyes while talking to me seemed to glow even brighter with the slap.

She touched the spot where he'd hit her, tears welling, the look on her face saying she'd stepped behind the looking glass and, instead of Alice, found Hannibal Lecter. She glanced at me. I gave her a little Paul Newman wave. Tough guy.

A cell phone rang. Wozniak suddenly didn't look so happy. He yanked it from his pocket. When he checked Caller ID, however, he nodded and the tension left his face. He told Grum to watch us and walked into the next room, phone to his ear.

"Asshole," Moira muttered. Grum leaned against the counter. Without taking his eyes off her, he fished out a coffee bean and threw it into his mouth. She met his gaze.

"Duane, I'm your lawyer. I'm trying to help . . ."

Child-like, he placed a finger across his lips. "In this house, you get punished if you talk when somebody's on the phone." I tried to see his eyes behind the dark lenses. Wasn't happening.

Moira fell silent. I concentrated on trying to listen to Wozniak's phone conversation. I wondered if Theo Zak was on the other end.

Wozniak wasn't whispering but, even so, I only caught about every third word. Until he said, *"Bounty hunter or not we'll take care of her, too."*

My throat went dry. *Sunny?* Was he setting Sunny up for a hit? I glanced at Grum. The dark glasses seemed fixed on Moira. No telling which of us he was watching.

Woz came grinning back into the room a minute later. He still carried the Glock but he had another pistol stuck down the front of his pants. He stopped next to Grum.

"Time to get started, bro."

I lifted my chin. "Is that the .38 you took off the Hayden kid?"

He touched the .38's grip. "One and the same. The piece that started it all." Then to Grum, he said, "Get them downstairs."

"Wait a minute," I said. "Let me see it."

"The fuck I will."

"What's the harm? Unload the damn thing. C'mon. Did Zak tell you the story behind it?"

"Why would I need its pedigree? It's not some priceless antique. It's a fucking gun."

"Just the same, it's got a colorful history. I'm surprised Zak didn't tell you the story. Why did he send you after it, by the way? He must have plenty of guys to do that kind of stuff."

"He trusts me."

I chuckled. "Yeah. Theo Zak trusts a reporter? That'll be the day."

"We go way back."

"But he didn't trust you enough to tell you why he needed it stolen, did he?"

"What difference does that make?"

"The difference between Zak trusting you and Zak setting you up as his patsy."

"I'm nobody's patsy!" Once again, his grin turned off and fury flashed on.

"Wait a second." I snapped my fingers. "Your mom worked for him, didn't she? In the state's attorney's office."

"Yeah."

"How old are you anyway, Woz? Twenty-eight? Twenty-nine? Let me guess. She was working for Zak when you were born. Maybe even before."

"So what?"

"I was just thinking. Good-looking woman. Powerful man. Late nights together in the office. Now he has you to run his errands."

Moira's bark of a laugh startled even me. "I should have

known. You're Zak's little bastard!"

He took two steps and grabbed her by the hair. I jumped up. Without looking my way he jabbed the Glock into my stomach.

"You dyke bitch." Wozniak yanked her to her feet. She gasped and grabbed his hand with both of hers. He lifted the Glock away from me and jammed it up under her jaw. All the color drained from her face. But it was the break I'd hoped for. Him between me and Grum.

"You screw cops. You screw state's attorneys. You fuck another *woman!* And you think you can call *me* names?"

I snapped out a hand, grabbed the .38 from his waistband, and reached a finger toward the trigger. Grum spotted my play. Darting to his right to get clear, he one-handed the shotgun in my direction. With double-aught buck, he might still clip his brother, but I would take most of the load.

I let go of the .38. It clattered to the floor. Wozniak jumped back, swung his Glock toward my face. I braced for death.

We stayed that way for a long moment. Neither of them fired. Instead, Wozniak's crazy-ass smile returned.

"Good one, Reno. Good one! You almost made it. Almost."

He backed a couple of arm-lengths away from us. Slipping the Glock into the back of his trousers, he picked up the .38. He gave a laugh.

"You want to see this piece of crap? Okay. Why not?"

He pushed the release, swung the cylinder out, and dropped five hollow-point slugs and one empty casing into his hand. Then handed the pistol to me, butt first.

I started to breathe again.

It was an old Smith & Wesson Model 10 Military and Police, the stalwart duty weapon of police departments from the '50s through the '80s. I ought to know. I'd fired my dad's often enough. On this one, the checkered grips were worn and the blueing pitted in several places, but it looked eminently service-able.

"Just an old pistol," Wozniak said.

I peered down the barrel. The smells of oil and gunpowder mingled. The cylinders had a slick residue inside. Trey Hayden had gone a little nuts with the oil as amateurs often do. My fingers felt a slightly raised area under the butt from something that had been stamped there a long time ago. Faded, it looked to me like a four-leaf clover followed by the numbers "1" and "2."

"No, not just any gun." I handed it back. "Tell me something. Did Zak order you to rape Lindsey Sears before you killed her?"

"Can't rape the willing, McCarthy. She offered it to us. Both of us. Said she'd do anything as long as we didn't hurt her." He glanced at Grum. "Guess we lied, huh, bro?"

Grum giggled.

Wozniak jerked his head at me. "Now get down in the fuck-ing basement."

I didn't move. "You think Zak's going to let you live with what you've got on him? Especially after all the heat that'll come down if Moira and I disappear? Better start running now, sicko."

"What heat? Yeah, there'll be lots of media for a while. But all I gotta do is write a few articles, maybe hint at a relationship between the two of you. Pretty soon, the excitement dies down. I know it's a blow to the ego, man, but you'll be old news in a month."

"People saw me leave that Mexican joint with you."

He shrugged. "So what? The cops ask, I tell 'em I last saw you headed over to Moira's office to get some nookie. Hey, I know all those guys. You think they'll see me as some kind of master criminal? Good ol' Woz the cop shop reporter?"

"I know them, too," Moira reminded him.

"Yeah? What about it? You think your blowjobs are so good the Wihega County cops are going to search forever for you? You're living in la-la land." He opened the basement door.

"You perverted—" Moira began.

Wozniak put his hand on my shoulder and shoved. I lunged for the banister, grabbed it, and managed to avoid taking a header down the stairs. Moira fell against my back.

The door slammed behind us.

"You're a fucking asshole!" Moira shouted and punched the door so hard it rattled on its hinges. A lock snapped into place. Wozniak's voice came through the wood.

"Hey, you should thank me. This'll give you a chance for a goodbye fuck. Try the bathtub why don't you?" I thought I heard him chuckle.

I waited a moment. There was a soft creak of a floorboard as he walked away. Moira started to say something, but I covered her mouth.

Wozniak said, "Get her car into the shed. Then come back here and help me wipe the place down."

Heavy steps. Then the opening and closing of a door.

"Bastard," Moira whispered.

"C'mon." I touched her arm.

She let me lead her down the stairs. The basement hadn't gotten any less dark. I felt her shudder.

Voice just above a whisper I asked, "What the hell are you doing here?"

"I told you I'd try to get Duane to surrender."

"You knew he was here all along?"

"I didn't *know* anything. A while back, I overheard Duane say something to him about their mother's house. A week or so ago, I thought to check the property tax records and found the address. It's . . . abandoned. I didn't think I'd find anyone here but I wanted to check just the same."

"You didn't happen to bring a cell phone did you?"

"I left it in the car. Wozniak killed the Hayden boy didn't he? He killed them all."

"Take my hand."

Layout clearly in mind, I led her across the basement. She impressed me by walking with assurance she couldn't have felt.

When we reached the door I'd discovered on my earlier reconnaissance, I rattled the knob, then put my foot up on the wall next to it and yanked. My head and back screamed in protest. The door moved about a half an inch, scraping reluctantly against the concrete floor. I tried again. Still just the slight give. Ran my hand down the jam. All that effort hadn't left enough of an opening to stick a nail file through. It made sense. I couldn't see Wozniak locking us down there and leaving a back way out.

"This place smells like a bathroom," Moira said.

"It gets worse." We re-crossed the basement to the place where I'd envisioned arms coming from the darkness. I told her about the crawlspace and how Wozniak referred to the basement as Duane's "crib."

"I think he lives in the crawlspace," I said. "Make a step with your hands. I want to get in there and see if I can find a weapon."

"It better be something good and you better find it fast."

The stench thickened as she helped boost me into the opening. Think windowless, dank high school locker room filled with filthy clothes and broken toilets. The entry I climbed through was partially blocked by a heavy bag of something that gave off the earthy, baseball field smell I'd recognized earlier. I pushed past it and deeper into darkness. Above me I could hear footfalls as Wozniak moved through the house.

For a crawlspace, it had quite a bit of room. Not enough to stand upright but as wide as three men standing shoulder to shoulder. I moved back as far as the space would allow, imagining Duane as an animal hiding from whatever he feared the most. His mother? His brother? I crouched and moved crablike, sweeping my hands to the sides and out front, staring into the darkness. Twice I paused to keep from sneezing and once nearly choked with the effort. Something fell on my back and I was sure I felt crawly tentacles squeezing into my shirt and down my spine.

I found mattress, sheets, and a tattered blanket and pillow first. Kept searching for anything heavy or that might have hard edges. Toppled a couple of empty beer cans and swore to myself. Nothing useful came to hand. I was about to reverse direction and crawl back to Moira when I ran my fingers under the oily pillow. At first, I thought I'd found a skinny harmonica. When I realized what it was, I ran my thumb along one edge, found a button and pressed.

I didn't have to see the blade jump out of the handle to realize I was holding a switchblade knife.

CHAPTER THIRTY

I'd only seen one switchblade since coming to Wihega County. Lindsey Sears had it in her hand in Wiley's parking lot when she threatened to amputate Lucas Bremmer's balls for shooting at the cat. This didn't have to be the same one but instinct told me it was. Even while being questioned by the cops, she'd managed to hold onto it. Until Wozniak took it away from her. A souvenir? Sexual psychopaths are known for doing such things. I slipped it in my pocket and worked my way back to the opening in the wall to the basement.

"God, it you took long enough," Moira breathed when I poked my head out. She patted the bag I'd clambered over getting into the crawlspace. "What the hell do they have a sack of quicklime for, anyway?"

Lime. Of course. Used to chalk the foul lines on a baseball diamond. Also used to speed the decomposition of corpses in mass graves in places with names like Treblinka and Sobibor and Auschwitz. Also popular with some serial killers. Suddenly the bathtub made sense.

Sometimes I hate being excellent at Trivial Pursuit.

Wozniak's recipe for our disappearance: Kill, place in tub, salt down with lime, and leave to marinate. Assuming no one else came into the basement for a few months, eventual disposal would amount to a sack full of white bones.

I shared my suspicions with Moira. No reason to hold anything back from her. I also handed over the knife. Given

Grum's history with women, I figured she might have a better chance to use it close in than I would. She shuddered as she took it.

"This isn't happening. This *can't* be happening. I'm a criminal defense attorney for God's sake." She grabbed my arm. "Wait a minute. That door in the back. Maybe we can use the knife as a wedge!"

"No. Blade's too thin and not strong enough. Save it."

"Then we're going to look for something else."

We made the trip through the dark again and this time she insisted we search the room the way I had done the crawlspace, on hands and knees. While we worked, I said, "Wozniak thinks he knows you pretty well."

I figured she wasn't going to answer. Then she did. "He knows enough."

"How did he blackmail you into defending his brother?" My hand closed around something long and wooden. A shim but, like the knife, not substantial enough to be of any use. I left it and kept moving. The concrete under my knees was hard and damp. I could still smell the lime.

"I was in a relationship with . . . a woman who worked for the sheriff's police. She's married. We were discreet, almost to the point of being obsessive about it, actually. After the rape video surfaced and I agreed to represent Lucas, Woz showed up in my office one day. He had credit card receipts and even pictures of Donna and me going into a hotel in the city. It just . . . floored me. He promised he wouldn't tell anyone but only if I kept the case from going to trial."

"Why you? There had to be other lawyers . . ."

"I knew the system for logging evidence to the sheriff's vault from when I clerked in the state's attorney's office. They never changed the procedures. And my friend had access to the combination. I told Woz the state's case was weak and I could probably get the girl to admit she hadn't been raped, but he insisted on the sure thing. So we did it his way." The last words spilled out quickly, like she was ashamed and wanted to rush past the memory.

"And he's owned you both ever since." A door slammed upstairs and heavy clunking steps told me Grum had returned. In the back of my head I heard a whisper. *Won't be long now.*

"He knew Duane would get in trouble and need me again. After the rape case and all the bad publicity about the sheriff's police, Zak put out the word that he'd take it as a personal insult if any attorney in the county ever represented him. So Woz left me alone. But he kept pestering my friend to give him inside information about cases he covered for the paper. It got so bad right after the first of the year, she finally took the risk and quit."

It was my turn to fall silent as pieces of the Hayden murder case assembled themselves in my head. I watched them drop into the right slots and then sat back on my heels.

"Your friend went to work for the school district, didn't she?" I asked. "Donna Teague. In Security."

A moment passed, and then Moira gave a tiny laugh from the darkness. "You're pretty good, McCarthy. How did you know that?"

I was about to tell her when Wozniak threw a fit right above our heads.

"Cops! That fucking bastard. That *fucking bastard!*" Footsteps pounded across the floor.

"Oh my God," Moira said in a very small voice.

"How many of them, goddamnit?" Wozniak snapped. I couldn't hear Duane's answer but it propelled Woz to even greater volume.

"Shit!" More running footsteps.

Moira moved close, startling me. "What do you—?"

I didn't take time to think.

"Stay here. In fact, get over in the corner. As far away from the stairs as you can."

She put a hand on my arm. I stepped away from it and rushed through the dark basement. By the crawlspace, I ditched my shoes and used my teeth to rip open the bag of lime. The powder dried my mouth and the acrid taste came close to closing my throat. Too late, I wondered if I'd just poisoned myself. Not to worry. Wozniak or Grum would probably kill me before it ever had a chance to work. I grabbed a thick handful of the chalk-like substance and climbed the stairs quiet and fast.

Duane was in the kitchen and must have been close to the door. I could smell his body odor and the coffee beans. He sounded excited. "I can't see them from here. I could go and—"

"You stupid piece of shit. You don't get it, do you? We've been set up! That bastard Zak *set us up!* You open that door, a sniper's probably ready to blow your ass away."

"You don't have to call me names!" Duane said in the hurt voice of a child.

Wozniak said, "Christ, I don't need this . . ." I heard touch tones being punched.

I should have been thrilled to hear about the cops but, even when the police perform superbly, hostage situations don't always end well for the hostage. It wasn't much of a stretch to assume Zak wanted this one to go south.

There was a muffled click and then a distant screech of feedback through a loudspeaker.

"Duane Grum!" A magnified voice. Teague. *"This is the Wihega County Sheriff's Police!"*

"Motherfuckers," Wozniak muttered.

The loudspeaker cut off at the same moment Wozniak started talking. Cell phone?

347

"It's Woz," he said quickly. "We're cool in here. You've gotta back off."

A pause.

"Yeah, we got McCarthy and Cullen," Wozniak said, louder now. "Lemme do it my way."

Again a pause. This one shorter.

"You may have to act like a hostage negotiator because you got other cops all around, but I *know* you don't want us coming out with our hands up, you prick. Zak wants us dead, doesn't he?"

Wozniak's breathing was audible. Almost hyperventilating.

"Yeah. Yeah, I understand you got problems, too. Just stay put out there. Duane's gonna take care of it. A couple more minutes." A phone snapped closed.

"What did he say?" Grum asked.

"They're trying to fuck me, that's what! But we're good. We're gonna be okay." Wozniak sounded like he was trying to convince himself.

"You listen to me," he said. "They've got to be dead for this to work. Get down there. Use the shotgun. Do it quick and make it messy."

"Wait. If I kill them now, aren't the cops gonna know . . . ?"

"It's okay." Wozniak's laugh was hollow. "Haven't I always been there for you? We'll both walk outta here. Don't worry about it. I got your back."

I'd heard used car salesmen sound more convincing at the end of a brutally slow month. Duane wasn't really that dumb, was he?

Whether out of stupidity, brotherly trust, or something darker, Duane apparently bought the package his brother was selling. And it happened so fast he almost caught me off-guard. I'd expected him to agree or argue. Say *something*. Instead, the door banged open and there he was, shotgun coming down off his shoulder as he charged forward to follow his brother's orders.

The fact he was wearing glasses made it tougher. I was crouched against the wall with my right hand balled into a fist around the clump of lime. When he crossed the threshold, I uncoiled my legs and lunged, coming up past the gun, driving the flat of my hand directly into his face, slapping the lime against the glasses with all the strength in my arm, shoulder, and back. Sort of like throwing a pie but staying with it to make sure it mashed flat.

His glasses snapped at the bridge and fell away. He bellowed once as the lime made it to his eyes. The shotgun boomed. Pellets rushed over my head and punched into the ceiling. Duane staggered, off balance. Dropped the shotgun. I caught one quick glimpse of Wozniak's shocked expression over his shoulder then I lowered my head and rammed it into Duane's belly.

It was a dumb move. His abs were like rocks. And, while sudden blindness would immobilize any normal person, I hadn't counted on his reflexes. He snapped both powerful arms around me like pincers and used his massive bulk to counter my charge. I felt myself propelled backward. I lost my footing but, in the last moment before I fell down the stairs for the second time that night, I hooked a hand in Duane's belt. That, and his forward momentum, dragged him with me. I twisted hard in mid-air. My back rammed painfully into the banister. He hit the wall opposite. For an eye-popping instant we were face to face. Then gravity did its thing and we crashed together, rolling head over ass, to the bottom of the steps.

I got lucky. Had he landed on top, he would have crushed me like a Ping-Pong ball under a dropped brick. Instead, he slammed face first into the basement floor, then came down with a "Whump!" on his right shoulder. With his howl of pain ringing in my ears, I dropped onto his back, got my arms under me, and vaulted past him.

I hit the floor on my hands and knees. Stunned, I tried to scramble to my feet but he grabbed my ankle and yanked me back toward him. I kicked him in the head. He pulled harder. I lashed out again with my foot and got his bad shoulder. He grunted and loosened his grip. Slipping my foot free, I stumbled away across the pitch-black basement completely disoriented, gasping for breath. Behind me, I heard him make a sound that was as inhuman as I'd ever heard. Part fury, part fear. An animal denied its prey but with every intention of setting out to corner it again. And we were in his lair.

I took four steps and caromed off a wall. Pain ricocheted through me top to bottom. Far off, I heard the bullhorn voice again but couldn't distinguish words. No matter. I'd covered plenty of hostage incidents. The script doesn't vary much. The shotgun blast had set things in motion. Whether the cops wore white hats or were the forces of evil, they'd be storming the house momentarily. Unless Wozniak delayed them. In which case, they might hold off just long enough for Grum to kill us. Either way, we were about to be dead.

"Duane! Listen to me. Your brother's going to kill you!"

I should've kept my mouth shut. Blinded or not, he knew this basement and I'd just targeted myself. He came at me in a rush. All the warning I had was shifting shadows and his huff of breath. I dodged to my right. Wasn't quick enough. He tagged me on the left shoulder with one of those big fists and my arm went numb. We were even now. I tried to run. He kicked the back of my left knee. I flopped to the floor.

"Where's the bitch?" he panted. His breath and body stank, a vile odor that had nothing to do with sweat and everything to do with a killing lust.

"Duane, your brother's only looking out for himself . . ."

A kick, this one just shy of collapsing a couple of ribs.

"My brother takes care of me," he wheezed in that awful

voice of his. "You're the one that's gonna die. Where's the bitch? I want the bitch first."

I covered my head just in time to take a kick to my right forearm.

"Where is she?"

Bodies collided above me. Moira screamed. I sensed violent motion. Grum bellowed like a child in pain but the cry cut off, abruptly replaced by the slurping sound a dentist's vacuum makes as it sucks up blood and saliva.

I eeled away on my back as fast as my damaged parts could take me. Something large thudded to the floor. More sobbing. A moment later, hands on my arm shocked me. I shied away. Then I realized it was Moira and she was trying to pull me to my feet. I felt wetness where she touched. I tried to rise with her but all my strength was gone. I sank against the wall behind me. She crouched at my side.

"I think he's dead," she whimpered. "I think I killed him. I think he's dead."

A blaze of white light cut through the darkness.

"Duane? Bro?" Wozniak's feet thundered on the stairs. The light danced crazily, floor to ceiling. "Duane, goddamnit."

The flashlight beam came to rest on a form not ten feet away. Time ground to a stop.

Duane Grum knelt on the hard basement floor facing the stairs. When he saw his brother, his mouth began to move but all that came out was the wet cawing sound produced by a torn windpipe. He was twisted to the right. Both hands stretched up over his shoulder, gripping the handle of the switchblade imbedded in his neck. From the looks of it, Moira had nicked his carotid artery on the way through. A bright arterial spray of blood pumped the last of his life into the air. It weakened as we watched.

I'd expected his eyes, uncovered for the first time, to be a devil red. Instead, they were childlike brown and leaked tears. His mouth moved and stopped. His body remained upright.

Wozniak, backlit by the light from upstairs, flashlight still on his brother, took a careful step out of range of the diminishing red fountain.

Neither Moira nor I spoke. She was shaking against me.

"Damn!" Wozniak pointed the flashlight at us. "Moira. You've got my brother's blood all over your blouse. You know that?"

The flashlight moved away. He brought up the Glock with his other hand. Moira gripped my arm so hard her fingers squeezed bone.

Wozniak licked his lips. "Teague said if I wanted to walk, I was going to have to do Duane. But that would have been different. A mercy killing. This . . ."

He crouched to peer into his brother's face. Then at us again. In the backsplash of the flashlight he looked stunned. Fury overrode his disbelief. "You butchered him."

"Woz, listen to me, man," I said. "The cops want you dead. Work with me and we all have a chance of walking out of here."

"Are you kidding? Sure they will. They know nobody else can spin the story the right way for them. I already have the headline: 'My Brother Took Me Hostage.' Has a Pulitzer sound, doesn't it?" His knees cracked as he stood.

"I couldn't stop Duane from shooting the two of you, see? So I stuck him."

Keeping the gun on us, he shoved the flashlight under his arm. Then he pried his brother's fingers off the handle of the switchblade. Grum's arm flopped down but he remained kneeling. No more cawing sounds. I couldn't see if he was breathing but his eyes were open.

"Stuck him with this before he could shoot me." Wozniak placed his hand where his brother's had been and squeezed. "Not world class improvisation but I think it'll get me by."

He drew himself up straight. "Should I kill McCarthy and fuck you, Moira?" he asked conversationally. He cocked his head. "No. I'll just kill both of you."

I swear I saw his finger tightening on the trigger even as an explosion blasted the once jammed-shut basement door behind him off its hinges. Two people burst into the room shouting.

To give him credit, Wozniak spun around like a pro and actually got off one shot. Then a pinprick of red light appeared on his chest, another danced on his forehead, and a volley of responding gunfire blew him apart like a tornado funnel ripping into a scarecrow.

Moira screamed. I wrapped my arms around her, expecting any second to feel the next set of slugs tearing into me. Wozniak's flash spun on the floor where it had dropped from his dead fingers. In the strobe-effect lighting, I saw two figures in black advancing toward us. Their weapons were up at eye level and they wore night-vision goggles.

It took me a second before I realized who they were.

CHAPTER THIRTY-ONE

Sunny lifted her goggles and produced a flashlight that brought near-daylight to the subterranean space. In two steps she was beside me, hand on the back of my neck. "You okay?"

"Never better. What the hell—"

"Tell you later. Wihega County SWAT is gonna blow in here and we need to get ready. Russ?"

Russ Traynor used his foot to slide the Glock away from Wozniak's corpse and checked Grum. "Dead."

I helped Moira to her feet as the radio strapped across Sunny's chest crackled: *"Entry team in position. We have shots fired. Repeat, shots fired."*

"Entry team, go!" came another voice. Teague.

"Shit." Sunny lifted the radio and keyed up, "Wihega County, stand by! There are four friendlies in the basement and two suspects down. Be advised, when your team makes entry they will be on live television. Repeat: live television."

"Who the hell is this? Get off the channel . . ."

"I'm a licensed bail enforcement agent. My partner and I have secured the scene. We will have our weapons on the floor and our hands in the air. Repeat: our weapons are on the floor. Don't forget. You're going to be on camera, guys."

She'd been talking while she and Russ laid their rifles on the basement floor and Russ unclipped a mini-camera from a Velcro mount on his shoulder. It was the same kind my I-team used for undercover stuff. It fit in the palm of his hand with room left over. A small Wi-Fi antenna stuck out the top. He pointed it at Moira and me.

Sunny said, "Kneel down, face forward. Put your hands behind your head." She dropped down next to me. Russ found a shelf in a corner and put the camera on it, facing the room, and then joined us.

We heard a crash upstairs, followed by multiple footfalls.

"Sheriff's police!"

"Reno McCarthy!" I yelled back. "There are four of us down here. We're not armed."

There was a pause and a helmeted head appeared for just a moment through the doorway at the top of the stairs. None of us moved. Then, almost as one, several bodies thundered down the stairs, weapons at eye-level aimed at us. Shouts bounced off the walls.

"Get down! Get down! Get Down!"

"On your bellies! Do it now!"

Three guys, one behind the other. One more kept the high ground at the top of the stairs, providing cover. They were dressed in black and carried the same type of rifles as Sunny and Russ. Theirs, however, had sound suppressors. Kill quietly amidst the noise and haste.

"Face down on the floor! Facedown!"

I dropped to within inches of Wozniak's body, face in his blood. His frozen-open eyes staring into mine looked dazed. My stomach twisted again. If I puked on the cops' shoes, would they open fire? A moment later I was frisked and my hands yanked down and flex-tied behind my back. I tried to lift my head, but the barrel of a gun jabbing behind my left ear persuaded me to keep still.

"Remember the camera!" Sunny said.

"You don't have any fuckin' camera."

"Video and audio is being monitored and taped in my office.

My staff has orders to duplicate the tapes and take them to the TV stations."

"Shut up bitch!"

"Shut up . . ."

"Shit, boss, there's a camera on this shelf . . ."

"Get 'em moved out. This way . . ."

Powerful hands wrapped around my biceps and hauled me upright. Another SWAT officer clumped through the door Sunny and Russ had blown off its hinges. Fingers in my back prodded me forward past him, up a flight of stairs that smelled of damp soil and wet leaves and out into the night where thick, swamp-wet air greeted me.

A figure in a windbreaker stood there waiting, partially illuminated by a flare of light seeping around the corner from the front of the house.

"What the fuck have you people done now?" Commander Gary Duvall asked.

"The gun. Tell your dad," I said. Fear mingled with the lime dust in my mouth and I gasped, choking. "In Wozniak's belt."

The same tactical guy who had pointed the rifle at me outside Grandma Bremmer's house propelled me past Duvall and the light from a thousand suns blinded me while the chatter of two-way radios from all directions swept my words into the darkness.

They put me in an eight-by-eight interrogation room with pale gray walls, a steel table and one chair. They also took off the handcuffs and gave me a cardboard cup of lukewarm coffee that tasted like they'd used it to marinate cigarette butts. When I asked about Moira, a moon-faced detective with a face pitted by acne told me to mind my own business. The sounds outside the room were muffled. The air stank of food grease and sweat and the light fixture buzzed like a bug-zapper in a rain forest. By my watch, I waited two and a half hours.

Most of the time, cops talk to witnesses right away. Suspects get to sit and consider their sins. What did that make me?

Teague came in a little after midnight. He wore a muted blue and white Hawaiian shirt with sweat-soaked armpits and an empty holster on his right hip. He threw a folder down on the table. I was standing at that point so he slid the chair around and sat.

"Your friend DeAngelis is fucked," Teague began. "At the very least, murder, home invasion, and obstruction of justice, but the state's attorney is a creative guy so I think there's a lot more to come. Maybe even some federal charges on the illegally modified weapons they had and illegal use of a police radio. Cute, but illegal as hell. That's federal, too. Her private detective license is history."

"Stop trying to bait me, Teague. Sunny can take care of herself. I'm tired and you've kept me here eighty-nine minutes longer than you needed to. If you want my statement, start acting like a real cop and let's get it done."

He tried to stare me down. "Okay, hotshot. Dig the hole deeper. Tell your story."

He took me through it twice. He was starting a third go-round when the interrogation room door banged open without a knock and Barnett Tanner stalked into the room looking like he'd been summoned from a party he hadn't been happy to leave. Chief Droot hovered behind him, along with Gary Duvall and another white-shirt I didn't recognize.

Barney is to Chicago defense lawyers what Mike Ditka is to coaches, minus the histrionics. He trailed the smell of expensive bourbon and high-dollar aftershave, white hair exquisitely barbered, jaw set as though daring the cops to take a swing at him.

"Barnett Tanner. I'm representing Ms. DeAngelis, her associate Mr. Traynor, and Mr. McCarthy. You okay, Reno?" He put a hand on my shoulder.

"Tired, hungry. Pissed off."

Tanner stared at Teague. "This interview is over. My clients and I are leaving."

"Wait a minute," Teague sputtered. "We're holding—"

Tanner held up a hand. "You're not holding anyone. I just explained the facts of life to your chief and the youngster from Felony Review outside. Ms. DeAngelis was legally representing one of your local bail bondsmen tonight and thus entitled to use whatever means necessary to make entry to the premises of a wanted felon. And I think it's obvious that she and her associate were defending not only themselves but also Mr. McCarthy and Ms. Cullen when they took Mr. Wozniak's life. *Regretfully* took Mr. Wozniak's life," he added.

"What the fuck are you talking about?"

"Duane Grum failed to appear in court three days ago on a felony DUI. In doing so, he forfeited his bail. If you recall, Ms. DeAngelis is a bail enforcement agent. Are you familiar with the United States Supreme Court ruling in *Taylor v. Taintor?*"

Holy shit. It took all the self-control I had to keep from laughing out loud. How the hell had Sunny managed to arrange all of that in a couple of hours?

Teague's jaw knotted but a gesture from Droot made him step aside.

The only car in front of the police building was a white stretch limo. Tanner grinned when he saw my expression. "Hey. Johnnie Cochran traveled first class. I might as well."

Inside, Sunny sprawled on the back seat, holding an open can of beer against her forehead, eyes closed. Russ was in one of the jump seats. He'd braced a highball glass filled with dark liquid on his knee and had an open bag of cashews in his other hand.

"Where's Moira?" I asked.

"Sorry slick. Your buddy Callahan already took her home,"

Sunny said, eyes still closed.

I pushed her legs off the seat and dropped down next to her.

Tanner asked where we wanted to go. I gave him the address of the motel. He offered me a beer. My stomach cringed. I declined.

"Sunshine, how the hell did you pull all that off?" I asked.

"Remember me telling you Grum had gone down a couple of times for DUI? He was due in court for an appearance this week. I called around and found he was a no-show. Guy who wrote his bond sounded happier than a hog in slop when I said I'd be glad to go looking."

"They had Grum's address?"

"They had his *brother's* address. I about fell over when I saw Wozniak's name on the bond sheet."

"How'd you know I was there?"

"Didn't. When you didn't answer your cell, I called Russ and we decided to drive by and scope the place out. We were coming through the woods from the back when Wihega County started talking on the radio about a hostage situation."

"So you were out there when Duane—"

"We saw him grab Cullen," Russ said. "I wanted to take him down then, but we didn't know the situation."

"He forced her inside," Sunny said, "and we listened. That's when we realized they put you in the basement."

"Listened . . . how?"

"Spike mike," Sunny said. "Not great quality through those stone walls but good enough to know you were in trouble and the way the county was lollygaggin' they'd never get to you in time. When we heard the fight start, Russ set a Detasheet strip charge and blew the door."

I massaged the base of my skull with both hands. Pain shot clear through to my forehead. I told them how Wozniak suckered me into his trap.

"He was going to kill me and come after you. He sure as hell wasn't expecting Moira to show up. Or those cops. Zak double-crossed him. I think Teague was there to make sure nobody came out of that house alive."

Sunny and Russ exchanged glances. "We thought the whole thing sounded a little . . . staged."

Tanner interrupted. "You're saying the chief of detectives of this bohunk police department was using his SWAT unit as a hit squad?"

"Maybe just one guy on the entry team. Remember, Moira and I were supposed to already be dead. Probably Grum, too. Wozniak could have been a tragic accident."

"Jesus Christ," Tanner said. The limo glided to a stop in front of the motel office. "If you have any evidence of all that, we need to bring in the FBI, the state police . . ."

"All I've got are guesses based on Wozniak's phone calls."

He wiped his mouth. When we got out of the limo he was pouring himself a Scotch.

I called the newsroom and related the evening's details to a wheezy, bored editor. He didn't sound bored for long.

"Jesus Christ! Chucky left a memo that if you called in we're supposed to tell you you're suspended and not to bother him. But he's gonna want to hear this . . ."

CHAPTER THIRTY-TWO

I fell asleep faster and harder than if one of the SWAT guys had smacked me in the head with a rifle butt. Awoke suddenly about an hour later, almost in a seated position, feet and legs tangled in the sheets, my throat raw and tears streaming down my cheeks. Vinnie's face in front of me. Oddly, given my tears, he was smiling and nodding. As if *approving* of me.

The damn thing was I couldn't remember the dream that set me off. Something about Vinnie backing me up in the basement and Duane going after him . . .

It had to have been a doozy from the look of the sheets. The phone, clock, my watch, and a bottle of water I'd put on the nightstand were now on the floor.

Trying to get away from something or someone. Duane? Wozniak? I realized I was shaking. Jesus.

Headlights flashed across the windows and a car slid to a stop in the slot outside my room. I glanced at the clock. Almost two. I listened for a door to open and close. Nothing. And the .45 Sunny had loaned me was under the seat of her Expedition.

The room phone rang. I jumped, swore, and leaned over to pick it up.

"Reno?" Moira's voice, small, shy, and hoarse. "I'm outside your room. I didn't want to startle you by knocking. I'm really scared and don't want to be alone . . ."

I opened the room door and swept her into my arms.

★ ★ ★ ★ ★

We yanked the mattress to the floor.

Our lovemaking was as fierce as hand-to-hand combat but mostly silent. She cried out twice, once when I entered her and again as she climaxed, but other than that we expressed our passion and relief at being alive with hands and tongues and teeth. When she finally mounted me and clenched her legs around mine, I felt the strength in them and in the wire taut-ness of her shoulders and arms.

Afterward, almost dozing, I said, "You left with Callahan?"

"God, Reno," she murmured. "Why are you asking me that *now?*"

"I'm curious how he fits in with you and Wozniak."

She came up on one elbow. "I sleep with Cal. He didn't know about Woz. He gives me information. He's well connected politically in the department so it's very good information."

"Gotcha."

"I sleep with two guys in the state's attorney's office, too. I'm very ambitious," she said. And then surprised me by burying her face in the pillow and starting to cry.

"Doesn't matter," I said. And it didn't. Nothing mattered at that moment except the fact we still breathed.

When sleep arrived it was deep and dreamless.

Until the goddamn phone rang at five a.m.

We had curled into spoons, my face pressed into the back of her head. She didn't stir at the noise and I didn't want to move and wake her. The phone stopped. The tension started to flow out of my shoulders again.

The ringing started up fifteen minutes later and continued, relentless, until I knew without a doubt who it was and how I planned to torture him to death.

"God," Moira moaned. "Stop that awful noise." When I didn't comply right away, she yanked my pillow out from underneath me and covered her head.

I rolled off the mattress and grabbed the receiver.

"What do you want?"

"Ah, Reno? Is that you?" Chucky said. "Sorry to, uh, wake you, man, but I heard you had a helluva night."

"Which is why I was sleeping."

"We need you for six, seven, and eight. Al's almost to your motel. He can set up right outside your room if you want. You don't even have to prepare a piece, just do Q and A with Franny and Giselle."

I filled my lungs, held the breath to a count of ten, and slowly exhaled. "I thought I was suspended?"

"Suspended! Where the hell did you get that? You're our star on this story, man. With you and the video that private eye sent us, we're going to close out this one on top."

"Then I handle it my way from now on. No asking permission. No arguments."

"Well," he chuckled. "I don't know if we can give you quite *that* much latitude."

"Then you can watch Goudie over at Seven get the exclusive."

"Reno, you know I need to have oversight . . ."

"Bullshit. You don't like the deal, get off the damn phone, and let me go back to sleep."

"Okay, okay. Take it easy. You're not a morning person are you?"

Even a shower couldn't wash away the clammy, closed-in feel left over from our experience in Grum's basement. If I took a deep breath I could still smell his coffee beans and body odor and, as many times as I gargled with mouthwash, the lime grit stayed caught in the back of my throat. I had a purple knot in the middle of the forehead but it didn't hurt unless I pressed it. I felt sluggish, old. Used-up.

Moira was asleep again by the time I got out of the shower. She lay on her side hugging the longest of the pillows and didn't move while I toweled dry, dressed, and left.

Al was set up for the live shot at the far end of the parking lot where Sunny and I had climbed the fence to chase Grum. He saw me coming and surveyed me with a critical eye.

"Fortunately for you, you look like shit. That's exactly what Chucky wants. Like you been smacked around all night. Go get your coffee. Thermos on the front seat."

I thought of Grum and his coffee beans. "I'm going to pass this time."

"Starbucks."

"Yeah? Well maybe . . ."

The morning, dawning clear, carried just the hint of heavy humidity that could turn uncomfortable later. The chugging of the truck's generator was the only sound in the parking lot. A guy named Raviv tinkered with the truck's electronics. I nodded to him as I climbed into the passenger seat and found the thermos. Al finished setting up the camera and a fill light to complement those on the side of the truck and slid behind the wheel.

"They transferred Eddie to Loyola's burn unit. He's not doing so good. Lotta pain. You doin' okay?"

"At least I didn't kill anybody this time."

"Call the desk. Franny wants to go over your Q and A before you get on the air."

By the time we went live, I'd given Mary Frances Fitzgerald, Channel 14's star morning anchor, enough background that she led me point by point through the events of the night before like a prosecutor parading a star witness. I followed up by linking Grum and Wozniak to the assaults on Eddie and Jody and revealed Wozniak's admission that he'd killed Trey Hayden.

"Wihega County Police have issued a news release claiming

Wozniak and Grum were part of a burglary ring," Franny persisted. "Was that the motive for Trey Hayden's murder?"

I looked directly at the camera. "All I can say right now, Mary Frances, is that Wihega County's news release is bunk. For lack of a better word."

Surprise crossed her features. "Well! Stay tuned to Channel 14 for details, huh Reno?"

I finished my live shot and was about to duck back into the truck when a Jeep Cherokee rolled into the lot and Frank Duvall motioned to me through the driver's window.

"Thought you'd like to see what they're saying about you." He handed over the morning Wihega County paper.

Wozniak and Grum looked out from side by side above the fold, under the shouted headline: "Journalist, Brother Killed in Shootout." Moira's photo was farther down, as was a publicity still of me off Channel 14's Web site. A stark picture of the house, lit by portable lamps, took up a good portion of page two. Its ordinariness surprised me. Some enterprising photographer had even gotten inside to grab a shot of the bathtub. The cut line under the photo referred to the lime.

A small, cold worm crawled along the back of my neck.

I skimmed the story and saw a quote from Teague about my "meddling that got a couple of people killed." The bulk of the story quoted Callahan from a news conference well after I'd gone to bed. He "revealed" that Wozniak had a juvenile record as a Peeping Tom and "speculated" it wasn't much of a jump from that to burglary.

I glanced from the paper to Duvall. "Burglary ring? Home invasion?"

"They had to manufacture something. This makes it look like they're on top of things."

"If you say so. Back on Planet Earth did the evidence techs find anything that links Wozniak and Grum to Hayden?"

"You gonna quote me?"

"No. But if you've got something I'll use it."

He nodded. "In Woz's briefcase. Pictures of the Hayden house and of the daughter with her boyfriend, plat of survey, some sketches. They took Wozniak's shoes to check for tile paste."

I cocked my head.

"They found tile paste in the Hayden house that matched what the county's using to replace the floor in the courthouse. That's what made them think a cop screwed up at the scene. They have other stuff that Teague's keeping hush hush. Gary's not in the loop for it."

"Gary got Wescott's .38 from the basement, though, right?"

He shook his head. "No chance."

"Goddamn it!"

"Right after they extracted you and your people, Teague ordered the place sealed. Just him and the ETs inside. They shot video for the other dicks to watch. Claimed he wanted the scene pristine."

"Goddamn it!"

Duvall held up one finger. "Hold them horses, son. You aren't the only one who needs that gun. Just because Teague got his hands on it first doesn't mean I'm going to let it disappear. I got a thirty-year-old case I'd like to close. Point of fact, Teague having it may help us."

He shoved open the Jeep's door and got out, holding his coffee aloft.

"Gary says they didn't inventory the piece with the rest of the evidence from last night. That means Teague stuck it in his desk drawer."

"Or its on the way to Zak."

"Nah. That's what I mean about an advantage. Teague's got a little gambling problem. Zak keeps him out of trouble in Vegas.

In return, Teague does all Zak's scut work inside the department."

"Like sanitizing crime scenes and running rogue SWAT operations?"

He nodded. "Everything that's happened, you better believe Zak wants only one guy knowing he's interested in that gun. Teague drove straight from the scene last night to the courthouse. Hasn't left. As of when I pulled up here, he was sleeping in his office."

"How the hell do you know that?"

"You think my son and me are the only ones who don't like what's happened to this county? We got good eyes and ears keeping track. It's when he leaves the building we could use a little help." He gestured toward the live truck.

"I figure we follow Teague every goddamn minute until he makes the delivery. Last time I looked at the statute books, stealing evidence was a felony. Wouldn't hurt to have your camera there when he makes the handoff. We nail him like that I'm betting he'll flip."

Devious, these old farts.

We woke up Sunny and then went over and got Russ out of bed, too. I had to be on the air for the seven o'clock show and, while I did my Q and A, Duvall brought the two of them up to speed. Afterward, I checked on Moira. If I'd popped a few rounds from Sunny's .45 through the ceiling, she wouldn't have heard me.

Sunny made a call and, just as Al and I got off the air after my last live hit at nine, one of her guys drove into the lot in a custom-built Cadillac Escalade outfitted for surveillance work. She laid a map out on the hood and we gathered around it. We were discussing strategy when Duvall's cell phone rang. He conferred with someone for a moment.

"Chief's called a noon meeting. Status report on last night's investigation. Teague'll have to be there so figure we've got three hours to figure how to work this and get into position."

I left them to their planning session. Duvall looked like a big old bird dog allowed out on the hunt one last time. I wandered across the parking lot to make a call of my own. JohnElla Perkins picked up on the first ring.

"I am very glad to hear from you. I began my morning working on the two brothers," she said. "Are you all right?"

I assured her I was fine. "Did you get the package I left and is my favor do-able?"

"Reno . . . would you come to my office? We need to discuss this."

The same dour receptionist wearing a cordless headset and a frown got up from behind a Formica-topped counter to guide me through a security door and down a short hallway. On my right were half a dozen tiny offices containing only desks and computers and on my left a window that ran the length of two autopsy suites. A Hispanic man wearing a green smock and bio-hazard gloves and boots was scrubbing down the table in the far room. He didn't look up. The hall smelled of an industrial cleanser that always makes me think someone just threw up.

JohnElla, wearing scrubs, came around her desk to hug me like a relative returning from a war zone. She'd changed in the three years since I'd last seen her. She was in her late forties, black hair in a short afro beginning to go gray, and a round, open face with kind eyes. While she'd been vastly overweight before, the woman holding me at arm's length had the broad-shouldered build of a serious athlete. She saw me noticing and laughed.

"My husband told me when I first brought up running for this job, 'Oprah gets to have a big butt because she's a household name. You ain't got a household name.' One of the investigators in the office was a physical fitness trainer so I started working with him. Quit smoking, too. I ran two marathons this year if you can believe it."

"You look great."

She squeezed my arms and released me. "I wish I could say the same about you, my friend. Have you had any sleep since you arrived in town? I am speaking as a physician now."

"Too much happening . . ."

"Yes, and if you are the Reno I remember, you are the cause of it." She sat in a leather armchair that had seen better days and motioned me to its twin beside her. "You and your anomalies," she chuckled.

"You found one, didn't you?"

"First, let me say this. My predecessors maintained the most convoluted records system I have ever seen. In addition to case files, there were separate records containing transcriptions of pathologist narration during postmortem. The play by play, you might call it. I now have a better idea why the two sets of documents were seldom consolidated." She sighed.

"I asked my pathology student who is supervising the system updates to make sure all of our cold cases included the transcriptions whenever possible. She found a transcription of Dr. Gore's comments as he did his external exam in the Forge case, otherwise we would not be having this conversation. She told me that, while it was in the drawer with the other transcriptions, it was out of order. Included with a different file, in fact."

"Hidden?"

"Yes. Given the information it contained that appears to have been the intention." She lifted a folder and held it in her lap. "Reno, how do you plan to use this information?"

"I think the circumstances of Elaine Forge's death impact the Hayden case."

"The repercussions of the revelations do not concern you?"

"You mean what happens to Wescott if this comes out?"
She nodded.

I shrugged. "No more than killing Elaine Forge meant to him."

"Do not be so quick to judge, my friend. In this office, I tell my people we leave our preconceptions at the door. They are often misleading."

She opened the file and sifted through several sheets of paper. I saw Duvall's photos.

"Elaine Forge received a .38 caliber bullet wound to the left side of her face and skull." She touched the side of her head as Duvall had done.

"We have both an entrance wound at the hairline one point five centimeters anterior to the tip of the left ear here, and then the exit, hidden by her hair, thirteen centimeters superior to the tip of her ear but two point five centimeters left of the mid-sagittal plane. Stellate pattern, lateral to medial at a fifty-degree angle. I suspect she moved her head as she was hit." She traced the bullet track as she spoke.

I cleared my throat. "The Dick and Jane version?"

She looked up. "Sorry. When Dr. Gore first examined the body, he saw the wound entered at her hairline, tracked to above her ear and exited. In other words, the bullet entered and exited her skull. His final report, the official document taken to the inquest, states that this wound caused her death. Between the transcription and the final report, however, I found several inconsistencies. In fact, his conclusions swerve substantially from his exam notes. This wound would have bled like the dickens, yes, but as far as I can tell from the shallow angle of entry and location, it never penetrated deeply enough to cause death."

"You're saying Gore altered his findings in the final report."

"Yes. The more I read, the more obvious it became. Most significantly, he discovered water in her lungs and obvious asphyxia." Her eyes sought mine.

"She drowned?"

"Yes. The water in her lungs tells us she was breathing after she was shot. Here is another pertinent fact. Gore made a comment during his exam that is missing from the final report." She held out the closeup photo that showed the gouge of the bullet track. She tapped it with her pen.

"He noted premortem trauma to the back of her head, here. You can see the beginnings of it, even though her hair is in the way. He questioned how it might have occurred and mentions checking her eyes for hemorrhage, which he did not find. Yet in his synopsis of the case, he writes this: *'Observation of the immediate area indicates victim was shot while standing next to pool and expired, falling backward into the water.'*"

She held up a form in one hand and a sheaf of papers in the other. "I am sure Dr. Gore never expected this report and this transcription to ever wind up in the same file. They are completely at odds with one another. I would put my money on the transcription being the most accurate representation of his findings."

I thought about Duvall's memories of the crime scene. It had looked to him, he said, as if someone hosed down the pool area.

"So she fell on concrete, not into the water?" I asked.

"Yes. Gore described her trauma as consistent with a fall backward onto a hard surface."

"Would that have knocked her out? Completely?"

"Without being able to examine the injury, I cannot say for sure but, yes, I believe the fall would have incapacitated her."

"She wouldn't have woken up? Or moved around?"

"Not in my opinion."

"Then how did she get into the pool?"

"Based on Dr. Gore's initial findings, I would have to conclude someone put her there."

There it was, I thought. Duvall had been right. Zak's secret little crime wasn't a secret anymore. I felt more awake than I had all morning.

Awake enough, in fact, to pop up from the chair, thank a suddenly wide-eyed JohnElla for her help, and scram out of there like one of her patients was chasing me.

I heard chatter from the Motorola radio I left on the passenger seat when I got back to the Expedition. Listening to a couple of the exchanges between Sunny and her guys, I gathered Teague was taking longer in his meeting than expected. I held a brief debate with myself. Sit and wait for something to happen or go talk to an old cop? Action won out. I made an extended phone call, scribbled some notes, and then drove to the address Duvall had given me.

Ernie Mueller, lead detective on the Forge case, lived in an elderly six-story apartment house with brick walls the color of nicotine-stained teeth. A picket fence circled a patch of Bermuda grass and a tiny garden where stakes through their centers held up seven oversize rose bushes. I clumped up two flights of outside stairs and found Mueller's unit. A jar of what looked like sun tea sat on the porch railing outside his door. A light breeze carried the smell of the river a block away. Mostly dead fish and marine gas.

The way Gary Duvall described him, I expected to find an unshaven drunk in his bathrobe nursing a little hair of the dog that had bitten him the night before. Mueller might have awakened hung over, but when he answered my knock he was clean shaven and on his way out carrying a stack of magazines under one arm, a half smoked cigar in his other hand.

"Ernie Mueller?"

"I'm already late for an appointment, and I got all the subscriptions I need right here. Taking these with me to the hospice. Patients there love to read. It's like they don't want to die without knowing who's doing what to who out in the world."

"Reno McCarthy. I'm a reporter looking into the murder of Elaine Forge."

That won me a flicker of the eyes and a squaring of the shoulders. He went from friendly old retired guy to suspicious old retired cop. About sixty, I guessed, he had the red nose and prominent vein structure common to heavy drinkers. As with many alcoholics, the smell of the booze he'd imbibed over the years leeched from his pores and, along with the cigar smoke, gave off the odor of an after-hours saloon before the janitor comes in. He was a couple of inches taller than me but not as well dressed. A scarred leather coat he might have bought while working the Forge case hung open to reveal a black shirt and a wide tie that hung halfway to an oversized belly.

He gave an uneasy little laugh. "Forge. That happened what, twenty, thirty years ago?"

"It's still an open case."

"Yeah, well, lotta cases never get solved, buddy."

"Lot of *murder* cases where the victim is the wife of the wealthiest man in the county? You were the lead investigator weren't you?"

He'd been shifting his weight from foot to foot, ready to leave. At my words, though, he stopped fidgeting. "Hey, hey. What're you trying to do here? You trying to make me the fall guy for some exposé or something?"

"Not at all. I figured, as the lead, you might remember more than the other investigators on the case. I thought I'd do the story from your point of view. You know, retired cop, thinking about the big case you were never able to solve. I just need a few minutes of your time . . ."

"Not interested." His hand slid to the doorknob. "Gotta go."

"You were new to the detective division when the murder

happened, right? Couple weeks or something? Hell of a time to transfer in."

"Like I said. It was a long time ago. I don't remember."

"C'mon, Sarge. Sure you do. There you were thinking you'd just gotten this nice cushy assignment and then a heater murder drops in your lap? Bet you were sorry you ever asked for *that* favor, huh?"

He scowled. "What are you talking about? What favor?"

"Your transfer. You used some clout to get it, right? What do they call the guy who watches out for you, helps you move up? Your rabbi? Your Chinaman? Who was your rabbi, Sarge? Uncle Theo Zak?"

He shoved past me. "I don't have to listen to this bullshit." He headed for the stairs.

"The question is, what did you do to make Zak feel so obligated? Or was it something you saw?"

He turned and pointed a finger at me. "I said no fucking comment! You got that?"

Technically he hadn't said anything of the sort but why get picky? I pointed a finger back at him.

"Zak get you the job at the Arena, too? A last favor for the guy who helped him cover up a murder? That doesn't seem like much payback to me. Unless it's all off the books . . . ?"

"That's none of your business!"

"You keep yelling like that, Sarge, and the IRS is liable to find out you're not being square with them. Man, they hate that. You ever been questioned by the IRS?"

"You dirty fuck," he said but he brought the volume down to inside voice level. "I live on a goddamn pension, and you're gonna take away the little extra I get that helps make ends meet? You'd do that to an old man?"

"Yes I would."

★ ★ ★ ★ ★

I was just about to unlock the Expedition's front door when my phone buzzed. Duvall said, "Where are you? You listening to the radio?"

"I was off the air. What's up?"

"Teague's on the move. He's just leaving the law enforcement center. One of my guys saw him put the gun in his briefcase. Sunny's guy is two cars behind him. The rest of us are spread out for a couple of blocks."

Teague was hotfooting his county car, the way cops are prone to do, heading away from downtown. I was tempted to run stoplights to catch up to the little procession. I held back. This was Duvall's show. He had said the trip to Zak's place would take about fifteen minutes in midday traffic. If that's where he was headed. Within a minute or so, though, the laconic voice of Russ Traynor came over the radio net. He sounded surprised.

"Heads up, guys. It looks like our subject is taking a detour."

Crap. All this and the guy was going to lunch? We were set up to tag along whatever he did, but the idea of following him while he ran errands made the back of my neck spasm.

Moments later, Russ again. *"He just took the turnoff for the Heights . . ."*

What the hell? My cell phone buzzed again.

"Son of a bitch is heading for Wescott, not Zak," Duvall said.

"But he's Zak's guy, right?"

"Always has been. Two possibilities. Zak ordered him to return the gun—"

"No. Zak wouldn't give up the leverage. Wescott's convinced he killed Elaine Forge with that gun."

"Then I suppose Wescott could have found out the gun was recovered last night. Sidestepped Zak. If he waved enough money in Teague's face . . . yeah, Billy would take it. But we're talking a life-changing amount."

The gun had changed Wescott's life. What was it worth to him, I wondered. Millions? I swerved around a woman in a Volkswagen talking on her cell phone. "Damnit. I don't want Wescott. I want Zak."

"I'll take what I can get," Duvall said.

Russ came back on the air a couple of minutes later. *"Subject is approaching the Wescott residence. Move the Escalade into position."*

"Copy." Al was in back of the Escalade with another of Sunny's colleagues driving.

I pounded the Expedition's steering wheel. He needed to be right on top of anything that happened. For TV purposes, the video had to be clear and crisp and absolutely damning.

"Subject's car is entering the driveway," Russ reported.

By that time, I was manhandling the big SUV into a parking space around the corner. I jumped out and sprinted down the block clutching the Motorola.

More radio traffic. *"Subject is out and carrying a briefcase."*

I reached Wescott's street and slowed to a walk. A wrought iron fence ran along the front of his property. Heavy undergrowth prevented me from even seeing the house from where I stood, but my heart leaped when I realized the Escalade was nearly at the foot of the driveway. An unmarked Chevrolet eased to a stop behind it. Sunny would be inside along with two young guys who were the key to our operation.

"OK everybody, stand-by . . ."

My heart hammered against my ribs. I stood in the middle of the street, radio volume turned all the way down, unit at my ear.

"Wescott's in the driveway. I think they're going to make the exchange outside."

Al, I hope you're getting this, I thought.

He'd be shooting through the specially made glass on the

back of the Escalade. I held my breath.

"The handoff's been made. Wescott is opening the package. We're moving—"

With those words, the guys in the car with Sunny jumped out, guns in their hands, and ran onto the property. I took off, too, as the back door of the Escalade popped open. Frank Duvall's Jeep plowed past me and screeched to a halt behind the van.

"Police! Internal Affairs!" The two guys from the car yelled. "Stay where you are and put your hands in the air, Commander! You too, sir! Hands up. Hands up!"

Teague didn't resist. As I turned the corner into the drive and started up, one of the detectives had him spread eagled on the hood of his own squad and was lifting his gun from its holster. His briefcase lay open on the ground in front of Wescott, who had his hands at shoulder height and was shaking his head, as though denying he had ever touched it.

I reached the group as the IA cop snapped handcuffs on the man who outranked him and muscled him upright. Teague didn't see me right away.

"Fucking Tyner," he snapped. "You're suspended. You too, Kremansky. Goddamn it, get these cuffs off me. I'm here on official business you assholes . . ."

When he caught a glimpse of me, a vein started pulsing in his forehead.

"You do not have my permission to put this on television!"

"Quiet down, Billy," Duvall said, striding forward. Teague blinked like he'd been backhanded.

"What the fuck is *this* . . ."

Duvall brushed past me and went face to face with the man, so close that Teague stumbled against his car and would have fallen if the IA cop hadn't had one hand on his upper arm. The other IA detective ushered Wescott inside the house.

"You don't see me. I'm a figment of your imagination," Duvall said in a low, hard voice. "So if I have to break your jaw to shut your mouth, it goes down as you falling on your face during the arrest. Just like any other clumsy mope."

The IA detective named Tyner stooped and looked at the gun Teague had brought. It lay inside the open briefcase in an evidence bag.

"I'd say we got you by the nuts, Commander. You want to explain this?" If putting the arm on his supervisor bothered him, Tyner's expression didn't show it.

Teague's face, on the other hand, was slowly turning gray. "You can't . . ."

Duvall tapped him on the chest. "Attempting to sell evidence you've removed from a crime scene? That's one felony, probably two."

"It's not evidence," Teague sputtered. "It's recovered property. I was returning it—"

He suddenly went as silent as if someone had switched off his voice box.

"To its rightful owner?" Duvall prompted. "What did he offer you anyway? A million? Two? You think Zak's ever gonna forget you double crossed him like this?"

Teague stayed mute. I've seen better looking corpses.

"What's the matter, Billy? Didn't think you'd get caught?" Duvall took a deep breath and seemed to bring his anger under control. He turned to Tyner.

"Take this piece of shit down to your car and hold him there. If he starts flapping his gums about anything as stupid as wanting a lawyer, we'll give him to the FBI."

Tyner walked Teague away. Sunny came up the drive and stood next to me.

"Al got it all. You can even see Wescott's hand on the briefcase."

"How do you want to work this? You need me in there with you to question him?" Duvall asked, adding in a low voice, "Assuming he's got anything to say."

Sunny shoved her hands into her pockets. Her face looked troubled. Neither of us had expected Teague to lead us to her client's doorstep.

"I want to keep it as low key as possible. Just Reno and me. Anything more than that, I'm sure he'll circle the lawyers. He may anyway."

Duvall grunted. "Given what just went down, he's going to need one."

CHAPTER THIRTY-THREE

We walked into the house, Sunny and I, each of us aware we had no right whatsoever to be there. Wescott and the second IAD detective, Kremansky, stood in a large, marble-floored foyer. Wescott's voice echoed under the vaulted ceiling.

"I demand you tell me what is going on."

Kremansky wore a neutral expression, hands folded in front of him. He didn't answer.

A vase filled with sweet-smelling flowers sat on an antique table off to the right, and a formal oil painting of a gray-haired man with a vibrant, younger blonde graced the wall on the left. Eldon and Elaine Forge. Beyond the painting was a curved flight of stairs with a large grandfather clock at its base and a hallway that disappeared into shadows. Straight ahead was a living room the size of my house.

Wescott wore a suit that looked so natural, yet elegant, on his narrow frame it had to be handmade. The creases in his slacks were as sharp as the gaze he turned on us when Sunny closed the front door.

"Ms. DeAngelis . . . Sunny? What's going on here?" He wore a slight, puzzled smile that dipped toward condescension. He flicked his eyes at me.

"You're the fellow from TV. I've enjoyed watching you the last few days, but you have no right to be in my home. That applies to all of you."

Kremansky asked, "You need me?" When Sunny shook her

head, he left without another word. His part of our slapped-together stage play was probably over. No need to put him at further risk. The curtain might close on us, too. I wasn't sure.

I glanced around the foyer, spotting a black leather briefcase on the floor by the door. I picked it up. Wescott put out a hand.

"That is private property. Give it to me." Was the hand trembling?

I popped the latches. Stacks of one-hundred-dollar bills lay nestled in the soft interior.

"This is absurd," he said.

"And this," I hefted the briefcase, "is what the lawyers call attempted bribery."

He put his hand into his pocket and withdrew a tiny cell phone. "The police and my attorneys aren't going to be nearly as patient or polite as I am." His hand was shaking.

"In case you hadn't noticed, that was a cop who just left. Internal Affairs. They investigate the crooked ones. They're about to question your friend the commander about the briefcase he brought you."

"I hope they'll enlighten me when they find out what that was all about. I can't imagine. Commander Teague merely said he was going to stop by. He didn't give a reason."

"Old friends?"

"We've played golf together, yes."

"My photographer has video of you accepting the gun, Mr. Wescott," I said. "And we know its pedigree. If I tell the story on the air the way I've put it together the last couple of days, Osama Bin Laden's more likely to be running Forge Global tomorrow than you are."

"Elise Hanratty allows her reporters to resort to blackmail?"

"We want you to tell us your side of what happened to the Hayden boy," Sunny said in a soft voice. "And what happened to Elaine Forge thirty years ago."

Not even a blink of surprise. Except for the hand he couldn't control, this guy was good.

"You obviously don't understand a whit about corporate America. Either of you. Why do you suppose there's never been a *60 Minutes* segment done on Forge Global? Why hasn't *Dateline* ever touched us, or CNN or Fox or any of the other network news programs for that matter? It's not like we don't have our share of whistleblowers! Hell, it's not like we don't have all kinds of secrets the TV people in New York would love to know about." He held up his cell phone.

"One call from us and their satellite infrastructure collapses! One call and it's weeks before they can use their cellular phones again. One call and their boards of directors start making noises about more oversight and less funding for news operations. And I haven't even touched on how slowly the gears at the FCC can be made to turn on any regulatory appeals they have pending. You think we can't keep one story off the local news?"

Wescott pressed the *send* key and lifted the phone to his face. "You're fools. Get out of my house."

I said, "The only chump here is you. For believing Theo Zak when he told you that you killed Elaine Forge."

His expression didn't change but he closed the phone.

"What sort of foolishness is this?"

"Let me ask you a question. Did you ever read the coroner's report on Mrs. Forge's death?"

"Mr. McCarthy, this is not a subject I wish to discuss with you or anyone else. Elaine Forge's death was a tragedy. It haunts me to this day. If you attempt in any way to disparage her or myself, please be assured I will bring legal action."

With that, he turned and headed toward the stairs, back rigid.

I took the copies of Dr. Gore's report and the transcription of his examination notes out of my pocket and called to him.

"Dr. Gore was in on it. His report was a lie. Zak put the

whole thing together to blackmail you."

He put his hand on the banister and started upward.

"She drowned, you asshole!" I shouted. "Unless you held her head under water after you shot her, you didn't kill her."

Wescott stopped as if he'd seen Elaine's ghost at the top of the stairs. He turned to face us. I walked over and thrust the documents at him.

It ran four and a half pages. I watched him read each one, snapping them back over their staple as he finished. By the time his eyes stopped moving, a bead of perspiration the size of a tear appeared just below his widow's peak. It trickled slowly down to his jaw line and dropped on the papers he held. He didn't move or speak. The mechanism of the grandfather clock behind me whirred. I heard a click as the minute hand on its face moved forward.

After two more clicks he asked, "The coroner gave you this?"

"Yes."

"And she will corroborate that this is an official document?"

"Yes, she will."

Wescott reached out and lightly touched the banister. Then he strode past me, across the foyer and into what might have been a study just off the living room. I glimpsed paneled walls, glass cabinets, and golf trophies before he closed the door behind him.

He hung up the phone.

He sat in the paneled room behind the wooden desk with the scarred top which had been his mentor's, surrounded by his golf trophies and pictures of himself with celebrities from Paul Newman and Clint Eastwood to Tiger Woods and Norman Schwarzkopf. There was a single photo on the blotter in front of him.

Eldon and Elaine Forge looked up at him with smiling eyes

from a table in the dining room of Cardinal's Manitowish Lodge in Northern Wisconsin. The three of them had stayed in a cabin there the summer before her death. She sat in a chair, her husband behind her and slightly out of focus the way Wescott planned when he snapped the shot. She was front and center wearing a low-cut blue and white sundress with spaghetti straps that looked great against her dark tan. Wescott's wife had hated the picture the first time she saw it, but he left it in a position of prominence on his credenza.

Elaine.

The first time she fucked him, he awakened to find her straddling him, naked. She begged him afterward to keep it their little secret. Told him she'd hungered for him since the moment he moved in. He hadn't had the slightest idea, he said. She giggled. He wasn't like other boys who slobbered and stared at her, she said.

They took to spending the summer afternoons together. Mornings he worked at the Forge plant. His job was to conceptualize new ideas and rough them out for the technicians and scientists in Research and Development. He was very, very good at his job, so good Eldon Forge saw the potential for teenage burnout and allowed him to have half his summer days free.

His hunger for her became a constant flame, fed by her lust. They adhered to only one rule. No touching when the old man was at home. It made Wescott crazy, but he understood why it had to be. The old man's love for his young wife might make him oblivious, but he was far from stupid.

Sometimes, in the middle of the night, he dreamed they would run away together. They weren't that far apart in age. Until he turned twenty-one, they could live as brother and sister. After, they could get married. What would it matter that she was a few years older?

Wescott touched the glass of the frame and wondered if he

should kill himself. He closed his eyes and felt his stomach heave. He wanted to disappear.

We stood outside Wescott's study door like a couple of groupies waiting for their favorite band and listened, hearing nothing except the ticking of the grandfather clock in the hall.

My cellular rang. I wandered through the living room, finding myself in front of a set of French doors overlooking a wide patio with a concrete balustrade. Beyond it, the broad backyard sloped downward to where water glistened. The pool.

JohnElla said, "Wescott just called me. I hope someone is keeping an eye on him. He sounds awful."

"Awful as in suicidal?"

"I will just say when he asked his questions he was full of bluster. By the time I finished telling him what I told you, he sounded . . . diminished."

"We're at his house," I said. "Actually, we're in his living room."

"Good heavens. I hope he does not have other guns." She hung up. She sounded irritated. Probably thinking she'd be getting more customers.

The bruise on my forehead started to itch. I rubbed it as I walked back to join Sunny.

The study door swung inward. Wescott blinked when he saw us. His tie was still exquisitely knotted, suit coat buttoned and unwrinkled, shirt and slacks crisp, but there was something wrong with his posture. And his eyes. The earlier anger was gone, replaced by the focused-on-a-distant-point gaze familiar to anyone who has dealt with trauma victims. I felt a moment of déjà vu, remembering when I'd seen a similar look in my own eyes. Way back inside of me, locked in the trunk where my most bitter and terrifying experiences hide, something rose up, stretched, and settled again.

After weeks where they did nothing but spend the afternoons romping together in Wescott's bed, Elaine suggested the target shooting. It was something she said she had done often as a child with her father on their farm in southern Illinois. She told him the feel of the weapon and its power turned her on. She took him to the woods, where he was surprised to see a makeshift target range. Something she'd set up to remind her of home, she said. Heretofore, she had used it mostly in the mornings while he was at work, she said.

Forge, he reminded her, despised guns.

She smiled and kissed him lightly.

This will be another of our secrets, she promised him.

Wescott touched the doorframe. As with the banister, the contact with something solid and familiar seemed to rouse him.

He drew himself erect and his eyes returned to this century.

"Is this part of your security audit, Miss DeAngelis? Bringing this . . . amateur Inquisition to my door?" Like asking the maid why she'd used the wrong cleaning product.

I knew how conflicted Sunny was about taking part in our little scenario, but her reply gave away nothing. "We have some questions, sir. My best advice is to be forthcoming with your answers."

"As I recall, the Spaniards said something to that effect as well. Don't you have to warn me against incriminating myself?"

"We're not police officers. We're trying to understand the circumstances surrounding the deaths of Elaine Forge and the three young people this week."

"And you think I can help?" Wescott looked at me. "You want to make me the lead story on your newscasts this evening, don't you?"

"You're already the lead. But I'd like to hear what you have to say."

"My side." He folded his arms against his chest, hands gripping his upper arms. It was the first defensive gesture I'd seen him make. "What is it you expect from me?"

"The truth," Sunny said. She gestured toward the study behind him. "Why don't we sit down?"

"My relationship with Theo Zak . . . let me put this as politely as I can. I will not discuss my business associates with you and certainly not for broadcast on the evening news."

"What's it take for you to understand that your 'business associate' has been playing you for a sucker since Elaine Forge died?" I said. "He saw everything that afternoon, didn't he?"

He shook his head. "I beg your pardon? I told you—"

"Wait." Sunny held up her hand in a calming gesture. "You need to know that both of us think the shooting was an accident. We're not accusing. We need your help to understand what happened to her and the Hayden boy and the others."

"So I should just relax while you pry into a very painful time in my life?"

I said, "When Zak offered to cover up what you'd done, did he say no one would believe it was an accident once they found out you'd been sleeping with her?"

Wescott's knuckles went white.

Her last day on earth they shot in the woods behind the house, then made love in the leaves near the trees where they hung their targets.

It was a new place for them, one he had always wanted to try. She had been oddly reluctant about it before, even frightened. Said someone might see. But that day was different.

He couldn't recall their actual lovemaking.

He remembered firing the pistol into the target, aiming carefully, concentrating. Then, feeling her naked breasts against his back, he lowered the gun and turned to discover she had stripped completely. Everything else after they fell to the ground was missing.

He couldn't forget their poolside conversation afterward. When she announced that their lovemaking would have to stop. Would stop.

They had, she said, been together for the last time.

He didn't believe her.

Maybe she'd drunk more wine than usual. Maybe it was the wine talking.

She said he was getting too serious. Told him someone else knew, had threatened to tell Forge about them if they didn't stop.

Why, he asked, voice shaking. Why would anyone do such a thing?

She cried a little then. The first time he'd seen her weep.

He broke down, too. Then rage seized him.

Tell me who, he said, and picked up the gun from the table. The empty *gun. He stood up. In his dreams, the standing up took forever. He towered over her.*

Who, damnit? I'll kill him. I really will. I'll go and shoot him now.

Oh Bobby, she said and shook her head. She looked so lovely in that moment. Naked and tan, tears streaking her face. He wanted her then. Felt his arousal. Saw her smile. She knew.

It was impossible. He couldn't not *have her again. Couldn't bear to be near her and not touch her. He raised the gun to the side of his head.*

If you won't tell me who he is, I'll shoot myself, he said. The wine talking. And panic.

That brought her to her feet, hands reaching out to wrap around his. She drew the pistol down between them. No. It will be okay. No, Bobby.

She tried to take the gun from him as they stood by the pool. And in the very instant before the explosion that changed him forever, she smiled and told him she loved him.

The blood. He saw the blood erupt from the side of her head and the expression of surprise on her face as she took a step and fell backward. The gun. He hadn't felt the recoil. He looked at his hands. They were empty. The gun now lay on the concrete next to the pool. He knelt and picked it up. A tendril of smoke drifted from the barrel.

She was utterly motionless, blood forming a black halo around her head on the concrete apron.

The gun had been empty. She had unloaded it. Or had he? The wine made everything cloudy and hard to remember. He opened the cylinder. The barrel still hot to the touch. The smell of gunpowder. Five live shells remained.

Her eyes closed, she lay on her back and bled and bled.

He saw himself put the gun on the table. Saw himself take several steps away and punch at the air. He could see he was sobbing, but he heard no screams. He fell to his knees beside her.

Heard his name called. "Robert!"

Saw the man running down the hill from the house.

"Robert," Theo Zak said. "Robert, my God. What have you done?"

He watched himself cry. The words tumbling out.

I didn't . . . she grabbed . . . I didn't mean to do it . . .

Zak knelt and touched her.

Touched her face. Touched her arms.

"I was on the patio. I saw you shoot her. Don't try to deny it!"

Pike Wescott remembered growing cold when the look on Zak's face appeared to mirror his own feelings of horror. He knew then it was real and not a dream.

"She's dead," Theo Zak said with blood on his hands. "You killed her."

"You're disgusting. Suggesting I had sex with her. She was Eldon Forge's wife, for God's sake!" Wescott said.

"His cheating wife. You weren't the first. The cops used to find her parked with other guys your age."

"Where on earth do you get this drivel?"

I wondered if he was aware of the way his hands clutched his arms. As though his head and body were two separate entities, telling different stories.

"Did Zak tell you she was dead? Maybe make a big deal of checking her pulse? You read the coroner's transcript. She was still breathing when he dumped her in the pool. He knew that."

Sunny softened her voice. "Sir, I've seen a lot of head wounds. It's understandable if you thought she was dead. You were seventeen."

Wescott stared at her as though transfixed. She kept her expression sympathetic.

"Zak was a grown man and a law enforcement officer. He would've known what to do. He could have helped her. Instead, he decided to make you the villain in your own eyes. All these years he's been making you pay him back. Hasn't he?"

After a moment, as he stood there frozen, not knowing what to do, Zak spoke again. The horror was gone from his voice. He sounded the way he always did. Uncle Theo. Always with the answers, the phony smile. His eyes looked as dead as Elaine's.

"Go inside, Robert. Stay there until I come for you. Go on. Go up to the house and wash your hands. In fact, take a shower. Change your clothes. You have blood on you."

"But Elaine . . ."

"Listen to me! There's nothing you can do for her. We have to work on protecting you now. Go up to the house and wait for me."

Wescott took a step back. Zak went to the hose that was coiled up in a faux planter next to the pool house and started to unravel it. Without turning he said, "Go up to the house, Robert."

Wescott slipped the gun into his belt and ran.

He couldn't stop shaking yet he felt numb inside. The images kept playing in his head. Her smile. The blood. The gun in his hand.

The gun was in his hand again as he stood at the French doors opening out to the patio balcony overlooking the backyard. He could see nothing save for the aged willow tree in the middle of the yard. He raised the gun to the side of his head.

Resolve hardened Wescott's features. His hands dropped away

from his arms.

"There is no purpose to these questions. I want both of you to leave. Elaine Forge died a long time ago. Let her rest in peace."

"There are a couple of other things I think you should know," I said. "One of them is that a city police officer, a sergeant by the name of Mueller, handled a call at the Forge residence one morning a couple of weeks before Mrs. Forge was killed. It was a complaint about shooting in the woods. I read some of the articles about you. You worked at the Forge plant in the mornings, didn't you?"

"I told you I don't intend . . ."

I slipped my digital recorder out of my pocket.

"Given what happened to the witnesses in the Hayden case, I took the precaution of recording ex-Sergeant Mueller's story. He told me he found Mrs. Forge having sex with the man you're protecting, Mr. Wescott. Theo Zak."

"No!"

A couple of years ago, I covered the demolition of a CHA high-rise on the south side. Lined with dynamite it imploded, the walls disintegrating as they sank into the ground. Wescott didn't go down but he seemed to shrink inside his elegant clothes.

"That's ridiculous."

I showed him the recorder. "You want to hear Mueller tell it?"

He shook his head.

"Zak promised him a promotion if he kept his mouth shut. A few weeks later, the chief of police transferred him into Detectives. Jacked up his pay grade a good bit, I imagine."

Wescott crossed the study past pictures of him playing old golf courses like Augusta, Pebble Beach, and St. Andrews and opening new ones, too, surrounded by the likes of Tiger, Mickelson, and Leighton Bruss.

Bumping the edge of his desk, he dropped into a leather swivel. Sunny moved to one side, where she could watch him if he opened a drawer. Instead, he reached out with both hands to grasp a gold-framed eight-by-ten photo that sat in the middle of the blotter.

He drew the picture to the edge of the desk with a trembling hand.

"Last night, I handled your gun. The .38," I said. "I noticed a mark on the frame. A four-leaf clover and a couple of numbers. Did Mrs. Forge ever say where she got the weapon?"

He didn't seem to hear my question but then, just as I was about to continue, he answered hoarsely, not taking his eyes off the photo. "She told me . . . her father bought it. In Saint Louis."

"She lied."

I waited the moment it took for him to process my words and look up at me.

"In the nineteen-fifties, whenever Smith & Wesson sold more than fifteen handguns to a police agency, they offered to die stamp the agency's identifier into the metal. They numbered each weapon, too. Sometimes small town police departments can be very helpful. I made a phone call this morning. I called Cloverdale, Wisconsin. Does that sound familiar?"

Wescott shook his head.

"The chief said back in the fifties, town marshals supplemented the department's manpower. He checked the records. Badge number twelve was issued to Marshal Nicholas Zacharias. Apparently, his son didn't like his last name so he shortened it."

Wescott settled the round opening at the end of the barrel against his temple, hand holding the heavy weapon out at an awkward angle. It was hard to keep steady. He pressed in harder. Pressed until it hurt, knowing he could end all of his pain with a pull of the trigger. He looked through the French doors across the balcony toward the pool. He had to see her one last time. The hanging branches of the willow prevented that.

"I figure it this way," I said. "Zak discovered his girlfriend was sleeping with you. Who knows why he showed up that afternoon. Maybe by accident. Maybe to watch the two of you. In any case, he saw the shooting. He checked. He realized Elaine was still alive. But, in his mind, she'd cheated on him. And you were the one she'd cheated with. That must have pissed him off."

I settled on the ottoman of a swivel chair two feet from where he sat staring at the picture on his desk.

"I give him credit. He thought fast. He knew he couldn't allow her to recover. What if she woke up and felt the need to confess everything to her loving husband? Zak wouldn't have lasted a day as state's attorney if Eldon Forge found out he'd been screwing his wife *and* had provided the gun that wounded her." I leaned in toward him and lowered my voice.

"You were another loose end. Someone else he couldn't control. Even if Elaine kept her mouth shut, maybe *you* knew about *him*. But if you had a guilty secret, you'd never talk to Forge or to the cops. Zak knew Mueller was inexperienced at best and a drunk at worst and would do a crappy job so he made sure the chief put him in charge of the investigation. He probably told the coroner to lose his initial exam notes and write the final report so Elaine Forge's death would appear to be a gunshot murder. From what I understand, Gore was the kind of guy who'd go along with that kind of deal.

"Zak finessed all that and he was home free. And when you got the top job at Forge, he could sit back and ride the gravy train. Did he start asking for insider information right away or did he wait? Did he say you would have gone to prison for murder if not for him? Does he remind you every so often that there's no statute of limitations on murder?"

Wescott didn't stir. If anything he seemed even more lost in his memories.

I slammed my hand down on his desk. "*He* killed her! Yet everything I have points to you. I'm going to put a story on the air tonight. People will think *you* shot her and *you* pushed her into the pool. They'll think *you* hired Wozniak to cover it up by killing Hayden. If you don't go on the record and implicate Zak, I have to give him a pass. He gets to walk. Again."

Sunny spoke up. "He hired the men who killed Hayden, Sears, and Bremmer, didn't he? Help us put him away for that."

I thought we had convinced him. He surprised me. Whether fanned by rage or guilt, embers of the fire I'd seen when we first confronted him still glowed in his eyes.

"Eldon Forge had a saying." Wescott's voice, crusted with grief, came out just above a whisper. "He said, 'You can admit your mistakes or take the path of least resistance and hide them.' None of this would have happened if it weren't for me. I'm the reason Elaine Forge died. I took the path of least resistance. I ran away. And now those three young people are dead because I ran."

"Then stop running and help us," Sunny said.

"You may need my help. I don't need yours." He licked his lips. "I trust you can see yourselves out?"

CHAPTER THIRTY-FOUR

During our time inside the Wescott house, coal-colored clouds stole the day's bright sunshine. They oozed fat droplets of rain that left marks like bullet holes on the hood of Teague's car, still parked in the driveway. We decided to make a run for our vehicles but, before we took two steps into the open, the storm ramped up from benign to vicious and pushed us back under the arch-covered entranceway.

I stared at the way the rain battered the late-blooming flowers arrayed in cement urns on either side of the entrance. Some of the leaves and petals had already been ripped from their stalks and lay on the driveway. The more sheltered plants bounced and swayed but seemed unaffected by the punishing sheets of water.

"Goddamn it, Reno!" Sunny fumed. "What the hell did we accomplish in there? I thought the point of the exercise was to get Wescott to link Zak to the murder of the Hayden kid. Not take it all on himself."

"We blew it."

"You aren't woofin'! Let's see. We have your theory about a case that's so cold it's in the deep freeze and Wescott all but confessing he personally whacked Hayden and the others. That may give Duvall a woody, but I didn't join up with you on this just to help my client put a noose around his neck."

I wanted to say something to calm her, but I was just as frustrated. The information I'd gotten from JohnElla had been within Pike Wescott's grasp all along. If he'd just allowed himself a whisper of doubt and gone looking. Like so many of us, though, he'd been too busy hiding in the closet of his fears. As a result, three innocents died. He wasn't wrong in accepting responsibility, but I sure wished he'd taken one more mighty step and tagged Zak for us, too.

As quickly as it attacked, the storm backed off, leaving warning growls of thunder in its wake. At the end of the driveway, Al stood under some trees talking to Kremansky, both of them looking waterlogged. The IAD officers' Crown Vic was parked halfway down the block, idling. I saw two heads behind the fogged-up glass of the rear window. Duvall and Teague, still conversing. I wondered how that was going. Duvall must have been watching for us because he climbed out and walked our way.

"Anything?" I asked.

"He goes back and forth between crying for a lawyer and claiming he was just doing Wescott a favor. I try to tell him he might as well give it up because once Zak hears he tried to return the gun to Wescott, they probably won't be dating any more. He's not listening. You know who the attorney is he wants us to call? Zak's daughter Sheila. I always knew that boy was dumber than a box of rocks. Get anything from your man in there?"

As Sunny briefed him, I tried to answer that question for myself. Had we learned anything or just given Wescott a nuclear-sized wakeup call?

"The attorney general's people are coming out to interview Teague," Duvall was saying. "She wants to make a case. It may take awhile, the politics being what they are and all. But she's hot to bring Zak down before the Bureau can get its hooks in 'im. Wescott, too."

"Wescott? Based on what evidence?"

Duvall gave her an odd look. "Based on the gun Teague hand-delivered to him."

"Receiving stolen property? Pretty lame."

"Not if they match it to a slug they found in a tree trunk outside the Hayden home." He must have seen surprise on both of our faces.

"When I called to tell him we recovered the gun, Gary said one of the guys in the crime scene unit was bragging how they went back and climbed a tree outside the Hayden house yesterday. Spent a couple of hours looking and found the slug. A .38. They get a match, and with the video you people shot, Wescott's going to have some hard questions to answer. Like why he was willing to pay Teague a million bucks for an old Smith & Wesson."

"Son of a bitch," Sunny said.

"AG's bringing me aboard as a special investigator. If you can persuade your man to roll over on Zak, I'll push him as a material witness. Meanwhile, I'm going to go lean on Teague some more." He damn near skipped back to the Crown Vic. Probably the most fun he'd had since he turned in his sap.

Whether Wescott became a material witness or not, I doubted Attorney General Jean Bolander would feel very sympathetic toward him. While state's attorney in DuPage County she'd put one of her more illustrious predecessors in prison and won the moniker Clean Jean the Prosecutin' Machine. Convicting both Zak and Wescott of criminal conspiracy and three murders would lift her up more than a few rungs on the ladder to Higher Office.

"They'll hammer him with everything they've got to make him testify," Sunny said, reading my mind. "He'll refuse, play martyr, and go to prison."

"But damnit, that doesn't make any sense. If the way he fondled that picture is any indication, we just told Wescott that

Zak killed maybe the only woman he ever loved *and* set him up for lifelong blackmail. I guarantee that guy in there is pissed off. I know something about feeling manipulated, Sunshine. Vinnie puts Zak to shame—"

"Horseshit. I don't buy that. You're not Wescott and Vinnie isn't Zak."

I started to snap a smartass response but the tiniest bit of guilt twisted in my gut. Like I'd just said something shameful and she'd caught me at it. What was that all about?

"Reno?"

I shook off my Dr. Phil moment. "All Wescott had to do to pull Zak down with him today, right now, was to go on camera and tell his side of the story. Even the Wihega County state's attorney would have been forced to start an investigation. And you can bet the AG would come in faster, too."

"Where are you taking this?"

"Maybe Wescott knows Zak is insulated so well he can beat a court case."

"C'mon, Reno. Sure he's a big cheese in Wihega County, but he's not God."

"Just suppose. Humor me. What does Wescott do then?"

One eyebrow went up. "Somehow I don't picture Wescott pulling a Rambo if that's what you're getting at."

"Maybe not mano a mano. He's a techno geek, right? All sorts of patents for electronic gear? Suppose he recorded the conversations where he asked Zak for help getting the gun?"

"Doesn't fly. Second-party consent."

"Crap, that's right." Without a judicial order, Illinois law requires both parties to a conversation must agree before it can be taped.

An SEC bust for insider trading? Tax evasion charges? How could Wescott bring Zak down? I leaned against the Expedition and closed my eyes. Something in his study had caught my attention while we were talking. What was it?

The photos on the walls. Celebrities. Golfers. Wescott on golf courses, old and new.

Oh, man. Golf courses.

CHAPTER THIRTY-FIVE

Wescott fumbled the cellular phone out of his jacket the moment the security monitor showed McCarthy and DeAngelis walking down the driveway. He felt a lump the size of a golf ball in his throat. He swallowed once and then twice, even though he knew the obstruction was imaginary. His doctor called it *globus hystericus,* a nervous disorder that often affected him before major meetings with the watchdogs from DOD and congressional oversight investigators. A glass of Scotch frequently worked to "dislodge" it, but he couldn't afford the luxury of alcohol. No, that wasn't accurate. This time he would experience the pain. No alcohol. No drugs.

Leaving the cell phone on the desk, he went behind the bar and poured water into a highball glass, gulping it down and then drinking another. He felt his hand shaking again. He raised the glass to eye level and watched the surface of the water tremble.

"I'm evil," he thought and hurled the highball glass at the wall across the room.

"I'm a goddamn evil *mess!*"

The glass shattered an autographed photo of Tiger Woods striding toward the eighteeenth at Augusta. Wescott felt a visceral rip he hadn't experienced since the temper tantrums of his childhood as the liquid blurred Tiger's image and sparkling shards rained onto the couch. It spiked an urge in him to rampage through the house and smash everything he saw. He picked up a bottle of Cutty Sark, weighed it in his hand, and then, taking it by the neck, slammed it down against the edge of the bar the way the cowboys in the saloons had done it in the movies of his youth. It didn't break, but the impact left a deep groove in the bar surface and sent a vibration up his arm.

He pointed the bottle at another photo, this one of Theo Zak behind the podium at the opening of the Forge Technology Center at Wihega County College.

"Don't try to deny it. You killed her. I know you did, you son of a bitch."

His eyes fell on the picture of Elaine Forge. He swung the bottle that way.

"You! I loved you! And you were screwing everyone, weren't you? Were you laughing at me behind my back, too? When I told you I wanted to marry you, was that funny? I *meant* it."

In three strides he reached the desk and raised the Cutty Sark bottle over his head with both hands, not seeing a picture but Elaine, only Elaine, lovely Elaine. Ready to crush her skull.

Wescott stared at Elaine until emotion overwhelmed him and the first sob escaped his throat. He let go of the bottle, heard it thud to the carpet, and then followed it down, down to his knees, hands over his head, tears scraping his cheeks like fingernails, and he cried as he had not done in years, crying for Elaine and himself and a childhood lost and the lives of three young people who hadn't needed to die.

Ten minutes later, he stopped crying as though an internal timer had clicked the "off" switch. He straightened. Saw his cell phone on the desk. Brushed his cheeks with the heel of his hand and sat in his chair. Glanced out the window toward the pool.

He realized Zak had watched them that day. Maybe from one of the chairs under the willow's branches. Had Zak been nearby every time they were together? Was that why Elaine never wanted to make love in the woods? Had Zak always been there? Furious because his lover was cheating on him and with a teenager no less. Plotting revenge?

If Elaine had just . . . told him. Why play with him the way she had? Like he meant nothing to her. All a game, he thought. All a game to her the way everything since had been a game to Zak. His way of pissing on the boy who became the man who was really a boy. Making sure the boy paid for his lust for the rest of his life.

Wescott's hands curled into fists as though a spasm of pain had coursed through him.

And he remembered . . .

Every demand. Every demeaning word.

Every under-the-table tip he provided that allowed Zak to make a killing on Wall Street.

His contacts in government that kept the FBI away from Zak's many "business ventures."

Their "arrangement" about the casino project.

Wescott focused once more on Elaine's picture, but this time her image seemed to melt away and he saw the greenhouse, the gun, his office, the gun, the study where he now sat, Eldon Forge's expression after he learned his wife was dead, the faces of his parents.

The smug and awful face of Theo Zak.

He laid the picture frame down. Hands shaking, he pushed back the metal snaps and removed the cardboard backing. He lifted out the photo. He carried it to the fireplace. He took a long match from the mantel. He struck it against the slate of the hearth. He watched the tip bloom into red flame and then turn briefly to blue as it touched the edge of the picture.

As the paper curled and smoked, something like a chill went through Robert Wescott. Not fear. For the first time in his adult life, he felt . . . anticipation.

He would move forward, he thought. After all, wasn't that Eldon Forge's advice? Not Forge the friend he had cuckolded. Forge his mentor. His teacher.

"You may stumble. Take the loss. Move on. Move ahead."

The scenario sketched out for him by McCarthy and DeAngelis amounted to no more than an engineering problem. His strengths lay in technology, and it was beyond time to put his skills to work.

Move *forward*.

Once again he sat at his desk. He tapped his password into the computer.

An hour later, Wescott exited the site. He left no clue to his presence. As a final act, he picked up his cellular phone.

Four rings later, a harried voice answered.

"Robert, Jesus! You caught me in the middle of a meeting with the fairway grass people. We're going with that mix of bent and—"

Wescott interrupted. "Plan B. You need to tell the governor you're not interested. And call the U.S. attorney."

A long pause. Then "What the hell? You told me everything was in order."

"Not any longer. You'll get your money. You must notify the governor today. Immediately. Fax the letter and make it public. When the press asks your reason for withdrawing, tell them about the phone calls. You remember the script?"

"Of course. Have you—?"

"Just now. Just as we planned."

"You know, Robert, you're not my only investor. I have others to protect. Be honest with me. Is there any chance at all someone will find out about this? The Feds, the press, anyone?"

Wescott summoned up his second smile of the day.

"None whatsoever. That I guarantee. You and I are completely in the clear."

CHAPTER THIRTY-SIX

I thought about the photo on his study wall of Wescott, Tiger, and Mickelson at the golf course groundbreaking. A Leighton Bruss golf course.

Gennaro had told me of Bruss's imminent appointment to the Illinois Gaming Board. *"Bruss has no connection to Zak. Nor the Outfit."*

Of course he didn't.

I asked Sunny to go online and look for any connection, public or private, between Bruss and Wescott. It took her an hour to key into the appropriate database and then two quick phone calls to her contacts in the right state departments before she discovered that the "WesFam Trust" belonged to Wescott and was a significant investor in "GCP Limited," the real estate partnership chaired by Leighton Bruss.

"So?" she turned away from her computer to ask. "Wescott's a golfer. His buddy is going to build golf courses. What's felonious there?"

"Is it public record?"

"No. Probably won't ever be, the way it was filed. Thanks to the Bush administration, people who know how to wiggle the rules can cloak their sweetheart deals. Sometimes even from the SEC and IRS."

"In this case, I'm guessing Wescott wants it hidden because the money he used to finance his buddy's new venture didn't come from him."

"Zak?"

I nodded. "It always bothered me why Zak agreed to go after that gun. Sure it linked him to the Forge case but so what? He's a lawyer. He'd know that was no big deal after all this time. But if Wescott was the key to getting his casino approved . . . hell, for once Zak wasn't calling the shots. He couldn't afford to have Wescott get distracted. He was humoring him. That's all."

"Maybe that's why he had Wozniak do the burglary instead of one of his goons. He didn't want it getting back to his buddies in the Outfit that he and Wescott were joined at the hip. If they found out Wescott was the key to the casino vote, they wouldn't need Zak."

"Gennaro says Bruss came up clean. No organized crime contacts, no connection to Zak. Wescott passed along the cash in the form of that partnership and who knows what other incentives," I said.

"I don't hear you using the word 'proof.' "

I looked at my watch. "Let's go see how Mr. Bruss reacts to hearing his name and the words 'organized crime' used in the same sentence."

Leighton Bruss was a fit-looking man in his late sixties whose features, voice, and the sweater tied around his shoulders all reminded me of a gruff but approachable and grandfatherly Paul Newman. Sunny, Al, and I sat across from him in his putting-green-sized office in Hoffman Estates. Artist renderings of his first several golf course projects sat on easels along one wall and landscape designs hung on another. Two large windows behind his desk overlooked a Forest Preserve where the trees were just beginning to shed their summer colors. From beyond his closed office door, voices murmured and phones rang.

"You have excellent sources, Mr. McCarthy. How did you find out so quickly that I turned down the gaming board appointment? My staff hasn't even finished writing up the press release. Hell, I just got off the phone with the governor a half-hour ago."

My stomach felt like I'd stepped into an empty elevator shaft.

"The way I understood it, you were at the top of the governor's short list."

"Oh, I don't know about 'the top.' He asked me some time ago if I would be interested in sitting on the board. I told him I'd never gambled in my life. He said that's precisely why he wanted me." He chuckled. "Nothing like being chosen for one's skills, is there?"

"What changed your mind?"

He gestured at the design boards across the room. "I'd like to say business is booming. We have an even dozen projects in the works and that's double what I expected at this time a year ago."

"Your investors must be pleased."

"Why, yes. Yes they are." A slight hesitation and then he chuckled again, tapping a pen on his desktop.

"But that's not the reason for your decision?"

The tapping stopped. He fingered the knot that held his sweater on his shoulders. And then, with all the dexterity of a TV anchor switching from happy talk to fatal car crashes, he took on the expression of a man burdened by the information he's about to share.

"Unfortunately no, Reno. It's not the reason. I have received some disturbing phone calls. Several in the last couple of weeks. One today as well."

"What kind of calls?"

"They began as offers. They turned into threats. That's another reason we're a little behind in sending out our news release. I had to call the state police." He glanced at Al.

"You might want to turn your camera on now . . ."

Back in the live truck, I slapped the dash hard enough to make my hand sting.

" 'You might want to turn your camera on now,' " I mimicked. "The son of a bitch was just waiting for the chance to start his spiel. He and Wescott are playing us. Hell, they're suckering any news organization that uses the story."

"That'll be every last one, if he gives them the same peek at his Caller ID he gave us," Al said.

I stared out the windshield at the front of the corporate complex that housed Bruss's office. It gleamed pristine white, the windows reflecting soft cirrus clouds that were breaking up and reforming at high altitude. The tinted glass, however, allowed no glimpse of the maneuvering going on inside.

Had Mike Wallace ever been sandbagged the way Bruss clobbered me? So much for taking him off guard and grilling him about his connection to Wescott.

"Goddamn it," I said. "I can't use that interview on the air. It's bullshit."

"Are you sure?" Sunny asked.

"Oh, come on, Sunshine! We put Wescott into meltdown mode against Zak. A couple of hours later, Wescott's buddy Bruss conveniently claims that Zak has been calling him and demanding he vote for the casino plan when he gets on the gaming board 'or else.' And then comes up with 'evidence' on his Caller ID guaranteeing Uncle Theo guest appearances before a couple of grand juries."

"Why are you pissed? You don't want Wescott going down alone any more than I do."

"No I don't. But Bruss's story doesn't prove anything. We air this and we're helping the two of them run their con."

"You don't know that. Proof or not, you can bet the AG's office and probably the FBI will investigate. Sounds like legitimate news to me."

"You're saying Wescott couldn't rig having Zak's number pop up on Bruss's phone?"

She grinned. "Sure. It's possible. For a few bucks, there are spoof sites on the Internet that'll let you display any number you want on somebody else's Caller ID."

"So it can be tracked?" I said.

"Wescott wouldn't use the Internet, Reno. He wouldn't have to. You saw Bruss's phone. It's a SekureTek from Forge Global. Wescott's own invention. Chances are Zak has one, too. They're encrypted. Probably gave Zak a nice rise in his Levis knowing his chats were so private."

"But if Zak didn't make the calls, his records will clear him. Besides, what if he can prove he was doing something else at the times Bruss claims the calls came in?"

"Techno-geek stuff, remember? I'm just speculating but, to convince an investigator, Wescott would have to plug outgoing call data into Zak's phone records that echoed the incoming calls Bruss received. As for the dates and times, I'm guessing again but Wescott and Zak probably had more than a few conversations in the last week or so, don't you think? If someone was so inclined, I imagine he could take the billing records of *those* calls and substitute them to match the readout Bruss showed us on his Caller ID. If that someone just happened to be the guy whose company makes the software most of the cell providers use."

My irritation slowly dissolved into an appreciation of the artful way Wescott had manipulated technology to wrap a frame around the man who had manipulated him.

"And it's all invisible?" I asked.

"The Feds might be able to track how he did it if they tried. Bush let the National Security Agency get pretty good at playing with cell phone records. But why would the FBI bother? Bruss's story puts Zak over a hot spit ready for them to baste."

"What about Zak's lawyers? If they hire their own techs . . ."

She snorted. "Without the NSA's computers? Not in a million years. Not unless they figure a way to pop open Wescott's brain so all his secrets spill out."

The only thing that might have cast a shade of immediate doubt on Bruss's story was his secret partnership with Wescott. Sunny asked me not to use that information because it had come from her confidential sources. I wrestled with my conscience for fifteen seconds and agreed.

And, as I figured he would, Chucky axed running what we'd gathered connecting Wescott and his gun to Forge, Hayden, and the rest. After all, why let nasty, confusing facts get in the way of a great story? Bruss was on the record pointing to Theo Zak as a mob-connected guy trying to buy the votes needed to approve his casino. Nothing else mattered.

"Reno, Reno. You're gonna break the Bruss story, dude, you're my hero. At this point, anything else is soft porn. Hey, aren't you the one who's been telling me all along Zak is the major bad guy here? Save what you have on Wescott for tomorrow. It'll make a great second-day lead. Third day even. But for now we're out in front on Bruss. Let's keep it simple for the viewers, okay?"

Theo Zak's really bad day began at four that afternoon.

Through his attorney-daughter, he refused to comment on Bruss's allegations. I hoped our call convinced him to be watching when I stepped in front of the camera for my first live shot of the afternoon.

"In a startling development today, Channel 14 News has learned that the man reported to be the governor's hand-picked choice to join

the Illinois Gaming Board has decided to take a pass. Former Boeing CEO Leighton Bruss claims that before he could even formally accept the appointment he was targeted with threats and intimidation, all designed to force his vote in favor of a casino for Wihega County.

"What's even more startling is evidence Bruss has provided indicating the man behind the harassment is former Wihega County board chairman and chief casino backer, Theo Zak. Bruss alleges that Zak invoked the name of a well-known organized crime figure as part of his effort to guarantee Bruss's cooperation in the voting scheme . . . and his silence about it afterward."

As soon as I got off the air, people started to call, taking shots at Zak.

The first was the publisher of the Wihega County *Examiner.* He claimed Zak convinced him to hire Wozniak despite the fact the paper knew about Wozniak's record as a Peeping Tom. The tradeoff Zak offered? An inside track to information about county government stories. He also told me the West Wihega Wildlife Sanctuary where Wozniak's home stood was Zak's land, part of a real estate trust.

"You don't plan to use this information in your stories?" I asked.

The publisher's voice made me think of the late actor Don Knotts.

"We may but I thought it might . . um . . get wider play coming from you. Chicago TV has a bigger reach than our little hometown rag."

Sunny was sitting with her feet up in the back of the live truck. When I disconnected, she raised an eyebrow at me. "A rat deciding to disembark after sensing ol' Uncle Theo's rowboat is starting to take on water?"

"He figures if Zak manages to come out of this unbruised, he can say he never ran anything damaging against his friend. Plus, if he gives us a tip, maybe we'll give him a pass if his name comes up connected to something dirty later."

"Your thoughts on that?"

"Why should he get a break?" I turned to her. "By the way? Your client or not, the first chance I get to run what we have on Wescott, I'm going to do it."

"He hired me for my advice. I gave it to him." She shrugged.

"Funny. You don't sound pissed."

"And you don't sound nearly as balls-to-the-walls to nail him as you did a couple of days ago. In fact, Mr. McCarthy, you seem almost laid back."

"I think . . ." I scratched a couple of notes for my next live shot then brought my eyes back up to hers.

"I think Attorney General Bolander will convene her own grand jury to investigate Zak, Wescott, and Wihega County. By the time she's finished, either Wescott will talk or he won't. If he doesn't, she'll probably ask for some kind of murder or conspiracy indictment against him. At that point, he'll either listen to his lawyer and go with a plea to some lesser charge or Clean Jean the Prosecutin' Machine will put his brilliant inventor ass in prison."

"That's if the Feds don't get to him first."

"Either way."

"But you're sympathetic."

"To a point," I said. "He couldn't have known the Hayden burglary was going to go sour. Or that Wozniak and his pet alligator were going to kill the girl or Bremmer. But the casino deal with Bruss . . . that wasn't blackmail or manipulation or accident. I'm betting that was plain old greed. Sort of mitigates my sympathy."

"You're saying at some point he realized Zak was running him and he decided to join up rather than fight back."

"And got in over his head."

411

★ ★ ★ ★ ★

I called Moira Cullen after my last live shot at six, thinking she might want to have dinner. Instead of spaghetti I got spite.

"Do you know what you've done, Reno? The casino is dead for sure. That was one way we might have brought this county back from economic catastrophe. And with all the rumors you've started about Pike Wescott, Jesus Christ! Forge Global may go into the tank, too! They're our biggest employer!"

"He's an accessory before and after the fact to murder. We should ignore that?"

"Unlike you, I'll wait until all the facts are in before I convict him. And goddamn you, you promised you'd tell me before shit hit the fan."

"No," I reminded her. "I said if I could, I'd let you know what I found out about Wescott before we aired it. We haven't aired anything. How does any of this hurt you, anyway? I have a feeling Wihega County is going to be looking for a new prosecuting attorney pretty soon. Maybe even before the next election."

"There's nothing to indicate he's—"

"Wasn't it you who told me Zak owns the state's attorney? How long do you think the SA will last when Bolander starts her housecleaning? If a majority of your buddies on the Leadership Council can manage to avoid getting indicted themselves, I'd say you could be moving your stuff into the courthouse before Christmas. You're just pissed because you didn't know ahead of time and you're scrambling."

She was quiet for a moment. "You're an asshole."

"Tell me I'm wrong."

"Get your own fucking dinner!"

Reno charms another one.

Al and I brought chili con queso and chips, nachos, tostadas, burritos, and three bottles of cheap wine back to the motel.

Beer, we felt, would give us gas. Hell, it was time for a celebration. Tomorrow, we'd begin the stakeout in front of Zak's place with every other media organization, waiting for him or one of his attorney children to come out and try to spin the story in a way that would be the least damaging. Attorney children. Al and I both had a good laugh at the phrase and kept coming up with variations of it all evening.

Sunny didn't answer her room phone or her cellular. That was fine. More food and wine for us. Somewhere after consuming half the wine and at least half the food, I called for a medium-sized crane to lift me out of a chair in Al's room and stash me on the bed in mine. I fell asleep atop the covers, wearing most of my clothes. I slept through the night except around midnight when I got up to puke. For the first time in months, however, I had decent dreams. Go figure. Had to be the wine.

Five a.m. found me slumped in the shower stall under the coldest water the motel's ancient pipes could produce. The Boston Pops Orchestra was playing the 1812 Overture complete with cannons exploding on either side of my head. Even so, I heard Sunny's voice calling my name from the Nextel on the bedside table. I stumbled out of the shower without turning off the spray and ran to grab the infernal device, swearing I'd hammer it into dust before the end of the day.

"Wescott's disappeared," she said.

CHAPTER THIRTY-SEVEN

Sunny was at Wescott's house. I threw on clothes, collected Al, and was there in twenty minutes. Along the way, I managed to piss off most of the morning news staff, including Giselle and Mary Frances, by announcing we would probably have to throw any prewritten scripts out the window. Sort of like yelling "stop the presses!" back in the old days.

Sunny answered the door, phone to her ear. She waved me inside. To anyone else, she might have seemed calm and in control, but I recognized the signs. Her hair was pulled back, there were smudges under her eyes, and she spoke in a clipped monotone, giving rapid instructions to someone about checking airline reservations. As she talked, she led me back to Wescott's study. She was off the phone inside a minute and looked at me in exasperation.

"Mrs. Wescott comes home from a night with friends about three-thirty and sees the door open to his study and a light on. Since he's been keeping the door locked in the past few months, she thinks that's odd so she goes to check. She finds two folders and a note to her on the desk."

"A confession naming Zak?" Sometimes my optimism rages out of control.

"One was a letter of resignation from Forge Global, along with five pages of instructions to the CFO that basically are suggestions to cushion the fallout from his sudden departure. The second one was private. Family stuff, she says. But she did say he included his will."

I leaned against the doorway.

"The CFO is crapping his drawers," Sunny said. "He's afraid Wall Street's going to find out before he can notify all the board members. He knows he's going to have to bring in the FBI, given the kind of stuff Wescott's been working on, but he wanted my take. I think he's hoping for a kidnapping."

"And your take is?"

"It's not a kidnapping. Other than that . . ." She shrugged, mouth tight, and glanced around the study. "I don't have a god-damn take."

"The will is a nice theatrical touch, don't you think?"

She ignored me. "I tipped Duvall so he can get some people to cover Zak. Just in case Wescott snapped and went hunting. I've started a track on his credit cards and have some people covering all the usual stuff. It's obviously too early to ask about bank withdrawals, but he's not exactly the kind of guy who needs to raid the family checking account on his way out the door. He could have squirreled money anywhere. Here, Switzerland, Grand Cayman . . ."

The house smelled of fried bacon, which made me a little queasy, but was as quiet as it had been the day before. If the domestic staff was around, they'd been told to stay out of sight. I asked about Wescott's wife and kids.

"Mrs. Wescott's upstairs on the phone talking to the family lawyer and their daughters. She told me I could use the study if I needed a quiet place to make calls of my own. The girls are staying with friends on Wescott's suggestion last night."

"This is an asshole thing he's doing to them."

Sunny expelled a breath. "I've got to admit. He blindsided me. Taking off is the one option he had for dealing with all this that I didn't even consider."

"You know I can't keep it off the air," I said. Wescott in the wind would be major news. I had a half an hour before my first live shot of the day.

"I've already convinced the missus to go public with a plea that he call her. I don't get the feeling they're huggy-kissy lovebirds, but she's . . . concerned. The CFO isn't happy with the idea of news coverage, but I told him to wake each board member if he wants them to know so badly."

"You make a pretty good producer. Want to give all this up and come back to show business?"

That didn't even rate a smile. She gestured at the expanse of room that still held the sweet aroma of cigar and wood smoke. "I never would have expected him to give all this up."

"You really think he wanted it in the first place?"

Chucky reacted to the news of Wescott's disappearance with absolute glee. He sounded so excited it wouldn't have surprised me to find out he was bouncing from wall to wall in the newsroom.

"The fucking CEO of Forge Global on the run because of a Channel 14 investigation? Larry King's people are going to be calling before noon. They'll want you for all the network shows, too. I knew keeping you in place was the right move. He knew you had him by the balls so he decided to split. First Bruss and now this. I love it! Wait. You think your private eye friend can find him? I'll put her on the payroll!"

"Does that include international travel?"

"Well," he stopped. "Naturally she'd have to take care of her expenses."

I broke Wescott's disappearance as the lead for six a.m. At noon, I reported that Chicago police had found Wescott's Cadillac Escalade parked in a garage near Union Station. The ticket under the windshield, together with the time Olivia Wescott had last seen him, made it reasonable to surmise he drove straight there after leaving home. FBI agents interviewed station personnel and, in other cities, boarded several trains that left Chicago within hours of when Wescott parked the Escalade. Police talked to cabbies and private livery drivers in the area of the station and pulled tapes from a dozen surveillance cameras. Sunny told me there had been no transactions on his credit cards.

Late in the day, after numerous television and radio stories had aired both locally and on the networks, I got a tip from Ken Herzlich, a freelance cameraman who's tight with cops in the 18th District. A man walking his dog between North Avenue and Oak Street Beaches had found Wescott's wallet in the grassy area between the parking lot and the cement walk along the water.

Chucky sent a crew from the station but insisted I come in from Wihega County for a live shot at ten from the deserted beach. Al and I got there just as the police marine unit and Coast Guard were giving up the water search for the night. We'd missed the formal news briefing but, off camera, I corralled a tactical sergeant I knew who'd been leading the hunt for more Wescott evidence along the lakefront.

"I don't know what I can tell you, Reno," he said. He wore a leather jacket and blue jeans, his star and a .45 automatic clipped to his belt. A Motorola handie-talkie stuffed into his inside jacket pocket murmured while we talked and he kept one hand wrapped around a steaming cup of coffee. With the breeze off the water it was about thirty-five degrees in the park.

"Wallet was over there, next to those trees. No cash but two credit cards and his driver's license still in their slots. That's almost a miracle."

"That could mean he dropped the wallet there a few minutes before your guy found it. Your witness see anyone else around?"

He grimaced. Eyes, red-rimmed from the cold, fixed on my face. "Anybody ever tell you that you think like a cop? Off the record, our 'witness' is about a thousand years old and should have a seeing eye dog instead of that smack-a-doodle or peek-a-doodle or whatever he was walking. Lucky he took the wallet home to show his kid. I had my guys spread out and check all the way up to Oak Street, the beach house here, the parking lot. The ones who walk into the water, sometimes they leave their clothes. We didn't find squat. Then again, somebody coulda took 'em when they grabbed the cash from his wallet."

"What's your gut tell you?"

"Who knows? Could have gone the way you said. Your guy was here, dropped the wallet so somebody would find it. Or it could be he'll wash up after the next storm. I'll tell you this. I heard the Coast Guard tell the other reporters that the boats'll be coming back to search some more in the morning? They do, they'll be in 'recovery' mode."

CHAPTER THIRTY-EIGHT

At ten, I summarized the facts we had about Wescott's disappearance but emphasized there was no proof he had killed himself by walking into Lake Michigan. Caroline, who had been assigned to get reactions from Olivia Wescott and Wihega County, made it sound like the family was mourning and his coworkers were devastated.

The truth, Sunny told me, was less colorful.

She was waiting as I stepped away from the camera. I'd thought she'd still be in Falcon Ridge. She looked as worn out as I'd ever seen her.

"Forge Global terminated my services a couple of hours ago. The CFO is now the CEO and he's not so hot to find his former boss anymore. I think he likes his new office. He told one of his assistants he's gonna turn Wescott's private lab into a sauna. All he wants from me is the security audit report. He has full faith in the FBI and the cops. Blah, blah, blah."

"How about Olivia Wescott? She doesn't want your help?"

"Not so much. She told me she hardly ever saw him, and the girls saw him less. The past few years he spent more time in that lab of his tinkering with projects than he did with them. Besides, she found out he signed over the house and a couple of brokerage accounts to her."

She turned to look at the water. I went to stand beside her.

"You think he's out there?" I asked.

In the spillover from the lights Al had set up for the live shot

I saw her tired grin. "You don't?"

"If he turns up as flotsam on Wilmette Beach in the next couple weeks, then I'll believe. Or is it jetsam? I never get that straight. Anyway, until there's a body, nope."

"Don't tell me. You're holding out for Helen Brach, too."

"Face it, Sunshine. Wescott learned from Zak. He played us with the Bruss stuff. He's still playing us."

They could have heard her sigh in Michigan.

After a moment she asked, "Want to grab a drink?"

"Rain check." Something she'd said after we questioned Wescott was niggling at me. Had been all day. I told her what it was. She smiled.

Roosevelt-Lakeshore Hospital is just off Lake Shore Drive a couple of blocks south of Oak Street Beach. As you get into the neighborhood, the old-fashioned kinds of signs you always used to see near hospitals warn, "Quiet—Hospital Zone." I guess that's so no one decides to hold a block party. As I pulled into the parking garage and took a ticket from the automatic dispenser at the foot of the drive, my stomach clenched the way it had in Grum's basement, and I could feel the metronome thudding of my heart against my rib cage.

I don't have to do this, I said to myself. Wescott had run from his past. Why couldn't I?

Sunny's words intruded again, as they had in every spare moment since she had uttered them.

"You're not Wescott . . ."

But, like him, I'd been running in fear ever since I shot and killed that Russian thug. Hiding behind my rage.

Rage at what? Maybe I needed to give that some thought.

The garage after visiting hours was silent save for the buzzing of the florescent lights overhead and the occasional thrum and rattle of the elevators. Little traffic moved on the adjacent streets and even the Drive was quiet. I encountered no one as I trudged across the pedestrian bridge and into the hospital proper.

"*. . . and Vinnie isn't Zak.*"

No, Vinnie wasn't Zak. Or Wozniak. Or Grum. Major difference. Vinnie had a soul.

And were his manipulations what drew me onto the killing field or had I put myself there?

More to think about.

I expected Security to brace me as I made my way to Cardiac Intensive Care, but the only people I saw in the halls were janitors in dark green uniforms pushing wheeled carts stocked with cleaning supplies and trailing the smell of disinfectant. Maybe it was the lighting, but every face I glanced at looked pale and exhausted. Did I appear the same way to them?

This time I checked in at the nurse's station. An oversized black woman holding two clipboards asked if she could help me. She wore a stethoscope around her neck and an orange and yellow top with a pager and ID badge clipped to her pockets. The top of a drug interaction book stuck out the top of one of the pockets. When I told her who I was, she nodded, smiled, and began rustling through another stack of clipboards lying on the counter in front of her.

"Dr. Fong said you might be stopping by. We've been waiting for you." She came up with the clipboard she wanted, added it to the two already in her arms, and motioned for me to follow her into a room that was no more than ten feet away.

"I'm Victoria and I'm taking care of Mr. Seamans this shift. We moved him to this room so we can keep a closer eye on him."

For a moment I had the irrational notion that her statement meant he'd awakened and caused some kind of disturbance, maybe wanting his clothes or to be discharged. One look at the form on the bed, however, and all my hopeful thoughts vanished.

Vinnie's face was grayer and his head and neck, all that was now visible above the bed linens, had swollen to half again their normal size so that his closed eyes seemed shrunken and buried in skin. More machines surrounded him, their digital readouts green and yellow and clicking away like the time on a digital clock. Drip lines ran to where I couldn't see them under the covers.

"Has he . . ." I cleared my throat. "Has there been any change since he was brought in?"

"I'm sorry Mr. McCarthy. No. We're keeping him as comfortable as we can." She touched my shoulder. "You can sure talk to him, though. At some level, they hear you." She added the last with a kind of wistfulness that made me suspect she wasn't new to the unit or to watching the approach of death.

I tried to think of a question. By the time I came up with one, she was gone.

I walked around the bed. Two small flower arrangements sat on a windowsill. I read the cards. One was from the Fraternal Order of Police lodge that represented Chicago police officers and the other from the Cook County state's attorney's office. Both offered wishes for a speedy recovery but each card had been computer generated. The rote sympathy and lack of a more personal message ticked me off. I wondered if the state's attorney, who hired Vinnie as a sort of freelance troubleshooter when he retired from the cops, had even been in to see him. I suspected not. No chance for a photo op since hospital rules banned cameras.

The room's window looked out on a small courtyard in the rear of the hospital and over the top of another wing to the lake beyond. The carbon arc lights on Lake Shore Drive appeared as yellow smudges. Out on the water, I could see lights of a couple of small pleasure craft and the larger profile of the Odyssey dinner boat moving sedately back toward its berth alongside Navy

Pier. Beyond them, the darkness was an impenetrable curtain. I wondered if Wescott was out there somewhere. If he was running, I wondered if he sought only his freedom or some kind of redemption. Or both.

I closed my eyes. The flowers were a mix of mums and something else I couldn't identify. I could smell their fragrance over the room's odor of illness and decay.

My father died before I could reach him, alone in the middle of a small field not far from our house. My mother collapsed of a heart attack while I was in college and was dead before I was even notified she'd been taken to the hospital.

Vinnie had been the one to deliver the news both times. He had to walk across the street to tell me about my dad but flew to Kansas when my mother died. Ever the master of the flat expression, he couldn't hide his tears.

I turned and looked at him. The rise and fall of his chest continued at a machine-measured pace. Otherwise he was still.

There was a plastic chair next to the bed. I sat down beside my oldest friend.

And for some damn fool reason, I started to cry.

. . . LATER

It rained the day they delivered the high-end computer gear to the two-story brick house in the Potwin neighborhood of Topeka, Kansas. A hard, driving, January rain that brought with it a surprising rumble of thunder. The two men who lifted the expensive equipment out of their vehicle and carried it inside glanced skyward, worried about the threat of lightning.

A realtor met them at the door and let them in to stack the boxes they'd brought on tables in a book-lined study in the front of the house. Large windows overlooked a tiny backyard. The men saw a set of flat-screen video monitors hanging from a rack in one corner of the room and noted how they displayed alternating views of the front and back entrances and all around the exterior. They discussed the customer's paranoia on the way back to their shop. Later, though, they forgot about it. The customer's order had been sizeable, but the house certainly wasn't of the type or in a location that suggested he was a terrorist or drug dealer. Besides, Topeka wasn't quite overrun with either, although the gang violence on the east side sort of made the guy's security setup understandable.

Their customer watched the delivery from behind the wheel of a new, brown Ford Aerostar van parked down the street from the Potwin house. His surveillance went unnoticed by anyone in the quiet neighborhood, even the realtor who had last seen him driving an economy rental sedan. He wore a cap pulled down over his eyes and occasionally scratched at the thick beard that covered the lower half of his face. It had grown in red with streaks of white at the chin. Its roundness made him think he looked like an 1800s gold prospector. The protruding belly added to the image. He wore jeans, a red and white checkered shirt, and a shapeless blue sport coat with a splotch of something unidentifiable on the lapel. Probably ketchup, he thought. He'd been eating fast food almost exclusively for the past few months. Particularly hot dogs and cheeseburgers, favorites from his teenage years.

The laptop on the seat next to him drew his attention. Checking Chicago news that morning, as he had each day for the past couple of months, he'd found an item of interest on Channel 14's Web site. He clicked "play" and watched streaming video as Reno McCarthy's voice came over the laptop's speakers.

"Authorities announced indictments Tuesday against former Wihega County Board Chairman Theo Zak and another man in an alleged conspiracy to open and run a mob-connected gambling casino in Falcon Ridge. The seventy-year-old Zak, along with thirty-seven-year-old Jack Wiley, face charges of extortion, attempted bribery, and intimidation of a witness. Illinois Attorney General Jean Bolander says the men are accused of plotting with organized crime figures to influence the votes of at least two members of the Illinois Gaming Board and one appointed member who had not yet taken his seat. No gaming board officials face charges, although the governor has asked for the entire board to resign in the wake of the probe. Bolander says additional charges against Zak and Wiley are pending. In a separate, but related, investigation state police and the FBI are looking into the way three murder cases were handled in Wihega County last fall. So far that's resulted in indictments of the Wihega County state's attorney and Falcon Ridge chief of police. U.S. Attorney Thomas J. Keevers admits the disappearance of Forge Global Technologies CEO Robert Wescott has slowed the investigations but will not damage them . . ."

The men from the computer store drove away. As they passed him, the van's occupant ducked his head. He'd placed his order online and they had never seen his face but, why should they get even a quick glimpse now? Absolute caution had carried him this far and he could think of no reason to relax his vigilance. Besides, he was finding he liked the cloak and dagger nature of his life these past few months. He seemed to have a talent for it.

When the realtor left, the man waited fifteen minutes. Then he got out, opened an umbrella, and strolled across the street and up his new driveway. The online research that led him to this neighborhood, this *block,* indicated all of his nearby neighbors worked during the day and had small children in school. If he kept to himself, he was sure he could maintain an unremarkable lifestyle here.

He entered through the rear door and briskly inspected the house. Kitchen cupboards and refrigerator full, Sears and J.C. Penney furniture arranged in the living areas, bed made and ready for use, towels set out in the bathroom. Good. He'd paid a substantial premium in a private deal with the realtor, also arranged online, to assure the house would be prepared for him to occupy.

He smiled and scratched his beard. All that remained were tasks he intended to handle himself. Installation of a transmitter that would alert his beeper if anyone tripped the alarm system when he was away from the house. Application of a specially treated and virtually invisible film on each window to block any view into the house day or night. And of course, setting up and interconnecting his four new computers.

After all, his contacts at the Department of Defense, unconcerned about the personal problems that had caused him to relocate, were waiting for him to get back in touch. And he had some ideas for a complex encryption code that he'd been scribble-scrabbling in his notebook and his laptop over the past several months.

He was eager to get to work.

ABOUT THE AUTHOR

Doug M. Cummings is the author of the top-selling *Deader by the Lake,* the first Reno McCarthy novel. An ex-cop, former security consultant, and award-winning Chicago broadcaster, Cummings has worked the street on both sides of the crime scene tape. His reports have been heard on every major network. Cummings lives in suburban Chicago. More information about him can be found at www.dougmcummings.com

Email Doug at: doug@dougmcummings.com